13 Stops

When considering the people I felt compelled to thank, not only for their support and encouragement as I worked my way through this project, but also for their contributions to it, God would have to be at the very top of my list. After all, this novel is my story, and for whatever His reasons, this is the story He's given me. It's a very rare thing for a man to reach this stage of his life, finding himself grateful for everything he has lived through or experienced, but that's exactly where I find myself as the writing of this novel came to a close.

Babs & Doug, without your kindness, compassion, hospitality, and generosity, this book would have never seen the light of day. I cannot possibly express the sense of gratitude I feel toward both of you.

Corey & Heather, I love both of you like crazy, and now you'll know why none of us are quite right in the head.

Pastor Steve, your unending support, guidance, and encouragement throughout this process has been absolutely priceless. Thank you for holding me accountable throughout this process. I couldn't have done it without you.

Debbie Jo, I can't thank you enough for always being there with continual support and encouragement. I will always be grateful.

Finally, Angel, had you never been a part of my life, this story would have been only half of what it is. Thank you for showing me beauty I never imagined possible.

To Kalia Rose;

May you thoroughly enjoy every minute you spend

singing and dancing through the streets of heaven

until we're invited to join you.

ONE

The train bursts from within the tunnel, moving swiftly into the wide uncovered space before it as the high grass along either side rolls away and is blown violently by its wake. The dense black smoke billowing from its stack leaves a constant trail of rolling clouds which change form as they are taken by the wind and are scattered across the countryside.

As the sun rises to the east, the impression is given of a new beginning in a previously untouched and unspoiled world, never before seen by human eyes or touched by human hands.

The thick steel of the train glistens in the early morning sunlight, seemingly floating as if there were no track to direct it. The powerful moan of the engines cuts through the air with tremendous force as they pull the cars effortlessly across the terrain.

The train's interior is finished for the most discriminating of tastes. Each car's ceilings are eight feet high, covered in pleated burgundy velvet and trimmed with polished walnut.

Crystal chandeliers sway slightly with the movement of the train as they hang from the center of the car, throwing bright prisms of dancing light throughout, while gold and etched crystal wall fixtures illuminate each row of seats.

Every seat is a beige leather high back, fully reclining with ample space to do so. The carpeting is a thick, white Berber, trimmed in polished walnut, and the windows are framed in rich mahogany.

At the front of the car is a small, circular bar with four seats. The neatly dressed bartender leans forward as he wipes down the bar with a large towel.

There is a small group of passengers, most of them looking very comfortable and relaxed. Some of them are looking out their windows at the passing scenery, some speaking in hushed tones to the passengers seated next to them, while others are reading to pass the time.

The conductor - a large, elderly man with a contagious smile and warm, knowing eyes - stands in the front of the first car. He's wearing a well-tailored black tuxedo with gold cufflinks, a white shirt and nicely polished black shoes. His hair is mostly gray and neatly combed.

As he studies the passengers, he fixes his gaze on a man sleeping in the first row on his left. The man looks completely out of place in these surroundings. He's wearing an old pair of blue jeans, torn slightly at the knees, and a faded Chicago Bears t-shirt. His tattered construction boots are unlaced with the tongues hanging down to the toes. His hair is dirty and uncombed, and he has what appears to be a four or five day whisker growth. The beam of sunlight coming through the window next to his seat casts dark shadows on the deep lines in his face.

The conductor leans toward him closely and taps him lightly on the shoulder.

"Sir," he said with a warm smile. "Would you care for something to drink?"

The passenger, startled at first, rubs his eyes as he turns his head to look at the conductor. He has a very confused look on his face as if he has no idea where he is or how he'd arrived here.

"No....no thank you," he replied as he looked through blurred vision at the
conductor's face, then down to the name 'Gabriel' on his nametag.

"Very well," Gabriel said as he turned to the next passenger.

The man shifted in his seat as he looked around the car, his eyes squinting and slightly out of focus, irritated by the bright light inside. He had absolutely no recollection of boarding any train. He reached into his pockets, searching for a ticket stub, but finds only a dirty piece of gum, a few singles, and twenty-seven cents in change.

"Where the hell am I?" he thought. "Must have been a good night."

Sam had experienced quite a few 'good nights' in recent years. In reality,
they weren't very good at all. He had spent most of them alone with a bottle since his divorce.

"Next stop, Reuben," Gabriel shouted from behind him.

"Reuben?... Where the heck is
Reuben?...Wow. I *am* lost," he thought to himself. Glancing through the window next to him, he stared at the platform, noticing a ruggedly handsome man leaning against the outside wall of the train depot. He had the appearance of someone who might be cast in the role of the main character in an action-adventure movie, with striking good looks and manly facial features. Next to him were three fishing poles, and a small tackle box sat on the ground next to his feet. Just to the man's left was an elaborate set of gates leading to what appeared to be a courtyard of some sort. Within these gates stood a large multitude of people, looking as though they were awaiting something.

Apparently this train was not what they were waiting for, as none of them boarded. Just as the train began to move again, the rugged man looked directly at Sam, nodding his head politely with a strong, confident facial expression. Sam let out a sigh as he looked away, and then let his head fall back into the headrest, deciding that he might as well just enjoy the ride. After all, it wasn't as though he had anywhere to be.

He had lost his job a few months earlier due to his heavy drinking. He had been surviving on a small amount of money he had left after being forced to sell his home, but that had gradually disappeared as he failed to find another job. He had no money, and due to the severity of his alcoholism, he was completely unable at this point to provide for himself in any way. His entire family had completely given up on him after many attempts to help. Even his own children, who were now in their early twenties and had moved out on their own, had left him behind as they moved on with their lives, not wanting anything more to do with him. There was simply no one left who he could turn to.

He had recently rented a small basement apartment on the west side
of Chicago. It was not so much an apartment as it was a dark, dusty, partially finished basement of a home he had rented from the owners who lived upstairs.

They were an elderly couple whose children were Sam's age and had moved out long ago. Their children had repeatedly tried to convince them to sell their home as the neighborhood had changed and had become increasingly dangerous, but they'd lived there for so many years it was impossible for them to imagine living anywhere else.

The space which Sam called home was approximately 600 square feet and was paneled in dark, wood-grained paneling with a white dropped ceiling. Various ceiling tiles were either broken or water stained and were loaded with cobwebs in the corners. A single fluorescent fixture in the center of the room was the only source of light he had, as the windows had been painted over or paneled shut long ago. The floors were covered with cheap vinyl tiles, some of which were either broken or missing completely, exposing the concrete floor below.

He liked this situation because he had his own entrance and the owners never bothered him as long as the rent was paid on time. The only thing he didn't like about it was the way that the church bells down the street would chime every few hours, seemingly mocking him with their joyous tones while he sat in his misery.

He had no television; just a cardboard box full of clothes, some old pictures that he kept in a worn out plastic bag, and a filthy twin mattress shoved into the corner without any sheets or blankets. His pillow was nothing more than a pair of dirty rolled up jeans.

Strewn throughout his apartment there were empty cigarette packs, full ashtrays, fast food wrappers, and empty liquor bottles.

It was there that he'd spent the majority of his time lately, drinking whatever he could afford as he tried unsuccessfully to drown the sadness of what had become of his life. He would find himself wandering the streets for hours, far past the point where there was any hope of redemption from a life that had somehow gone horribly wrong.

His concentration and his desire to accomplish anything meaningful had faded to nothing over the past few years. In his eyes, there was simply no way out of his current situation. There was no hope for the future, and nobody left who cared about the past.

He turned in his seat to look back at the other passengers. It was an odd mix of people. Near the back of the car was a man dressed in a very nice suit with a briefcase on the floor next to the aisle. Across the aisle, near the middle of the car, there was a very attractive woman in a red dress. A few rows behind her, there was a family who looked as though they were on a vacation. Their little boy looked to be about five years old and it was quite obvious that he wanted to get off of the train. He kept trying to get out of his seat and climb over his father to get to the aisle. His father, losing his patience, grabbed the boy by the arm and jerked him back into his seat.

"Peter!" the mother shouted. "Don't jerk him like that, you'll hurt him!"

The boy started to cry and turned to his mother as she put her arm around him. Peter looked directly at Sam, causing him to turn around in his seat, sensing the father's embarrassment.

Next stop, Simeon," Gabriel shouted as the train once again slowed to a stop.

Still being completely confused as to his whereabouts, Sam turned to look at the approaching station.

As he gazed through the window, he saw a neatly carved sign over the train station with the name "Simeon" written upon it. There was a large group of people at the station, but apparently none of this group needed to board the train either. They all stood on the platform, looking at the train with blank, emotionless faces. Nobody spoke as the train waited. They just stood in place, motionless, staring at the passengers through the tinted glass until the train began to move again, at which point they turned and began to walk away slowly. In the midst of the crowd, one man stood alone, apparently unaware of any movement around him. He looked directly at Sam through the glass with a cold stare, glaring at him as if he was this man's worst enemy. It appeared as though he was an extremely angry man, standing motionless with both of his fists tightly clenched. Behind him, Sam could see another set of gates, very similar to the ones at the first stop.

"This looks like a Twilight Zone episode," Sam

thought to himself.

As the train pulled slowly from the station, Sam started to close his eyes when he was suddenly startled by a young boy, who ran quickly past him down the aisle. He looked ahead to see that the little boy from the vacationing family had broken free and had run to the front of the car. He looked at his parents, expecting them to be chasing after him, but they had apparently given up. They remained in their seats, keeping a close eye on him to ensure that he wasn't getting into any trouble. An ear to ear grin broke across his face as he realized that he was free to roam for a while.

"Hey there, tiger!" Gabriel bellowed to the boy, a huge smile on his face.   "Tiger?" Sam thought to himself, raising one eyebrow.

Tiger was a nickname that Sam's father had given him as a young boy; a nickname he had always liked.

The little boy stopped and looked up at Gabriel with a big smile on his face.

"What's your name, big guy?" Gabriel asked.

"Jonathon," the little boy replied, looking back at his parents for
approval.

"Jonathon, huh? Well, let me ask you something Jonathon. How would you like to take a walk up to the front of the train with me and meet the engineer?" Gabriel asked excitedly as he kneeled down next to Jonathon and winked at his parents.

"Maybe he could even teach you how to drive the train," he continued.

"Can I mom?" he asked, his voice raised in excitement as he spun around
to look at his mother.

"O.k., Jonathon, but you *behave* yourself up there."

Gabriel took hold of Jonathon's hand and began to lead him through the front door of the car, disappearing as it closed behind them.

Sam again closed his eyes, thinking back to when he was that age. It was a very long time ago, far longer in emotional years than in actual.

In a classic case of the sins of the father being visited upon the son, Sam was never able to shake himself from the demons that had also plagued his dad. Although he had grown up swearing to himself that he would never succumb to them, they were, in the end, his absolute downfall.

His father, Lee, was an enormous man of 6'4", 260 pounds. His hair, which
was mostly gray, had begun receding rapidly when he was in his very early twenties and he was now completely bald on top. As was the style in the mid-to-late 60's, he wore thick sideburns down to his jaw line.

He had a struggled from a severe drinking problem through the majority of his life, and would become extremely violent when he was drunk. While he was always the perfect gentleman when sober, he would show an utter disrespect for women while intoxicated.

He had quite the reputation of being nearly unstoppable when the mood struck him. Anyone who knew him well would agree that, once he had that certain look in his eyes, it was always a good idea to simply get out of his way.

He had another son, also named Lee, from a previous relationship who was ten years older than Sam. Little Lee, as family members called him, lived with his mother, and therefore he and Sam weren't able to spend much time together when they were young. Sam always looked up to him. He never bought into the half-brother idea. As far as Sam was concerned, Little Lee was his big brother, plain and simple.

Sam's mother, Dawn, came from a typical Irish-Catholic family in Chicago. She was a very attractive woman, catching Lee's eye the first time he had met her. Due to the dysfunctional living conditions within her own home, she had run away at 17.

She met Sam's father on a blind date, and was immediately swept away by his charm and personality. They were married at a justice of the peace office after dating for a short time and moved into a small apartment in Des Plaines, Illinois.

After being together just over a year, she gave birth to Sam's sister, Suzanne. Sam would arrive in their family one and a half years later.

In time, they were able to purchase a small, three-bedroom house in Arlington Heights, Illinois, about 30 miles northwest of Chicago. It wasn't much, but it was all that they could afford on Lee's meager earnings as a bartender at a local country club. Sam's mother had worked as a waitress at the same club, but had eventually stopped working in order to stay home with Sam and his sister.

Sam couldn't remember his parents ever being happy in their marriage. There were always loud arguments, and his father would disappear for days on end on a fairly consistent basis.

Sam's very first memory of his home life came when he was about five years old, on a night when his parent's fighting seem to come to a head. There had been a lot of late night arguments between them throughout the prior week, causing Sam and his sister to wonder what was going on. They had heard their parents arguing earlier in the day, and their father had stormed out of the house immediately following it. From all of their prior experiences, they knew that he would come home later that night, intoxicated and out of control. Out of a sense of morbid curiosity, they decided to set up their blankets by Suzanne's bedroom door so they wouldn't miss any of the action when he finally came home. They both stayed up as long as they could but eventually drifted off to sleep.

A few hours later, they awoke to an explosion of sound coming from the living room. The entire house shook as they heard broken glass falling to the floor. Sam opened his eyes and looked down the hallway. The lamp which was usually on the end table in the living room was now lying on the floor, the shade bent and broken, casting eerie shadows of Sam's father on the far wall. Sam couldn't see his mother, but he could hear her crying. His father staggered backward toward the rear wall of the living room, letting loose with a mouthful of obscenities.

The hallway that led to Suzanne's bedroom was directly in line with the rear wall of the living room, giving Sam and Suzanne a clear view of their father. He was having a hard time standing and was swaying from one side to the other as he wiped the sweat from his forehead with his arm.

He was wearing his work clothes, a pair of black dress pants, a white shirt, and a black tie. The tie was hanging loosely from his neck and the top few buttons of his shirt were opened. His hair, which was usually neatly combed, was standing up on one side, looking as though he had been wrestling with someone.

He stood directly in their line of sight, seething at Sam's mother across the room. He turned his head to the left and saw Sam and Suzanne lying in the doorway at the end of the hall. Sam was suddenly gripped with fear as he realized that his father had turned his attention to him. He had a crazed look in his eyes - one which Sam had never seen before, but one which he would see many more times during his lifetime.

"Oh, you want to see what's going on?!" his father bellowed with a voice
that sounded like thunder.

"Come on out here then!" he continued, motioning toward them.

Sam could see that his father was holding

something in his right hand, but he couldn't make out what it was. He could feel himself tremble with fear as he and Suzanne stood up and started down the hallway, Suzanne slightly behind him.

As they turned the corner into the living room, they could see that their mother had a cut over the bridge of her nose. She was sitting on the sofa; her face turned toward the floor as she attempted to cover the damage he had done to it with her trembling hands. Her shoulders were jerking sporadically as she drew in short, shallow breaths, crying uncontrollably. Suzanne ran to her mother and threw her arms around her.

The living room furniture had all been shoved out of place, and a large painting on the wall had been knocked sideways. Sam looked to see what his father was holding in his right hand. He could now see that it was a gun. Lee had come to the conclusion that Sam's mother was having an affair and he had come home with the gun to end it.

"Sit down!" his father yelled, waving the gun wildly as the sudden sound of
his thundering voice caused the three of them to jump.

Sam could feel his heart pounding so hard in his chest it felt as though it might explode.

"Stop it, you're scaring the children!" his mother cried.

"I'm not scaring anybody!" he shouted back as he leaned in toward her.
He then turned his head to look at Sam.

"Am I scaring you?!" he yelled with his eyes full of rage.

Sam couldn't control himself any longer. His chest began to heave as he
burst into tears, shaking with fear. He sprang from his seat and ran to his mother, wrapping his arms around her with all of his might. With that, his father turned away in disgust, let out a growl, and then turned

around and headed toward the kitchen. The whole house shook with every step he took, culminating with a loud crash as he stormed through the front door. A few seconds later, they heard his car screech out of the driveway and take off down the street.

They all listened intently as the powerful moan of the car's engine gradually faded off into the distance. None of them dared to move. They sat holding each other and crying for a short while, all of them hoping and praying that they wouldn't hear his car pull back into the driveway.

Dawn lifted her head and began wiping the tears from her cheeks with the back of her hand.

"Are you o.k. Mom?" Suzanne asked as she looked up at her mother's face.

"Yeah, I'm okay," she replied, her voice still shaking.

"Come on, guys. You two should be in bed," she said as she stood up, holding her hands out to them.

They each took hold of one of her hands and the three of them made their way down the hallway toward their bedrooms. When they reached the bedroom doors, she leaned down and gave them both a hug.

"Go ahead now…Everything's alright," she said through a forced smile.

Sam let go of his mother, walked slowly to his bed, and then climbed in, pulling the covers up under his neck. He watched his bedroom door as it closed slowly behind her. He stared at the light coming through the crack between the bottom of the door and the floor and listened intently as his mother began cleaning the mess in the living room. He was sorry that he and Suzanne had decided to sleep in her bedroom doorway that night. He wasn't sure what they had expected to see when their father came home, but he never expected to see *that.* All he knew for certain at this point was that he never wanted to see anything like that again. He laid awake in his bed, replaying everything he had just seen over and over again until his eyes became too heavy to keep open anymore. He closed them, still afraid that he father would return and continue his assault. Eventually his exhaustion got the better of him, and he drifted off to sleep.

When he awoke the next morning, Sam emerged from his room and quietly peered into his parent's bedroom to see if his father had returned home, seeing that he had not.

He walked to the living room and turned on the television, spinning the dial through the eight channels that were available in those days. Before he could find anything worth watching, he heard his father's car pull into the driveway. Jumping to his feet, he bolted through the kitchen and then out the front door. Deep down inside, he was still a bit frightened about what his father's demeanor might be, but he desperately wanted everything to be o.k. again.

"Daddy!" he yelled as his father stepped from the car and closed the door.

"Hey there, Tiger," Lee said with a smile as Sam slammed into his legs and hung on, playfully trying to pry Sam from his leg as he walked toward the house.

For a brief moment, Sam had all but forgotten the events of the previous evening. Everything was right in his world again. In his eyes, his dad was home again, and that's all that mattered.

"Where's your mother?" Lee asked as they entered the kitchen.

"She's in your bedroom, dad," Sam answered.

"O.k., go watch t.v… I'll be right back," he said as he began walking toward the bedroom.

Sam smiled to himself after he had left the room. He knew that his parents would talk things over, and before too long, everything would be back to normal. He was still young enough to believe that saying you were sorry was the magic formula to solving any and all of your problems. He knew that his father would apologize and that his mother would accept his apology. Beyond that, there was no reason to remain angry, nor was there anything to fear.

Dawn hadn't slept much through the night. Her thoughts had been spinning constantly as she tossed and turned, wondering how her life had come to this. Lee had been verbally abusive from time to time, but this was the first time he had ever physically abused her. Her mind raced back and forth, one minute thinking about how wrong he was to have done so, and the next minute wondering if she had somehow done something to deserve it. She was also torn between wanting to take the kids and leave, and feeling paralyzed with the fear of having nowhere else to go.

As he stepped into the bedroom and quietly closed the door behind him, Lee looked over at Dawn. She had heard him come home and sat up on the far side of the bed, her back toward the bedroom door.

The only light in the room was the small amount that made its way through the heavy gold curtains that covered the small casement window. He stood silently for a moment, searching for the right words to say as his eyes adjusted to the darkness. He took in a deep breath as he shifted his weight from one foot to the other. He had rehearsed everything that he would say on his way home, but the words escaped him as he looked at her.

"Dawn...I, I'm sorry," he stuttered nervously as he wiped a bead of sweat from his brow.

Dawn sat quietly at the edge of the bed, waiting to hear what he would say next. She knew that this was very difficult for him, and she wanted it to be.

"I didn't mean to hurt you," he continued.

Dawn's shoulders began to tremble slightly as the tears started to well
up in her eyes. She leaned over toward the nightstand and picked up a tissue.

"Well, you did," she answered quietly as she brought it to her face and
began to wipe her eyes.

Lee walked slowly to the edge of the bed and put his hand on Dawn's
shoulder. Her entire body stiffened when she felt his touch. She wanted to throw his hand off of her and run out of the room, but she couldn't move. She felt nearly paralyzed in a dense fog of fear and confusion.

Lee pulled his hand away, feeling a sense of coldness from her body language.

"What do you want me to do?" he asked quietly. "What do you want me to say?" I'm sorry, I made a mistake."

A million answers to his question raced through her mind as she sat in silence, but she could verbalize none of them.

"Lee…you can't do that to me…You can't do that to the kids. You scared the hell out of all of us last night."

Lee's heart dropped as he began to think about how frightened Sam and
Suzanne must have been. He loved them very much, and he would never want them to be afraid of him for any reason. He stood silently as his hands dropped slowly to each side. After a minute or so, he turned and opened the bedroom door. As he stepped through the doorway, he paused for a second, looking back at Dawn.

"I'm sorry," he said again, turning his eyes to the floor as he continued into the hallway, closing the door quietly behind him.

When he entered the living room, he saw that Suzanne had joined Sam, both of them sitting on the living room floor in front of the television. He walked past them and sat on the sofa, lighting a cigarette as he contemplated what he might say. He was never very good at expressing his feelings to anyone. He wanted to say that he would never act that way again, but he knew better. He was who he was, and even though his actions might have been over the top, he also believed deep down inside that Dawn had brought most of this upon herself.

Over the course of the next few weeks, all was relatively quiet in their home. Lee had been on his best behavior, giving Dawn and the kids hope that he had seen the error of his ways.

As she did every morning, Dawn hurried to get the kids ready for school, seeing them off as they headed down the driveway on their bikes. It was a relatively short ride to school, a trip that Sam and Suzanne made on a daily basis. They lived in a very quiet, safe neighborhood, and there was no reason to fear that anything would happen to either of them along the way.

She had recently taken on a part time job as a keypunch operator to help make ends meet. With the kids being in school for most of the day, she could do so without leaving them alone for long periods of time.

"Have a good day!" she yelled after them with a smile as they rode away.

They followed one another through the quiet, suburban neighborhood, past the small homes with neatly manicured lawns, eventually passing a growing number of schoolmates as they neared the school.

Pulling up to the bike racks, Sam began to have second thoughts about going inside. Suzanne had raced ahead of him and had already locked up her bike, heading inside to start her day. He remembered going to the Y.M.C.A. about six blocks away and playing basketball with a few friends earlier that summer. He looked at the school, and then looked back down the block at the other students who were heading his way.   Suzanne being no longer in sight, he backed his bike away from the rack, coasting slowly away from the school, keeping a sharp eye out for any teachers who might see him leaving. He knew that it was the wrong thing to do, but how would anyone know? He rode the six blocks to the Y.M.C.A. and went inside, grabbing a basketball as he entered the gym. He shot baskets and played by himself for most of the day, and then spent a few hours riding through the neighborhood and taking in the sights.

As he coasted slowly down the tree-lined streets, he looked at all of the homes he passed along the way, never imagining that the families inside were any different from his. He just naturally assumed that all of the fathers yelled and screamed at all of the other mothers, and that sometimes they probably even hit them if they became angry enough.

As he finally made his way to the school property, he was completely unaware that the school principal had called Dawn at work, informing her that Sam was nowhere to be found.

With her heart in her throat, she had driven to the school as quickly as possible. When he had finally returned to the school, she was standing next to her car speaking with the principal.

"Sam!" she shrieked as she saw him riding up to them. "Where the hell have you been?"

Sam suddenly realized that his cover was blown, and that he was in big trouble.

"What do you mean?" he asked, playing dumb.

"Don't give me that crap! You haven't been to school all day! Where did you go?" she demanded.

Knowing that he'd be in serious trouble if he told the truth, he blurted out the first thing that came to mind.

"I don't know...I was riding my bike toward the school...and I just kept going. I got a little lost for a while, and before I knew it, I was at the Y.M.C.A.."

A look of concern grew on Dawn's face.

"What do you mean, you just kept going? And why did you go to the Y.M.C.A.?"

"I don't know, mom. I just kept going. I knew that I should go to school, but I got confused. I didn't really know where I was until I got to the Y.M.C.A."

Dawn wasn't sure what to think. She leaned over and hugged him, and then leaned back to look into his eyes. He looked sincere in his explanation, and she began to wonder if everything that he'd been through over the past few months had taken its toll on him. She began to consider the thought that something may be going on in his mind that needed to be looked into.

As they were driving home, she began thinking about an old friend who was a psychologist, wondering if he'd be willing to talk things over with Sam to see if he was alright. She couldn't afford to pay for any type of counseling, and she hoped that he might just do it for her as a favor.

She had first met him while he was playing part time in a jazz band back when she and Lee worked at the country club together. The band played there quite often, and they had become casual friends, talking every so often when they would take their breaks. At one point, he had given her a business card from his office, which was located in a state run mental institution in Chicago.

Once they arrived at home, she looked for his card, remembering that she had tucked it inside of her phone book. She thought again about whether or not it was a good idea to expose Sam to any type of therapy at such a young age. Knowing that the only other alternative would be to do nothing and wait to see if he developed more serious problems, she picked up the phone and dialed the number.

"Mental Health," a pleasant voice answered.

"Yes, I'm looking for Will Rohdes," she said quietly.

"Hold one second please."

Dawn twisted the phone cord between her fingers as she waited for Will to answer.

"Will Rohdes speaking."

"Will, hi. I don't know if you remember me. I used to work as a waitress at the Old Orchard Country Club...Dawn Grace?"

"Oh, hi Dawn. Sure I remember you. How are you?"

"Well, unfortunately, not too well."

"What's wrong?"

"It's my son, Sam. For some reason he decided not to go to school today. He says that he doesn't know why, that he just forgot where he was going and kept on riding his bike. I'm a little worried, Will."

"Really?... Huh... Has he ever done anything like this before?"

"No. Never."

"Have you talked with Lee about it?"

"No. I don't know if I should. You know how his temper is. If Sam is having some sort of problems, I really wouldn't want Lee to explode. That might just make things worse."

"Well, what would you like me to do?"

"I don't know. Would it be possible to have him come in and speak with you? Maybe you could see what's going on in his mind. I just don't know how to talk with him about it."

"Sure, Dawn. I can see him here at the office. How does next Wednesday at 4 sound?"

"That would be great. Thank you so very much...Will, there's one more thing."

"Go ahead."

"You know that Lee and I can't really afford to pay for any counseling. Is there any way you could do this as a favor?"

Will paused for a few seconds, not sure how he wanted to answer. He felt a little annoyed that someone would actually call him out of the blue, asking him to render his professional services without some form of payment.

"Hello?" Dawn said quietly.

"Yeah...That's fine, Dawn," he answered reluctantly.

"You're the best, Will! Thank you so very much!"

She hung up the phone and walked over to Sam's bedroom. Looking in through the doorway, she was pleased to see him sitting in on the floor in front of his bed playing with his cars, oblivious to the concern that she was feeling.

Once Wednesday had arrived, Dawn brought Sam to Will's office and took a seat in the waiting room, wondering if she was doing the right thing. She looked around the waiting room at the other patients, some obviously suffering from serious mental disorders. This was, after all, a state run mental facility where the sickest of the sick came for treatment. She hoped to herself that Sam didn't belong here.

The receptionist slid the glass window to the waiting room open and leaned forward.

"Mrs. Grace?"

"Yes?" she answered, startled by the voice.

"Mr. Rohdes will see you now."

"Sam, wait here for a few minutes. I'll be right back."

"O.k. mom," he answered with a smile.

She turned and walked through the door, being led to Will's office by the receptionist.

"Dawn, how are you?" Will said with a smile as she entered the room. "Please, have a seat."

"Thank you," she responded as she took her seat, feeling very uneasy about being there.

"So, what's going on with Sam?" he asked as he took a yellow legal pad from his desk drawer and set it on his desk.

Dawn let out a deep sigh, obviously very

nervous about her young son's condition.

"Well, the other day, Sam left early with his sister to ride their bikes to school. They've both taken their bikes to school on many occasions, so I had no reason to believe that they wouldn't make it there. While I was still at work, the principal called from the school. He told me that Sam hadn't been in school all day. I was scared to death, Will. I didn't know if Lee had come to get him or if somebody had grabbed him before he made it inside. I had no idea what to think."

"I understand," Will said as he scribbled on his pad. "Please…go on."

"As we were standing there, Sam rode up on his bike as if nothing had happened. When I asked him where he had been, he seemed confused."

"What do you mean, confused?"

"It was as if he had no idea why he hadn't gone to school. He said that he started riding his bike toward the school and just kept on riding."

"Did he say why?"

"No…He said that he didn't know why."

"And he's never done anything like this before?"

"No, never."

"Has he had any times where he seemed confused or delirious."

"Not that I'm aware of."

"Have there been any changes in his typical behavior lately? Has he been less communicative or depressed?"

"No, not at all."

Will was well aware of Lee's drinking, as well as his volatile temper. While working at the country club, he had heard countless tales of his legendary outbursts, and had personally witnessed a few of them as well, watching from a distance as Lee bounced a few obnoxious customers out of the bar. He looked up at Dawn, watching to see her facial expression before asking his next question.

"Has anything happened at home lately that might be causing him to be upset?"

Dawn looked away briefly before she answered, her thoughts returning to the night of Lee's melt down.

"No," she replied unconvincingly.

"I see....Are you sure?" he asked after studying her for a few seconds.

"Yes.....I'm sure," she replied, still looking away.

"O.k.. Well, why don't you send him in and let me speak with him for few minutes. Maybe I can find out if there are some issues going on in his mind that led to this. We can talk again when we're done, alright?"

"Alright...Thank you very much, Will," she said quietly as she stood and turned toward the door.

"Oh...there's one more thing," she said, pausing briefly.

"What's that?"

"I know that you see Lee at the club from time to time. Please don't tell him anything about this."

"You have my word, Dawn."

"Thank you, Will."

Dawn walked back into the waiting room and looked at Sam, who was looking toward the other side of the room, observing a man in his 20's who seemed to be having a heated disagreement with himself.

"Sam, come here for a minute," she said with a smile.

Sam jumped from his seat and walked over to Dawn as she squatted down slightly and whispered in his ear.

"The man in the office over here wants to talk to you about the other day when you missed school. There's no reason to be afraid or nervous. You're not in any trouble. He only wants to talk. Just tell him the truth, o.k.?"

"O.k. mom."

Sam walked into Will's office and sat in the seat in front of his desk.

"Hi there, Sam," Will said with a friendly smile.

"Hi," Sam replied quietly.

"I'm going to ask you a few questions, o.k. Sam? You're not in any trouble or anything, so you don't have to be afraid. I just want you to tell me what's on your mind."

He studied Sam's facial expression and body language for a few seconds, noticing that he appeared to be anxious. He then turned the first page over on his legal pad and folded it underneath.

Do you understand?" he asked.

Sam nodded, his palms beginning to sweat as he awaited the first question.

"Sam, how do you like school."

"It's alright."

Will looked down as he scribbled on his pad.

"Do you have a lot of friends there?"

"Yeah."

"Has anyone been bothering you there?"

"What do you mean?"

"Has anyone been making fun of you or picking on you or anything like that?"

"No."

"Are you sure?...Nobody?...How about Suzanne? Has anyone been bothering her?"

"No. I don't think so."

"What do you think of your teachers?"

"I don't know. They're nice, I guess."

With every answer that Sam gave, Will wrote down more notes on his legal pad. The sound of the felt tip pen squeaking across the paper was starting to annoy Sam. He began to wonder what he had said that was interesting enough to write down. He looked around the cramped office, and then back at Will.

"Sam...I know your dad, and I know that he can get very angry at times," he said as he looked up at Sam to see the reaction to his next question.

"How do you feel about that?"

Sam didn't answer, looking down at his shoes to avoid making any eye contact.

"Sam?... How do you feel about that?"

"I don't know," Sam answered, still staring at his shoes. He hadn't thought much about how *he* had felt about it.

Will could see that Sam was becoming uncomfortable with his line of questioning, so he decided to go another direction.

"Sam, do you ever have times when you feel confused or feel like you can't concentrate?"

"No, not really."

"Why don't you tell me what happened the other day at school."

"I don't know," Sam replied, looking back at his shoes. "I was riding my bike to school and I just forgot where I was going. I just kept riding. Before I knew it, I was at the Y.M.C.A.."

Sam found it impossible to look Will in the eyes as he answered his questions. He knew that his story didn't make much sense, but it was all that he had. He was desperately hoping that Will would change the subject.

Will stared across his desk at Sam, the silence becoming uncomfortable as Sam began to pick at the seam on the arm of his chair. He wondered whether or not Will was buying any of this. He could feel his face getting hot and his stomach starting to tighten as he waited for Will's response.

"Did you have something on your mind that you were thinking about as you were riding? Was something bothering you?"

"No...not really."

"How are things at home, Sam?...Is there anything happening at home that's been upsetting you?"

"No."

"Nothing?...Are you sure?...You can tell me if

27

there is, Sam...You're not going to get anyone in trouble."

"No...nothing."

"All right, buddy...Thanks for talking to me. Listen, I think we're done here. Why don't you go outside and ask your mother to come in."

Sam couldn't get out of the office fast enough. He walked into the waiting room and sat down, letting his mother know that Will wanted to speak with her.

"Well," Will said as she sat down across from him. "I talked with Sam about what happened the other day. I also asked a few questions about his home life, his friends, etc.. I really don't think that he has any serious issues or anything like that.

"Oh, thank God!" Dawn replied with a sigh of relief.

"I do think that you should keep a close eye on him, though. Please call me if you notice anything different about his behavior or if more episodes like this one occur."

"Absolutely. Thank you so much Will," Dawn said as she stood and reached across the desk to shake his hand.

"No problem...but I do have another question."

"Sure..."

"I've noticed a similar reaction from both you and Sam when I've asked either of you if anything has been going on at home that's been bothering you...I know I'm not there, and it's really none of my business, but judging by your body language, I can see that neither of you are being honest with me about that."

"Will...it's really complicated."

"It usually is, Dawn...but if you don't talk about it, I can't help you through it."

"Maybe another time, Will...There's just too much there, and I can't leave Sam in the waiting room that long," she said with a nervous laugh as she stood up again.

"Thanks again for your time, Will…I'd better get going."

"No problem, Dawn…anytime."

Dawn walked out of his office, satisfied in Will's opinion that Sam wasn't experiencing any serious problems. She couldn't wait to get out of this creepy building and away from the patients who roamed the halls wearing hospital gowns and speaking to imaginary friends with far away looks in their eyes.

As evening fell, Lee still hadn't returned home from work. This wasn't out of the ordinary. He would frequently stay after hours for a few cocktails before returning home.   Dawn tucked Sam and Suzanne into bed and began to straighten up the house. Sam loved listening to the white noise of the vacuum cleaner and watching the light under his door as she made her way down the hallway. In a matter of minutes he was sound asleep.

He awoke at about 3:00am, having an intense urge to use the bathroom. Being half asleep, he exited the bathroom, and without realizing what he was doing, entered his parent's room instead of his own. He crawled into their bed and immediately fell back into a deep sleep.

Feeling the bed move, Dawn awoke. As she lay in bed still half asleep, she thought for a moment that there was a slight odor of smoke in the room. Thinking that she was just imagining things, she rolled over, pulling the blanket up to her shoulders and trying to fall back to sleep. Opening her eyes for a moment, she saw that Sam was in the bed next to her.

"That's odd," she thought. "Why is Sam in here?"

As her senses began to awaken, she again smelled smoke, this time more strongly than before. Panic ran through her as she threw her blanket to the side and sprung out of bed. She instinctively made her way to the door through the dark bedroom, stumbling as she tried to move as quickly as possible. She hesitated for a second after clutching the doorknob, fearing what she might find on the other side.

Flinging the door open, she stepped backward, her eyes wide open as she
struggled to see in the darkness. She could barely make out anything through the layer of dense smoke working its way down from the hallway ceiling. She watched, terrified as it rolled under the top of the door frame and into her bedroom.

She reached quickly behind the door, grabbing her bathrobe which was hanging on a hook on the back side and brought it to her face, covering her mouth and nose. As she stepped into the hallway, she looked frantically in every direction trying to see where the smoke was coming from.

Thinking that it may be coming from the kitchen, she ran down the hallway.
As she entered the living room she saw Lee, still in his work clothes, sound asleep on the sofa, an orange glow illuminating the room from the cushion next to him.

After working very late, he had sat on the sofa to have one last cigarette before going to bed and had fallen asleep with the lit cigarette in his hand.

"Lee, wake up! The sofa's on fire!" she screamed as she ran toward him.

Lee immediately jumped to his feet, looking back at the smoldering cushion.
He lunged forward, grabbing the cushion by the corner and ran to the back door. After fumbling with the lock for a moment, he threw it open and flung the cushion into the back yard.

He then walked back toward the sofa, which had also begun to smolder underneath where the cushion had been.

"Hold the storm door open!" he barked as he bent over to pick up one end.

Dawn wrapped her robe around her shoulders and stepped through the
doorway, holding the storm door open as wide as she could as Lee began to drag the sofa toward her.

With brute force, Lee dragged it through the doorway, scraping it along both sides until it was out of the house. He then continued to drag it until it was about 30 feet away. He set it down and immediately ran to get the garden hose which was hanging near the back door. Turning back with the hose in his hand, he began to soak the cushion and sofa until he could see no more sign of smoke coming from either.

"Are you all right?" Dawn asked as he walked back toward the house and
turned off the hose.

"Yeah, I'm fine," he replied, looking down at his legs to make sure.

"What did you do?! Did you fall asleep with a lit cigarette or something?!"

"Yeah, I must have."

"Lee, how could you do something like that?!"

"It's not like I did it on purpose!" he replied, becoming agitated. "I must have been really tired!"

"You have to be more careful."

"Really?! No kidding?!" he asked sarcastically. "I'll keep that in mind."

Lee stepped back through the doorway and walked over to the living room
window, opening it to let the smoke out. He then continued through the rest of the house, opening all of the windows as Dawn went to check on Sam and Suzanne. Both of them were sound asleep, completely unaware of what had just happened.

When they were satisfied that all of the smoke had cleared, they closed the
windows and walked to their bedroom.

As he entered the room, Lee walked over to his bed and leaned over, picking
Sam up in his arms, and turned to take him to his own

bed. As he tucked him
in, Lee began to think about what might have
happened had Dawn not awoken him. He stared at
Sam for a few minutes, and then returned to his
bedroom.

Dawn had already climbed into bed, her heart
still pounding from the excitement.

"Were you awake this whole time?" Lee asked
as he began to undress, wondering to himself how
she knew to come into the living room.

"No, I was sound asleep. Sam came into our
room and woke me up when he
climbed into the bed."

"Why was he up?" he asked.

"I don't know," she replied. "Thank God that he
was. We could've all been dead."

As she rolled over onto her side with her back
to Lee, she began to
wonder how much Lee had been drinking before he
came home. Her stomach was
in knots as she stared at the wall, thinking about what
might have happened had Sam not come into their
room. She knew it was a miracle that he had.

Although she had never had much of a
relationship with God, she quietly
offered up a quick prayer of thanks.

TWO

As the train continued its journey across the countryside, Sam looked through the window at the passing scenery, thinking to himself that he would have caused far less pain to those around him had he never climbed into his parent's bed that night. It would have been over long before he had the opportunity to screw things up the way that he had.

He had listened to many people talk over the years about their childhood, conveniently placing the blame for all of their failures squarely at the feet of their parents, but he never bought into that. In fact, he had always been disgusted by that mindset. As far as he was concerned, everyone receives ample opportunity to take control of their own lives. He had no one but himself to blame for the mess he had made of his life.

He looked toward the front of the car as the man in the nice suit walked past him and took a seat at the bar.

"Can I help you sir?" the bartender asked with a smile.

"I'll have a rum and coke, please," the man said as he reached for his wallet.

"Right away, sir," he replied as he reached for a glass and filled it with ice.

The man looked back at Sam and nodded as he waited for his drink. Sam offered a half smile as he nodded back.

"Here you are," the bartender said as he placed a cocktail napkin in front of the man, setting the drink on it.

The bartender then turned away and began wiping down the shelf behind him.

"Excuse me," the man said as he pulled a few bills from his wallet. "How much do I owe you?"

"Oh, the drinks are complimentary, sir," he replied as he looked back at the man and smiled.

"Really? Well, here, take this," he responded as he slid a couple of singles across the bar.

"I cannot accept tips, sir. All gratuities are included in the ticket price."

"Wow…Okay."

He looked back at Sam and shrugged as he picked up his money and put it back in his wallet.

Sam was in desperate need of a drink. His hands were shaking slightly as is common with alcoholics when they haven't had a drink in a while. He wanted to say yes when Gabriel had asked him if he wanted one earlier, but having just a few dollars, he decided to pass. Hearing that the drinks were on the house was too much for him to resist. He immediately stood up and walked to the bar, taking a seat at the far end away from the man in the suit.

"Can I help you sir?" the bartender asked with

a smile.

"Uh, yeah. I'll have a vodka and tonic please," he said nervously as he ran his hands through his hair in an attempt to make himself look presentable.

"Yes sir," the bartender replied.

Sam turned in his seat, looking back at the rest of the passengers as he waited for his drink.

"Here you are," the bartender said as he set the drink in front of him.

"Thank you," Sam replied as he picked up his drink. His hands were shaking slightly as he brought it to his mouth and tipped it back, finishing half of it with his first sip.

"Not a bad deal, huh?" the man in the suit asked as he looked at Sam.

"Excuse me?" Sam replied.

"Free drinks. That's not too hard to take," he said as he raised his glass in a toast and winked.

"Oh...yeah. Not bad," Sam replied with a laugh.

Sam threw back the rest of his drink and set the empty glass back on the bar.

"Would you care for another, sir?" the bartender asked.

"Yes, please."

The bartender took his empty glass, placed it in the sink and grabbed a clean one, filling it with ice.

"Excuse me," Sam said to get the bartender's attention.

"Yes sir."

"Is there a bathroom in this car?"

"Yes sir. All the way to the back on the left," he replied, pointing to the back of the car.

"Thank you."

Sam stood up and began walking down the aisle toward the bathroom. The woman in the red dress flashed a warm smile at him as he walked past her seat. He couldn't put his finger on it, but there was something very familiar about her. Her warm smile, her eyes, and the way that she tilted her head slightly to one side as she smiled all reminded him of someone, but he couldn't place who she was. Sam returned her smile and continued to the rear of the car.

He entered the bathroom, turning to lock the door, and then turned back to look at himself in the mirror as he leaned on the sink.

"I look like hell," he thought as he turned the water on and bent down to bring the cool water to his face with his hands. After repeating the act three or four times, he wiped the water from his eyes and turned to look for some paper towels. As he looked behind him, he saw that there was a stack of clean white cloth towels, folded neatly on a large shelf.

"This is too much," he thought as he reached for one.

After drying his face, he again looked at himself in the mirror. His hair looked as though he had just crawled out of bed.

"No wonder she was smiling at me. I look like an idiot," he said under his breath.

He bent down again, this time putting his entire head under the faucet. He stood up slightly as he turned the water off and dried his hair with the towel. Grabbing his comb from his back pocket, he looked back into the mirror as he combed it back.

"There, that's better," he said out loud, feeling refreshed.

"Next stop, Levi," he heard Gabriel shout through the closed bathroom door. He shook his head and laughed to himself as he stared at his reflection.

"Levi, huh? Are all of these damn stops named after people? What the hell ever happened to names like Pleasantville?" he laughed to himself.

Before leaving the bathroom, he reached into his pocket and pulled out his only piece of gum, picking the lint from it before putting it in his mouth. Giving himself a quick smile in the mirror, he turned and opened the bathroom door.

He walked down the aisle back to his place at the bar where a fresh drink was waiting for him.

"Feel better?" the man in the suit asked as Sam sat down.

"Much," Sam replied with a smile as he picked up his drink.

The man watched carefully as Sam started his third drink. Sam could feel the man staring at him, which made him begin to feel a bit uncomfortable.

"What the heck is this guy staring at?" he thought to himself, feeling a little self-conscious about being watched so closely. With his tolerance for alcohol being as high as it was, most people he knew were amazed at how much he could consume in one sitting. All of his closest friends and family members knew he had a serious problem, and many had suggested that he seek help. This was something that was completely out of the question for him. He had been to a few alcoholics' anonymous meetings in the past and was nauseated by them. The way he saw it, attending one meant meeting with a bunch of losers every week to discuss how miserable their lives were. That was something he saw no point in doing.

Sam turned on his bar stool and glanced across the cabin. He felt out of place as he looked around at the other passengers. This wasn't the type of crowd that he was used to drinking with at the local gin mill. Although he still had no idea as to how or when he had boarded the train, he didn't want to give anyone the impression that he was lost. After all, if he were to clue anyone in to the fact that he had somehow boarded the train accidentally, he was certain that he would be escorted off of it. Having absolutely no clue where he even was would make that problem even more serious. He would much rather ride things out on the train and see where it led than to be dropped in the middle of nowhere with no money and no way to get back to his apartment.

He took a sip of his drink and looked back at the man in the suit.

"So, are you going to introduce yourself, or are you planning to just sit there and stare at me?" he asked.

"Pardon me?" the man asked, surprised by Sam's question.

"Do you have a name?" Sam asked sarcastically.

"Oh, Paul...My name is Paul...And yours?" the man asked as he held out his hand.

"Sam...Nice to meet you," Sam replied as he shook his hand.

"Pleased to meet you, Sam."

"So, where are you headed, Paul?"

He truly didn't care about Paul's destination, but was instead just trying to get an idea of where the train was going.

"Oh, I'm just on another business trip. With all of the trips I've been on, I sometimes have a hard time remembering exactly where I am."

"I know the feeling," Sam replied with a smirk as he finished his drink.

"What do you do that forces you to travel so much."

"I'm what you might call a project coordinator. My boss likes to have me oversee various projects due to my experience in working with people. My job is to ensure that things go as planned and to calm everyone down when the pressure is on."

"This guy is really full of himself," Sam thought. "Project coordinator...He probably never had to work a day in his life," he muttered to himself as he stared down at his empty glass.

"Would you care for another, sir?" the bartender asked, looking at Sam.

"Yes please," he replied as he slid the glass toward him.

"Sounds like a stressful way to make a living,"

Sam said with a smirk.

"It can be if you let it. I've found that it really helps to dive into various projects in my free time just to blow off some steam and take my mind off of work. I've recently started a new one."

"Oh? What type of project?" Sam asked as he took his drink.

"Well, I enjoy restoring classic cars. I've completed 6 so far."

"Really? What are you working on now?"

"Oh, she's going to be a beauty. It's a 1965 Pontiac Bonneville convertible that I picked up out west."

"No kidding?" Sam replied with a stunned look on his face. "My dad had 1965 Bonneville convertible when I was a kid. That car was absolutely gorgeous. It was white one with burgundy leather interior," he continued.

Sam could still picture the proud look in his father's eyes as he pulled into the driveway with the top down. It was a beautiful summer's day in 1969. The sun nearly blinded Sam as it reflected off of the wide chrome trim surrounding the front windshield.

Lee and Dawn had left a few hours earlier, telling Sam and Suzanne to stay at home because they would have a surprise for them when they returned. They had no idea that their father had seen the car sitting proudly on the lot of the Pontiac dealer a few blocks from their home and had fallen in love with it. He couldn't drive past the lot without staring at it as he passed.

"Wanna go for a ride?" Lee shouted with an enormous smile as he brought the car to a stop next to Sam, his face beaming with pride.

"Wow!" Sam screamed as he stared at the car. "Yeah, dad! Let's go!"

Lee put the car in park and opened the driver's door, standing up and pushing the driver's seat forward as Sam ran to the car and climbed into the back seat. Suzanne ran excitedly to the passenger side and climbed in behind Dawn.

"Here we go!" Lee bellowed as he began to back down the driveway.

Sam and Suzanne couldn't help but to stare at each other with enormous smiles on their faces as Lee punched the gas and headed down the open road.

They stared up at the passing trees, taking in the incredible feeling of freedom that came from cruising along with no roof over their heads. It was such a wonderful feeling to have the entire sky open as they sped down nearly every road in their neighborhood, the warm sun on their faces as Suzanne's and Dawn's hair blew wildly in the wind.

After a few hours of joy riding, Lee turned back down their street and pulled into their driveway. They all climbed out of the car and looked back at it in disbelief that it was really theirs.

"I'm going to call the babysitter," Dawn said, looking at Lee.

"Babysitter?" Sam asked. "Where are you going?"

"Your mom and I are going out for dinner," Lee replied.

"Awe, can't we go?" Suzanne pleaded.

"No. We want to be alone for a little while."

Although Sam wanted to go out for dinner too, he wasn't overly disappointed. Cindy, their usual babysitter, was absolutely beautiful in Sam's eyes. He'd had a crush on her since the first time that she had watched them.

The four of them walked back to the house, Lee stopping at the doorway and turning back to take one last look at his new car before going inside. Sam and Suzanne walked into the living room and sat down in front of the television as Lee and Dawn went to get ready for their night out.

After Cindy had arrived, Lee and Dawn gave

Sam and Suzanne hugs and headed toward the door.

"You two be good for Cindy," Dawn said, looking back at them as she opened the door.

"We will, mom," they both replied.

Lee and Dawn stepped outside, closing the door behind them and walked toward the car.

"Why don't you two watch some t.v.," Cindy said with a smile. "I have to make a quick phone call."

They both ran into the living room and plopped down on the floor in front of the television as Cindy picked up the phone.

Dawn was very excited as she and Lee made their way to the restaurant. With two small children and a limited amount of income, it wasn't often that they had the chance to go out alone. It was turning out to be a beautiful summer's evening. She felt as though she were on top of the world as she watched the sun begin to set on the horizon. She took in a deep breath as she looked up at the beautiful colors splashed across the warm summer sky.

They arrived at the restaurant and were seated at a dimly lit, private table. She had noticed a definite change in Lee's demeanor on the way there. He seemed to be in a great mood throughout the entire afternoon, but was becoming far more solemn as the evening progressed.

"Lee, is something bothering you?" she asked, thinking that something must be on his mind.

"No...no. I'm fine," Lee responded, shifting in his seat.

Their waiter walked up and handed them their menus.

"Hi, I'm Frank and I'll be serving you tonight. Can I get you something to drink?"

"Yes, I'll have a glass of white wine please," Dawn said with a smile.

"And for you, sir?"

"I'll just have a cup of coffee."

"Very well."

Lee avoided making any eye contact with Dawn as they waited for their drinks. They both looked around the room, feeling a bit of tension building between them.

"Here you go," Frank said as he set their drinks in front of them.

Dawn took a sip of her wine, then set it down and looked at Lee.

"Lee, there's something on your mind. What is it?"

Lee let out a heavy sigh and rubbed his forehead, obviously nervous about what he was about to say. He picked up his coffee and took a sip, setting it back down slowly as he searched for the right words.

"There's something that I need to tell you. In fact, I've wanted to tell you for a while," he said as he reached into his shirt pocket.

"What is it?" she asked hesitantly, afraid to know what he was about to say.

Lee pulled a picture from his shirt pocket and handed it to her across the table. Dawn took the picture and stared at it for a few seconds. It was a picture of a baby girl, the newborn daughter of her best friend, Ronnie.

Having no idea why he would be showing her a picture of Ronnie's daughter, she glanced up at him with a puzzled look on her face, and then stared back at the photo.

"I don't understand, Lee. Why are you showing me a picture of Ronnie's baby?"

"It's...it's a long story," he replied, struggling to find the right words.

"You and I were going through a tough time, and..."

Her heart suddenly became heavy in her chest as she made the connection in her mind. Her body began to feel numb as her eyes filled with tears. Everything around her started to move as if it were in slow motion as she set the photo down on the table directly in front of her and took a drink of her wine. Her palms began to sweat as she built up enough courage to ask the obvious question.

"Why are you showing me this?" she asked with a trembling voice, her tightened chest barely able to produce enough air to get the words out.

Lee let out another heavy sigh and looked down at the table.

"Why are you showing me a picture of Ronnie's baby, Lee?...Tell me!" she demanded in a firm voice as she glared across the table.

Lee looked up at her, hesitating for a second.

"Because she's my daughter," he said in a quiet voice.

Dawn gasped as the tears welled up in her eyes and then began to roll down her cheeks. She picked up her napkin and brought it to her face. She had thought for quite some time that Lee had been unfaithful in their marriage, but had never before been faced with the absolute truth.

Her mind raced through a thousand incomplete thoughts as she struggled to put just one of them to words. She began thinking back to the way that Lee had acted when the two of them had visited Ronnie to see the baby after she had returned home from the hospital. She pictured him holding the baby in her mind's eye, as well as the way he and Ronnie had looked at each other as he held her. Not once had she even imagined that he was the father.

"You bastard!" she said with a clenched jaw as she picked up the picture and threw it at him.

"Don't make a scene, Dawn," Lee said impatiently as he looked around the room.

"Don't make a scene?!" she answered in a loud voice as she slammed her fist on the table.

"You take me out to dinner to tell me that you've fathered a baby with my best friend and then tell me not to make a scene?! Oh, I'll make a scene, you jerk!" she yelled as she stood up from the table, grabbing her glass of wine and throwing it in Lee's face.

She then slammed the empty glass down on the table and ran out of the dining room.

Lee picked up his napkin and slowly wiped his face.

"That went well," he said under his breath sarcastically.

He turned in his seat and looked around the room to see the other customers staring at him in dead silence.

"What the hell are you all looking at?!" he bellowed as he stood up from the table, his face red with anger, and threw his napkin down on his seat. The other customers immediately looked away, not wanting to become involved.

Lee turned and walked through the dining room toward the waiting area, handing their shocked waiter a twenty dollar bill as he passed.

"Here, sorry about the mess," he said, glaring as he stormed out of the room.

He caught a glimpse of Dawn as she threw the door open to the ladies restroom and stepped inside.

As she entered the ladies room, she immediately ran into one of the stalls, closing the door behind her. She began sobbing uncontrollably as she sat down, grabbing a handful of tissue and holding it to her face as she rocked back and forth. She screamed into her hands as she thought about how her best friend and her husband could both betray her in such a way.

She had been so excited for Ronnie when she had learned that she was going to have a baby. She had even helped with the baby shower, thinking that the baby belonged to Ronnie's husband, who had recently passed away.

Lee stepped through the restaurant entrance and stood outside, waiting for Dawn. He regretted his decision to tell her about the baby, especially in a public setting. But he knew that he had to tell her. If he hadn't, he was certain that Ronnie would have at some point. He knew that it would be best if she'd heard the news from him. He lit a cigarette and began to pace back and forth as he waited, wondering what Dawn's response would be once she had some time to compose herself.

After a few minutes, Dawn wiped the tears from her face and left the stall, walking over to the mirror. She had spent a good amount of time fixing herself up for what she thought was going to be a romantic dinner with her husband. As she looked at her reflection, she started to feel ashamed and foolish for doing so. She began to wipe away her mascara, which by now had run down her cheeks and smeared around her eyes.

After she had gathered herself, she left the bathroom and walked to a nearby payphone in the lobby. Her hands shook wildly as she dug in her purse for change and placed it in the slot. She struggled to turn the large rotary dial and then waited impatiently for a voice on the other end.

"Hello?"

"Doris, its Dawn. Can you do me a favor?" she asked as her voice began to break.

"Dawn?" she replied, having a hard time making out her words.

"Yeah. Doris, I need you to come pick me up."

"Are you o.k.?" she asked, hearing the desperation in her voice.

"Yeah... Well, no, I'm not. Please just come and get me."

"Where are you?"

"I'm at the Country Club. In the lobby."

"All right. I'll be there in fifteen minutes."

"Thank you, Doris," she said with a relieved voice, looking around the lobby for any sign of Lee.

Doris had been a good friend to Dawn for a

number of years and was very aware of Lee's drinking and violent outbursts. She had always suspected that he had been unfaithful to her, but wasn't entirely certain that was the case. She had tried repeatedly to convince her to take the kids and leave him for her own well-being. She had told her many times to call if she needed any help, but this was the first time that Dawn had done so, which made Doris fear the worst when she heard tone of Dawn's voice.

Dawn hung up the phone and walked back toward the dining room. Looking inside, she saw that Lee was no longer at the table, which had been cleaned and had a fresh table setting on it. She walked over to the bar to look for him. Not seeing him there, she walked back through the lobby and out the front door. Lee spun around and looked at her as she stepped outside.

"You can just get the hell out of here!" she said, pointing her finger at him.

"Dawn, please. I'm sorry. Come on, let's just go home," he pleaded.

"I'm not going anywhere with you, you bastard!" she snapped back.

"And just how do you plan to get home? Are you going to walk?" he asked, his voice beginning to rise in anger.

"Maybe I will!" she replied. "Or maybe I just won't be coming home!"

"Oh, is that right?!" he asked sarcastically.

"Yes it is!"

"Fine, have it your way!" he shouted, throwing his hands up and turning to walk toward the car.

Dawn returned to the lobby and sat down near the front window, watching Lee through the glass as he reached the car, opened the door and sat in the driver's seat, slamming the driver's door shut. She tried to lean back, away from his line of sight as he glared back at the restaurant through the windshield.

"Why isn't he leaving?" she thought to herself

as she watched him. Her heart was racing as she began to think about what he might do next. She desperately wanted Doris to arrive, but at the same time she was afraid of what his reaction would be once he saw her. She could barely make out his silhouette in the dim parking lot lights. He sat motionless as the smoke from his cigarette drifted from the driver's window, his face illuminated every so often by the lit end as he took a long drag.

After what seemed like an eternity, he threw it out of the window and started the car. He sat for another minute or so after turning the headlights on, then slammed the car into gear and raced out of the parking lot.

Dawn took a deep breath, relieved that he had left. A few minutes later, she watched as Doris drove up to the restaurant, parking in front of the entrance. She stood up and walked quickly through the front door as Doris got out of the car and began walking toward her.

"Are you o.k.?" she asked as she walked around the back of her car.

"Please, let's just get out of here," Dawn pleaded as she opened the passenger side door and climbed inside, fearing that Lee could return at any moment.

Doris returned to the driver's seat and put the car into drive as she closed her door.

"Dawn, are you all right?" she asked as she drove through the lot, looking over at her.

"No, I'm not."

"What happened?"

"Please, just drive," Dawn said in a panicked voice as she looked around for any sign of Lee.

"Where are we going?" Doris asked.

"Anywhere but my house."

After they were a safe distance from the restaurant, Dawn again started to cry uncontrollably. Doris reached into her purse and took out a tissue,

47

handing it to her.

"Dawn...please talk to me. What just happened?"

Dawn did her best to take a deep breath and force the words out.

"Lee's been screwing around on me," she said as she wiped her face with the tissue.

"How do you know? Did you catch him with someone?"

"He came right out and told me, Doris."

"Did he say who he was seeing?"

Dawn paused for a second, not believing the words that were about to come from her own mouth.

"Ronnie."

Doris let her foot off of the gas briefly as her head snapped to the right to look at Dawn.

"You have got to be kidding me...Ronnie?!" she replied in a shocked voice.

"I wish that I was."

"Oh, honey. I'm so sorry!" Doris said as she brought her right hand up and rubbed Dawn's shoulder.

"Why her?" Dawn pleaded. "What does he see in her?"

"I don't know, Dawn," Doris answered in a calm voice, shaking her head.

"When did this happen?...Was it just one time, or has it been going on for a while?"

"I have no idea...He showed me a picture of Ronnie's baby, Doris...He showed me a picture and told me that he was the father."

"Oh my God...So, what are you going to do?"

Dawn was at a loss as she considered her options. She knew in her heart that her marriage was over, but she had no idea what to do next.

"Listen, you're more than welcome to stay by me until you sort things out. You can sleep in the spare bedroom. We can go get the kids and bring them there too."

"Thank you Doris. Are you sure that I won't be imposing?"

"Are you crazy? Of course you won't be imposing. Should we go and get the kids?"

The last place that Dawn wanted to go right now was home. She knew that Lee would go home to look after Sam and Suzanne if he took her threat of not coming home seriously. She also knew that he wouldn't raise a finger to hurt them. If anything, he would send them to bed as soon as he arrived in hopes that they would be sleeping before she returned.

"No, the kids will be alright tonight. They're with a babysitter and Lee won't be out long."

"Are you sure?"

"Yeah, I'm sure."

Doris turned onto Northwest Highway and headed toward her home.

After Lee had left the restaurant, he stopped at Vicki's Place, a local tavern not far from their home. He was a fairly regular customer there, stopping by every so often since he and Dawn had bought their home just a few blocks north.

He walked inside and took a seat at the end of the bar, lighting a cigarette as he scanned the room. It was a quiet evening at Vicki's. There were two men in their mid-twenties shooting pool in the corner and a man sitting at the other end of the bar, slumped over his drink as he muttered to himself.

He reached into his pants pocket, pulling out a twenty dollar bill and set it down on the bar.

"Hey, Lee," the bartender said as he walked over, placing a beer in front of him.

"How are ya, Frank?" Lee responded.

"Good, and you?"

"Oh, just great," Lee answered sarcastically as he picked up his beer.

Lee looked down at his watch. It was only 9:00. He remembered Dawn telling Cindy that they would be home by 11:00. As he sat at the bar, he continued to think about Dawn's reaction to news he had given her. The more he thought about it, the more he drank. The more he drank, the angrier he became.

"How dare she embarrass me like that? Making a scene in front of all of those people," he thought to himself.

He finished a few more beers, keeping an eye on his watch. At 10:45, he stood up, taking his change from the top of the bar and leaving a few dollars for Frank.

"Are ya taking off, Lee?" Frank asked as he noticed Lee gathering his change.

"Yeah, we have a babysitter watching the kids."

"All right," Frank said as he took Lee's empty bottle and threw it in the trash. "You have a good night."

"Thanks, Frank. You do the same," he replied as he turned and walked toward the door.

He stepped outside and paused by the door as he lit a cigarette. He could feel his blood pressure rise as he walked to his car.

"So, this is what I get for being honest," he muttered as he sat down and started the car. He slammed the transmission into reverse, kicking up a cloud of gravel and dust as he backed out of his parking space. The tires shrieked as he pulled out of the lot, heading north toward home.

The living room lit up from the headlights on Lee's car as he pulled into the driveway. Cindy stood and walked toward the kitchen, greeting Lee as he stepped inside.
She could immediately sense that he'd been drinking.

"Hi Mr. Grace," she said nervously.

"Hi Cindy."

He was not in the mood for any small talk, and wanted her to leave quickly in case Dawn returned home. The last thing that he wanted was to be involved in another embarrassing scene.

"How much do I owe you?" he asked as he pulled out his wallet.

Cindy turned to look at the clock on the kitchen wall.

"Oh, I got here at 8:00…so three hours… um… is $4.50 o.k.?"

"Sure, that's fine."

"Here, just take five," he answered, pulling out a five dollar bill and handing it to her.

"Oh, thank you Mr. Grace," she said with a wide smile as she took the money and turned toward the front door.

"Do you need a ride home, Cindy?"

"No, that's o.k.. I'll walk."

"All right. Have a good night"

"You too, Mr. Grace."

Lee tossed his keys on the kitchen countertop and walked through the house, looking for Sam and Suzanne. Finding them sound asleep in their rooms, he walked back to the living room and turned on the television, waiting for Dawn to return.

A few blocks away, Doris pulled the car into her driveway.

"Are you o.k. Dawn?" she asked in a quiet voice as she turned off the car.

"Yeah, I'm fine," Dawn responded as she looked at the passenger side floor.

"I'm so sorry, Dawn," she said, leaning over to put her arms around her.

"Thank you for being here for me Doris, and for being such a good friend," she replied, reaching up to hold her arm.

"Don't be silly. Where else would I be?" she answered with a smile.

"Come on inside. I'll put on some tea."

Doris lived alone in a large, red brick, four bedroom, colonial style home. Her husband had passed away a few years earlier and their only son was away at school.

As they entered her home, Doris walked to her bedroom while Dawn took a seat at the kitchen table. A few minutes later, Doris entered the kitchen carrying a thick, terrycloth bathrobe.

"Here sweetie. You can use this."

"Oh, thank you," Dawn answered as she put the robe on her lap.

Doris turned and took the tea kettle from the top of the stove, turning toward the sink to fill it with water.

"Are you hungry?" she asked as she turned the stove on. "I have some leftover chicken."

"No, thank you. I really don't have much of an appetite right now."

Doris turned and sat down across the table from Dawn. They sat in silence as they waited for the water to boil, neither of them able to think of the right words to say. After a few minutes, the tea kettle began to whistle.

Doris stood up and walked over to the counter next to the stove and took two cups from the cabinet above. Placing a tea bag in each, she filled them with the hot water and turned toward the table, setting a cup in front of Dawn. She then returned to her seat.

After a few more minutes of awkward silence, Doris looked across the table.

"What are you going to do, Dawn?" she asked in a quiet voice.

Dawn took a deep breath as if she were going to speak, and then exhaled slowly while staring into her tea as if the answer to Doris' question could be found there.

"I don't know," she answered softly, her eyebrows raised as she slowly shook her head from side to side.

"You *do* know that you can stay here as long as you need to. The spare bedroom is just collecting dust, and you're more than welcome to it. We can pick up the kids in the morning and bring them here too. They can sleep in there with you or we can let them camp out on the living room floor."

Dawn nodded. She knew that Doris was sincere in her offer, but there was so much more to consider. She and the kids would be welcome there for a few weeks, maybe even a few months, but then what?

"I've been such a fool," she said quietly.

"You have not, Dawn," Doris responded sympathetically.

"Yes I have. I've been a fool for trusting him all of these years. I've been a fool for believing that Ronnie was such a good friend. How could I have been so blind?"

"Dawn, you had no way of knowing that any of this was going on. I never would have believed it. You can't blame yourself for any of this. What you need to do now is to figure out where to go from here."

"I think that what I'd really like is to go to bed. There's so much that I need to think about and I'm just too tired right now. It's been a long day."

"I know," Doris answered. "You finish your tea. I'll go make a bed for you."

Doris stood up and walked to the spare bedroom, stopping at the linen closet to pull out some clean sheets. Her heart broke for her friend as she thought not only about what she had just been through, but also about the long, hard road that she was facing. When she had finished making the bed, she returned to the kitchen and walked over to Dawn, holding her arms out.

"Come on, honey. You need some sleep."

"Thanks again, Doris," she replied, standing to hug her.

"You're more than welcome."

Dawn turned and walked down the hall, quietly closing the bedroom door behind her. She couldn't help but to feel out of place as she looked around the room. She knew that she had every right to leave Lee, but still felt as though she was doing something horribly wrong. She was at the brink of making one of the biggest decisions in her life, one that would not only affect her, but also her children for the rest of their young lives.

She wrapped the bathrobe around her shoulders and laid down on the bed, staring at the ceiling as her mind raced back and forth from thoughts of absolute determination to get through this, to the crushing realization that she had been betrayed so severely by the two people she had trusted most, to a state of complete and total confusion as to what she should do next. Every muscle in her body was tied into knots as the events of the evening played over and over in her mind. Every time she tried to relax in an attempt to fall to sleep, her mind would once again begin to race, and her body would tighten up. She knew that she would need to be very strong to deal with this, but she wondered if she had that kind of strength within her. After tossing and turning for quite some time, she eventually fell asleep.

She slept well into the following afternoon. Doris didn't want to awaken her, as she knew that Dawn would need a good night's sleep to deal with the crisis at hand. When she finally awoke, her memory of the previous evening immediately enveloped her as if it were a thick, suffocating cloud. As much as she dreaded the mere thought, she knew that she had to call Lee and tell him that it was over between them. After having a few cups of coffee to clear the fog, she talked everything over with Doris for a while. The more she thought everything through, the more certain she became that leaving Lee was the only logical choice. She picked herself up from the table and left the room, walking over to the phone in the kitchen. She hesitated briefly, and then dialed the number, feeling her chest tighten as she waited for an answer.

"Hello?"

"Lee? It's me."

Lee paused for a moment.

"Hello?" Dawn said quietly.

"Yeah. I'm here. Where are you?" he asked sharply.

"Lee, I have something to tell you."

"Where are you Dawn?" he asked again, his voice rising in anger.

"Where I am isn't important. I have something to say to you and I want you to listen carefully."

"Oh yeah? And what's that?" he snapped back.

"It's over between us, Lee. I want a divorce. I just can't take it any longer. I want you out of that house today."

"Really?" And where would you suggest that I go?"

"I really don't care where you go. Why don't you go by Ronnie's house? I'm sure that she'd take you in!" she responded sarcastically.

"Oh, that's funny Dawn. And what about the kids? Have you thought about that?"

"The kids are staying right where they are. The three of us will stay in the house until they're finished with the school year. After that, we'll sell the house and go our separate ways."

"So that's how it is, huh?"

"Yes, Lee. That's how it is."

"Hey, fine. You do whatever you feel you have to do."

"Oh, I will. I can guarantee that." she answered, looking at the clock on the kitchen wall.

"It's 2:30 right now. I'll be home at about 7:00. I don't want you to be there."

"Believe me, I won't be!" he responded in a matter of fact tone.

Dawn pulled the phone away from her ear as he slammed the phone against the kitchen wall. After hanging up, she picked up the phone again and called her sister, Sophie. Without getting too much into the details, she asked her if she could please meet her at Doris' house, promising to fill her in on all of the details once she'd arrived. Not being exactly sure about what was going on, but wanting very much to be there for her sister in her time of need, Sophie readily agreed to do so.

As they were playing together in Sam's bedroom, Sam and Suzanne heard the loud crash of the phone slamming against the kitchen wall and walked toward the kitchen to see what had happened. As they entered the room, they saw Lee, his face red with anger as he paced back and forth with his hands on his hips.

"What's wrong, dad?" Sam asked as they stopped in the doorway.

Lee spun around and glared at them, enraged by what Dawn had just said to him.

"Nothing's wrong!" he snapped. "Just go and play, would you!"

They turned quickly and hurried back to Sam's room, closing the door behind them.

Lee wiped away the sweat that was beginning to build on his forehead. He took a deep breath, and feeling badly about shouting at them, walked down the hallway and opened Sam's bedroom door. The two of them immediately backed away, fearing the worst.

"I'm sorry, you guys. Come here," he said as he held out his arms to them. He grabbed both of them and hugged them tightly, kissing each of them on the top of their heads. He then turned and left the room, walking immediately to his bedroom and closing the door. He opened his closet door and grabbed a pair of suitcases, throwing them on the bed. He then began to stuff as much of his clothing as he could fit into each of them.

After he had finished doing so, he quietly opened his bedroom door and looked out into the hallway. He didn't want them to see him with the suitcases, knowing that if they did, he'd have to explain to them where he was going and why he was leaving. Hearing them playing in Sam's room, he quickly grabbed the suitcases and walked outside to his car, opening the trunk and throwing them inside.

He walked back into the house and picked up the phone, dialing Cindy's number.

"Hello?"

"Cindy?"

"Yes."

"Cindy, It's Lee Grace."

"Oh, hi Mr. Grace."

"Listen, I need you to watch the kids for about an hour tonight. Can you do that?"

"Sure. What time?"

"Can you be here at about 6:00? I have to be somewhere and Dawn won't be home until about 7:00."

"O.k., I'll be there at 6."

"Thanks Cindy."

"You're welcome."

Back in Doris' kitchen, Dawn sat down at the table and lowered her head. She reached up with trembling hands and covered her face, letting out a heavy sigh.

Doris walked over and began to rub her shoulders, knowing that she had just made what was possibly the toughest decision of her entire life.

"Everything is going to be fine, Dawn," she said softly.

"I'm not so sure, Doris. You don't know Lee like I do. He really frightens me sometimes."

Doris walked around her and sat on the other side of the table, taking hold of her hands and pulling them from her face, looking directly into her eyes.

"Dawn, why don't you just pick up the kids after he leaves and bring them back here? I'd really feel much better about this whole thing if you were all here instead of in that house. You can take them to Sophie's house later if that's what you want to do."

"Thank you, but no. I really need for them to stay there while I figure out what we're gonna do next. They don't need to know what's going on just yet. I don't want them to worry about what might happen in the future. I want them to have some sort of stability right now. I'll be fine, Doris, I promise. Sophie's coming out tonight and I'm sure that he won't do anything crazy with her there."

Doris let go of Dawn's hands and sat back into her chair. While this whole idea frightened her, she understood why Dawn would feel this way. It would be difficult enough for Sam and Suzanne to deal with the thought of their parents getting divorced without the added shock of leaving their home.

"Hey, should I put on some tea for us?" she asked quietly.

"Yes, please...I'd like that."

A few hours later, Sophie arrived at the front door.

"Hi sis!" Sophie said with a warm smile as she entered the living room.

Without saying a word, Dawn walked over to her and embraced her, the tears beginning to well up in her eyes as she hung on, savoring the warmth of holding someone who truly cared about her.

"It's all right. You're going to be fine," Sophie whispered into her ear as she patted Dawn on her back.

"Would you like something to drink, Sophie?" Doris asked.

"Oh, yes. That would be great!" Sophie replied as she released Dawn, stepping back to look into her eyes. She could see the fear and exhaustion on her face as she reached up to wipe a tear way.

"Why don't we sit down so you can tell me what's going on?"

Dawn nodded silently as the three of them

turned and walked to the kitchen, Dawn and Sophie taking a seat at the table as Doris walked over to the cabinet where she kept her glasses.

"What would you like Sophie?"

"Would some coffee be too much trouble?" she replied.

"No, not at all," she answered as she put on a new pot.

Dawn looked across the table at Sophie, offering a half-hearted smile before looking down at her hands as she rubbed them together.

"Are you okay sis?" Sophie asked quietly.

Dawn let out a sporadic sigh as she leaned back in her seat, closing her eyes briefly before looking back at Sophie.

"Yeah, I'm fine...Well, as good as I can be considering the circumstances."

After taking a deep breath to compose herself, she went on to explain to Sophie the details of what had happened the previous evening. Sophie was very aware of Lee's shortcomings and was always very outspoken about how she'd felt about him. She had secretly wished that Dawn would leave him for a number of years, but tried her best to keep that to herself. She had no second thoughts when she agreed to stay with Dawn for a few days, knowing that Lee would more than likely avoid doing anything crazy if he were to stop by while she was there.

"Here you go," Doris said as she set their coffee and tea on the table and took a seat next to Dawn.

"Thank you Doris," Sophie said with a smile.

The three of them talked for a few hours, discussing the situation and what Dawn's options were.

"It's almost seven," Sophie said with a heavy sigh as she looked down at her wristwatch. "Do you suppose that we should head over to your place soon?"

"Yeah, we probably should," Dawn responded nervously. "Lee should be gone by now."

"You two be careful," Doris said in a concerned voice as the three of them stood up from the table. "Remember, you're more than welcome to come back here."

"I know. Thank you, Doris," Dawn said as she leaned over to give her a hug.

"Thank you for everything, Doris," Sophie said as she put her hand on Doris' back.

"Anytime, Sophie."

All three of them could feel the tension beginning to build as they walked toward the front door. Dawn turned back and gave Doris a silent smile as they stepped outside, then walked quickly to Sophie's car.

Sophie sat in the driver's seat and started the car, taking a deep breath and looking over at Dawn before putting it into drive.

"Are you sure that you're ready for this, sis?" Sophie asked.

"Yeah. As ready as I'll ever be," Dawn responded in a tense voice.

Sophie put the car into drive and pulled away from Doris' house. Dawn could feel the adrenaline rushing through her body as the car began to move. Doris lived just a few blocks from her house and they would be there in less than a minute.

Dawn's breathing became very shallow as they turned onto her street. She strained to look around the corner, watching nervously for any sign of Lee's car in the driveway. A single light from the front porch shone on the empty asphalt driveway.

"It doesn't look like he's here," Sophie said in a relieved voice as she pulled into the drive and put the car into park. She looked around for a few seconds before turning her lights off.

"No, he's not. Good!" Dawn responded as she let out a deep breath and reached for the door handle.

The two of them stepped from the car and walked along the front of the house, looking inside through the kitchen windows as they passed. Dawn fumbled nervously with her keys as she looked for the right one. Just as she reached for the door, it flew open with a crash.

"Mommy!" Suzanne shouted as she ran through the doorway and wrapped her arms around Dawn's legs.

"Suzanne, you scared me half to death!" Dawn said in a relieved voice as she hugged Suzanne's head.

"Hi Suzanne!" Sophie said with a warm smile.

"Aunt Sophie!" Suzanne shrieked as she spun around to look at her. She reached over with one of her arms, wrapping it around Sophie's leg as she continued to hold onto her mother.

"Mommy! Aunt Sophie!" Sam shouted from inside the kitchen as he ran through the front door and wrapped his arms around the three of them, nearly knocking all of them over.

"Woah guys. Take it easy!" Dawn said as she reached down and patted Sam on the head. They both let go as the four of them stepped into the kitchen and closed the door.

"Hi Mrs. Grace," Cindy said as she entered the room.

"Oh, Hi Cindy. How long have you been here?"

"About an hour, I think."

"All right. Hang on a second," Dawn said as she set her purse on the kitchen table and pulled out her wallet.

"Is two dollars okay?"

"Oh, yeah. That would be fine," Cindy said as she took the money. "Thank you."

"Thank you Cindy."

"I'll see you all later."

"Bye Cindy," Dawn replied with a smile.

"Mommy, where have you been? Why didn't

you come home last night?" Sam asked in an angry voice.

"I stayed by Doris' house. She wanted me to help her with a few things. It's okay. I'm home now. Have you two eaten anything?"

"No. Not yet", Suzanne responded.

"Well, why don't you go watch t.v. while I make you some dinner."

Sam and Suzanne turned and ran into the living room, playfully fighting for the best spot in front of the television.

Sophie walked over to the kitchen window and looked outside. Not being able to make out much from inside with the lights on, she pressed her face against the glass and cupped her hands around it to get a better look.

"You don't think that he'll be coming back, do you?" she asked as she backed away from the window.

"I certainly hope not. That's all we need."

"So how are things going with you and Frank?" Dawn asked as she pulled out a frying pan and put it on the stove.

"Good," she replied. "We've been looking at homes down in Alabama for quite some time now. You know how much Frank wants to move back there."

"Do you have any idea when that might happen?"

"Hopefully by the end of August. We'd hate to have Julie change schools in the middle of the year, so we're taking our time."

"Have you found a place yet?"

"Yes we have. There's a nice little ranch that we have our eyes on. It's on 5 acres just outside of Decatur. We're probably going to head down to take another look in a few weeks."

"How much are they asking for it?"

"$18,000."

"Oh, that's not too bad."

"Frank has been talking to a lot of people down there. He thinks that we might be able to get it for around $15,000."

"Have you told mom that you're planning to move?"

"Yeah. We talked a few weeks ago. She sounded like she was happy for us, but you know mom."

"Yeah, don't I though. Has Frank found work down that way?"

"Actually, the company that he works for has an office in Decatur. They said that they could transfer him without a problem."

"Wow. That's great, Sophie. It sounds like things are really coming together for you two."

"Well, we're keeping our fingers crossed. Frank really wants to be closer to his mother. She's not getting any younger. He's afraid that she doesn't have much time left."

"Come on, kids!" Dawn shouted as she put the sandwiches on two plates and walked them over to the table.

"Are you hungry, Sophie?"

"No...No thank you. I ate before I left the house."

Sam and Suzanne ran into the kitchen, taking their normal seats at the table. After they had finished eating, they returned to the living room to watch t.v. while Dawn and Sophie remained seated at the kitchen table. They were finally beginning to relax a bit and were feeling confident that Lee wasn't going to return. As Dawn walked to the sink with a handful of dishes, the phone rang, startling her for a moment. She looked back at Sophie with a stunned expression as she set the dishes on the counter and answered it.

"Hello?" she said quietly.

Nobody answered, but she could hear the sound of people talking and laughing in the background.

"Hello? Is anybody there?" she asked, raising her voice a bit.

"Hello Dawn," Lee responded with a growl, his speech slightly slurred.

"What do you want, Lee?"

"Who's there with you?" he demanded.

"What do you mean, who's here with me? Nobody's here."

"Who's car did I see in the driveway?" he bellowed.

"Oh, that's just Sophie's car. Sophie drove me home."

"Really? Well I want you and Sophie to know something."

"And what's that, Lee?" she snapped back sarcastically.

"I have a gun, and I'm just about to come over there and blow both of your damn heads off."

Dawn gasped and covered her mouth with her hand as she immediately slammed the phone down, disconnecting the call and then backing away to the far wall with a look of absolute panic in her eyes.

"Mommy?" Sam called out from the living room upon hearing the phone slam. "Are you okay?"

"Kids, come here," she said in a panicked voice as she held out her trembling arms.

"Dawn? What's going on?" Sophie asked.

"Kids, I want both of you to go into my bedroom and hide under my bed. Don't come out until I tell you to."

"Why, Mom? You're scaring me!" Suzanne cried out.

"Just go! Now!" Dawn shouted as she pushed the two of them from behind.

"Sophie, can you please take them back there?"

"Come on kids. I'll go back with you," Sophie said as she took their hands and led them out of the room.

Dawn picked up the telephone as soon as they turned the corner, dialing as quickly as she could.

"Arlington Heights Police. How can I help you?"

"Yes, my name is Dawn Grace. I live at 1107 Wilke Road. I have an emergency."

"Go ahead, ma'am."

"My husband has been out drinking. He's an extremely violent man and he just called here saying that he has a gun and he's coming here to kill me and my sister."

"What's your husband's name, Ma'am?"

"Lee. Lee Grace."

"You said that was 1107 Wilke Road?"

"Yes."

"Hold on one second. I'm going to contact one of our officers so he can get there right away."

"Thank you."

Dawn could hear her heart pounding in her chest as she strained to see outside through the kitchen window. She slapped at the light switch, missing it twice before finally turning the light off. Seconds seemed like hours as she waited for a voice on the other end of the line, watching intently for any sign of Lee of his car.

"Ma'am?"

"Yes," Dawn said with a quick burst of breath.

"We have officers on the way. I want you to lock your doors and stay inside until they arrive. Do you understand?"

"Yes, I understand. Thank you."

Sophie entered the room as Dawn hung up the phone and reached immediately for the dead bolt on the door, locking it with a quick twist.

"What's going on, sis?"

"That was Lee."

"Yeah. I figured as much," Sophie said sarcastically. "What did he say?"

"He said that he has a gun and he's going to

come here and kill both of us," she whispered, not wanting the kids to hear.

"Oh my God! Did you call the police?"

"Yes. They're on their way. Where are the kids?"

"They're fine. They're in your room."

Sam and Suzanne sat in the dark, having no idea what was happening back in the kitchen.

"Suzanne?" Sam whispered.

"What, Sam."

"Why was mommy so scared?"

"I don't know. I think that was daddy on the phone."

"Was he mad?"

"I don't know, Sam."

"Suzanne?"

"What, Sam?" she replied impatiently.

"I don't like it when daddy gets mad," he said, looking down at the floor. "It scares me."

"I know, Sam...It scares me too."

The two of them sat quietly for a few more minutes, listening carefully for any sound of their father. After squirming around a bit, Sam stood up and walked toward the door.

"Sam! Come back here!" Suzanne whispered as emphatically as she could.

Sam ignored her, opening the door slowly and peeking down the hallway.

"Oh my God! He's here!" Dawn said breathlessly as she began backing from the window. Sophie looked out to see Lee's car pull slowly into the driveway and stop just behind hers.

He sat in the dark, leering at the house as he finished his cigarette. They could see his face glow in the red light every time that he took another drag.

"There's the police!" Sophie said excitedly as she looked across the street. Both of them moved closer to the window to get a better view. One squad car had pulled over with his lights off directly across the street from their house, while another pulled up to the edge of the driveway. From what they could see from their vantage point, there appeared to be two officers in each car. All of them remained in their cars watching Lee as he sat in the driveway, waiting patiently for him to step out of the car. Knowing that he could very well be armed and dangerous, they didn't want to do anything to alert him to their presence.

"What is he doing?" Dawn asked impatiently. "Why is he just sitting there?"

A third squad car pulled slowly down the street with his lights off as Lee began to open the driver's door. He stepped out and turned back toward the car, reaching over to the passenger seat to pick something up.

There was a sudden explosion of light as the officers in all three squad cars turned on their spotlights and aimed them at Lee. The third squad to arrive drove directly onto the front lawn, directing his headlights toward Lee also.

"What's going on, mommy?" Sam asked as he entered the kitchen.

"It's o.k., Sam. Come here," she replied as she held out her hand behind her.

"Put your hands up and step away from the car, Lee!" one of the officers shouted.

Sam looked out the window to see six police officers with their guns drawn, surrounding his father. He could see a pained look on his father's face as he turned around, holding a pizza box over his head.

"I just came home to bring my kids some pizza!" he shouted back angrily.

"Put the box down on the roof and step away from the car, Lee!" the officer demanded as all of them moved gradually closer, their guns aimed directly at him.

Absolute panic filled Sam as he watched the officers pointing their guns at his father, moving closer like a squad of assassins. Believing that they were about to open fire on him, Sam couldn't take it anymore. He ran to the front door and unlocked it as fast as he could, throwing it open with a crash.

"Sam, No!" Dawn screamed as she realized what he was doing.

"Daddy!" Sam shrieked as he ran toward his father, slamming into his legs and wrapping his arms around them.

"Leave him alone!" he screamed at the officers, tears streaming down his cheeks as he hung on to Lee's legs as tightly as he could.

"Don't shoot my daddy! He didn't do anything! Leave him alone!" he begged them as terror filled his heart.

The officers stopped dead in their tracks and looked at one another, all of them knowing that the situation had instantly become much more complicated.

"Lee, please. For your son. Put the box down. We don't want anyone to get hurt here," one of the officers pleaded.

Lee took a deep breath, reaching down to put his hand on Sam's head.

"I just wanted to bring my kids some pizza. That's all I'm doing," he said, his voice cracking as the tears began to well up in his eyes.

"It's all right, Lee. Put the box down."

Lee turned toward the car and slid the pizza box on to the roof, reaching down to hold Sam's head tightly against him.

"I love you, tiger," he said quietly as he rubbed Sam's head, and then held his hands back up in the air.

"You'd better go back inside now. I'm okay."

Sam turned to see two of the officers moving in slowly as they put their guns back in the holsters. He looked back up at Lee, who had his eyes closed as he held his hands high in the air. He let go of Lee's legs and walked slowly back toward the front door where Dawn was waiting for him. He looked back to see one of the officers bring Lee's hands down behind his back and put his handcuffs on him while another grabbed the pizza box and walked away, opening it to investigate its contents.

"It's just a pizza," he said with a relieved look on his face as he looked inside.

Dawn opened the screen door just enough to grab Sam and pull him inside, wrapping both of her arms around him. Sam strained to see what was happening through the screen door as one of the officers helped Lee into the back seat of the squad car and closed the door.

The officers searched Lee's car thoroughly, but found nothing. Once they had determined that there was no longer any threat, they all gathered in the driveway and talked for a few minutes before heading back to their cars. As the rest of them began to pull away, one of the officers walked to the front door.

"Mrs. Grace?" he asked with a polite smile as he removed his hat.

"Yes."

"Is everyone o.k.?"

"Yes. Thank you for coming so quickly."

She wanted to invite him inside, but with Lee sitting in the back of his car, she was eager to see him leave.

"He didn't have any weapons, ma'am. We're going to take him to the station and let him sleep it off. If you'd like to press charges, you'll have to come down and do so."

"Thank you, officer. Do I have to come right now?"

"No ma'am. You can wait until tomorrow morning if you'd like."

"Alright. Thank you again."

"No problem."

The officer put his hat back on as he turned to

walk away, then hesitated for a second, looking back at Dawn as she stood in the darkened doorway holding Sam and Suzanne. His gut told him that she would probably decide not to press charges after sleeping on it for the night.

"You know, I've seen this kind of thing before," he said, taking a deep breath. "If you decide not to press charges, we'll probably end up back here again. These things don't ever fix themselves." he continued, looking her in the eyes to ensure that she understood what he was trying to say.

"I understand," she replied with a trembling voice.

He stood in the doorway for a few more seconds, offering a warm smile to Sam. He then looked back at Dawn, who was avoiding any eye contact.

"Good night, ma'am."

"Good night."

Dawn turned and closed the door as the officer walked back toward his car.

"Dawn? Are you all right?" Sophie asked as she held out her arms.

"No... No I'm not."

"Listen to me. I want you to go and pack up whatever you and the kids need. You're not staying here anymore. You're coming home with me. Do you understand?"

As much as Dawn wanted to keep the kids at home, she knew that Lee would eventually return. She also knew that, when he did, she might not walk away so easily. In fact, there was a very good chance that she wouldn't walk away at all. She packed up as much as they could load into Sophie's car, and then left, never to return again.

THREE

Sam finished his drink and returned to his seat. Now that he had some alcohol in his bloodstream, the shaking of his hands settled down a bit and his thoughts began to clear. He leaned back in his chair, letting out a deep sigh as he gazed out the window; his nerves soothed by the beauty of the scenery. He had seen beautiful country sides many times throughout his life, but somehow this was different. Somehow this was cleaner and more pristine than he'd ever seen before. Everything from the nearby, wide open fields to the mountains far in the distance; from the brilliance of the sunlight to the depth of the clouds, was somehow crisper, cleaner and clearer.

His thoughts returned to the day before he had arrived on the train, but as hard as he tried, he could remember very little. He remembered collecting the last few dollars that he had and then leaving his apartment to buy whatever food he could afford, but after that he could remember nothing. He knew that he had been drinking that morning, but not anymore than he had on any other morning. He had suffered from blackouts in the past after drinking far too much, but he couldn't recall any of them being as thorough as this one. His previous blackouts usually involved just a few hours of time. This one had lasted throughout an entire day, through the evening, and into the following morning when he awoke on the train.

He looked out the window again as he tried to remember something…anything. He was still at a complete and total loss as to where he was or even how he had wound up here. It didn't make any sense, but then again, nothing in his life had made any sense for a very long time. For a brief moment, he allowed himself to consider the possibility that maybe it was fate that had landed him here. He began to consider the possibility that maybe the gods had finally decided to smile upon him, causing him to stumble inadvertently onto a train that was taking him to a place far away from the ugliness, pain and fear that he had known so very long. Maybe this was a brand new start for him – one which he hadn't chosen or planned, but one which would somehow work out for him due to the universe suddenly smiling upon him.

"Next stop, Judah," Gabriel bellowed from the front of the car.

Sam looked out the window and saw twelve men standing on the platform; eleven of them surrounding the twelfth man, who stood taller than the rest. He was a very handsome man, dressed in nicer clothes than those gathered around him. As he spoke to them, gesturing with his hands as if he were explaining something of great importance, they all stood silently, nodding in agreement from time to time.

As he looked to the man's left, Sam saw another set of gates with the name 'Judah' written across the upper frame above them. On the ground, on either side of the gates, there were large sculptures of lions – one on each side. The lion's faces were turned in opposite directions, one facing east, and the other west, as if they were keeping watch over anyone who might approach.

Just as Sam looked back at the group of men, the taller one who had been speaking to the rest of them looked at him through the window and pointed directly at him. Upon doing so, the rest of the men turned their heads, looking back at Sam for a brief moment. One by one they turned away, looking back at the man, all of them eventually nodding in agreement once again as he continued to speak.

"What the heck was that all about?" Sam thought to himself, wondering why this complete stranger standing on a train platform would decide to point at him out of the blue like that. He turned away, thinking that maybe the man was just pointing in his general direction. Still, he felt a bit confused, because it certainly looked as though he was pointing directly at him.

As the train began to pull away, a young man in his early twenties, wearing a clean, neatly pressed

U.S. Marines uniform entered the car and walked toward Sam, taking the seat next to him.

Sam had always felt a deep sense of respect for any man or woman who would volunteer to serve their country. He was a Navy veteran himself, and while he'd never served during war time or experienced the sacrifices of those who had, he knew firsthand what life in the military was like. He watched the young man closely from across the aisle, sensing from the excited look on his face that he might be on leave, heading home to see his friends and family. Thinking back, he could remember that feeling very well.

"On your way home, son?" Sam asked, thinking that he might be able to gather some information as to where they were and where they were headed.

"Yes, sir!" he replied with a wide smile.

"Where are you stationed?"

"Lejeune base camp, North Carolina."

"Wow...we're a long way from North Carolina."

"We sure are! And I couldn't be happier about that!"

"What's your name, son?" Sam asked, reaching over to shake his hand.

"Andrew. And yours?" the man replied, returning his handshake.

"Sam...Nice to meet you, Andrew."

"Likewise."

"So, what's the first thing you're gonna do when you get back home?"

"Oh, I'm not sure," he replied. "But I can't wait to take this uniform off, put on some old, comfortable clothes, head down to the old creek and do some fishing!"

"Where ya from?" Sam asked, hoping to learn where they were heading.

"Alabama, sir. Decatur, Alabama."

"No kidding? I spent some time there as a kid."

"Really? Did you like it?"

"Yeah, it was nice," Sam replied, not wanting to insult the young man's hometown by sharing his true feelings.

Sam looked out the window, thinking back to the summer he had spent there. He remembered it being the hottest, most humid, God forsaken place he'd ever been. Then again, he probably hadn't given it much of a chance. After all, he was still reeling from everything he'd gone through at home before he'd arrived.

It was early summer, 1970, when he was just eight years old. His parents had divorced a year earlier, and not long after they had sold the only home he had ever known. After living with his Aunt Sophie and Uncle Frank for a while in a small apartment on the west side of Chicago, they moved into an apartment of their own in a suburb about five miles northwest of the city. His mother had taken on a new full-time job and was doing all she could to keep her head above water. This wasn't easy, being a single mother with two kids to feed, especially since she was receiving no child support whatsoever from Sam's father.

Will, the psychologist whom Dawn had taken Sam to see, had heard through the grapevine that she and Lee had been divorced. Having always been attracted to her, he called to ask if she'd be interested in getting together for a drink some time.

Will had come from a highly dysfunctional family himself, and by the time he was in his early 20's, he found himself in a place where he felt as though he had no control over anything or anyone in his life. He came to the realization that what he truly wanted was not healthy, functional relationships with others, but relationships within which *he* would be the one who called all of the shots. Relationships where he could control and manipulate others to get whatever it was that he wanted, without being forced to care about what would be best for the other person or what they might need to be truly happy. In an effort to achieve this sense of power and control, he went back to school and earned himself a master's degree in psychology, emerging from that experience with all of the knowledge he would need to force his will upon anyone who might have the unpleasant experience of crossing his path.

By the time they went on their first date, Dawn was at a place in her life where she was exceptionally vulnerable. She had just recently escaped from an extremely abusive relationship, had two young children she needed to care for, and was at a loss as to what direction her life would eventually lead her. What she wanted more than anything was security and stability for both her and the kids.

Will knew more than enough about the inner workings of the human mind to tell her whatever it was she needed to hear. His ultimate goal was never one which included truly loving her, but instead being one of owning her as a possession. He had never been married, had no children of his own, and never seriously considered the idea of having any in the future. Being 40 years old and living alone in his small, one bedroom apartment, he liked the idea of dating an attractive, 29 year-old woman whom he was fairly convinced he could manipulate and control. He wasn't particularly interested in the idea of stepping into a ready-made family, but he knew that if he could simply deal with it and wait things out long enough, there was a good chance he could eventually have her for his own.

He did his best to assure her that he could be the source of stability and security she so desperately wanted. He was also able to convince her that he was not only fine with the idea of raising the kids with her, but that he also eagerly wanted to do so. He remained on his best behavior around the kids, giving her no reason to believe that he didn't want the family life she wanted as well.

After dating for just under a year, they were married. It was a small wedding, held in the home of Will's mother, who was an ordained minister.

Wanting to spend some time alone together after their wedding, Dawn arranged to have Sophie and Frank take the kids to Alabama for a few months. They readily agreed, and once it was over, they loaded up Sam and Suzanne along with their clothes and some of their favorite toys, and then headed back home to Decatur. The kids had been sound asleep in the back seat for quite a while as they pulled into the driveway, so Frank picked them up and carried them inside, putting them to bed in their cousin Julie's room.

Frank and Sophie's home was a small, white, two bedroom frame home built in the late 1950's. It sat on the top of a hill on a very large lot surrounded by dense woods. The front yard had small patches of grass sprouting up sporadically in the midst of the dry, cracked dirt. An abandoned, 1961 Chevy station wagon sat off to the side of the gravel driveway.

The back yard was very large, sloping downward toward the dense woods behind it. A pink Nash Rambler with no windows or tires sat off of the rear corner of the home, rusting quietly in the intense heat.

The paint on the exterior of the home was old, faded and peeling, but the inside was always clean and full of love. There were no screens in the windows, which were always left open to allow whatever breeze might be available to blow through and carry off with it the intense Alabama heat as the curtains swayed back and forth with the wind. The only item in their home that resembled air conditioning was a small box fan which sat in one of the living room windows.

Sam awoke the following morning and looked around the bedroom. The warm morning sun broke into shafts of light as it beamed through the open window. The sheer curtains blew softly in the cool morning breeze. He wondered where he was for a few seconds as he wiped the sleep from his eyes. He looked to his left to see Suzanne and Julie sleeping on the bed across from him. A smile broke onto his face as he realized he was at his Aunt Sophie's home. He climbed from the bed and walked slowly out into the hallway, where he began to hear the sounds of pots and pans being moved around and dishes being placed on the kitchen table.

"Well, good morning, sleepy head," Frank said with a broad smile as Sam entered the kitchen.

"Hi, Uncle Frank!" Sam replied with excitement as he ran up and hugged him.

Sam spun around and saw his Aunt Sophie pouring pancake batter into a large iron skillet on the stove.

"Hi, Aunt Sophie!" Sam shouted as he ran over and wrapped his arms around her legs.

"Ooh, be careful, sweetie. This is very hot," she replied as she leaned down and kissed him on the head.

Sam couldn't wait to start the day. He had never been to Alabama before and he wanted to see everything. After breakfast, Julie took Sam and Suzanne out into the neighborhood to show them around. Their eyes were huge with curiosity as they took in their new surroundings. From the slightly rusted 7-up sign that swung back and forth as it hung out in front of the general store to the large pasture where Starlight, a neighbor's horse, would run through the many acres that were sectioned off with a barbed wire fence, everything was very new and different. They walked around the neighborhood most of the day, stopping back home just briefly for a quick sandwich around lunchtime.

This was a whole new world for Sam. Yesterday he was living in the shadows of a major city like Chicago, the only reality he'd ever known. Today he was in the deep-south; in a small town in Alabama which was just a few years removed from the civil rights marches of the late 60's. Although the turbulence of those days had subsided to a degree, racism was still very much a part of the culture. People thought differently, acted differently, and looked different from what Sam had always known. He was mostly unaware of these differences, but he was as much a foreigner here as he would've been had he traveled to a completely different country.

They finally came back home just as Sophie was preparing dinner. At the dinner table, they talked constantly, excited about everything they had seen. She and Frank listened politely, both very happy that Sam and Suzanne were excited about being there.

Frank was a bear of a man who had spent most of his life employed as a steel worker. He had broad shoulders and hands that could crush a billiard ball. He had flaming red hair and enough freckles on his face to play connect the dots for days. Behind his strong appearance was a gentle man with a heart of gold. He was never in a hurry to do anything, but instead moved along with a slow determination.

"So, Sam," Frank said in his slow southern drawl. "How would you and Suzanne like to go swimming tomorrow?"

"Really!?" Sam shrieked. "Yeah, we'd love to. I've never gone swimming!"

"You've never gone swimming?"

"Nope. Never."

"So, you don't know how to swim?" Frank said asked a perplexed look.

"Nope."

"Well then, that settles it. Tomorrow, I'm gonna teach you how to swim."

Sam could hardly contain his excitement. He leaped from the table and ran around the kitchen. He'd been wanting to learn how to swim for at least the past two years, but with all of the mayhem going on back home, going to the local pool was never very high on anyone's priority list.

The following morning, Frank and Sophie loaded up the car with a basket of sandwiches and drinks, stopped at the local store to buy bathing suits for Sam and Suzanne, and then headed to a beach along the Tennessee River. Sam couldn't get out of the car fast enough once they had parked. He grabbed whatever he could carry and ran toward the beach. Once everyone caught up with him, he began begging Frank to teach him to swim.

"Come on Uncle Frank! Teach me to swim! Teach me to swim!" he shouted.

"Hang on there," Frank said with a smile as he took his time helping Sophie lay out blankets in the sand. He knew the anticipation was killing Sam, and he was loving every minute of it.

"Come on Uncle Frank! You promised!"

After what seemed to be an eternity, Frank finally turned and looked at Sam.

"Are you ready, Sam?" He asked with an enormous grin.

"Yeah! I'm ready! Let's go!!"

"Alright. Let's go," Frank shouted as he bent over.

He lifted Sam up and sat him on his shoulders, and then turned to walk toward the water. Sam was beaming with excitement as they neared the shoreline. Frank began walking straight out into the water, Sam smiling ear to ear. As he continued moving forward, away from the shoreline, Sam began looking down to see how deep the water was. Once it was up around Frank's chest, Sam started to get a little concerned. Frank didn't say a word, but kept on walking away from shore until the water was just under his chin.

"Are you ready, Sam?"

Feeling Frank reaching back to pull him off of

his shoulders, Sam didn't like where this was going. He grabbed onto Frank's head with all his might.

"Hang on, Uncle Frank. What are you doing?" Sam shrieked.

"I'm teaching you how to swim!" Frank shouted with a laugh as he picked Sam up off of his shoulders and threw him into the deeper water.

"Swim, Sam!" Frank yelled as he laughed, turning away and starting to walk back toward the shore.

"Uncle Frank!" Sam screamed in a panic, barely able to keep his head above water as he paddled wildly.

"Swim, Sam! Swim!" Frank shouted back.

Terrified that he was about to drown, Sam began to kick and paddle as hard as his little body would allow him to. He turned himself toward the shoreline, flailing at the water with every ounce of strength he had. He eventually made his way to water shallow enough to walk in, and then immediately stood up and started running toward Frank, who had just made himself comfortable on a beach towel next to Sophie.

"Uncle Frank, you lied to me!" Sam shouted as he ran up to them.

"How did I lie to you?" Frank replied with a smile.

"You said you were going to teach me how to swim!"

"Well," Frank said with a pause. "You just learned how, didn't you?"

Sam thought this over for a second. He was still angry, but a smile began to break over his face. Uncle Frank was right. He *did* learn how to swim. Frank saw him starting to smile and hollered.

"Woo-hoo! Little Sammy's a swimmer now!"

Filled with excitement about his newly acquired skill, Sam started to jump up and down in the sand, waving his arms over his head in own impromptu victory dance.

"Sammy is a swim-mer, Sammy is a swim-mer!" Frank started to chant with an enormous smile.

Sam broke into laughter and began dancing on the beach to Frank's chanting.

"I'm a swim-mer! I'm a swim-mer!" he shouted back as he danced and waved his hands over his head.

Sam turned in excitement and ran back to the water, continuing away from shore until the water was deep enough to swim in. He quickly realized that this swimming stuff was a lot more fun when the fear of imminent death wasn't hanging over his head. He spent the next few hours swimming through the deeper water until he was exhausted, returning to the shore to rest until the excitement gripped him again, causing him to run back to the water and try it again. By the time they packed up and left the beach, he could barely move his arms anymore.

After leaving, they spent the rest of the day giving Sam and Suzanne a tour of the entire area, driving through a variety of small towns as Sophie, Frank and Julie pointed out anything they thought Sam and Suzanne might find interesting.

As the day progressed, Sam began to notice that Suzanne and Julie were paying more attention to each other than they were to him, excluding him from their conversations to the point where they were almost completely ignoring him. As the three of them sat in the back seat of the car, the girls began to whisper things to each other, laughing when they looked over at him. It bothered him that they would act this way toward him, but he tried his best to ignore it, looking out the car window and taking in the sights.

By the end of the day, they were all exhausted. They returned home and started to get ready for bed as soon as they walked in the door. After putting on his pajamas and brushing his teeth, Sam walked into the living room with a big smile on his face and hugged Frank and Sophie.

"I love you Aunt Sophie. I love you Uncle Frank," he said as he turned to walk back to the bedroom.

Sam was very excited about staying here. With all of the distractions of this new environment, he had completely forgotten about the chaos his life had been before coming here. He missed his mom, but he felt happy. He felt loved.

He turned the corner and walked into Julie's room, heading over to his bed and climbing in. Julie and Suzanne were already in their beds, talking and giggling as he entered.

"What are *you* doing in here?" Julie said sarcastically.

"Hi, Julie!" Sam replied, laughing at her sarcasm.

"I don't want you in here. Go sleep in the yard," she said with a biting tone as Suzanne giggled.

"Yeah, go sleep in the yard with the dogs," Suzanne chimed in.

"*You* go sleep with the dogs," Sam snapped back.

"No, you belong with the dogs, cuz you smell like a dog," Julie replied

Sam got up and went back into the living room, confused as to why Julie and Suzanne were being so mean to him all of a sudden.

"Aunt Sophie, Julie and Suzanne are being mean to me," he said with a sad voice.

"Julie! Suzanne! You both stop being mean to Sam!" Sophie hollered from the living room.

"Go back to bed now, Sam. It's past your bed time," she continued.

Sam walked back into the bedroom, feeling vindicated that Sophie had scolded them. He walked over to his bed and climbed back in.

"I'm sorry, Sam," Julie said with false sincerity. "You're not like a dog. You're more like a pig."

"Yeah, a chubby little pig!" Suzanne chimed in.

"Leave me alone!" Sam answered as he rolled over to face the wall.

"Oink oink, said the stinky little pig!" Julie said mockingly as she and Suzanne burst into laughter.

"That's enough, girls!" Sophie shouted from the living room.

"Sammy is a pi-ig. Sammy is a pi-ig," Julie and Suzanne began singing in a whisper, just loud enough for Sam to hear.

Sam pulled the blankets up and pressed his pillow over his ears until he couldn't hear them anymore. Tears began to fill his eyes as he faced the wall. As hard as he tried to hide it, Julie heard him starting to cry.

"Oh, is the little baby pig crying? she whispered mockingly. "Cry little piggy. Cry little piggy."

Sam pressed the pillow harder against his ears, trying his best to ignore her as he eventually drifted off to sleep.

The following morning, Julie and Suzanne awoke before Sam. They hurriedly ate breakfast, and then walked quickly toward the front door as they heard him coming down the hallway.

"Hey, where ya goin?" Sam called out as they stepped outside.

"Nowhere," Julie shouted back, walking through the front yard toward the dirt road that ran past their house.

Sam walked quickly toward the door and held it open.

"Hey! Where are you guys going? Wait for me," he shouted.

"We don't want you coming with us. You stink like a pig," Julie shouted back.

The two girls laughed loudly as they turned and headed down the dirt road as Sam ran into the kitchen.

"Aunt Sophie! Where are they going?!" he

pleaded. "They just left without me!"

"Oh, don't you worry about them, Sam. They'll be back They're just going for a walk," she replied. "Why don't you sit down and have some breakfast?"

Sam was heartbroken. For as long as he could remember, Suzanne was more than just a sister. She was his very best friend. Through all of the dark times and challenges they had to face growing up with their father, she was the one person who was always there for him. Julie was also like a best friend to him. He couldn't understand why they were suddenly being so cruel to him.

The sting of loneliness began to fill his heart. His father was no longer in his life, and his mother seemed as though she was a million miles away. Now the two people he felt closest to throughout his young life didn't want any part of him. He suddenly felt more alone than he had ever felt in his life.

"Aunt Sophie?" he said softly as the tears began to trickle down his cheeks.

"Yes, Sam. What's wrong?" she replied as she walked over to him and put her hand on his shoulder.

"I miss my mom," he said as his head sank, the tears now falling on his shirt.

"Oh, honey, I know. Come here," she said softly as she turned his chair toward her and wrapped her arms around him.

"When is she coming back to get me?" he asked quietly.

"Soon, honey. I promise...Very soon."

"Can I call her?" he asked quietly.

"Not right now, Sam."

"When?"

"I don't know, honey. Maybe tomorrow, ok? Hey listen. I made you some pancakes. Why don't you eat some breakfast, and then you can go outside and play, ok?" she said in a consoling voice.

Sam gathered himself, finished his breakfast, and walked into Julie's bedroom. In the corner next to his bed was the only thing Sam had brought with him to Alabama. It was an old shoebox filled with Matchbox cars. A plastic model of a 1965 Bonneville convertible that his father had built for him was placed carefully on top. It was Sam's prized possession, and the only thing he had left that was from his father. He pulled off the cover and took the car out, looking at it closely. He then put the lid back on the shoebox and headed out into the front yard.

Sam loved his Matchbox cars. He could play with them for hours on end, and he often did. He would divide them into equal groups, and then invent imaginary battles between the two. During these battles, the Bonneville was always the king of the cars. It was never involved in the battles per se, but would instead sit off in safety, shouting out orders to the rest of the cars.

He picked the perfect location for the next battle - a hilly area of the yard with tufts of grass for the cars to hide behind as they waited to ambush the others - and sat down in the dirt, pulling his cars out to array them in battle.

He played for a couple of hours, occasionally looking down the dirt road for Julie and Suzanne to return. As cruel as they had been to him earlier, he still hoped they would come back to play with him.

"Hey Sam," Frank said with a smile as he walked out the front door and saw Sam sitting in the yard.

"I think there's a bike around back. You can take it for a ride if you want to."

"Really?" Sam asked with excitement.

"Yup. It's out back against the house."

Sam quickly picked up his cars and put them back in the shoebox, placing it out of the way on the front porch, and then ran around the house. He grabbed the bike and climbed on, riding back around to the front yard.

"How far can I go?" he shouted out to Frank.

"You can go all the way down this road and back, but stay off of Danville road. That's a very dangerous road," he replied.

"Thanks Uncle Frank! I will! I promise!" Sam shouted back as he rode through the yard and onto the dirt road.

After riding about a block, he saw a large lot where someone had dumped small piles of dirt long ago. Through many rainstorms and countless hot summer days, the piles had hardened into row upon row of small hills. Sam turned into the lot and began riding over the hills, trying to jump from one to the other. He stayed there for a couple of hours, until he ran out of energy, and then made his way back to the dirt road and headed toward home.

As he cleared the top of the hill, he saw two boys playing in the front yard. Getting a little closer, he could see that the boys were playing with his cars in the dirt. Panic began to fill his heart as he rode faster toward the house. He jumped off of the bike and ran into the yard, where he saw his prized possession, the Bonneville his father had built him, smashed and broken, lying in pieces in the dirt.

"No!" he shouted as he ran over and picked it up. All of the wheels had been broken off. The plastic windshield was shattered. The bumpers and mirrors were gone, nowhere to be found.

"What are you screaming about?" Sophie shouted as she came outside.

"They broke it, Aunt Sophie! They broke my car!" he cried out.

"Sammy, you stop your shouting," she demanded. "You played with their bike, and they played with your cars. You all have to share."

"But they smashed it!" he shouted back.

"Did you break his car?" Sophie asked the boys.

"Yeah...We were just playing with it and it broke by accident," one of them replied.

"You say you're sorry, then," she said with a stern voice

"We're sorry," he replied as they walked away, leaving the rest of the cars scattered throughout the yard.

Sam looked down at the shattered piece of plastic that was – in reality – the only connection that remained between he and his father. Symbolic of what had become of their relationship, it was smashed, shattered, and left behind in the dirt. It didn't even slightly resemble the car he had walked away from just a short while ago. He picked up the shoebox and walked slowly through the yard, searching for any small pieces he could find. He gathered up what he could, along with the rest of his cars, and put them back into the box. He then closed the lid, his stomach feeling sick over what had just happened.

He began to hate being here. Everything seemed to be going wrong for him at every turn. The excitement of his new surroundings had been quickly washed over by a strong sense that he simply didn't belong here. He began to feel completely isolated, abandoned, and alone.

The next few weeks brought more of the same. The longer he stayed in Alabama, the less time Suzanne and Julie spent around him, and the more cruelly they treated him. Whenever they would spend time with him, which wasn't much, they would mock him relentlessly, making fun of everything about him from the way that he looked to the way that he walked and talked. He would continually try to think of something funny to say, hoping that they would laugh with him like they used to: hoping that they would play with him again, but to no avail. Growing weary of trying, and not wanting to be teased anymore, he instead began to spend countless hours playing alone with his matchbox cars, avoiding any communication with either of them.

Although he would use all of the rest of his cars to play, the Bonneville never came out of the box again. It sickened him to even look at it.

There wasn't a day that went by when he didn't ask where his mother was, why she was gone, or when she would be coming back. Aunt Sophie and Uncle Frank did their best to distract him from thinking about it, but those questions were continually on his mind.

As the heat of the summer raged on, the violent storms soon followed. On one of those summer days, Sophie and Frank had heard reports that some dangerous storms were moving into the area, and would arrive early in the evening. They brought the kids inside and turned on the old black and white television in their living room. Trying to keep them occupied and unaware of what was coming, Sophie made a big bowl of popcorn and brought it into the room, telling the kids that they were going to stay inside and have a family movie night.

As Sam laid on his stomach on the floor, looking up at the t.v., the winds began to pick up as the cooler night air moved in, combining with the hot air that had been present throughout most of the day. He looked over at Frank, who had a concerned look on his face. This was peculiar to Sam, because his usually easy going, calm uncle had never shown any signs of fear or concern about anything. He watched Frank closely, paying attention to his seemingly strange behavior.

As they began to hear the winds howling, Frank would get up occasionally, walk to the window, look outside for a few seconds, and then return to his chair.

"What's wrong, Uncle Frank?" Sam asked.

"Nothing, Sam. How's that popcorn?" he replied with a smile.

"It's yummy," Sam said with a grin.

Frank brought a few kernels to his mouth, and

then looked out the window again. The window fan in the living room was on, drawing in the cooler air. Sam could hear its motor beginning to strain as the winds started to blow with more and more force. The thin curtains that hung in the other window began to blow with more frequency and intensity. The thunder that was off in the distance was getting closer, and the lightening appeared to be getting brighter and brighter. Sam could see that Frank was becoming more and more concerned.

"Frank, should we head down to Mama Staggs'?" Sophie asked

"No, it's not time just yet," Frank replied with his slow southern drawl.

Mama Staggs was the nickname the family used for Malcom's mother. She was a sweet, heavy set southern woman who lived in a small brick home down in the valley. Whenever there was a threat of severe weather that might lead to a tornado, the whole family would drive to her home where they could wait safely as the storms passed. It was a much safer place to be than their small, wooden frame home that rested on the top of a large hill.

Sam looked at Frank again as he again stood up from his chair and looked toward the window. Just as he took a step toward it, a very strong wind struck the house, sucking the fan out through the open window and sending it tumbling down the hill.

"Sophie?" Frank said in his usual calm, slow voice. "I think it's time."

"Kids, get your shoes on. We're going to Mama Staggs'," she said as she began picking up their shoes and handing them out.

"Why are we goin to Mama Staggs'?" Suzanne asked.

"Just get your shoes on, honey. It's okay," Sophie replied.

They all sprang to their feet and headed for the front door as Frank went through the house, closing all of the windows and turning off the lights. As the front door opened, the strong winds knocked Sam sideways, almost causing him to lose his balance completely.

"Hurry, Sam! Get in the car!" Sophie demanded with a sense of urgency.

They all piled into Frank's old Chevy station wagon as he got in the driver's seat and started the car. Sam could feel the entire car rocking from side to side as it was buffeted by the winds. Frank headed down the old dirt road, and then turned onto Danville road. It was a very dangerous, narrow, twisting undivided two-lane highway that led toward the lower valley, about two or three miles north.

Sam was becoming increasingly nervous as he looked at the enormous trees on either side of the road being bent over and twisted by the progressively violent winds. Lightening flashed in every direction, followed quickly by earth shaking thunder. The rain poured down in heavy sheets, seemingly following a direct horizontal path in front of them. Along with the rain, various pieces of debris could be seen flying across the highway in the beam of Frank's headlights.

"Did we wait too long?" Sophie asked Frank in a nervous voice.

"No, we're ok," Frank replied, both hands tightly gripping the steering wheel as he made his way through the mayhem. Sam didn't say a word as he watched the road in front of them. He was now absolutely terrified by what he was seeing. He had never seen such a violent storm at any point in his life.

"We need to pick up Dave on the way," Frank said quietly.

Dave was Frank's brother who lived between Frank's home and Mama Staggs' home.

"What? Why do we have to pick up Dave?" Sophie protested. "We need to just get to Mama Staggs'."

"We *have* to get him, Sophie," Frank replied. "He has no car, and he needs to get outta here too. He has no way to get there."

A few minutes later, Frank turned into a gravel driveway on his left and pulled close to the house. The front door immediately flew open as Dave and his wife, Marla, stepped outside. Before they made it down their front steps, a blinding flash of lightening exploded just twenty feet to the right of the car, splitting in half a large tree that stood in the middle of their front yard. Momentarily blinded by the brilliant flash, Sam looked to his right to see what was left of the tree falling to the side, and then landing with a thunderous crash that shook the car violently. After being knocked back a step by the lightening, Dave and Marla regained their footing and ran to the car.

"Wow! That was something, huh?" Dave said with a touch of sarcasm as he climbed inside, attempting to catch his breath.

Frank backed out of the driveway and headed once again down Danville road. Within a few minutes, he pulled into Mama Staggs' driveway. As Sam looked down the road past her house, he could see large tree branches lying all over the ground in every direction. The traffic signals at a nearby intersection were all flashing red, and downed power lines danced across the asphalt pavement as arcs of live electricity shot from them, lighting up the nearby ground. Mama Staggs threw open the front door, motioning to everyone to come inside. The house was eerily dark behind her with the exception of the flickering background light from candles she had placed on her dining room table.

"Hurry up y'all!" she shouted at the car. "It's getting real bad out here!"

All of the car doors opened simultaneously as everyone was very eager to get inside to safety. Once inside, Mama Staggs ushered all of the children into her bedroom, telling them all to take cover under her large cast iron bed. None of them said a word, shaking with fear. They quickly followed her instructions and huddled up underneath as the lightening continued flashing, the thunder shaking the entire home to its foundation. They stayed there, completely silent for about twenty minutes until the storm began to sound as if it were calming down a bit.

"Alright, kids, you can come out now," Mama Staggs said in a sweet southern drawl as she stood in the doorway.

She could see that they were all visibly shaken by what had just taken place, and she wanted to calm their nerves and reassure them that they were perfectly safe.

"Why don't y'all set up here on my bed for a while," she continued.

She walked out of the bedroom for a few seconds, and then returned with a harmonica in her hand, taking a seat in a rocking chair across the room without saying a word. As the kids kept turning to look out the bedroom window to see if it really was safe, she raised her harmonica and began playing very softly. She rocked back and forth slowly in the chair, her eyes closed in the darkness as the lightning gradually became more and more distant, and the sound of thunder waited a little longer to sound after each flash. Before long, Sam stopped looking out the window, his eyes fixed upon her as she played. He put his head down on a pillow, listening to the soothing sound mixed with the slow creaking of her rocking chair as it moved back and forth across the dusty hardwood floor. He could feel his heart rate beginning to slow, his breathing becoming deeper and more relaxed, and before long he closed his eyes, drifting off to sleep.

As the weeks turned into months and the hot Alabama summer raged on, Sam continued to become more and more isolated from everyone. He had eventually given up on the thought of being accepted and loved by Julie and Suzanne. All he could think about was going home and leaving Alabama far behind him. Maybe then, he thought, he and Suzanne could become close once again, away from the influence of his cousin who had somehow turned her against him.

As more time passed, he started to feel as though his mother might be gone forever. As unthinkable as it was for him to imagine, he began to wonder if she had left him behind for good. While he loved Frank and Sophie, and as chaotic as his home life had been, they could never replace his mother and father. In an effort to draw him out of his own silence and isolation, they continually tried to find ways to keep him involved and occupied with various activities that might bring him some sort of happiness. In spite of their efforts, they could see him slipping away. His questions about where his mother was and when she'd return became less and less a part of their daily conversations. At just 8 years of age, he had begun to accept a reality in his life that no child that age should ever have to consider. As lonely as isolation was, it was far less painful than feeling the continual rejection and abandonment from the people he loved the most.

FOUR

"Next stop, Naphtali," Gabriel announced from the back of the car.

Sam glanced through the window at the approaching station. He was becoming increasingly disturbed about not knowing where he was or where he was going. As he studied the landscape leading to the station, the beautiful, rolling hills and scenic landscape fascinated him. As the train continued from station to station, Sam noticed that it seemed to be following a large river. He'd seen many rivers in his days, but this one was very different. The clarity of the water was astonishing, and there was a living quality about it that he'd never seen before in any body of water. It was absolutely crystal clear, and the trees growing along either side of it were exceptionally vibrant and healthy. He would occasionally see groups of people gathered at its banks, drawing water out of it. There was a sense of celebration surrounding it as the people approached. Children ran playfully into it, while adults walked up and stood alongside of it, apparently in awe of what they were seeing. He would occasionally see various people dipping their hands into it, and then bringing it to their lips to drink, while others peacefully immersed themselves into its depths.

He looked away from the river and fixed his gaze upon the station. Off in the distance, still a long way off, he saw a man running toward it.

"Better get moving, pal," Sam chuckled to himself, thinking that the man was running to catch the train.

As he looked more closely, he could see what looked like deer running with him, surrounding him on all four sides as he ran through the tall grass. Sam was amazed at how they seemingly had no fear of the man, looking as if they were even going as far as slowing down to allow him to catch up when they began to run too far ahead. They stayed with him all the way to the platform, wandering around it casually as if they were waiting for him as he stopped to catch his breath for a moment. He paced back and forth across the platform, his hands on his hips, taking deep breaths much like you'd see a runner do upon completing a marathon.

Behind him, Sam saw yet another set of gates, these with the name 'Naphtali' written on a sign above.

"What is with these gates, already?" Sam thought to himself.

He looked back at the man on the platform as the train began to move once again. As their eyes locked, Sam could see a sense of sadness in his eyes. They continued to look at each other until he was nearly out of sight, at which point the man nodded, and then started running back in the direction from which he had come, his deer friends following close behind.

Sam turned in his seat and looked over the other passengers. Many of them appeared to be a bit less comfortable than when he had first boarded the train. There was less talking amongst them, and most of them were staring out the windows with distant looks on their faces.

He looked at the woman in the red dress who had caught his eye earlier. She seemed to have a sadness in her eyes that reached down deep within her, as if she had lost something or someone very important to her. As he scanned her profile, then glanced down at the shape of her body, Sam was awestruck at her incredible beauty. He had no idea why, but there was just something very familiar about her. From looking at her, he knew that there was no way they would've run with the same crowd. She was in a completely different league, far out of his range. He thought that maybe she was an actress or a model, and that it was possible he had seen her in a movie, or possibly a magazine. As he looked up to her face, she turned and looked at him, breaking into a warm, kind smile.

Shouts of joy and a loud burst of laughter broke out in the front of the car, startling Sam and drawing his attention up front.

"Mommy!" a young boy, about 8 years old, shouted as a middle aged woman entered the car.

"I thought you'd never get here!" he continued.

"Now, why did you think that? I told you I'd be back," she replied with a warm smile.

"But it took you soooo long!" he insisted as he wrapped his arms tightly around her legs.

He hadn't seen either of them on the train prior to this point, but it was clear to him that they were meeting here after being apart for some time. As Sam watched this joyous scene unfolding, another man approached the woman from behind.

"Hey, sweetie," he said, putting his hand on her shoulder.

"James!" she replied with a wide smile, turning to give him a hug. "I missed you so much!"

"I missed you more," he replied, leaning over to give her a kiss.

"It's so good to be back home," she said with a sigh as they took a seat in the row directly in front of Sam, the young boy climbing up into her lap.

"It's good to have you back," he replied.

"I'm so sorry it took so long. You know how these business trips can be."

"I know. It's okay. Was it a good trip?"

"Yes, it was very productive," she said with a pause. "Well, it was when the guys weren't partying in the hotel bar until 2am."

"Was there a lot of that?"

"Not a lot, but enough."

"Did you join them?"

"Not really. I did the first night we arrived, just to relax after the long trip. They were driving me crazy, calling my room every night and asking me to come down, but I just didn't feel right about it."

"Why not?"

"Because it wouldn't be right for me to be drinking in a hotel bar with a bunch of other men while my husband was sitting home alone on the other side of the country."

"Ah...," he replied, waving his hand. "I trust you, sweetie."

"I know you do, James. You don't have a jealous bone in your body. I love that so very much about you."

Wanting more of his mother's attention, the little boy suddenly stood up on the edge of the seat in front of her and fell into her chest, wrapping his arms around her neck.

"I love you so much, mommy!" he exclaimed, looking over the back of the seat at Sam as he held her.

Sam smiled warmly at him, knowing exactly how this moment felt for him. As he continued to watch, he began to think back to the day his mother returned to Alabama to pick him up, and the incredible joy he felt when he first saw her.

He woke up in Julie's bedroom, just as he had every day for the past few months. He looked around the room and wiped the sleep from his eyes as the sun beamed in through the bedroom window. A slight breeze blew the curtains softly as he laid there for a few moments watching their gentle movement. He could hear voices in the kitchen, and the sound of Sophie banging pots and pans around as she prepared breakfast. He could smell bacon and eggs cooking, and suddenly felt a little hungry. He casually climbed out of bed, and then made his way down the hallway toward the kitchen.

"Good morning, Aunt Sophie," he said with a sleepy voice.

"Good morning, Sam," she replied with an enormous smile.

"Do you see anyone here you recognize?" she continued.

Sam turned and looked toward the kitchen table, his eyes lit up and his heart jumped in his chest when he saw his mother sitting at the table with a cup of tea.

"Mom!" he shrieked as he ran to the table and wrapped his arms around her as tightly as he could.

"I missed you so much! Where were you?!" he shouted.

"Oh, I missed you so much too, Sam," she replied.

"Are we going home now? Did you come to take us home?!" he pleaded.

"Yes, Sam, we're going home," she replied as she laughed.

"Oh, you don't like it here, Sam?" Sophie asked jokingly.

"I missed my mommy so much! I wanna go home!" he shouted.

"I missed you too, but I'm here now, ok? We're going home soon."

"When?! When are we going home?!" he

demanded.

"We're leaving this afternoon, ok?"

"Yaaaaay!" he shouted as he began dancing in circles around the kitchen table.

Sam was so excited he felt as though his heart was going to explode in his chest. Dawn spent a good portion of the day visiting Sophie and Frank, with Sam and Suzanne clinging tightly by her side the whole time. When it was time to leave, Frank drove them to the Greyhound bus station, where they boarded their bus back to Chicago.

Sam and Suzanne were very optimistic about their future in the new home. Will had always been very nice to them, and they were happy that he and their mother were now married. They loved their new home, and they loved the idea of living in the city. They had no thoughts in their mind about this being a *new* family. It simply hadn't been discussed. In their minds, their mother had married Will, they were happy together, and he was now going to be simply an addition to the family they already were. All of that changed very quickly during a conversation at the dinner table a few days after they had returned home.

Will wanted nothing more in his life than to be able to assert his absolute authority over anyone who had chosen to be in a relationship with him. He had no interest in real relationships. He wanted only absolute control. Of course, he would need to be able to gain that control without Dawn being even remotely aware of his ultimate goal. It would have to be disguised in such a way that he would look like the good guy in her eyes, no matter how it turned out. He knew that that the only way he could achieve the absolute control he was seeking would be to begin with isolating them from anyone who might get in the way; namely, their father. He was aware of the damage that had been done to their relationship with him in the past, but knowing the forgiving nature of children toward their own parents, he couldn't risk the chance that they might someday turn their loyalties back toward him. Due to his experiences with troubled families as a psychologist, he was well aware of the potential for even the most dysfunctional of families to find healing and restoration over time. That thought was completely unacceptable to him – at least for the next ten years; after which he could finally be rid of Sam and Suzanne so that he could be alone with his wife. He needed to draw a definite line which, once crossed over, he would no longer be just a new member of their already established family, but the complete and total replacement of the father they once had. He discussed it with Dawn, convincing her that he wanted only what was best for the children, without giving her even the slightest hint that he wanted anything out of it for himself other than the family she had always wanted.

"Kids," Dawn said quietly. "Will and I have been talking, and there's something he wants to say to you."

Same and Suzanne turned to look at Will.

"Listen," he began. "I'm very happy that I married your mom, and I'm very happy that we all live here together now. From now on, I don't want you guys to call me Will anymore. I want you to call me dad."

Sam and Suzanne looked across the table at each other, confused by his request.

"You want us to call you dad?" Sam asked with a confused expression.

"Yes, Sam. I want you to call me dad."

Sam paused for a moment, not sure of exactly what to say. It had never occurred to him that he would want to do that. After all, no matter how bad his relationship with his father had been, he was still his father and nothing could ever change that. He looked back at Will, who had sat back into his chair with a bit of a proud smirk on his face, feeling as though he had just offered them something very important and valuable.

"Bu…But you're not my dad," Sam replied.

"Well, I know I'm not," Will answered impatiently. "But your dad's not here, and I am, so I would like you to call me dad."

Sam looked at Suzanne again, who also had a very uncomfortable look on her face.

"But you're not my dad," Sam repeated. "My dad is my dad. I know he's not here, but he's still my dad."

"So, you're not going to call me dad, then?" Will asked impatiently, leaning forward in his chair with a more confrontational disposition.

"No…I can't," Sam replied.

"How about if we call you something else…like pop?" Suzanne chimed in cheerfully, attempting to defuse what was becoming a very uncomfortable conversation.

"Pop, huh?" Will asked sarcastically. "You want to call me Pop?"

Both Sam and Suzanne could see that Will was becoming very upset at the way the conversation had turned. He began to move around in his seat a bit, his face turning red as his breathing became more labored.

"Hey, listen, if you don't want to call me dad, that's fine! Don't call me dad!" he barked as he stood up, threw his napkin down on the table and then stormed off down the hallway.

Sam and Suzanne looked at their mom, who looked very uncomfortable.

"What the heck was that all about, mom? Suzanne asked. "Why did he get so angry?"

"I don't know, kids. I guess he just really wanted you to call him dad," she replied, seemingly disappointed they hadn't agreed to do so.

Sam and Suzanne felt bad about hurting Will's feelings, but they just couldn't imagine calling him dad while their father was still alive. They sat in silence for a few minutes until Dawn stood up from the table and followed Will into the bedroom, closing the door behind her. Looking at each other in disbelief as they heard them arguing in the bedroom, Sam flashed a confused expression at Suzanne, shrugged his shoulders, crossed his eyes, and then brought his finger up to his temple, rotating it in circles to make the international sign of "This guy's crazy."

What neither of them understood was that their refusal of his request would change how Will looked at everything with regard to his relationship with them. He knew what they had been through with their father, and had assumed they would eagerly push their father aside and look to *him* as a father figure, feeling very grateful that he was willing to step into that role for them. Coming to the realization that they fully rejected the idea of giving him the role of being their father, and in doing so, rejected the absolute control he had sought to gain over them, left him feeling no desire to even pretend as though he wanted any sort of true relationship with them from that point forward.

As the next few months went by with Will and Dawn having full-time jobs, it was agreed that Sam and Suzanne would be assigned daily chores to help in keeping the house clean. They were assigned a rotating schedule of duties, and were told they would earn a weekly allowance for performing those duties. It seemed like a good plan to Dawn and Will, not only to help in keeping the house clean, but also to teach the kids a sense of responsibility. Sam and Suzanne liked the idea too because it put money in their pocket on a weekly basis, which was something they'd never experienced before. What they didn't know was that they had just been employed not by a fair boss, but instead by an unforgiving taskmaster who would prove to be impossible to please. Suzanne learned this truth almost immediately. Her job on that day was to clean the kitchen, and a list of items that needed to be done was given to her. She was actually a little excited as she began by washing the dishes, cleaning out the sinks, wiping down the countertops, and then finished by sweeping and washing the kitchen floor. She worked diligently for about an hour, and then stepped back to look over her work. She was very pleased with what she saw, and she was very proud of herself. In her eyes, everything looked clean and in its proper place. She went to her bedroom, closed the door, and turned on her stereo to listen to some music as she lied on her bed.

A few hours later, she heard Will come in the front door. Feeling excited to show him her work, she turned off her stereo, arranged her stuffed animals on her bed, and then walked into the kitchen to find Will on his hands and knees, picking at the corner of the floor with his fingernail.

"Suzanne?" he said in a stern voice.

"Yeah, Will," she replied, a bit confused at what she was seeing.

"Did you sweep and clean the kitchen floor today?"

"Yes, I did," she said with a smile. "Doesn't it look nice?"

"No, it doesn't," he barked. "There's still dirt here. Wash it again."

"Are you serious?" she replied in disbelief.

"Yeah!" He snapped. "You're damn right I'm serious! It's filthy!"

With that, he stood up and stormed past her without saying another word, leaving a small pile of dirt on the floor that he had dug out of the corner. She stood in the doorway, staring at the floor. She felt a little sick, having been so proud of her work, only to have it instantly rejected as inadequate. She went to the closet and got the broom, swept the floor again, then filled a bucket with hot soapy water to re-wash the floor. She spent more time on it than before, this time paying special attention to the corners where she had seen him digging with his fingernail. Once the floor had dried, she went into the living room where he was reading.

"Will?" she said quietly.

"Yes?" he replied without looking up from his book.

"I've finished the floor. Do you want to take another look at it?"

He put his book down and returned to the kitchen, getting on his hands and knees once again. This time he swept from side to side over a large section of the floor with the palm of his hand, then lifted it and rubbed his hands together. He felt a few very small crumbs of dirt, and stood back to his feet.

"Do it again," he said sharply as he showed her the palm of his hand, then walked out of the room and returned to his book.

Suzanne was so frustrated she wanted to scream. She let out a heavy sigh that Will heard from the other room. He jumped up and returned to the kitchen.

"Do you have a problem with washing the floor the way I want it washed?" he snapped, his face turning red.

"Well, I just don't understand, Will," she pleaded. "I really took my time and I did the best job I could."

"Well, your best just isn't good enough!" he barked. "Do you want your allowance this week?"

"Yeah, I want my allowance," she replied in disbelief.

"Then do it again!" he shouted.

Suzanne went to the closet, got the broom, and started all over again. Once she had washed it a third time, she called Will back into the room. Will again got on his hands and knees. Finding no more dirt this time, he stood up, clapping his hands together.

"I guess that'll do," he said, seemingly unimpressed. "Where's your brother? He was supposed to take the garbage out, and it's still there."

"I don't know," she replied. "He's probably playing outside."

Will walked back into the living room and returned to his reading, waiting for Sam to come home. About 30 minutes later, Sam walked in the front door.

"Sam, weren't you supposed to take out the garbage today?" Will asked.

"Oh, yeah. I'm sorry. I forgot. I'll do it now," Sam replied nonchalantly

"You forgot?" Will asked

"Yeah, I forgot."

"Why did you forget?"

Sam stopped in his tracks and looked at Will, not expecting to hear that question.

"I don't know…I just forgot."

"Oh, I see," Will said with a hint of sarcasm. "And what were you doing that was so important it made you forget to take out the garbage?"

"Nothing, really? I was just playing, and I forgot."

"Okay," Will said as he nodded his head. "Then I guess I can forget about giving you your allowance this week."

"What?" Sam shot back. "Are you serious?"

"Yes, I'm very serious," Will said in a matter-of-fact tone. "You were supposed to take the garbage out before I got home. You didn't do that. You forgot. Therefore, you can forget about your allowance this week."

Sam stood speechless, having no idea how to respond. After a few seconds, he shook his head and let out a sigh, causing Will to explode.

"Hey, do you have a problem?!" Will shouted as he jumped to his feet.

"Well, I just don't understand," Sam replied. "I forgot. I'm sorry. I told you I'd do it now. I just don't understand why I should lose my allowance."

"Because that's just the way it is, little boy!" Will

replied, his face red with anger. "I asked you to have something done by a specific time, and you didn't do it!

"Okay, okay! I'm sorry!" Sam said as he backed away and went into the kitchen to get the garbage. He came back inside and went down to his bedroom, frustrated and confused about what had just happened. A few minutes later, Suzanne entered his room.

"What the heck is *his* problem?" Sam asked incredulously.

"I don't know. What a jerk," Suzanne replied.

She then went on to tell Sam about what had happened with the kitchen floor. Sam sat and listened, his eyes wide in disbelief. A few minutes later, Dawn returned home from work. Sam and Suzanne left his room, eager to tell their mother about what had transpired.

"Hi Will," she said with a smile as she entered the room.

"We have to talk," Will shot back

"Oh...okay...Is something wrong?"

Will stood up and stormed past her, walking into their bedroom without saying another word. Dawn looked down the hallway at Sam and Suzanne with a confused expression. They both shrugged, being very confused by the situation themselves. She set her purse on the table and followed Will into the bedroom, closing the door behind her.

"What's wrong, honey?" she asked quietly.

"I'll tell ya what's wrong," he shot back. "Your kids have no respect for my authority."

"What are you talking about?" she replied in disbelief.

She knew the various shortcomings her kids had, but she never knew either of them to be disrespectful in any way.

"I asked them to do their chores. It was very simple. Neither of them completed their work to my liking, and when I told them that I wasn't pleased with their work, they both huffed and puffed and gave me an attitude. I'm not going to stand for that, Dawn."

"Calm down, Will," she replied, seeing that he was very upset. "What did they do that wasn't to your liking."

"I asked Suzanne to wash the kitchen floor, and she did a horrible job. The whole floor was still covered with dirt, so I told her to do it again. She did a half-assed job the second time too. There was dirt everywhere. When I told her she needed to do it right, she let out a heavy sigh as if I was being unreasonable. Sam was supposed to take out the garbage before I came home. He didn't do it because he said that he forgot. I told him that since he forgot to take out the garbage, he could also forget about getting his allowance this week."

"Well, did he take it out, and did Suzanne eventually wash the floor the right way?" she asked quietly.

"Yes they did, but I shouldn't have to remind them to do what they've already been told to do, and I shouldn't have to baby-sit them while they do it. It should be done right the first time, when it's supposed to be done."

"Alright, I'll talk to them, ok? I don't understand why you're so upset about all of this," she said quietly.

"You don't know why I'm upset?!" he asked incredulously. "Look, I'm trying to teach these kids how to be responsible. That's something they've apparently never been taught."

"That's not fair, Will! I've done the best that I could!" she snapped back, hurt by his comment.

"I'm not blaming you, Dawn. Look, I know you've all been through a lot. Because of all that you've been through, those kids of yours have to be trained. If you want them to grow up as productive members of society, they have to learn how to be responsible. That's all I'm saying. What's most important is that you work with me on this. I know what I'm doing, and we have to show a united front. If we don't, they'll see that very quickly and they'll eventually begin trying to take advantage of our disagreements. That's just what kids do. Please trust me on this."

"I trust you, Will. I just think you need to be a little more understanding, ok? This is all very new to them."

"I will," he replied as he stood up to give her a hug.

When Dawn left the bedroom, Sam and Suzanne were waiting for her in the living room.

"Mom, can we talk?" Suzanne asked as she entered the room.

"Yeah, let's go in your room," she replied.

The three of them went into Suzanne's room and closed the door.

"Mom, I don't understand what Will's problem is," Suzanne said, looking at Dawn in desperation.

"I know," she replied. "I just had a talk with him. He told me what happened."

"Did he tell you that he acted like a mental case?" Sam shot back.

"Stop it, Sam," she snapped. "Listen, he just expects both of you to do what you're asked when you're asked to do it."

"I did, mom!" Suzanne replied. "I cleaned the whole kitchen! He got on his hands and knees and started picking dirt out of the corners! Then he made me wash it two more times! That's crazy, mom!"

"He just wants it done a certain way, Suzanne. You didn't know what he was expecting, but now that you know what he wants. There shouldn't be any more problems with that, right?"

Sam and Suzanne looked at each other, stunned by their mother's response.

"Are you serious?" Sam asked.

"Yes, I'm serious, Sam. And now you know that

you need to have the garbage out before he gets home from work. He told you that before, and you didn't do it. There's really no excuse for that, Sam. Listen, I have to get dinner started. I know that Will was very upset about what happened today. I think it would be a good thing if both of you would go into the living room and apologize to him."

With that, she turned and left Suzanne's room.

"Apologize to him?! For what?!" Sam demanded as he looked toward Suzanne.

"I don't know...Maybe she's right, Sam."

After talking things over for a few minutes, they agreed that maybe it was best if they *did* apologize. They didn't understand why he became so upset over what appeared to be such minor issues, but they both liked Will and they didn't want to disappoint him. They both said they were sorry, and believed that the issue would be put behind them.

Over the next few months, matters only became worse. There was no room for error, and any minor discrepancy in how or when their chores would be completed was met with harsh criticism and heavy punishment. More often than not, Sam wouldn't receive any allowance at all due to some minor rule infraction he'd commit over the course of the week.

Will became absolutely convinced that that any sign of irresponsibility from either of them was not a result of youthful irresponsibility, but instead direct rebellion against his authority. He began to regularly accuse them of purposely neglecting their responsibilities in a passive-aggressive effort to undermine his leadership in the home. In time, acts that would initially result in verbal abuse and the loss of their allowance also included random groundings for extended periods of time.

The longer they lived together, the more difficult their living conditions became. Will, being a very light sleeper, asked for absolute silence in the house after 10:00pm, when he'd go to bed. The only bathroom in their home was directly next to the master bedroom where he slept. If anyone had to use the bathroom after he had gone to bed, they knew that they had better be as quiet as a church mouse when doing so. If they weren't, and he awoke, there would be hell to pay. Sam and Suzanne tried as hard as they could to follow his instructions. They would tiptoe down the hallway, closing the door as slowly and quietly as possible, almost moving in slow motion until they were finished. But no matter how quiet they were, he would always wake up. He eventually demanded that nobody use the bathroom after 10:00pm. He told them to use the bathroom just before he went to bed, and if anyone woke up in the middle of the night having to go, they'd just have to hold it till morning. That was the rule, and there would be no exceptions.

Will's ultimate goal was never allow either of them to feel comfortable in their own home, because doing so would inevitably lead to both of them wanting to stay there longer than he had planned. He wanted both of them gone by the age of eighteen, with no exceptions, and he knew that the best way to accomplish this would be to make it absolutely clear to them that they weren't welcome there. While Dawn was away at work, he would regularly make rude comments to them, telling them that he couldn't wait until they were eighteen so that he could be alone with *his* wife. He also made it very clear to them on a regular basis that this was *his* home, not theirs.

As more time passed, and as more and more rules of acceptable conduct were enforced, Sam and Suzanne began to feel less and less like part of a family living at home, and more and more like unwanted strangers living in a prison camp. They would plead with their mother time and again to intervene, but she didn't want to confront him, believing that it would only make matters worse. She wanted to keep the peace, hoping that everything would calm down and they could become the happy family she had always wanted them to be. She believed that, if they could all just try harder to do things the way he demanded they be done, there would be no more confrontations. Due to that mindset, they never once witnessed her standing up for them or defending them in any way. Will's rules were Will's rules, she would say, and if they were all going to live in the same home, they would just have to deal with it.

Sam and Suzanne began to feel a deep sense of abandonment from their mother that they didn't understand. She had been with them through thick and thin, but those days were apparently over. They learned to accept that she would be no help, she was no longer on their side, and all they had was each other. Over the years, this would develop into an incredibly deep relationship between them. They would become more than just brother and sister. They would become best friends forever.

After living with Will for a little over a year, Dawn was cooking in the kitchen when the phone rang.

"Hello?" she said as she put it to her ear.

"Dawn?"

"Yes."

"It's Lee...How are you?"

"Lee?" she replied, taken aback that he'd be calling. "Um...I'm ok. Why are you calling?"

"I really miss the kids, Dawn," he said quietly. "I wanted to see if we could arrange a way for me to see them."

"I don't know, Lee," she replied, feeling the blood rush to her head.

"They're my kids, Dawn. I have a right to see them."

"I'd have to talk to *them*, Lee...I don't even know if they'd want to see you."

Lee paused for a moment to collect his

thoughts.

"Lee?…Are you there?"

"Yeah…yeah, I'm here," he replied. "Alright, well, can you do that? Can you talk to them and get back to me?"

"Ok…I will," she replied hesitantly.

"Alright…thank you.

"Goodbye, Lee."

"Goodbye, Dawn."

Dawn hung up the phone and stood motionless for a few minutes as her thoughts swirled over the possible implications of his request. She had no desire to have Lee come to her new home to pick the kids up, and even less desire to allow them to leave with him. At the same time, she didn't know if she could legally stop it from happening. She was almost certain the kids wouldn't want any part of him coming around either. If they refused to go, then the problem would be solved, but what if they wanted to see him? Panic began to fill her heart and mind as she thought through all of the possible implications.

She finished making dinner, and then called everyone to the table. After they had been eating for a while, Will noticed that she was being very quiet.

"Is something bothering you, honey?" he asked quietly.

With both of the kids being present at the table, Dawn wasn't sure if this was the right time to bring it up. She started to answer, but immediately stopped herself.

"Honey?" Will said as he looked up from his dinner plate. "Is something wrong?"

"Yes, something *is* bothering me," she replied.

"And what's that?" Will replied coldly.

"Lee called a little while ago."

"Lee?" he said sarcastically. "What in the world did *he* want?"

Dawn swallowed hard, not wanting to say why he had called. She looked at Sam and Suzanne, who had both stopped eating and were staring at her intently.

"He wants to see the kids," she replied softly, looking down at her food.

"Dad?!" Sam almost shrieked. "Dad wants to see us?!"

"Yes, Sam...Your dad wants to see you."

Sam and Suzanne looked at each other, their eyes wide in disbelief.

"When?!" Sam asked excitedly.

"I don't know, Sam."

Even though his father had been guilty of doing things that were incredibly destructive to their family, the long period of time that had passed since he had last seen him allowed Sam to think back about many of the good memories he had experienced with him also. He often wondered why his father seemed to have no desire to see them, leaving them behind so very long ago. Sometimes he wondered if it was because of the ways he had disappointed his father in the past. No matter what the answers were to those questions, finding out that Lee wanted to see him now brought him more happiness than anything that had happened in a very long time. To Sam, it meant that his father still loved him.

"I wanna see him, mom!" he replied with excitement. "I miss my dad!"

Will immediately raised the palm of his hand toward Sam's face in a gesture meant to shut him up as he turned to look at Dawn.

"You're not seriously considering this, are you?" he asked as he set down his fork.

"I don't know, Will," she replied impatiently.

"What do you mean, *you don't know*?" he asked, his voice rising a bit in anger.

"I wanna see my dad!" Sam shouted out, suddenly upset that Will might get in the way of that.

"Shut up, Sam!" Will snapped, raising his palm toward Sam's face again.

"Answer me, Dawn," Will insisted. "Are you seriously considering this?"

"I don't know, Will. I have to think about it. Kids, I really don't know if this is something that's going to happen. We have to talk about it and think it over for a while, ok?"

"I think we need to discuss this right now, Dawn," he insisted, standing from the table and walking toward their bedroom.

Dawn looked across the table at Sam and Suzanne, seeing the looks of excitement on their faces.

"Shhh," she whispered, raising her finger to her lips. "I'll go talk to him," she continued as she stood and followed him into the bedroom.

"I can't believe you're actually considering this!" he insisted, shaking his head at her as if she were insane.

"He's their father, Will."

"I understand that, but he gave up the right to be their father when walked away from them."

"He didn't walk away from them, Will."

"Oh really? He didn't? Then what would you call it?" he replied, raising his voice.

"I kept them from him for the first year because I was afraid. After that, they were in Alabama all summer. It wasn't as if he had any choice."

"I can't believe you're doing this to me, Dawn," he replied in disgust.

"To you?!" she answered in disbelief. "What am I doing to *you*?!"

"Do you have any idea how hard I've worked to correct their behavior over the past year?"

"I don't understand how that has anything to do with any of this!"

"Oh, you don't?" he asked in a mocking tone.

"No, I don't!"

"Well, let me explain it to you, since you apparently have no clue as to how any of this works," he answered in a condescending tone.

"Don't speak to me like that, Will," she insisted. "I'm not some kind of idiot.

"I'm sorry…I'm not suggesting that you are," he replied, lowering his voice. "Listen, over the past year or so, I have worked very hard to correct some things in your kids that were in desperate need of correcting. I've been trying to teach them how to be more responsible and respectful, and I believe that it's starting to work. If you allow Lee back into their lives, his influence is going to undermine everything I've been trying to do. His reckless attitude and behavior will have a definite negative impact on them, and it could very easily cause them to rebel against my authority."

"Will…," she replied in stunned amazement. "This isn't about you. This is about two kids who, in spite of everything, still love their father. It's also about a father who, whether you like who he is or not, has every right in the world to see his children."

"So, that's how you're going to look at this?"

"Yes, Will, it is."

Over the next few days, it was all Sam could think about. He hadn't seen his father in nearly two years, and he was beginning to miss him very badly. He didn't think back upon all of the bad memories he had of him, but of the many good ones that had been scattered in between. He remembered the Bonneville model his father had built him, and the proud expression on his face when he had handed it to him. He thought back to how happy his father was when they were riding in his convertible for the very first time. He remembered cuddling on the sofa with him when Sam was very small. In spite of the bad times, the frightening times, these were all very fond memories for Sam.

He then thought back to how upset his father would get when he cried. Sam felt ashamed inside that he had been so weak, and he wondered from time to time if his father didn't want to see him because he had cried so much when they were together. He remembered his father taunting him, mockingly repeating "*Crybaby, crybaby, crybaby.*" over and over again whenever Sam's eyes would well up from being hurt or upset. Sam knew how much his crying had upset his father, and he had promised himself very long ago that if he ever did see his father again, he would never again cry in front of him again, no matter what.

Within a few days, after much discussion between she and Will, and speaking to Lee in an effort to work out all of the details, the decision was made to allow Sam and Suzanne to begin having regularly scheduled visits with their father. After taking a deep breath, and still uncertain if it was a good idea, she broke the news to them.

"Sam? Suzanne?" she called out from the living room. "Come in here, Will and I have something we want to talk to you about."

They both ran into the living room, playfully pushing and shoving each other back and forth.

"Sit down, guys," Dawn said quietly. "We have something important to tell you."

Sam and Suzanne both knew what she wanted to talk to them about. They had been on pins and needles since first hearing that their father wanted to see them.

"Is it about dad?" Suzanne asked excitedly.

"Yes, it's about your father," she replied.

"Can we see him?" Suzanne asked, even more excited.

"Yes, but...,"

As soon as they heard the word yes, Sam and Suzanne both let out a jubilant shout, interrupting their mom as she was speaking.

"Hold on, guys!" she demanded, raising her voice. "There are some things you need to know about your father before you see him."

"What, mom?" Sam asked, suddenly a little afraid of what she might say next.

"Your father is married to another woman now. Do you remember my friend Ronnie?"

Sam and Suzanne looked at each other, confused. They didn't remember ever meeting any woman named Ronnie. They also had no knowledge of their affair or the baby girl who had been born because of it.

"No, mom," Sam said quietly. "I don't remember any Ronnie."

"Well, she was once a very good friend of your father and I. He told me that they started dating after the divorce, and they're married now.

"Alright...," Sam replied, surprised by the news.

"There's something else you need to know. Ronnie has a daughter. Her name is Sandy, and she's a few years younger than you, Sam. She's your step-sister."

Both of their eyes lit up when they heard the news.

"We have a step-sister?" Suzanne asked incredulously.

"Yes, you do," Dawn replied with a heavy sigh.

Dawn almost gritted her teeth as she mentioned Sandy. She saw no need in telling them that she was also their father's daughter, making her their half-sister.

"Where do they live?" Suzanne asked.

"In Ronnie's house, in Des Plaines," she replied.

"When can we see him?" Sam asked excitedly.

"Well, here's what we're going to do. We've agreed that you can see your father one weekend per month."

"When?" Sam asked impatiently.

"Starting next weekend. He's going to pick you up Saturday morning at 10:00."

Sam and Suzanne jumped to their feet, thrilled

at the news. Dawn wasn't nearly as excited. She had many reservations about this, knowing what Lee was capable of doing while drinking. Will sat absolutely silent during the entire conversation, his right hand covering his chin and lower lip as he looked directly at the floor across the room.

The next week seemed to take forever for Sam. All he could think about was how excited he was, and how different things were going to be between he and his father this time around. He wasn't a crybaby anymore, and he was going to prove it to him. More than anything, he wanted his father to be proud of him.

By 9:00 Saturday morning, Sam and Suzanne had their clothes, pillows, blankets, and toothbrushes packed and sitting by the front door. Both of them sat on the sofa, looking down the street through the living room window, their eyes opening wide with anticipation with every car that headed their way. At 10:15am, the sunlight caught the thick chrome surrounding the windshield of their father's 1965 Pontiac Bonneville convertible as it turned the corner. Lee was still very proud of that car, and he knew that both kids loved it and would be excited to see it. To make the moment even more special, he had washed and waxed it the day before, and had put the convertible top down before leaving to pick them up.

"He's here!" Sam shouted as he jumped from the sofa, grabbed his belongings and ran toward the door.

"Bye, mom! I love you!" he said breathlessly as he quickly hugged her waist, and then disappeared through the doorway, Suzanne close behind him.

"Daddy!" they both shouted as they ran toward the car.

Sam swung the door open and jumped into the back seat, throwing his belongings to the side, and then leaped over the back of Lee's seat, wrapping his arms around his huge shoulders and hugging him as hard as he could. Suzanne dove across the front seat and wrapped her arms around his waist.

"Hi, guys!" Lee replied with an enormous smile on his face. "How've ya been?" he continued, hugging each of them back for a few seconds.

"Come on, sit down. Let's get going," he said as he put the car in drive.

Sam could feel the intense joy pouring out of him, smiling a mile wide as he looked up at the passing trees overhead while Lee drove down their street. It instantly brought him back to the memories of getting into his dad's Bonneville and taking that first ride with the top down. The leather seats, the smell of cigarettes and Old Spice cologne from his dad, the way the engine sounded as he drove off, and right down to Suzanne's hair whipping him in the face from the front seat. For a brief moment in time, everything felt right in his world again.

Wanting to explain his current living situation to them before arriving at the house, Lee stopped at a local restaurant in his neighborhood so they could talk for a little while.

"Come on, guys. Let's get some lunch," he said with a smile as he pulled into the lot and parked the car.

They were both excited as they entered the restaurant and took a seat at the counter. Up to this point in their lives, they had never been to an actual restaurant before. Sam's eyes grew wide as his father handed him a menu. There were so many choices, and he had no idea what to order.

"Hey, I need to explain some things to you guys," Lee said with a bit of hesitation. "A lot of things have changed over the past couple years."

Sam and Suzanne nodded, waiting for him to continue.

"I married someone a while ago. Her name is Ronnie. She's your step-mother now."

"We know, Dad. Mom told us," Sam replied.

"She did?"

"Yeah."

"What did she say about her?" Lee asked, wondering how much they knew.

"Nothing, really. She just said that you're married now."

"Where did you meet her, Dad?" Suzanne asked, curious to know a little more about her.

"I've known her for a long time," he replied. "I don't remember where we actually met."

"Is she nice?" Sam asked, hoping that she wouldn't turn out to be as nasty as Will had been to them.

"Yes, she is…I don't know if you remember, but you've met her before. You were both very young at the time."

Sam and Suzanne looked at each other, not having any memories of anyone named Ronnie.

"No, I don't remember," he replied.

"Well, she remembers you, and she's really looking forward to seeing both of you again. The last time she saw you, you were only babies.

There's something else you should know," he continued, pausing for a few seconds. "You have a half-sister."

"We know, Dad. Mom told us."

"She did? What did she tell you about her?"

"Not much. She just said that Ronnie had a daughter."

Lee sat back, looking at both of them. He was relieved that their mother hadn't revealed to them that he was her father.

"Yeah…Her name is Sandy. She's a little younger than both of you."

"I can't wait to meet both of them, Dad," Suzanne replied with a smile. "I've always wanted a little sister."

The three of them finished their lunch, Lee filling them in on the many details of what had happened in his life since the last time they'd seen each other and asking them what had been going on in theirs.

The rest of their weekend together was very nice for all of them. They didn't do much other than stay at home and talk, getting to know Ronnie and Sandy and enjoying spending time together with their father for the first time in a long time. By the time Sunday evening had arrived, Sam and Suzanne started to dread the thought of going back home. They knew that their father had some serious issues, but none of those issues came up while they were there. Everything was very calm and low-key. They felt very welcome and comfortable in their father's home, which was a very different experience from what they'd been feeling in their own home. Neither of them mentioned it, but they were both feeling as though they'd rather stay with him than to return to the prison camp environment that Will had created.

"I love you, Dad," Sam said as he reached over the back of Lee's car seat after he had pulled in front of their house. "It was really great to see you."

"It was good to see you too, Sam," he replied, reaching back over the seat to rub the top of his head.

"When can we see you again?" Suzanne asked.

"I'm not sure yet. I'll call you, okay?"

"Okay," she replied as she stepped out of the car.

While they both started to dread going inside, they also felt very happy about how their weekend had gone. They opened the front door, and then turned to wave goodbye as Lee put the car in drive and pulled away from the curb.

FIVE

As he sat on the train continuing in his daydream, Sam was suddenly distracted as he heard a commotion coming from the front of the car.

"Look out, you idiot!" a young boy of about 12 said to a girl in front of him who was apparently his sister as he shoved her to the side.

"Knock it off, you jerk!" she shouted as she shoved him back.

Sam watched as they made their way through the car, taking their seats a few rows behind him, nudging and poking each other the whole way.

He laughed to himself, thinking back to how he and his sister had annoyed the heck out of each other for a number of years. There never seemed to be any sense to it other than pure sibling rivalry, constantly trying to 'one up' each other at getting under each other's skin.

That mindset eventually tapered off as they realized how they truly needed to be there for, and protect each other. Sam couldn't remember them ever having a conversation about it or making any sort of pact. It simply came about naturally as their living conditions with Will and their mother deteriorated even further, along with the relationships they would have with both.

They had settled into their new neighborhood, making some close friends along the way. Sam had become best friends with a boy his age named

George, who lived a few blocks away. They met on Sam's first day at his new school. As it had turned out, it was George's first day in the school also. George was seated next to him, and began talking to him as soon as he sat down. After a few minutes, George asked how long he had been at the school. When Sam replied that it was his first day there, George laughed and replied: "Hey, it's my first day too! Wanna be friends?" From that day on, they were nearly inseparable. They began to walk home from school together every day, usually picking on George's twin brother Bill along the way. They had no reason to pick on him, other than both of them finding him to be exceptionally annoying.

Suzanne had met and become best friends with Cathren, a girl in her class from a German family in the neighborhood. They too would become nearly inseparable as the years progressed.

By this time, Sam and Suzanne were becoming fairly popular in their neighborhood. Sam truly enjoyed making other people laugh, and was beginning to settle nicely into the role of the class clown, constantly cracking jokes and pulling pranks on his friends. While it got him into trouble from time to time, it also made him a lot of friends who loved having him around because he would always make them laugh.

As they grew closer to their friends, they began to openly discuss their living conditions at home with them, as well as with and their families. The more they did so, the more concerned their friends and their friend's parents became. There were many times when, after sharing some of the details of their home life, questions would be raised that neither of them had any answers for. It became clear to many of them that the way they were being treated by Will wasn't just different or strange, but downright abusive.

Such an event occurred just as Sam was entering 6th grade. In an effort to create space between himself and the kids, Will had spent the summer building bedrooms in the basement for them. This effectively moved them into the lower level of the home, while their mother's bedroom was on the upper level. They didn't think much about it, other than they were happy to have larger bedrooms.

They came home from school to find Will and their mother sitting at the dining room table, and to avoid any problems with Will, they immediately began doing their chores.

"Sam, Suzanne, come in here a minute. We have something we need to discuss with you," Will said in a firm voice.

What's up?" Sam said as he entered the room and sat at the table.

"You're aware of how light of a sleeper I am, right?" Will asked

"Yes," they both replied.

"Well, I've asked you two repeatedly to not use the bathroom after I've gone to bed, but you continue to do so. In doing so, you wake me up every single night. I need my sleep, and I can't continue to be awakened every single night, so here's my solution: From now on, if you need to go to the bathroom in the middle of the night, I want you to use the washtub in the basement. To ensure that you don't continue coming up here, I'm going to start locking the door leading to the basement before we go to bed."

Sam and Suzanne looked at each other in disbelief.

"Are you serious?" Sam asked.

"Yes, I'm very serious," Will replied sharply. "I'm tired of you two waking me up every night, so this is just the way it has to be."

"How am I supposed to use the washtub to go to the bathroom?" Suzanne cried out. "I mean, it's easy for Sam. He's a boy. But how am I supposed to do that?"

"Well, there's a simple solution for that," Will answered. "We'll leave a bucket next to the washtub. If you have to go, you can squat over the bucket, then pour it into the sink and rinse it out when you're done."

"What if we have to go number two? Then what?"   Suzanne demanded.

"If you have to go number two, then maybe you can take the bucket outside into the yard, do your business, and then throw it in the trash can out back."

Sam looked at his mother in disbelief, hoping that she would say something to put an end to this nonsense, but she didn't say a word. She simply stared down at the table, apparently in agreement with Will's idea.

"That's just the way it's going to be. You'll just have to deal with it. Now why don't you two get started on your chores," Will said as he stood up and walked away from the table.

"Mom?" Suzanne said quietly. "Do we really have to do this?"

"Oh, it's not a big deal, Suzanne," Dawn replied.

"Not a big deal? Are you kidding me?" Suzanne shot back

"Listen..... you know he's a very light sleeper. We tried to work it out, but you guys wake him up almost every single night. He works hard and he needs his rest."

"He wants us to go crap in the yard like dogs, mom! I think that *is* a big deal. I think that's a *very* big deal" Suzanne answered as her eyes welled up.

"Stop it, Suzanne!" Dawn snapped back. "You're making something out of nothing here. Now go get started on your chores. I'm going to start dinner soon."

Sam and Suzanne stood up from the table, looking at each other in disbelief.

"Unbelievable," Sam said under his breath as he shook his head

"What was that, Sam?" Dawn asked

"Nothing…Nothing at all," he replied as he walked away

He walked into the kitchen and grabbed the garbage, heading toward the back door as he could feel the heat rise to his head. He couldn't believe that Will would even suggest such a thing, and worse yet that his own mother would agree it was a reasonable idea.

Sam returned inside, finished his chores, and walked downstairs toward his bedroom. As he passed Suzanne's bedroom door, he could hear her crying in her room.

"Hey…sis?" he said quietly as he knocked on her door.

"Go away, Sam," she replied. "I don't wanna talk right now.

"Are you ok?" he asked through the door.

"No…I'm not ok, Sam," she answered, crying a little harder.

Sam opened the door to see her lying face down on her bed, her hands covering her face.

"Hey…it's gonna be ok," he said as he walked up next to her and sat down on the bed.

"I can't stand him, Sam…He's such an idiot. I wish he would just leave."

"I know…I wish he would too," he replied.

"And how could mom just sit there? How can she agree with this?"

"I don't know, sis…I don't get it."

Sam's heart broke as he reached over and rubbed Suzanne's back. As much as he hated the situation and how he was being treated, he hated that his sister was being treated this way even more.

"Hey…I've got an idea," he said with a sneaky smile on his face.

"What, Sam?" she replied, knowing that he was about to say something silly.

"He doesn't want us to use the bathroom, right? How about if I wait until he's sleeping tonight and then go upstairs and pee on his head?"

"You're sick, Sam!" she replied as she started to laugh.

"No, I'm serious!" he said as he began laughing even harder. "Or maybe I should just go upstairs right now and pee on the dining room floor!"

"Stop it, Sam...that's sick!"

"Sure it's sick...but it's kinda funny too, isn't it?"

Suzanne reached behind her and pulled out a pillow, swinging it around and hitting him in the side of the head.

"Sick, sick, sick!" She shouted as she began beating him up with her pillow as he ran from her room laughing.

A short while later, their mother called them upstairs for dinner. There was very little discussion at the dinner table that night. After they had finished eating, Will left the room and returned with a cup of coffee as Sam and Suzanne began clearing the table. Sam stopped and looked at Suzanne as she gathered a few dishes. When she looked up at him, he pretended like he was urinating on the floor as he batted his eyebrows.

She glared at him, mouthing the word 'sick' as she looked away. Sam laughed out loud as he picked up a few more items and headed toward the kitchen.

"What's so funny, Sam?" Will asked.

"Nothing, Will. I was just thinking about something," he replied as he left the room.

"Whatever," Will replied with a smirk as he took another sip of his coffee.

Later that evening, after he and Suzanne had finished cleaning the kitchen, Sam returned upstairs. As he was walking through the kitchen, he saw their coffee pot sitting on the stove. It was an old glass percolator, which would be filled with coffee and water, and then placed on the stove to be heated. Will would put fresh coffee and water in it every night before going to bed, and would then turn on the stove in the morning to make his coffee.

A devious thought suddenly entered his mind as he pictured Will drinking his morning coffee. He stopped in his tracks, staring at the pot and thinking that he had just come up with the perfect plan. He walked toward the t.v. room and looked around the corner. Dawn was reading a book as Will watched a television program.

"What's up, Sam?" Dawn asked as she looked up from her book.

"Oh nothing, mom," he replied. I was just seeing what you were doing."

He turned back toward the kitchen, looking back over his shoulder as he entered. He could feel his adrenaline start to flow as he picked up the coffee pot and headed toward the staircase. He stopped by the sink and poured a little bit of water out, placed the coffee grounds on the counter, and made his way to the stairs while unzipping his pants. He stood in the staircase, his shoulder against the wall, and began to urinate in it, filling it as much as he could. He knew the whole time that getting caught would mean certain death, but it was all he could do to keep himself from laughing out loud before he headed back downstairs. Once he was finished, he quickly made his way back to the sink, replaced the coffee grounds, and returned the coffee pot to the stove. He then made it back to his bedroom, pushed his face into his pillow, and started cracking up at the thought about what Will's facial expression would be after taking that first sip of coffee.

The following morning, he had forgotten all about what he had done. It was a Saturday morning and he was excited that his father was coming to pick him up at 10:00. He jumped out of bed and ran up the stairs to find Will standing in the kitchen.

"Good morning, Will," he said with a smile

"Good morning," Will replied. "Hey Sam, I have a question for you," he continued. "This morning, *my wife* and I got up and made ourselves a pot of coffee. We both spit it out as soon as we tasted it. It was absolutely horrible. You didn't put anything in the pot, did you?"

Having completely forgotten what he had done the previous evening, he was caught off guard by the question as he suddenly remembered.

"Um...no, I didn't," he said as he walked quickly past Will and entered the bathroom, looking to remove himself quickly from the conversation.

He closed the bathroom door and put his hand over his mouth, trying desperately to keep from laughing out loud. He knew that his mother never drank coffee, but drank tea instead, so he was certain that she hadn't also been a victim of his prank. This made him want to laugh even harder. He assumed that Will knew he had put something in the coffee pot, but had no evidence to support his suspicion. He also assumed that Will was simply trying to make him feel guilty by saying that his mother had drunk some also. In his mind, he had just gotten away with the perfect crime. Once he had composed himself, he brushed his teeth and left the bathroom, hoping that the conversation was over. Fortunately for him, it was.

He made himself a bowl of cereal and then got some clothes together to bring with him to his father's house. At about 9:45, he entered the living room and sat on the sofa, looking out the living room window and watching to see Lee's car. Suzanne joined him a few minutes later.

"Hey Sam," she said as she sat next to him

"Hey sis."

Sam was dying to tell her what he had done, but he was afraid of what her reaction might be.

"What are you grinning about?" she asked with a smile.

"Oh nothing," he replied. "I'm just excited to see dad."

"Yeah, me too," she responded with a smile. "And I can't wait to get out of here," she whispered.

"Me neither...You have no idea," he replied with a chuckle.

Sam looked down at his watch. It was now 10:05. Because Lee had a habit of showing up late, it didn't concern him too much, but by 10:30, he began to worry.

"Hey mom?" he called out to her from the living room.

"Yeah, Sam."

"Did my dad call?"

"No, he hasn't called Sam. I'm sure he'll be here. He's probably just running late."

"Can I call him?"

"No Sam, you can't call him. It's a long distance call," Will interrupted harshly.

Sam looked back down at his watch.

"He's coming, right sis?" he asked as his heart sank a little bit.

"Yeah...He'll be here," Suzanne replied, beginning to doubt it a little herself.

By 11:00, he still had not arrived. Suzanne got up and walked toward her room.

"Hey Sam, wanna play some cards or something?" she asked as she paused and looked back at Sam, her heart breaking a little bit as she watched him continuing to stare out the window.

"No...I'm gonna wait here," he replied.

Once noon had passed, Dawn entered the living room to find him still sitting by the window.

"Sam!" she demanded.

"What, mom?"

"Look, he's obviously not coming. Why are you just sitting there staring out the window? Why don't you go outside and find your friends or something? Go do something!"

Sam looked at her in silence for a few seconds and then looked back out the window without responding. "Maybe she was right," he began to think. "Maybe he just isn't coming."

"Sam...," she said softly, sitting on the sofa next to him. "I hate to see you sitting here waiting for him all day. I don't know what happened or where he is, but I really don't think he's showing up today. It's a beautiful day today. Why don't you go outside and see what your friends are doing? There's no point in just sitting here staring out the window."

"I'm just gonna wait a little bit longer, okay mom?" he answered, looking down the street again.

"Alright, just sit there then," she said in a sarcastic tone as she stood up and walked away.

Her harsh tone stung, but not nearly as much as did his father's failure to show up. Unfortunately, this wouldn't be the last time it happened. Over the next few years, Lee failed to show up for visitation on numerous occasions. Sometimes he would call to say he wasn't coming, but most times he would just fail to show, leaving Sam and Suzanne sitting in the living room, staring down the road for long periods of time waiting for his car to turn the corner.

There were a few times when he'd arrive hung over from the night before, and one occasion, he even showed up drunk. Once he picked them up and turned the corner where they were no longer in sight of the house, he told Suzanne to sit in his lap and steer the car while he operated the gas and brakes. Being just 13, she was terrified to do so, but excited to have the opportunity. She resisted at first, but Lee insisted until she finally agreed, ultimately driving the 7 miles from Chicago to his home in Des Plaines through busy city streets and crowded intersections.

Sam was happy that he was able to visit his father from time to time, but he hated it when Lee would drink. He never drank in front of them, but would sit in bars until the wee hours of the morning and arrive back home barely able to walk. Many times he wouldn't come home at all.

On one such occasion Lee had picked Sam and Suzanne up for visitation on a Saturday morning. By early Saturday evening he left the house, saying that he had some errands to run and left them with Ronnie and Sandy. Sam had become very close to them and always enjoyed being around them, but he hadn't come to visit them. He came to spend time with his father.

As the evening progressed, Sam began to wonder where his father had gone. He asked Ronnie repeatedly where he was and what time she thought he'd be back home. Not wanting to upset him, she flippantly shrugged off the question and tried to distract him by asking him to play cards or to watch some television with her.

Throughout the evening, Sam sat on the sofa and glanced outside from time to time for any sign of his father's return. As it grew dark, Sam's head would snap around to look out the window every time a car turned the corner near the home, sending beams of bright light across the room as its headlights shone through the panes of glass.

Eventually, Ronnie made a bed for him on the sofa and suggested that they all go to bed for the night, assuring him that his father would be home soon and that she was certain he'd say goodnight to him once he arrived. She then turned off the lights and made her way to her own bedroom, seething inside that Lee would do this to his own children.

Sam laid down on the sofa with his head propped up on his pillow and stared out the window into the dark night. He watched the headlights from the cars as they drove down the main road a few doors down from the house, watching intently for one of the cars to turn down their street and pull into the driveway. He'd perk up every time one of the drivers would turn on their turn signal as they approached the intersection, lifting his head up slightly to see if it was his father, but time after time the cars that turned drove right past, deflating Sam's heart from feelings of happy expectation to gnawing disappointment. After an hour or so, Ronnie opened her bedroom door and came down the hallway into the living room.

"Sam? Are you still awake?" she asked quietly.

"Yeah Ronnie," he replied.

"Why are you still up?"

"I'm just waiting for my dad."

"Sam, I think it might be awhile before he gets home," she said as her heart broke a little bit at how disappointed she knew he must be feeling. "Why don't you close your eyes and try to get some sleep? I'm sure your dad will wake you up when he gets home."

"Yeah, I'm pretty tired," he said quietly. "Maybe I will."

"Okay. Goodnight, Sam."

"Goodnight, Ronnie."

Sam rolled over on his side and closed his eyes, opening them occasionally whenever a set of headlights shone through the window, but as the hour grew later and his eyes became heavier, he gave up and fell asleep. His father never came home that night, nor did he show up the following day, leaving Ronnie to drive Sam and Suzanne home Sunday evening.

A deep sense of disappointment flooded Sam's mind as he continued to stare down the street waiting for him to arrive this time. As much as he hated to give up on the hope that his father would show up, he hated the feeling of waiting just to be eventually disappointed even more.

"Mom...," he shouted from the living room as he got up from the sofa.

"What, Sam?" she responded impatiently.

"I'm gonna go over to George's for a while.

"Okay, Sam. Have a good time."

He had mixed emotions as he made his way down the street heading for George's house several blocks away. As he turned to look back whenever he heard a car heading down his street, he was torn between wanting to see his father's car coming toward him and hoping that he'd reach the corner and be out of sight before his father arrived, wanting his father to somehow feel the same disappointment he felt as he sat by the window so many times before. He felt a combination of anger, sadness, and fear at the same time as he reached the first intersection and disappeared around the corner.

"Hey buddy! What are you doing here?" George said as he answered the door.

"Hey George. Can ya come out for a while?" Sam asked

"I thought you were going to your dad's house today."

"Yeah, I did to. He never showed up."

"Again?"

"Yeah, again. So do ya wanna go do something?"

"Sure, come on in," George said as he opened the door and stepped to the side.

"Hi Mrs. Pappas," Sam said with a smile as he entered the kitchen and saw George's mother.

"Oh, hi Sam. How are you?"

"I'm ok. How are you?"

"I'm good."

"Mom, me and Sam are going to go hang out for a while," George said as he looked for his shoes.

"I'm surprised to see you, Sam. I thought George told me you were going to visit your father today."

"Yeah...He never showed up," Sam replied as he looked down, not wanting to explain.

"He never showed up?"

"Nah."

"Why not? Did he call to say why he wasn't coming?"

"No…he never called…he does that sometimes."

"Did your mother call him to see what was going on?"

"No…She just told me I should go out and do something, so I came here."

George's mother looked at George with a sad, confused expression, and then looked back at Sam.

"Well, that's not right."

"Mom, leave him alone. It's ok," George spoke up

"No, it's not ok, George. What kind of a father tells his son he's going to visit him and then just never shows up? And what kind of a mother…?"

"Mom, stop!" George interrupted with a loud voice.

"It's ok, Mrs. Pappas," Sam replied. "It just happens like that sometimes."

"Well, ok," she replied sarcastically. "But I don't understand…It's just not right."

George looked at Sam and motioned toward the door as his mother walked to the sink and began rinsing off dishes.

"We're gonna go out for a while, mom," he said as he walked toward the door.

"Where are you going?"

"I dunno…out. Maybe we'll go over to the park or something."

"O.k.. Make sure you're home in time for dinner."

"I'll see ya later, Mrs. Pappas," Sam said quietly.

"Bye, Sam. You boys stay out of trouble, o.k.?"

Sam felt a bit ashamed as he walked outside. He had known George's family for a few years, and had spent a good amount of time around them. While all families have their issues and problems, there was something very different about their family. In fact, Sam was beginning to understand that there was something very different about the families of all of his friends. Whenever he would stop by their homes, he would be welcomed inside by them. They would ask him to sit at their kitchen tables and talk to him. They'd ask him if he was hungry, or even slide a snack on the table in front of him as he sat down without even asking if he wanted anything. They simply made him feel welcome in their homes as if he were part of their family. That never happened in his home. His friends were rarely, if ever, invited inside. None of them ever felt welcome there, so they never asked to come over. What made matters worse was that Sam didn't want them there. He was always afraid that Will would insult them or be rude to them while they were there. He knew how that felt for him, and he certainly didn't want them to feel that way.

He began to struggle with what a family was supposed to be. He knew what he had always seen in his family, but he hadn't spent enough time around other families to know what a close, loving family looked like. He didn't know what stability in the home looked like. He had always just assumed that his experiences at home weren't all that different than anyone else's, and he had learned to accept as normal what most people believed was unthinkable.

As he began to look around at the families he saw his friends in, he began to realize that none of these other families had gone through a divorce. All of their mothers and fathers lived at home together, with no need for visitation schedules that may or may not have to be kept. There was no alcoholism, no domestic violence, no controlling, manipulative step-fathers. While their families had their own problems, all of his friends seemed to be very comfortable in their own homes, and their parents all seemed supportive and protective of them. In short, he could tell that, in spite of their differences, they all just loved one another. If any issues would arise, they would come together as a family and work them out.

He began to struggle with the difference between what he had always been taught by the words and actions of his parents and what he was beginning to see in the lives of his friends. It began to make him uncomfortable when others would question what was going on in his home because he had no answers as to why he was being treated the way he was. Another glaring difference he saw when comparing his family to others was the reality that it was completely unacceptable for him to question the way he was being treated in his own home. If he said or did anything to suggest he was angry, upset, or even slightly confused by it, he would be told he was ungrateful or selfish and would more than likely be threatened with groundings, loss of privileges or even physical violence. With the exception of Suzanne, there was no one in his family he could turn to with his concerns or complaints about his home life. This led to him feeling afraid whenever he was at home or at Lee's house, and it also led to the feeling that he had no right to be angry, upset or disappointed with his parents or step-parents. After all, that type of behavior on his part was completely unacceptable, and if it were to be displayed in any way, it would be dealt with severely.

He and George spent a few hours walking around the neighborhood until it was time for George to go back home. They didn't talk much about his father not showing up that morning. George could tell that he was upset about it, but didn't necessarily want to talk about it, so he left it alone.

He walked back home, wondering if his father had ever shown up. He entered the back door and made his way upstairs, finding the whole house quiet. Believing that everyone had apparently left while he was away, he felt a sense of relief. He liked being home alone, because it was the only time he felt truly at peace there. As he entered the living room, he was surprised to hear Suzanne's voice coming from the front porch. Feeling playful, he decided to sneak up on her from behind. He walked quietly toward the door, then threw it open and yelled "Aha!" in a loud voice to frighten her. She spun around to face him, and let out a startled gasp while at the same time taking something in her hand and trying to hide it from his sight. He looked out on the front porch where he saw Beth, a neighbor girl from down the block, looking just as alarmed as Suzanne.

"Sam! You jerk!" Suzanne shouted. "I'll see you later, Beth," she said quickly as she turned back and closed the front door.

It was obvious to Sam that Beth had given her something she was trying to hide from him.

"What did Beth give you?" he said with a smile, knowing he had caught her doing something wrong, but he wasn't sure what it was yet.

"Nothing!" she said sharply as she tried to walk past him, putting it in her pocket.

"Come on!" he insisted playfully as he stepped in front of her. "What did she give you?"

"O.k., I'll show you," she replied, knowing that he wasn't going to let it go. "But don't tell mom and Will!" she insisted.

"I won't…I promise."

Suzanne reached into her pocket and pulled out two funny looking cigarettes with twisted ends. Sam stared at them for a second, confused as to what they were.

"What are those?"

"They're joints."

"Joints?" Sam replied with a laugh. "Really?"

"Yeah Sam…really."

Sam looked back down at the funny little cigarettes for a few seconds, and then looked up at her. He had heard about people smoking marijuana at school, but he'd never known anyone who had.

"Have you ever tried em before?" he asked with a sense of stunned excitement.

"Yeah, a couple of times."

"What do they do?"

"I dunno...they make you feel happy. They just kinda make you laugh."

"I wanna try em!" he replied with a wide smile.

"Are you serious?"

"Yeah, I'm serious. I wanna try!"

"Alright, but you can't tell anyone!"

"I promise!...Wanna try em now?"

"We can't. I promised Sandy I'd get these so we could smoke em together. We'll have to wait until we go by Dad's again."

"Sandy smokes pot?" he replied, shocked that his younger step-sister had tried it before he had.

"Yeah, and I promised her, so we have to wait. Dad called after you left and said that something came up, so he couldn't make it. He's gonna come get us next weekend."

"What came up?"

"He said that he went to pick up a puppy. It couldn't wait because the guy who owned it was going to give it to somebody else if he didn't come get it right away."

"Really? What kind of puppy?" he asked with excitement in his voice.

"A German Shepherd."

"Cool!" he said with a laugh. As any boy his age would, he really loved dogs. While they had still lived with their father, they had numerous dogs come in and out of their home and he loved all of them.

He was happy to hear that Lee had called, happy to hear about the puppy, and happy that Lee was planning to pick them up the following weekend. But for some reason he couldn't identify, he was somehow more excited about the possibility that he'd be able to see what it felt like to get high. He liked the idea of just 'feeling happy.' As the week wore on, he kept his word and never mentioned it to anyone. After they had arrived at Lee's house the following Saturday, he couldn't wait to go somewhere with Suzanne and Sandy to smoke the joints. After they had settled in for a while, he kept looking at them, waiting for the signal.

"Mom, we're gonna take a walk to the park," Sandy said as she entered the kitchen where they were sitting.

"Alright…take that stupid dog with you. He needs to go out," Ronnie replied impatiently, not at all happy with Lee's decision to bring a dog home.

"I'll walk him!" Sam replied quickly.

He took the leash as the three of them headed outside and began walking toward the park.

"Are we gonna get high now?" he asked impatiently.

"Shut up, Sam!" Sandy snapped back. "Don't be stupid."

"What do you mean?" he replied, not knowing what he had said wrong.

"Do you wanna get caught?"

"No…I don't."

"Then shut up and stop blabbing. I don't think this is a good idea, Suzanne. He's gonna do something stupid."

"No he won't…It's ok," Suzanne replied looking at Sam, not entirely sure that he wouldn't.

"I'm not gonna do anything stupid, Sandy!" Sam protested.

"You better not!" she snapped back.

Sam was growing tired of Sandy's attitude. He had gotten along with her when they had first met, but she had developed an attitude of superiority toward him in recent months that he didn't quite understand. He loved her because he considered her to be his sister, but at the same time he didn't know why she had started to put him down in front of others with rude comments or insults.

They reached the park and sat down on the merry-go-round, where Suzanne pulled out the joints and lit one, passing it to Sandy as Sam watched intently. Sandy then handed it to Sam.

"How do you do this?" he asked

"Take a drag off of it, inhale, then hold the smoke in as long as you can," Suzanne replied.

Sam took a drag and breathed in deep. He didn't feel anything unusual except an urge to cough.

"Keep it down, you moron!" Sandy demanded. "Do you want the whole world to see what we're doing?"

Sam turned his back to the street, hiding the joint in his hand.

"You probably won't get high the first time. I don't think anyone does," Suzanne said with a smile.

The three of them stayed at the park until they finished smoking, and then headed back to the house.

"Don't act like an idiot when we get inside, Sam," Sandy said sharply as they approached the front yard.

"What are you talking about?" Sam replied, feeling increasingly aggravated by her negative comments.

"Just don't do anything stupid. I don't want them to know we got high. We'll be in big trouble if they find out."

"You know something, Sandy?" he said, stopping in his tracks. "I'll bet you could end up being a pretty nice person if didn't try so hard to suck as a human being. You should try it some time. I think you'd enjoy not sucking."

"Screw you, Sam," she snapped back, waving her hand at him.

"What's wrong?" he replied, flashing a sarcastic smirk at Suzanne, who was trying not to laugh. "I'm not suggesting that you stop sucking as a human being forever. That would be impossible. Just take it a few minutes at a time. Here! I know! Try to not suck for just the next fifteen minutes and see how it goes. You might really enjoy it."

Nancy picked up her pace, ignoring him as she made her way to the front door.

Sam didn't feel any different than he had when they left the house. He was trying to be aware of how he was acting, but he didn't feel as though he was acting stoned at all. He brought the dog inside and took his leash off, and then called him over to play with him while he sat on the living room floor. The more he played with him, the more fun he began to have. Before long, he was rolling on the floor laughing, playfully shoving the puppy away and teasing him with his pull toy. He suddenly looked up to see Sandy scowling at him as she sat on the sofa. She mouthed the words "Knock it off" with an intense look of anger in her eyes, not wanting anyone else to notice.

He left the dog alone, got up and sat on the sofa next to her, laughing to himself as he sat down.

"So this is what it feels like to be high," he thought to himself, genuinely liking what he was feeling. He just felt happy, just as Suzanne had told him he would. He looked over at Suzanne, flashing a knowing smile at her. She smiled back, shaking her head slightly. She wasn't afraid of Sam getting them caught. For her, it was just good to see him laugh. He settled back into the sofa, feeling better than he had in a long time, and for the moment, he didn't have a care in the world.

"Dinner's ready. Come on and eat, kids," Ronnie announced from the kitchen about an hour later.

Sam got up and ran into the kitchen. For some reason he didn't quite understand, he was hungrier than he ever remembered being.

"I'm starving!" he said impatiently

"Well, help yourself, Sam. There's plenty here," Ronnie replied

"I will!" he said as he loaded up his plate with spaghetti.

"Wow...You really were hungry," Lee said with a chuckle as he watched Sam finish off the first plate and then load up a second. "Don't they feed you at home?"

Sam laughed as he dug into the second plate-full, thinking this was the most delicious spaghetti he'd ever tasted. He savored every single bite until his plate was empty, then leaned back in his chair with a very satisfied smile on his face. He eventually made his way back into the living room and sat on the sofa, falling sound asleep. When bedtime arrived, everyone else went to bed, leaving him by himself. He slept through the entire evening, waking up as the sun rose the following morning. He opened his eyes to see that Ronnie had covered him with a blanket at some point, but with no recollection of her having done so.

It was Sunday morning, and he knew that he and Suzanne would be returning home by the end of the day. He dreaded going back home, and his stomach began to tighten up just thinking about it. He sat up on the sofa and stared out the living room window at the early morning sunrise, wishing he could stay with his father a few more days. It was far from perfect there, but at least he didn't feel like he had to weigh every word that came out of his mouth or feel as though he was constantly walking on eggshells.

As the morning turned to afternoon, and the afternoon turned to dusk, his stomach grew more knotted up inside of him and his shoulders began to tighten. It was the kind of reluctant anticipation one might feel when leaving for the dentist to have a root canal done. You know that you have no choice in the matter, but you'd much rather go bowling.

As night fell, Lee turned the corner and headed down their block. There was dead silence in the car as they drew near to their home.

"Alright, kids," Lee said as he stopped and threw the car in park. "We're here."

"I love you, dad," Sam said as he leaned forward and hugged Lee's shoulders over the back of the seat.

"I'll see ya later, Tiger," he replied as he patted Sam's arm.

"I love you, dad," Suzanne said quietly as she leaned into him and hugged his waist.

"I love you too, sweetie," he replied as he put his arm around her, leaned over and kissed her head.

They grabbed their bags, got out of the car, and then made their way up the stairs to the front door, almost holding their breath as they unlocked the door and stepped inside. They saw a single light coming from the living room as they headed down the hallway.

"Hi Mom...Hi Will," Suzanne said as she stood in the doorway.

"Hi guys," Dawn answered with a smile.

"Hi...hey, if you two need to take shower before you go to bed, you'd better get in there now. It's getting late," Will said coldly, never looking up from his book.

"Uh...yeah...ok," Suzanne replied.

Will exhaled loudly as he set his book down on his lap and turned to her.

"Is there something wrong, Suzanne?"

"No...I'll bring my stuff downstairs first, then I'll come back up and get in the shower."

"What about you, Sam? Do you have a problem with that?" he demanded.

"What are you talking about?" Sam replied, taken aback by his tone.

"You know what?" Will started as he became more animated. "Every time you two come home from your father's house, you both come back with an attitude, and I don't like it one bit. I don't know what those two are saying to you when you're over there, but you'd better just knock it off."

Sam looked at Suzanne and rolled his eyes as Will picked up his book and began reading again.

"Alright...well, why don't you two take your showers and get ready for bed," Dawn suggested in a quiet voice.

They both turned away and made their way downstairs toward their bedrooms to drop off their things.

"Yeah, hey, thanks for the warm welcome," Sam said under his breath as Suzanne walked toward her door. "It's great to be back home, you big fat jerk."

"No kidding," she replied as she pushed it open.

Sam made walked to his room, dropped his bag, and plopped down on his bed, fuming over Will's attitude.

"Hey wait a minute!" he thought as a smile broke over his face. He got back up and hurried to Suzanne's bedroom.

"Hey, sis...Are you dressed?" he asked as he knocked on her door.

"Yeah, come on in," she replied.

"Hey," he said in a quiet voice. "You still have that other joint, right? I know we only smoked one with Sandy. Wanna smoke the other one?"

"Now?"

"Yeah, now," he replied.

"We have to take our showers, Sam. We're gonna get in big trouble if we don't."

"Okay...After we take our showers, then. Wanna smoke it then?"

"I don't know, Sam...we'll get caught."

"Okay...Never mind...Maybe tomorrow after they go to work?" he replied, batting his eyebrows playfully.

"Well see Sam...Now get outta here, you nut," she replied with a laugh as she shoved him toward her bedroom door.

After they had showered, they returned downstairs. Sam laid on his bed, listening to the floor creak with every step as Will walked across the kitchen and locked the door leading to the basement. He heard him walk to the living room, then back down the hall to the master bedroom and close the door. He always felt a sense of relief after Will had gone to bed because he knew there would be no more drama or arguments for the day. It was the only time of the day when he felt as though he could relax and not feel on edge awaiting the next confrontation.

He began to think about how calm he felt when he was high. He really liked that feeling. He got up and walked quietly to Suzanne's room. Seeing the light under the door, he knocked softly.

"Suzanne, are you up?" he asked in a quiet voice.

"Yeah, come in, Sam," she replied.

He entered her room, quietly closed the door and sat next to her on the bed.

"Why do you think he's like that, sis?" he asked quietly, his voice cracking a bit.

"Who? Will?"

"Yeah...Why does he always have to act like that?"

"I dunno, Sam...I don't get it."

"Neither do I...He seemed so nice when mom was dating him...He just changed...What happened?"

"I dunno, Sam."

He sat quietly for a moment as he stared at the wall across her room, thinking about everything that was going on in their lives.

"And what's up with dad?" he asked.

"What do you mean?"

"Why does he always go out drinking and not come home for days?"

"I don't know about that either, Sam."

"Why would he do that when we go to see him? I mean, we don't see him for weeks and then sometimes we go there and he's gone all weekend. Why would he do that? Is there something wrong with us?"

"No!" She insisted, hesitating for a second.

"Well, there's plenty wrong with you. There's nothing wrong with me," she said with a laugh as she whacked him with a pillow.

Sam let out a laugh and grabbed another pillow, whacking her back as he jumped to his feet.

"Shhhh!" she insisted, trying to keep her voice down as they both exploded into laughter. "You're gonna wake up jerk face!"

The two of them laughed until their sides hurt, covering their mouths as they tried not to make any noise. The harder they tried to be quiet, the harder they would laugh. Sam eventually buried his face in a pillow to keep from looking at her.

After they had settled down a bit, Suzanne took a deep breath.

"O.k., Sam. I'm really tired. Why don't we go to bed."

Alright, sweet dreams, sis," he replied as he got up and opened her door.

"Sweet dreams, Sam."

The next few weeks were filled more of the same hostile home environment, with Sam and Suzanne being confronted by Will on nearly a daily basis, being constantly accused of disrespecting him and his authority within their home. It grew to the point where neither of them wanted to be home at all when Will was there. When he *was* home, they would remain in their rooms to avoid any type of confrontation.

Late on one summer night, as Sam laid on his bed listening to music, Suzanne knocked on his door.

"Sam, are you up?" she asked quietly.

"Yeah."

She opened the door and stepped inside. He was surprised to see her dressed as if she were about to go out.

"Why are you dressed?" he asked with a confused voice.

"I'm sneaking out...Wanna come with?"

"What?!" He asked in a shocked voice. "Where are you going?"

"I'm going over to Dave's house to party with them. Wanna come with?"

Dave was a notorious stoner they both knew from school. His parents were oblivious to the fact that he and his friends were smoking pot, and would allow as many friends to come over and hang out in in their basement with him as he wanted, which made Dave's house the party house of the neighborhood, with many kids coming in and out through all hours of the night.

"No way!" he insisted. "We'll get caught!"

"No we won't, I promise. I do it all the time."

"Are you serious? How?"

"I climb out my bedroom window and leave it unlocked. When I get back home I just climb back in. I've done it every night this week."

"Get outta here! Really?"

"Yup...I do it all the time. Wanna come with me?"

"What about Dave's parents? Won't they tell on us?"

"Nope...We all hang out in the basement. They never come down there."

Sam thought it through for a second. He really wanted to go, but he was terrified of being caught.

"I'm leaving now...Are you coming or not?" Suzanne insisted with a sense of urgency.

"Yeah, ok.....Hang on.....Let me get dressed."

"Alright...hurry up. I'll be in my room."

Sam could feel the adrenaline pumping through his veins as he hurried to put his clothes on. He was excited about going out to party with the older, cool kids from school. Suzanne's friends at that point in her life were all the cool kids. The rebels, the stoners, the kids that everyone in his class seemed to envy because they did whatever they wanted to and didn't take any crap from anyone. Being accepted into that crowd moved him up a step on the food chain. At the same time, he was terrified at the thought of what would happen if they were caught. Somehow that just added to the excitement. After all, if he could get away with it, he'd be just as cool as the coolest kids he knew. He finished getting dressed and tiptoed to Suzanne's room, finding her standing next to her bed with the window open.

"Are you ready?" she asked with a devious smile.

"Yeah... let's go."

The two of them held the window up for each other and crawled out as quietly as they could, easing it down gently after they were both outside.

"Okay... let's wait here for a few minutes," Suzanne said quietly.

"Why?" Sam asked, feeling an intense urge to get away before they got caught.

"Because if Will heard us sneak out, he'll come running out here. If he does, we can just say that we came outside to sit in the yard. If he doesn't come out, we're home free."

Sam felt a smile break over his face. "Wow... That's pretty smart, sis."

"Yeah, I know... I'm the one with the brains, remember?"

Sam sat on the concrete of their backyard patio and waited for the o.k. to take off. As he looked up, he began to notice all of the stars in the sky. It was a beautiful summer night with a slight breeze from the south. The air just felt different for some reason.

There was a sense of freedom he could feel in his chest that he couldn't possibly define, much less explain. His normally busy neighborhood full of people, traffic and noise seemed eerily calm and silent. He wasn't afraid at all. He leaned back and took a deep breath, soaking it all in.

"You ok, bro?" Suzanne asked quietly.

"Yeah…yeah. I'm ok," he replied as he slowly opened his eyes.

"Alright…it's all clear…Let's go."

The two of them stepped quietly through the gate, and then crept down the alley, trying to stay away from the streetlights to avoid being spotted by anyone. They avoided the main roads, sticking to the darker, quieter side streets until they arrived at Dave's house.

"Hey! What's up?" Dave called out with a slow smile as they entered through the basement door. "Want a beer?" he asked, reaching into a cooler and then pulling two out.

"Absolutely!" Sam replied as he took it from him.

As he scanned the room, he saw a number of kids he knew from school. They were all sitting back, relaxing, with eyes that weren't much more than tiny slits due to having smoked a good deal of marijuana..

"Hey, Sam!" one of them called out, sliding over to make room for him on the sofa. "Wanna get high?" he continued, holding up a joint.

"Yes, as a matter of fact!" he replied. "Yes, I do!"

Sam and Suzanne stayed there, partying with their friends until the wee hours of the morning. Just before sunrise, they decided to head for home, not wanting to get caught climbing back in. While they could've explained why they were sitting in the back yard just before they had left, they both knew that they could never explain their way out of climbing back in at four in the morning, smelling of beer and pot smoke.

Sam felt as though everything was moving in slow motion as they made their way back down the city streets. After walking for what seemed to be hours, they finally arrived back home. Checking to make sure that nobody was watching, they carefully climbed back into the window.

"That was awesome, sis! Thanks for bringing me with," he said with a chuckle.

"Yeah, that was fun," she replied with a smile. "We should do that again!"

"You're right, we should...um...I'm gonna go to bed now."

"Good idea, Sam. Be quiet going back to your room. We definitely don't want Will coming down here now," she whispered.

Sam left her room, being as quiet as he possibly could until he was safe in his own bed. Not hearing any movement upstairs, he knew they had just gotten away with it. He laughed to himself, and then rolled over and fell asleep.

SIX

"Next stop, Zebulun," Gabriel shouted, jarring Sam from his daydream. As he opened his eyes, the memories seemed so very vivid and real to him he was surprised to find that he was on the train and not waking up in his bed back home.

Sadness filled his heart as he thought back to the days when he and Suzanne were so very close. They were partners in crime, so to speak. He couldn't remember a time during their childhood when he didn't love her with all of his heart.

Many years had passed since those days, and they had grown farther apart with each passing year until they rarely even talked anymore. He missed her very badly, but he was very ashamed at where his life had brought him. He was ashamed of the things he had done and who he'd become. He had picked up the phone on many occasions just to call her and say hello, but hung up before he dialed. She was married with four kids and seemed to make all of the right decisions with her life as an adult, while he had gone the opposite direction in making all of the wrong ones. He longed for the days when they were close, for the simplicity of the days when they would just sit and talk, not simply as brother and sister, but as best friends.

He shook these thoughts out of his mind and looked out the window as the train left the station, noticing what appeared to be a wedding. A beautiful woman stood proudly in a long white dress, holding hands with a man in a black suit, before a priest under a white arbor covered in brilliant red roses.

Off to the side, there was a large table covered with a multitude of beautifully wrapped gifts, while behind them stood a large gathering of well-dressed people, all of whom appeared to be overjoyed with what they had come to witness.

"Getting married at a train station?" Sam thought to himself. "Well, I bet the price was right," he thought with a laugh.

He continued to look over at the couple, considering the thought that maybe this place held some sort of romantic value for them. Maybe it was the place where they had first met, or maybe he had proposed to her here before leaving on a long journey of some sort. Even so, he thought, it was still an odd place to begin the rest of one's life with somebody.

As he was thinking these things over, the door at the front of the car opened, and a young man of about 25 walked in and took the seat across from him. He watched as the man put his belongings on a nearby seat and began digging through a well-worn leather bag.

He was dressed in an old pair of jeans and a t-shirt, wearing a pair of leather sandals with no socks. His hair was very long and looked as though it had been badly wind-blown. His hands were rough and his skin was weathered more than one might usually see of a man his age.

Sam continued to watch as the man pulled a beat up, dog-eared bible out of his bag and placed it on his lap. He bowed his head and closed his eyes for a moment, mouthing a few words under his breath, and then looked down and opened his bible to where a bookmark had been placed.

"Great...a bible-thumper," Sam thought to himself. "Of all the seats on this train, he's got to pick the one across from me."

He looked back behind him for an open seat he might be able to move to. He had enough on his mind, and the last thing he wanted right now was some Jesus-freak preaching to him. He began to feel more and more uncomfortable and anxious, hoping the man wouldn't notice him.

"Hi...How are you?" the man asked as he looked over at Sam.

"Damn it!" Sam shouted on the inside. "Just my luck."

"Hi," Sam replied in a dismissive voice as he looked away.

"Don't make eye-contact," he thought to himself. "These people are like junkyard dogs...If you make eye-contact, they move in for the kill."

"My name is Bart...What's yours?" the man asked as he offered his hand.

"My name is shut the hell up and don't bother me," Sam thought to himself.

"Sam...My name is Sam," he replied as he reluctantly shook his hand.

"Nice to meet you, Sam," Bart said with a wide smile.

"Likewise," Sam mumbled.

"So, what brings you here, Sam? Business?"

"No...fate," Sam answered with a sarcastic smirk, thinking about how much he hated being preached to. Throughout his adult life, it seemed as though religious people were always popping up out of nowhere, wanting to talk to him about God. It made him cringe every time it happened.

"Actually...nothing...just passing through," he continued.

"Yeah? I'm on my way home. I just got back from Zambia," Bart replied.

"Here comes the sales pitch," Sam thought to himself, not replying.

"I'm a missionary."

"Bingo!" Sam thought as he laughed out loud.

"Why do you laugh?" he asked with a smile.

"On, no reason…Hey, listen, I don't mean to be rude or anything, but I'm not much in the mood for conversation. I'm gonna go to the back and shut my eyes a bit," Sam said abruptly as he excused himself and walked to the back of the looking another seat.

Oh…ok. Have a nice nap," Bart replied from across the car.

Sam watched from behind as Bart appeared to bow his head again, and then looked down to read.

"Whew…Got outta that one," he thought.

Sam couldn't stand Christians…especially the missionary types. They never knew when to shut up, and they'd rarely take no for an answer. He always viewed them as snake oil salesmen, promising weak-minded people that if they turn their lives over to some imaginary God, everything would change and their lives would somehow get better. From his own first-hand experiences with these people, he knew that wasn't even close to being the truth.

The first time he'd ever met a missionary was in 1978, when he was 16 years-old. His mother and step-father had started to attend a non-denominational church in their neighborhood and had dragged Sam and Suzanne along with them. After visiting a few weeks, a young missionary named Steve stopped by their house for a visit. Will welcomed him in and the two of them sat in their living room to talk. Sam, curious as to what this was all about, took a seat on the living room sofa and listened as the conversation began.

"So, what brings you here, Steve?" Will asked.

"Oh, nothing, really. I just wanted to stop by and see how you're all doing and to ask you why you decided to visit the bible church," Steve replied.

"Well, my wife and I have been thinking about finding a local church, and a friend recommended yours."

"Oh…I see…And was there anything in particular that you were looking for in the church?"

"Not really," Will said with a bit of hesitation. "We just thought it might be a good idea to start going to church, and we thought it might be good for the kids too."

"How old are your kids, Will?" Steve asked as he looked over at Sam.

"Oh, they're not mine…They're Dawn's," he replied dismissively.

"I see…," he answered, feeling a little disturbed at how quickly Will had disowned them. "It must be kinda tough trying to pull a broken family together, huh?"

"To say the least," he replied as he rolled his eyes.

"Is their father…?"

"Oh, he's still around…It's a long story. I'd rather not get into it."

"Are they close?"

"Oh, definitely! They think he can do no wrong," he answered sarcastically.

Sensing from his reactions that the conversation was about to become uncomfortable for both of them, Steve changed his direction.

"Will, let me ask you a question. What are your thoughts about God?"

"I'm not sure what you mean."

"Well, when you think about God, how do you envision him? Do you see him as some far away, distant power who has very little involvement in our lives, or is he something more than that to you?"

Will sat back and collected his thoughts for a moment, not certain how to answer. After all, nobody had ever asked him to define God before.

"Well, I suppose he has some interest in us, but I'm not sure how much or how that applies to me."

"Well, Will, I'll ask you to look at God from your perspective. You've taken on the role of a father recently, right? How do you view these children? What is it that you'd want to give them? How do you see your role in their lives?"

"I'd want to teach them some responsibility, to give them a safe home, to provide for their needs, etc."

Steve sat back for a second considering the items Will listed, and then leaned in a little closer.

"What about love, Will? Do you love them?"

"Sure I do," he replied after a brief hesitation, not meaning the words as much as understanding that saying he didn't might sound strange to a visitor from a church.

His response surprised Sam quite a bit. He'd never heard Will say that he loved them before, and from the way he had always treated them, he was absolutely certain that he didn't.

"Will, I want you to think about their lives for a moment. Would you say that their relationship with their father has been damaged?"

"Absolutely."

"And what damaged it?"

"Well, a number of things," Will replied, not wanting to get into everything Lee had done to damage his relationship with them.

"I'm not asking you to give me a laundry list of everything that has gone wrong. I'm really asking you to simply look at their relationship with their father from the outside. Here you have a relationship that should be very close, and yet it's not. Whatever the reasons are for this, the fact remains that their relationship isn't what it was designed to be. That truth has caused a great deal of pain in all of their lives. Would that be fair to say?"

"Yes…absolutely."

"And how would you suggest they get past that and restore their relationship?"

Will thought this through and could come up with nothing. He wasn't at all interested in Sam and

Suzanne restoring their relationship with their father. In truth, he would rather that relationship end and free him from having to deal with any of it. He remained silent, staring at the wall behind Steve.

"Will, our relationship with God is very much the same. Damage has been done to that relationship through sin…Our sin. But God wants to restore that relationship with us, which is why he sent his son to die on the cross to pay the penalty for that sin. He did that so we might have a close, loving relationship with him once again. In fact, the bible teaches that we've all sinned and fallen short of the glory of God. Do you believe that you've sinned at some point in your life?"

"Of course I do. We all have."

"That's right, Will. We all have. But in John 3:16, the bible also says; *"For God so loved the world, he gave his only begotten son, that whoever believes in him shall have eternal life."*

"I've heard that before, Steve, but I'm not sure what that means for me."

"Well, do you believe that you're a sinner in need of forgiveness?"

"Yes."

"Do you believe that Jesus was the son of God, and that he died for your sins so that you would be forgiven?"

"Yes."

"Then all it takes is for you to pray, to acknowledge that, and to thank him for it. To ask for that forgiveness, and to ask him to be your Lord and Savior. Do you think you'd like to do that now?"

"I have to be honest, Steve. That sounds too easy. That would be like you telling me that if I sat in that chair over there, everything would somehow change. I don't know if I buy that."

"Fair enough, Will. But what if God himself sat here and told you that if you did sit in that chair, that's exactly what would happen? Would you sit in it?"

"Sure," Will said with a chuckle. "But he's not here."

"Oh, but he is, Will. His words are here in this book, and that's exactly what he says here. So tell me Will, do you believe God's words?"

"Yes...I do."

"Then are you ready to bow your head with me and pray that prayer?"

Will sat back in his chair for a few seconds. He wasn't sure what would change, if anything, if he prayed with Steve. He felt a sense of fear as to what might happen next, but he also knew that whatever happened, it probably wouldn't hurt anything to try. He liked the idea of God being on his side.

"Yeah...I think I am."

Sam watched and listened as the two of them bowed their heads and began to pray as a million different thoughts raced through his mind. He'd never heard anyone talk about God like that before. He didn't really believe there was a God somewhere out there, but he assumed that if there was, he was far too busy running the universe to care about him. At the same time he was hopeful this was true, because if it was, God would surely see all the horrible treatment he and Suzanne had been given by Will, and he would immediately change things. If God could change everything, he would surely start with Will. He never considered that the same message was true for him. After all, he didn't believe he had done anything wrong. He was just a kid, and an unwilling victim of all that had occurred to this point in his life. If any changes needed to be made, it wasn't with him. It was with those around him.

Steve let out a heavy sigh as they finished their prayer and opened their eyes.

"Congratulations, Will," he said with a smile. "You are now born again. I'll be praying for you and your family, you can believe that."

"Thank you, Steve," Will replied, reaching out to shake his hand.

Sam began to feel a sense of excitement. "Born again," he thought to himself. "Will is gonna change. Everything is different now."

He got up and followed Steve outside, feeling very happy about what he'd just witnessed. If there was any truth to any of this, things were about to be different, and he couldn't wait to see the changes that were sure to come in the near future.

Will was fairly quiet for the rest of the week. He seemed to be deep in thought about what he had just done, and what it meant for him. Sam took that as a sign that things had indeed changed in Will's heart. He began to believe that maybe there was some truth to all of this, that maybe Will really was going to be different.

He was even more excited when Will announced that they'd all be attending church again the following Sunday.   He couldn't wait to get dressed and get in the car Sunday morning, feeling very good about being there.

Once they arrived, he stood off to the side as Will and Dawn were introduced to the pastor, who mentioned how he'd heard of him through Steve, and was very pleased to see him there.

"I understand that God is doing some wonderful things in your life, Will," the pastor said with a smile as he shook his hand.

"He sure is," Will replied with a smile.

"Well, it's great to see you here. I'm glad you came."

Sam began to wander around the church, taking it all in. It was just a small, non-denominational church; nothing fancy like the Catholic or Lutheran churches in the neighborhood. There was no stained glass, no marble sculptures, and nobody was wearing robes or speaking in Latin. It was just a simple, plain building, full of everyday people. It didn't even smell like church.

They took their seats and listened as the pastor began to welcome everyone. Sam felt a little out of place in this new environment. He began to fidget in his seat a bit as the service continued, fighting the urge to close his eyes and nod off. He looked around the sanctuary as the pastor spoke, taking in all of the curious items he'd never seen before. There was a long table at the front of the stage with a pure white tablecloth on it. On top of the table were white candles, carefully placed in highly polished, gold plated candlestick holders. To the rear of the stage there were two flags; one the American flag, and the other an odd flag he'd never seen before with a cross set into the upper left corner.

As he took all of this in, paying no attention to what the pastor was saying, everyone around him stood up, leaned forward, and picked up little red books that had been placed in pockets on the backs of the seats in front of them. They all opened these books, apparently to the same page, and a pianist began playing music he'd never heard before. Everyone around him suddenly began singing as if they knew exactly what they were singing. He looked over at his mother, who was doing the same.

Sensing his confusion, she leaned toward him and pointed to a place on the page where the words of the song being sung appeared.

Sam wasn't interested in singing a song he'd never heard before, and didn't particularly enjoy. After all, this wasn't anything like the music he listened to.

He looked down at the top of the page. "Amazing Grace!" he thought to himself as he read the song's title. "Hey, that's me!" he thought with a chuckle, making the connection between the title and his last name.

After singing a few songs, everyone placed the books back in the seat pockets and sat down. With that, the pastor walked to his pulpit, opened a bible, and began to read aloud.

"If I speak with the tongues of men and angels, but do not have love, I have become a noisy gong or a clanging cymbal. If I have the gift of prophecy, and know all mysteries and all knowledge; and if I have all faith, so as to remove mountains, but do not have love, I am nothing," the pastor said in a firm, yet calm voice.

He then paused and looked around the room, allowing his words to sink in for a moment, and then looked back at his bible to continue reading."

"Love is patient, love is kind and is not jealous; love does not brag and is not arrogant, does not act unbecomingly; it does not seek its own, is not provoked, does not take into account a wrong suffered, does not rejoice in unrighteousness, but rejoices in the truth; bears all things, believes all things, hopes all things, endures all things."

Sam sat back in his seat as these words resonated deep within him. He knew in his heart that he wanted to love others like that. He knew that he wanted to be loved like that more than anything else in the world. He knew these things should be true within the relationships he had experienced with his family. But this was nothing close to the type of love he had experienced to this point in his young life.

As the pastor continued speaking, Sam began to rewrite these words in his mind, based upon his own experiences.

"Love is angry and threatening," he thought to himself. "Love demands perfection from those who are loved…Love is violent…Love is unforgiving…Love is fear…Love is rejection. Love controls all things, manipulates all things, destroys the hope and trust in all things," he continued in his mind.

He looked over at Will as the pastor continued. He seemed to be taking all of this in, nodding in agreement as the pastor spoke of this love that had been so foreign to Sam.

He then noticed something he had never seen before. From where he was sitting, it appeared as though tears had begun to well up in Will's eyes.

Sam sat in his place, confused, and having no idea what to make of this. As much as he was afraid to, he began to feel a sense of hope. Maybe it was true. Maybe Will was beginning to soften a little. Maybe these words being spoken by the pastor were somehow changing him on the inside. By the time the service was over, Sam began to feel hopeful and curious at the same time. He watched and listened carefully as Will approached the pastor before leaving. If Will was going to say anything to him about what he had just heard, Sam wanted to hear it.

"Thank you very much, pastor," Will said with a smile as he reached out to shake his hand. "Your words really hit home with me today," he continued.

"Oh, you're very welcome, Will. I'm glad you came. I'm assuming we'll see you next week, then?" he replied with a chuckle.

"Absolutely!" Will said with firm conviction in his voice.

Sam felt a smile rise up from deep within his soul as they walked toward the car. He began to feel a profound sense of hope that everything had somehow changed. He didn't understand how just a few simple words could change everything about a person, but he truly saw something very different in Will's demeanor. After they were all back in the car, he looked across the back seat at Suzanne and flashed a smile. By her facial expression, he could see that she was feeling the same things. She reached over and squeezed his hand with an enormous smile on her face.

"So, where to now?" Will asked as they pulled out of the parking lot.

"We have to stop at the shoe store on the way home," Dawn replied. "We need to get Sam a pair of shoes. The pair he's wearing are way too small for him and they're falling apart at the seams," she continued.

Will's facial expression immediately changed.

"Well, alright, but we're not gonna spend a lot," he answered dismissively.

Dawn paused for a moment, weighing her words before continuing.

"There's a pair that Sam and I were looking at the other day," she began. "He really liked them."

"How much are they?" Will asked impatiently.

"Sixteen dollars," she replied.

"Sixteen dollars?!" he snapped. "No...We can get him a pair that will be just fine for about twelve dollars," he insisted.

"But honey, he really liked that pair," she said in a soft voice.

"I don't care what he really likes!" he snapped back. "We'll get him a pair for ten or twelve dollars, and that will be the end of it!"

An uncomfortable silence fell over the car as Sam and Suzanne looked at each other, perplexed at why he would become so upset over just a few dollars.

"How do you feel about that, Sam?" Will asked sarcastically as he turned in his seat to look at Sam.

"I...I dunno," Sam replied under his breath.

"I can't hear you Sam!" he barked. "I asked you how you feel about that."

"I'm fine with that...I guess I'm just a little disappointed," Sam replied calmly.

"Oh really? You're disappointed? Why are you disappointed, Sam?"

"Well, I just really liked those shoes, so I'm kinda disappointed that I can't have em, that's all."

"Oh...you're disappointed!" Will snapped back. "Well I'll tell you what. If you're that disappointed, why don't you call your good for nothing father? Maybe he can buy you your God-damned shoes!"

"Will!" Dawn interrupted, reaching over to grab his hand. "It's okay. There's no reason to get so upset."

"I'm just getting very tired of his selfishness and ungrateful attitude, Dawn! It makes me want to vomit!"

Sam shrunk back in his seat, absolutely deflated by Will's response. It wasn't even about the shoes anymore. It was about the hope he had felt just a few moments ago being torn from him and thrown away violently. He sat in silence, feeling foolish for allowing himself to believe that a few words from a pastor would change anything. It was all just talk. It was all just empty words. After returning home, Sam changed his clothes and walked into the living room where Will and Dawn were reading.

"I'm gonna go over to George's house for a while, ok?"

"Alright, that's fine," Dawn replied with a sympathetic smile. "Be home in time for dinner, ok?"

Sam couldn't get out of the house fast enough. He stepped outside and began walking toward George's house, thinking over everything that had just occurred.

"What a bunch of crap, all of this Jesus stuff," he thought to himself. "These people say all of these things and act all nice and happy while they're at church, but the minute they walk out of the door they go right back to being the pieces of crap they were before they got there."

The more he thought about it, the angrier he became for allowing himself to believe it might be true in the first place. He couldn't believe he would be so foolish as to believe that whole line of garbage.

"Hey Sam! What's up, buddy?" George said with a smile as he answered the door.

"Nothing," Sam replied. "Can you hang out for a while?"

"Yeah, sure," George replied. "Hang on a minute."

"Mom, Dad, I'm gonna go hang out with Sam for a while, ok?" he shouted up the stairs to his parents.

"Where are you going?" his mother shouted back.

"I don't know...out," he shouted back with a laugh as he stepped outside and closed the door behind him.

"So, what's going on, man?" George asked as they made their way down the alley behind his house.

"Not much," Sam replied. "My step-father is just being a jerk again."

"Yeah? So what's new?" George replied with a chuckle. "What's his problem now?"

"I don't know. He's just a jerk. I think he probably woke up this morning in a good mood, and then looked in the mirror and suddenly remembered that he was an idiot."

They continued walking until they reached the playground of their old grammar school a few blocks away.

"Hey man, you seem really bummed out," George said with a grin. "I think I've got just what you need." He continued as he reached into his pocket and pulled out a joint.

"Wanna get high, buddy?"

Sam laughed out loud as he looked at the goofy smile on George's face.

"You know it," he replied as they sat down against the brick wall of the school, facing the playground.

George lit the joint, took a few hits, and passed it to Sam.

"So, what's up with this guy?" he asked as he exhaled slowly.

"I don't know, man. There just always seems to be something he's pissed off about, you know? I just can't catch a break."

"Yeah...he's a jerk, dude."

Sam sat in silence for a few minutes as the high began to wash over him. It felt nice...calm.

"George, let me ask you something."

"Yeah, sure."

"Does your family go to church?"

"Yeah, we go every week."

"What do you think about all of that church talk?"

"I don't know...what do you mean?"

"Do you think it really makes a difference to people?"

"I guess so...I don't know...I haven't thought about it much. Why do you ask?"

"Well, we started going to a new church this week, and the pastor was talking about some stuff, you know? It seemed to make a lot of sense while we were sitting there. But then we left, and everything went back to the way it was before we got there."

"What do you mean?"

"Well, the pastor was talking about love, and what that's supposed to be. My step-father was sitting there listening to this stuff, and I really started to think it was hitting home with him. But the minute we hit the door, he turned right back into the same turd he was before we got there."

George started to laugh to himself as a mental image came to mind.

"Why are you laughing?" Sam asked with a puzzled expression.

"What did you think was going to happen? Did you think you'd leave there and head straight toward the hippie commune?"

"What the hell are you talking about?" Sam replied as he started to laugh.

"You know…all of that peace and love and 'Age of Aquarius' nonsense? Is that what you expected? Did you think he'd stop at the head shop and buy some tie-died t-shirts?....Maybe a couple of James Taylor or Jefferson Airplane albums or something? Or did you think he'd buy an acoustic guitar and you'd all spend your evenings sitting around a fire singing Kumbaya?"

"You're such an idiot," Sam replied as he began laughing out loud.

"Yeah, I know," George replied with a smile as he held out the joint. "Want another hit?" he asked, batting his eyebrows.

"Yeah…why not," Sam replied as he took the joint and drew in another hit.

"Hey, Sam…screw that guy, you know? He's not gonna change, man. Don't let that crap bother you. He's just a really weird dude. Just do your thing and don't let him get to you."

"Yeah…you're right. He's not gonna change," Sam replied, staring off into the distance.

"You're a good guy, Sam…You don't deserve to be treated the way he treats you. Just do your own thing, man. Rise above it."

Sam leaned his head back against the cold red brick and closed his eyes for a moment as he felt a sense of calm wash over him. Getting high became something he was beginning to do on a fairly regular basis. He was very aware that pot didn't solve his problems, but for the time being, it sure felt as though it did. It gave him the ability to let his mind rest, which was something he desperately needed from time to time. It gave him the ability to forget about all of his problems and just laugh for a while, which was something he truly needed to feel.

Over the course of the next year, his family continued to attend the local church. Suzanne began to change as the lessons being taught there resonated within her. She stopped getting high, stopped hanging out with many of the friends she had spent much of her time with, and even went as far as throwing out many of the albums she had previously enjoyed listening to due to the lyrical content of the music.

While many of her friends rejected her due to her new beliefs, Sam stayed close by her side. He knew that this wasn't just a phase she was going through. He knew that she hadn't suddenly lost her mind as many of her friends had suggested. What he saw happening in her life seemed to be very real. She wasn't trying to be someone she was not. She had simply started to believe that there was a better way of life ahead of her, and she wanted to embrace that way of life with her whole being.

She would, from time to time, attempt to talk to him about her newly found faith and show him how that same faith and sense of purpose was available to him, but no matter how compelling her arguments may have been, he couldn't get past the hypocrisy he saw in Will and various other members of the church. He also couldn't get past the thought that if there truly was this loving God out there somewhere who loved him and wanted the best for him, why would this God allow him to have experienced the pain he had felt? Why would this God sit silently and watch as his father beat his mother? Why would this God allow he and Suzanne to be forced to urinate in a basement sink like a couple of animals instead of being allowed to use the bathroom like normal human beings? Why would he allow war, abuse, murder, corruption, and hundreds of other wrongs to continue unchecked in the very world he had created? All of these questions led Sam to the belief that if there really was a God, he wasn't the kind, loving God he had been told about in church. In his mind, this was a God who wanted to mistreat and demoralize him for some strange reason, and who was using the very people who claimed to believe in him to carry out that mistreatment.

Where he had seen Suzanne going in her life, and the hope that this new life had given her, were very good things in Sam's eyes. She had clearly been given a sense of peace and purpose in this, and he wanted her to feel that peace. She deserved that peace in her life. He wanted to feel that peace in his life too, but he knew that he would never find it where she had.

She had learned about a summer retreat at a Christian camp in northern Wisconsin that a group of high school kids from the church were planning to attend. There was going to be music, sports, horseback riding, and a bunch of kids sleeping in cabins for a few weeks. The more she learned about it, the more excited she became. After the year she had just experienced, and after all of the dramatic changes that had occurred in her life during that time, the idea of just getting away and having fun for a couple of weeks appealed to her deeply.

The cost of the trip was very reasonable, and she was certain that Will and Dawn would be more than willing to come up with the money she needed to attend. After all, they had encouraged her to attend the church and follow this new faith which they too had claimed to share. The pastor had mentioned the trip repeatedly during the weekly services at the church, and the majority of the church members who had teen-aged children were eager to send them, if for no other reason than to experience some peace and quiet in their homes while their kids were away learning more about their faith. To most of those members, it was a win-win situation.

She was eager to bring the topic up, convinced that they would jump at the chance to send her. After returning from a Sunday service when the pastor had mentioned it again, she brought it up as they were sitting down for lunch.

"Hey mom, Will, you know that summer camp that Pastor Terry has been talking about at church?"

"Yeah...what about it?" Will replied with indifference.

"I think I'd really like to go to that." she said excitedly.

"Really?...and how do you plan on paying for it?"

"Well...it really doesn't cost that much," she replied in a confused tone.

"How much is *really not that much*?"

"It's forty dollars, and that's for two whole weeks! It includes meals and everything!"

"Do you *have* forty dollars?" he asked sarcastically.

Suzanne looked across the table at Sam, who was shaking his head in disbelief. Dawn sat silently, looking down at her food.

"Well...no...I don't."

"Well then I guess you're not going," he replied in a matter-of-fact tone.

"Well...I was kind of hoping that you and mom would help me pay for it. I mean, I've been saving my allowance, but I don't have enough for the whole thing."

"How much do you have?"

"Twelve dollars so far, but I'll get another two dollars this week, so I'll have fourteen."

"Looks like you'll have to figure out a way to find another twenty six bucks."

"Mom?" Suzanne said, clearly pleading for her to intervene.

"Will, maybe we can talk about this later," Dawn said quietly.

"Talk about what? There's nothing to talk about," he snapped back. "It's very simple. If she wants to go to some summer camp, then she has to figure out how she's gonna pay for it. End of story."

Will took another bite of his lunch, and then got up and walked away from the table.

"Mom?" Suzanne pleaded under her breath.

"Shhhh…I'll talk to him a little later," she whispered, not wanted to upset him further.

Suzanne got up and went downstairs to her room, closed the door and laid down on her bed trying to fight back the tears.

Sam came to her door a few minutes later and knocked softly.

"Hey sis?" he called out in a hushed voice.

"Yeah, Sam."

"Can I come in?"

"Yeah," she replied, wiping her face with her arm.

"Hey…are you ok?" he asked as he sat down on the side of her bed.

"I can't believe it, Sam. I really thought they'd want me to go. I mean, it's a Christian camp."

"I know…I don't get it either."

"They've been talking about it at church for weeks. *Everyone* is going."

"I know…so what are you gonna do?"

"I don't know, Sam. I guess I can't go."

"Hey," he said, reaching into his pocket and then pulling it back out with a few dollars in it. "Here, sis…I want you to have this."

"No, Sam. I'm not gonna take your money. I'll have to figure it out somehow.

"Who knows? Maybe mom will talk him into changing his mind," he replied, wanting to give her some sense of hope.

"Yeah." She said with a laugh. "Good luck with that."

"Yeah, I know…Hey wait a minute!" he said as his eyes lit up. "Wasn't Pastor Terry talking about some kind of a fundraiser…selling candy or something?"

"Yeah, but I don't know how much that would help."

"Why don't call and find out? Maybe you could pay for it that way."

"Yeah, maybe I could," she replied as a small sense of hope returned to her.

"Thank you, Sam," she said as she sat up and gave him a hug.

Over the next few weeks, Suzanne spent every waking hour going door to door in the neighborhood trying to sell enough candy to fund her trip. By the end of the month, she had raised enough money to pay for the entire trip, leaving her the allowance money she had saved for spending money while she was there. She looked over at Sam as they sat in the back seat of the car in the church parking lot, waiting to board the bus for camp.

"Thank you, Sam...I love you so much." she said as she leaned over and gave him a hug.

"I love you too, sis. Have a good time, ok?"

"You know it!" she said with an excited tone in her voice.

Sam watched through the window as she got on the bus, and then waved at him after finding her seat. He waved back, offering a wide smile.

As the bus pulled away, he looked forward at Will and his mother, suddenly realizing that he was now alone with them. His stomach sank as he began to realize that he'd be without his best friend, and the one person who he could talk to about anything at any time. This would be the first time in their lives they would be apart, and he began to feel a deep sense of loss. He sat silently in the back seat on the ride home, wondering what the next few weeks would be like without her.

While she was away, Will directed all of his negative energy toward Sam. He seemed to enjoy the fact that there was one less person in his home to deal with, and he began to think about what his life with Dawn would be like without any kids around. He couldn't wait to be alone with her, and he made that very clear to Sam whenever he had him alone. He would never say anything about this when Dawn was around, but when he and Sam were alone, he would continually remind him of how he saw him as nothing more than an obstacle in the way of what he truly wanted.

Meanwhile, Sam began to look for ways to spend as much time as possible away from home. He applied for a part-time job at a local restaurant / ice cream parlor called Maloney's, which was only about a mile from home. To his surprise, they hired him immediately and trained him to work the ice cream counter, putting together their locally famous fountain creations.

While he wasn't crazy about wearing a bowtie and a paper hat, he enjoyed working at a job where everything he built made people happy. He would often watch the customers through the stained-glass partitions, and feel a deep sense of pride and joy as the smiles would break out on their faces as his fountain creations arrived at their tables. It wasn't much in the big scheme of things, but it was enough to make him look forward to going to work.

Before long, he found another reason to want to be there. As he was working the ice cream counter, one of the waitresses approached him.

"Hey Sam, I have a question for you," she asked with a smile.

"Yeah?"

"Hey, what do you think of Angela?" she asked, pointing over at one of the other waitresses.

Sam looked over the counter at Angela, who was putting together a food order, completely oblivious to their conversation.

"She's really nice," he replied.

"Do you think she's pretty?" she asked with a coy smile.

"Yeah…she's absolutely beautiful," He answered, looking back at Angela again.

"Really?"

"Yeah, really."

"Well, she kinda likes you too."

"Are you serious?" he asked in disbelief, thinking that Angela was way out of his league.

"Yeah, I'm serious...you should ask her out," she said with an enormous smile.

"Do you really think she'd go out with me?"

"I don't *think* she would...I *know* she would."

Sam spent the rest of his shift stealing glances at Angela. Her usual warm smile suddenly looked different to him. He couldn't wait for his shift to end so he could talk to her.

After the store had closed, he cleaned his station faster than he ever had before, desperately wanting to be done before she left for the evening. Once everything was cleaned properly, he punched out and headed for the front exit just as Angela was stepping outside.

"Hey Angela!" he called out, trying to catch his breath.

"Hi, Sam," she replied with a warm smile as she turned back to look at him.

"Hey, how are you getting home?"

"I'm gonna walk."

"Which way are you going?" he asked, hoping they were heading the same direction. Of course, it really didn't matter to him which way she lived. He would've walked 5 miles in the wrong direction just to spend some time with her.

"I live about six blocks that way," she replied, pointing the same direction that he needed to go.

"Really? Can I walk you home?"

"Sure," she replied with a warm smile.

Sam was beside himself with excitement. Not only was this incredibly beautiful girl apparently interested in him, but now she wanted him to walk her home. He wanted to pinch himself to make sure he wasn't dreaming. He tried desperately to think of something to say that wouldn't make him sound stupid.

"So, how long have you been working here?" he asked, only having been there a couple of weeks himself.

"About a year."

"Do you like it here?"

"Yeah, it's okay…I like the people."

"Not me…I hate people…I took the job for the free paper hats."

"Yeah…You're right. I lied. I can't stand being around people. To be honest, I took the job only because I love the figure flattering green apron."

"That's what caught my eye."

"My green apron?"

"Absolutely."

"Hmmm…Maybe I should've left it on for the walk home…We can go back and get it if you'd like."

"You'd do that for me?"

"Sure…What can I say? I'm a people-pleaser."

"Well, I'll tell you what. If you do that for me, I'll take it one step further and grab a paper hat. I know how sexy they make me look."

"They sure do. That's the first thing I noticed about you."

"My sexiness?"

"No, you're paper hat…I found myself mesmerized by it…I didn't notice your sexiness until a few seconds later."

Sam was beginning to feel his guard drop a bit. The nervousness he felt when they first left the restaurant was quickly fading as he began to realize that Angela's quick wit matched very well with his own. The more they talked, the more attractive he found her to be. He began to sense that there was something very special about her. He was feeling a sort of unexplainable bond with her on a level far deeper than he could understand; almost as if they were somehow kindred souls. He instantly felt more comfortable around her than he'd ever felt around any other girls his age. Their conversation didn't feel at all forced, but completely natural. No matter what they started to talk about, whether serious, funny, or just plain silly, the words just flowed from both of them.

As they continued walking down the busy city street toward her apartment, he became less aware of their surroundings. It was as if the lights of the city had been created for the sole purpose of accentuating the incredible beauty he was seeing in her. He found himself almost completely unaware of where he was or what he was saying, becoming increasingly lost in the moment, which at the core of his soul felt as though it had been designed to show him what true beauty really looked like. He felt an almost unstoppable urge to reach down and hold her hand as they walked side by side, but his insecurity stopped him.

"Well, we're here," she said with a warm smile as she pointed at her apartment.

"I'm sorry...what?" he replied, feeling mesmerized.

"We're here," she repeated. "That's my apartment."

"Oh...okay," he stammered. "Hey listen..."

"Yeah?"

"When are you working next?"

"I'm on tomorrow till closing."

"Me too!" he said with an excited tone. "Um...Would it be okay if I walked you home again tomorrow?"

"Yes...I'd like that," she replied with another warm smile.

"Yeah...Me too."

Sam stood in awkward silence for a few seconds, not at all sure how to say good-bye. Every part of him wanted desperately to wrap his arms around her and give her the kind of good-bye kiss that you only see in romantic movies, but he thought that would be pushing his luck. He reached down and took her hand for a second, then looked back into her eyes.

"Hey...I really like you, Angela," he said with a shy smile, feeling the heat rise to his face.

"I really like you too, Sam," she replied with a kind smile.

"Alright...well...goodnight...I'll see you tomorrow, okay?"

"Okay...Goodnight, Sam...I'll see you tomorrow."

He watched from the sidewalk as she turned and walked to her front door, glancing back at him with a kind smile as she opened the door and stepped inside.

He could hardly contain himself as he made his way around the corner, out of her line of sight. Every molecule in his body wanted to break into spontaneous dancing and singing. He felt like Jimmy Stewart in 'It's a Wonderful Life,' after Clarence had given him his new perspective on life. Everything around him had somehow become more beautiful, alive and vibrant. He felt as though he was walking on a cloud the entire way home, with a smile on his face that wouldn't leave, and which felt as though it came from deep places within his soul that he never knew had even existed. He couldn't wait to return to work so he could see her again.

Once he had arrived back home, he laid in his bed envisioning every smile he had seen flash across her face. He replayed in his mind every word she had spoken. He felt as though he had immediately fallen in love with everything about her, and somehow just being around her made everything feel right in his world.

When he awoke the following morning, his very first thoughts were of Angela. He jumped out of bed with an enormous smile and made his way upstairs to grab some breakfast.

Will entered the dining room just as Sam poured himself a bowl of cereal and sat down.

"Sam?" he said with his familiar, critical tone.

"Yeah?" Sam replied, beginning to feel as though all of the air had just been sucked out of the room.

"I went into the kitchen last night to get *my wife* a cup of tea, and I noticed that you didn't take the garbage out before you left for work."

"Oh…I'm sorry," he replied with a sigh. "I'll take it out now," he continued as he stood up from the table.

"Well, I'm sorry, sport, but *now* is too late. You were supposed to take it out last night."

"I know…I'm sorry. I was in a rush to get to work on time. It must've slipped my mind."

"Alright…well, you know what that means, right?" he replied with a matter-of-fact tone in his voice.

"It means that you've just lost your allowance, and you're grounded for a week."

"What?!" Sam blurted out, stunned at the severity of his punishment for such a small rule infraction.

"You heard me. You're grounded for a week, and you've lost your allowance."

"But I *can't* be grounded! I have to work tonight!" he pleaded.

"You can go to work tonight, but you're staying home during the day and you're gonna come home straight after work."

Sam began to feel an intense anger building up inside of him.

"That's crazy," he said under his breath as Will was walking out of the room.

"What did you just say?" Will demanded as he stopped in the doorway and re-entered the room, his face red with anger.

"I said that's crazy," Sam said in a firm tone. "I forget to take the garbage out because I was in a hurry to get to work, and I end up getting grounded for a week?!"

A look of rage fell over Will's face as he walked quickly over to Sam at the table, leaning in until his face was just inches from Sam's.

"Wanna hear something even crazier *little boy*?" he seethed, clenching his teeth as he spoke. "Now you're grounded for two weeks!" How do you like that, *little boy*? Do you have anything else you'd like to say?" he continued, almost daring Sam to say another word and worsen his punishment.

Sam sat silently, resisting the intense urge to take his spoon and stick it in Will's eye.

"That's what I thought," Will snapped with a cocky smirk as he backed away, confident that he had squashed any thoughts of rebellion Sam may have been considering. In his twisted mind, Will viewed any disagreement in his decisions as an act of rebellion that needed to be crushed instantly, before it led to more serious rebellious acts. What's more, he viewed any tone of disappointment with his decisions, or forgetfulness in carrying out his demands as yet another direct act of rebellion.

Sam knew exactly what Will was attempting to do by referring to him as a *little boy*. He was merely attempting to emasculate him, proving to himself that he was the *only* man in the house. He also knew that any further discussion would lead to even more severe punishment. He finished his breakfast and returned to his room, staying there for the remainder of the day to avoid any further confrontations. He began to miss Suzanne desperately, but at the same time he hoped that she was truly enjoying her time at camp, as well as her temporary freedom from Will's prison environment.

The day seemed to drag out forever. He couldn't get through the front door fast enough once it was time to leave for work. He felt a sense of excitement returning as he made his way to the restaurant, knowing that he'd be able to see Angela again.

"Look at that handsome guy in the paper hat," Angela said over the counter with a smile.

"Hey, Angela! You're looking pretty fine yourself in that green apron," he replied with an enormous smile. "How are you tonight?"

"I'm good…how are you?"

"I'm doing great now."

"Yeah?...Me too," she replied with a knowing smile.

"Hey, I need you to work your magic back there," she continued. "I've got a table full of hungry people over there demanding tulip sundaes *immediately*. I think they might be a little high, and you know how much those stoners love their ice cream," she said with a wink.

"Yes, we do…er…I mean, I'll do my best not to disappoint them," he replied with a chuckle.

They exchanged smiles back and forth throughout their entire shift. Whenever the action slowed down a bit, he'd find himself scanning the restaurant trying to steal a glance at her. All he could think about was how much he was looking forward to the walk home. Minutes turned to hours as he kept looking over at the large clock on the wall in his station. Finally, after what seemed like an eternity, their shift ended and they walked outside together.

"Hey Angela?" he said with a touch of nervousness in his voice.

"Yeah?"

"I was thinking about you all night last night, and again all day today."

"Really?...And what were you thinking?" she replied with a coy smile. "About how hot I look in my green apron?"

"Yeah, that's *exactly* what I was thinking," he replied with a laugh. "I have to be honest. I was a little disappointed when I realized you weren't gonna wear it home."

"Not as disappointed as *I* was when you threw out your paper hat."

"Yeah, sorry about that…I *had* to take it off…It kept giving me paper cuts on my forehead," he chuckled.

"Do you know what I really want to do?" he asked, trying to build up his courage.

"Ummm…Try to invent a more comfortable paper hat, patent it, and then sell millions of them to restaurants all over the world, much to the pleasure of uncomfortable sundae creators?"

"Wow…I think you might very well be brilliant," he replied, stopping to stare at her with an amazed expression.

"You could be a millionaire," she said with a nod and a wink.

"I sure could, and do you know what I'd do first if I was?"

"I can't even begin to imagine."

"I'd buy a piece of land in Maui, far away from everything, with a waterfall nearby."

"That sounds really beautiful."

"It would be, and then I'd build an enormous treehouse right in the middle of it."

"A treehouse? Why a treehouse?"

"What? You don't like treehouses?"

"I actually love them."

"Perfect! Because after I finished building it, I would come back here and get you so that we could spend all of our days together, relaxing in our treehouse and gazing out of the open windows at our own private waterfall."

"Whoa…You're moving a little fast there, aren't you Mr. Grace? I mean, I've just met you."

"Yeah…You're probably right. Maybe we should get to know each other a little better before we run off to Maui."

"Maybe just a little bit."

As they continued walking, not talking for a few minutes, Angela began thinking to herself how beautiful the scenario was that he had just painted. She knew that they had only met a very short time ago, but she was already beginning to feel some strong feelings for him.

"But if we did get to know each other a little better, and if you were up for it, that's exactly what I'd do," he answered quietly.

"Would you really?" she asked with a coy smile.

"I sure would," he replied. "And do you know what else I'd do?"

"I'm afraid to ask."

"I'd buy a little notebook that we could keep right by the front door."

"A little notebook? For what?" she asked with a confused expression.

"Well, every day, while the other person wasn't looking, we could each write little notes to each other in it."

"What kind of notes? Reminders to pick up a loaf of bread or to take out the trash?" she answered playfully.

"No, nice things. Things like '*I love the way you smile at me,*' or '*You look so very beautiful in the moonlight tonight.*'"

Angela could suddenly feel the blood rush to her face, feeling a sense of warmth deep within her that nobody had ever made her feel before.

"That's some pretty romantic stuff right there, Mr. Grace," she replied, turning away for a moment to hide her face.

"So, what were you really going to say before I interrupted you?" she asked, trying to change the subject. "You said there was something that you really wanted to do. What was it?"

"This," he said as he reached down and held her hand, looking over at her to see her reaction.

"That's nice...I like that," she replied, feeling too shy to look him in the eyes as a warm smile grew over her face.

"There's something else I've been thinking about."

"What's that, Sam?"

"Well, I've decided that we need to change your name."

"Change my name?" she replied with a tone of shock in her voice. "Why would you want to change my name?"

"Well...Angela is a nice name...A very nice name."

"But you like Agnes better?...Or Penelope perhaps?" she said with a laugh.

"Oooooh...Agnes...I never thought of that one."

"It's kinda hot, no?"

"Absolutely!....But here's what I was thinking," he said as his voice softened.

"Your name is Angela...but when I look at you, I see an angel...So I think we need to drop the second 'a,' and I'll just call you Angel from now on. Would that be okay?"

Angela gripped his hand more tightly as she felt her heart fill with butterflies.

"I would love that," she replied with a warm smile.

They held hands for the entire walk home, both of them feeling their palms getting sweaty, but neither of them wanting to let go. They arrived at her apartment far too quickly for Sam's liking. He would've walked with her throughout the entire city if he could've, not letting go of her hand until the sun came up the next morning.

"Well, we're here," she said as she turned and looked him in the eyes, taking his other hand.

"Hey listen," she continued. "My step-mother isn't gonna be home for a while. You can come in and talk for a while if you want."

"No...I can't," he replied, feeling his heart sink in his chest. "My step-father is gonna be waiting for me to get home. He told me to get home right after work."

"Oh...it's okay...I understand," she replied, feeling a bit rejected.

"I'm sorry...I *really* want to...I really like being with you."

"I really like being with you too, Sam," she said, looking him in the eyes.

"Can I..." he hesitated, having a hard time finding his courage.

"Can you what?" she asked with a smile.

He looked down at the ground for a few seconds, and then looked her in the eyes, glancing at her lips momentarily.

"You want to kiss me, don't you?" she said with a playful smile.

"More than anything in the world," he sighed.

"Well, what are you waiting for?"

He pulled her close and kissed her, immediately feeling as though every part of his body had come alive for the very first time. He held her as close as he could, wrapping both of his arms around her, wanting that first kiss to last forever.

"Excuse me!" she demanded as she pushed him away playfully.

"What's wrong?" he asked, thinking he might have over-stepped his boundaries.

"Did I say that you could hug me too?"

"Um...no. I suppose you didn't," he replied, taking his arms off of her. "It just felt like the right thing to do at the time."

"You're right...it was," she answered as she leaned in close, wrapping her arms around him.

They stood outside the doorway of her apartment, continuing to kiss each other as if their very lives depended upon it. It wasn't the first time either of them had kissed someone, but no kiss had ever felt so important or beautiful before.

"Hey..." Sam said quietly after a few minutes had passed. "I really have to get going," he continued, fighting every emotion in his soul.

"Okay...You'd better go...I don't want you to get in trouble."

"Ha!" he barked out. "Trouble?...That's my middle name! I always seem to be in trouble for something," he answered with an over-dramatic laugh.

"I know the feeling," she replied, rolling her eyes.

"Hey, Angel?" he said, looking into her eyes.

"Yes?" she replied, loving the sound of his voice speaking her new name.

"When can I see you again?" he asked.

"Well, I don't work again until the weekend...But you can come by before then if you want to."

"I can't," he replied with disappointment. "I'm grounded for the next two weeks. The only time I can leave the house is for work."

"Grounded?...What the heck did you do, you little trouble maker?"

"Eh...nothing, really," he replied, too embarrassed to discuss it.

"Alright...well...maybe I'll see you next weekend...Are you working next weekend?"

"Yeah...Saturday."

"Alright then...I'll see you on Saturday."

Saturday felt like an eternity away as Sam left and started to make his way home. He began to despise Will in his heart, not only for the way he had always treated he and Suzanne, but now for getting in the way of the most beautiful relationship he could ever imagine having. He felt himself falling very much in love with Angela, and he was beginning to believe that she was feeling the same way about him. Being grounded as often as he was for such minor rule infractions was only going to make it all but impossible to see her away from work. He felt an incredibly strong sense of resentment from this, and he couldn't wait to be away from Will and his dysfunctional ways. He also began to feel the same sense of resentment toward his mother for allowing Will to do these things without saying as much as a word in his defense.

Once he arrived back home, he walked straight downstairs without saying a word. He noticed a light coming from underneath Suzanne's bedroom door as he walked past her room. Not expecting her to return for another day or so, he was surprised to see her light on. He quickly walked over and knocked on her door.

"Hey sis?.....Are you in there?"

"Yeah, Sam.....Come on in," she replied cheerfully.

"Hey!" he said excitedly as he ran across her room and gave her a big hug.

"How was camp?"

"Oh, it was sooo much fun, Sam! I wish you could've been there! We had a blast! I didn't want to come home!"

"Why would you?" he replied sarcastically.

"I know, right?"

"So, tell me everything!"

"Well, I have some news for you," she replied, nearly unable to contain herself.

"News? What kind of news?" he asked, sensing her excitement.

"Well...I met a guy."

"A guy?....What kinda guy?" he teased. "A fat guy? A little guy? A homeless guy?"

"Stop it!" she shouted, shoving him playfully.

"His name is Jim," she continued. "He's a really good guy. We talked a lot while we were at camp, and...I really like him. He's coming down next weekend to meet all of you."

Jim was a seminary student at a local Christian college, and he had gone to camp as part of his internship. He had grown up in a very close Christian family in southern Michigan, and he immediately fell head over heels for Suzanne the first time they met. By the time camp had ended, they were both very interested in pursuing a relationship once they returned back home.

Sam noticed the warm smile that broke across her face as she described him, and he knew exactly what that felt like.

"So...he's gonna come down here and meet Will, huh?" he asked, not wanting to burst her bubble, but being concerned about how Jim might be treated once he arrived.

"Yeah...I've thought about that," she replied, feeling her heart sink a bit.

"He knows what to expect," she continued. "I told him a lot about what it's like being here. I think he'll be okay."

"I hope so, sis. Hey, I'm looking forward to meeting him!"

"He's looking forward to meeting you too, bro. I told him all about you...Hey, maybe we can go out for lunch or something so you guys can get to know each other a bit."

"Aint gonna happen, sis."

"What?...Why not?"

"I'm grounded for two weeks."

"Are you serious?" she replied, her heart sinking. "For what?"

"I beat up a midget."

"You what?"

"I beat up a midget," he repeated. "Actually, I only got grounded for one week for that. I got the second week because he was a homeless midget."

"Oh stop!" she said, starting to laugh.

"No, seriously!.....It's quite the sad story, really. He had a great career going with the circus...Got fired for making inappropriate advances toward the bearded lady...Hence the homeless situation."

"You are such a nut!" she replied, beginning to laugh out loud.

Over the course of the next few months, Jim proposed to Suzanne, and a wedding date was set for the month following her high school graduation. They planned to move to Jim's home town in Michigan after the wedding. Sam was heartbroken that she would be moving away, but he had grown to like Jim very much, and he knew that he was very good to her.

Sam continued to walk Angela home from work every time he could, and they fell very much in love with each other. Their home life, however, made it nearly impossible to truly cultivate a relationship.

Unbeknownst to Sam, Angela's home life was just as dysfunctional as his; maybe even more. Her father, whom she loved dearly, had passed away just months before they had met, leaving her to live alone with her step-mother who was a severe alcoholic, and who mistreated her horribly.

She was forced to work two jobs while finishing high school, which gave her very little free time. It became a continual hit-and-miss situation between them; Sam being grounded for various minor rule infractions for the vast majority of the year, and Angela being far too busy taking on the role of being the only responsible adult in their home. Along with Will's many controlling demands was one that restricted their use of the telephone. They were only allowed to use it for a few minutes at a time, and they were forbidden to use it at all if they were grounded, making it impossible for Sam to speak with her unless he was at work.

He was eventually fired from his job at the restaurant, leaving them literally no way to communicate. When he'd call, she'd be working, and when she wasn't working, she would wonder why he never came by to say hello. They never talked to each other in any depth about their home life. Neither of them wanted to. Being together when they could always made them forget about how bad things were for them at home. Neither of them wanted to ruin what they were feeling by talking about all of the negative drama in their lives.

Once Suzanne had married and moved to Michigan, Sam was forced to take on the full brunt of Will's displeasure in not being able to be alone with *his wife.* With Suzanne being gone, and with him being grounded constantly, he had found himself in a place of complete and total isolation. His mother was working full-time as well as going to night school, so he rarely had any opportunity to talk to her. He was completely shut off from the outside world. His friends, Angela, and even Suzanne were all far removed from his life.

He sat in his room listening to music for most of his days, thinking about Angela with every song that spoke of true love. For the time being, music had become his best and only friend.

He continued to see his father from time to time, if and when he decided to show up for visitation. Those visits became increasingly difficult for Sam. Most of the time, he'd feel like an outsider staying with his father's new family, which in the end was merely another dysfunctional home situation.

His father eventually hired him to help paint a house he had been working on. He thought it would be good to teach Sam a trade, but it became an experience that proved to be very painful for Sam due to his father's constant criticism of his abilities and work ethic. He learned very little about the trade itself, but he learned a great deal about how his father thought about him.

As he was finishing his junior year in high school, Dawn approached him with what she believed was some very good news.

"Sam, Will and I have been talking," she said with excitement in her voice.

"Yeah?....About what?" he replied, not sure he wanted to know.

"Well, Will is retiring, and we've been giving a lot of thought to where we'd like to live once he does. We've decided that we're going to sell this house and move to North Carolina. We think it will give all of us a chance to start over."

"North Carolina?" Sam blurted out. "Why would you want to move to North Carolina?"

"Oh, Sam, it's beautiful down there. The weather is far warmer, the country is beautiful, and I think you'd love it down there."

Sam felt a sense of panic fall over him. He realized immediately that moving to another state would mean complete and total isolation from any friends or family he had left. He knew it would mean being alone, in a strange environment, with Will. He also knew it meant that he would never see Angela again. He immediately rejected the idea in his mind, refusing to even consider the thought.

"I don't want to move to North Carolina, mom," he said firmly. "I want to stay here and finish high school with my friends. I only have one year left. Can't you wait until after I graduate?" he pleaded. "It's just one more year."

"No, Sam...we've decided. We're putting this place on the market next week. It'll be good for all of us. You'll see."

Sam couldn't believe what he was hearing. He couldn't understand how she could possibly think this was a good idea, or how she wouldn't even consider allowing him to graduate from high school with a bunch of strangers, far removed from all of the friends he had grown up with. In his mind, this was the last straw. He couldn't take any more. He immediately began trying to figure out a way to stay behind if they did eventually leave. It would be impossible for him to stay with his father, because his mother would never allow such a thing. He began to talk to his friends at school about the idea of running away. He'd need a place to stay temporarily, until he could get a job and support himself. He found a friend who's sister, Mary, was a few years older than him, and who had an apartment in the neighborhood with her boyfriend. They knew about his situation at home, and they agreed to let him stay for a few months if necessary. It was the perfect place to go because nobody from his family knew who they were, much less where they lived. It would be the best place to lay low until they were out of town and the heat was off.

Within a month, Will and Dawn had found a home they had fallen in love with in North Carolina. They worked out a deal with their realtor to sell their current home after they moved, and the moving date was set.

Sam spent the next few weeks lining up a move of his own. He knew it would be difficult, but he was determined. He arranged to have George meet him the night before they moved to give him a ride, and began to think about what he'd need to bring with him.

The night before their scheduled move, he sat alone in his room as the night wore on, keeping an eye on the clock on his dresser. He had stuffed all of his clothes into two large garbage bags and had set them on the floor next to his bed. He knew that Will and Dawn would go to bed a little after 10:00pm, so he planned to wait awhile afterward, until he knew they were sleeping, and then sneak quietly out the back door.

He sat in the silence of his bedroom, reasoning through his decision to end their lives together in this way. A big part of him was very much afraid of what might come, but deep down inside, he could see no other way. He wasn't nearly as afraid of the unknown as he was of what he knew his life would be like if Will were able to get him alone on the other side of the country. His heart was breaking inside of him, knowing how hurt his mother would be once she realized he was gone. He never wanted to hurt her, but he couldn't let that stop him. After all, from what he could see, she had no concerns of how he felt about anything. He'd known that for a long time. Will wanted to be alone with her, and as far as he could see, she wanted to be alone with him. The more he thought everything through, the more he believed that he'd be simply giving everyone what they truly wanted.

He continued to stare at the clock...9:45 and counting. His palms were wet with sweat as he thought about what he was about to do. His life was about to change dramatically, and forever.

Panic began to well up inside of him as he heard Dawn come down the stairs and make her way toward his room.

"Sam?...Are you still up?" she asked as she knocked on his bedroom door.

"Yeah, mom," he replied nervously.

"Hey," she began as she entered the room and sat on the edge of his bed. "I know this isn't easy for you," she continued. "But it's going to work out, I promise you."

Sam sat in silence, glancing back at the clock and hoping his ride wouldn't leave if he was delayed.

"Are you okay?" Dawn asked, bothered by his silence.

"Yeah, mom...I'm okay."

"Listen...why don't you go to bed and get some sleep. We've got a long ride ahead of us tomorrow."

"Yeah…I will. I'm just cleaning up my room and getting my stuff together. I have to take out some trash and stuff like that."

"Oh, don't worry about that tonight. Why don't you go to bed? We'll take care of that in the morning," she said, putting her hand on his shoulder.

Sam's heart began to break as he looked as his mother. He knew that this could be the last time he'd ever see her. He wanted to beg her not to go, but he knew that would be fruitless. He reached over and put his arms around her, giving her what he knew could very well be the last hug he ever gave her.

"I love you, mom," he whispered quietly, wanting to hold on forever.

"I love you too, Sam…Get some rest, okay?"

"Okay."

He sat back on his bed and wiped a tear away as she left his room and made her way upstairs. He listened carefully to their every movement as she and Will started to get ready for bed. On a trial run, he grabbed some garbage from his room and took it outside to the garbage can in the alley. He scanned the block to see if George's car was waiting, but saw nothing. Fear began to grip him as he wondered if he would be left alone to make his way to Mary's apartment. It would be a long walk carrying two full garbage bags of clothes up and down alleys and side streets – especially if his mother called the police after noticing his absence.

He walked back to the house and stepped inside, shocked to see his mother standing at the top of the stairs.

"What are you doing, Sam?" she asked, curious about his actions.

"I was just taking out some trash, mom…I have just a few more bags left."

"Okay…well, get that done and go to bed…It's getting late."

"I will, mom…good night."

Sam walked back to his room and listened again to the footsteps as Dawn walked to her bedroom. Feeling as though it was now or never, he picked up his bags of clothes and walked to the back door, pausing for a few seconds to listen for anyone coming back toward him. Hearing nothing, he walked outside, making his way calmly through the back yard. Once he hit the alley, he began running as fast as he could toward the end of the block, the large bags bouncing against his legs.

It was a warm, humid summer's night, and he could feel the sweat beginning to drip down his face as he ran with all of the strength he could muster. The end of the block seemed to move further away with every step he took, but he kept pushing forward with all of his might.

Freedom, in whatever shape it was about to come to him, was only a few houses away. With every drop of sweat than began to run down his back, he felt along with it the stripping away of every insult, every threat, and every brick of the psychological prison Will had attempted to bury him within. The bags he was carrying seemed to become lighter with every step. By the time he reached the end of the block, he was running faster than he had ever remembered running before.

He reached the end of the block and quickly turned the corner. Seeing George's car waiting on the side street, he ran toward it as if he were shot out of a cannon. He quickly opened the door, threw his bags inside, and jumped in.

"Go man, go!" he shouted breathlessly.

He ducked down in the back seat as the car took off down the street, not wanting to be seen if anyone came out looking for him.

"I was about to take off, man," George said with a chuckle as he looked at him in the rear-view mirror. "I thought something went wrong."

"Yeah…my mom kept coming downstairs to check on me," he replied, trying desperately to catch his breath. "I'm glad you waited, man. I would've been screwed if you split," he continued.

Sam felt as though the weight of the world had been lifted off of his shoulders as he looked out at the passing houses. Never again would he have to answer to Will. Never again would he have to feel trapped in his own home, feeling unwanted, unloved, and isolated. Everything about that moment felt as though he had been in the midst of serving a life sentence and had suddenly found a way to break out of prison. He didn't know what the future would bring, but he didn't care. Whatever it was, it was certain to be better than the life he'd been living.

"Hey man…" George said from the front seat. "You're free!"

"Yeah…" Sam said with a sigh of relief. "I sure am."

They arrived at Mary's apartment within just a few minutes. Sam grabbed his bags of clothes and walked over to the driver's window.

"Hey man, I can't thank you enough for helping me out," he said with a smile as he reached through the window to shake George's hand. "I'll never forget this, man."

"Hey, no problem, dude," George replied with a smile. "Just keep your head down for a while, man. You know they're going to be looking for you. Give me a call if you need anything."

"Yeah, I know. I'll be careful. Thanks again, bro."

Sam threw his bags over his shoulder and knocked on Mary's door.

"Hey Sam!" she said happily as she opened the door and invited him inside.

"Sit down," she said, pointing to the kitchen table. "Can I get you a drink?"

"Yeah....that would be great...thank you," he replied as he took a seat.

"So, what's the plan, Sam?" she asked as she set a drink in front of him and sat across the table.

"The plan?"

"Yeah, the plan...This is only a temporary situation. You know that, right?"

"Yeah, I know. Hey, I can't even begin to tell you how much I appreciate you letting me stay here."

"Don't worry about it, but we have to figure out where you're gonna go from here."

"Yeah, I know. I'm gonna go out and apply for some jobs first thing in the morning. Hopefully something will come up quickly."

"Okay. I laid out some blankets and a pillow on the living room floor. Just make sure to fold 'em up and put 'em away in the morning, ok?"

"I will...Thank you."

"So, do your parents know you're gone?"

"I'm not sure."

"How did you get out of there?"

"I just pretended like I was taking some garbage out and took off down the alley."

"Wow...that was pretty ballsy."

"Yeah, well, you do what you have to do, you know?" he replied with a shrug of his shoulders.

"Well I'm glad you're out of there. That was a pretty bad situation."

"I'm glad too...I already feel like a new man."

"I'm sure you do...Hey, wanna get high to celebrate your new freedom?" she asked, pulling a pipe out of kitchen drawer next to the table.

"I thought you'd never ask," he replied with a chuckle.

After talking for a while longer, Sam walked into the living room and laid on the floor, looking up at the ceiling as a million thoughts raced through his mind. He knew there was no way anyone would ever find him there. He also knew that he couldn't talk to anyone until the heat was off. He had no idea how his mother and Will would react to his being gone. Would they call the police? Would they hold off on the move and search for him? He knew that this would be his only chance to escape. If he were to be caught, he'd never get another chance at freedom. His mother and Will would definitely keep a constant eye on him until the move if they found him and brought him back home. He had to play it smart and lay low for a while, but for the time being, he knew that he was free and that was all that really mattered.

Dawn had heard him leave through the back door. Assuming that he was merely taking out more trash, she laid in bed, listening for him to come back inside. After not hearing him for a few minutes, she got out of bed and walked to the back door. Seeing it left wide open, she stood at the top of the stairs and waited for him to return.

Panic began to set in as she saw no sign of him. She closed her robe and walked hurriedly to the alley, her eyes scanning in every direction. Not finding him there, she ran back inside and hurried to his room. Finding it empty, her heart rose into her throat.

"Will!" she yelled as she ran back to the stairs.

Hearing the panic in her voice, Will sprang from his bed and ran toward the back of the house.

"Sam's gone, Will! He's gone!" she cried out.

"What do you mean, he's gone?" he shouted back.

"He's just gone! I heard him go outside a few minutes ago, but he never came back! He's gone!"

"Calm down, honey! I'm sure he's around somewhere," Will insisted.

"Don't tell me to calm down! My son is gone!"

"He probably took off to his father's house. Why don't you call over there to see if he knows anything."

Dawn ran to the phone and dialed Lee's number.

"Hello?" Ronnie answered, surprised that anyone would be calling at such a late hour.

"Ronnie, it's Dawn...Have you heard from Sam?"

"Have I heard from Sam?!...No. Why would I have heard from him?"

"He's gone, Ronnie! Is he there?! Did he say he was coming there?"

"No, I haven't heard anything from him," she replied, stunned by the news.

"Don't lie to me, Ronnie!"

"What?! I'm not lying! I haven't heard anything from him."

"Give me the phone, honey," Will insisted.

"Ronnie? It's Will."

"Hi Will...What's going on with Sam?"

"I guess he took off. We're supposed to be moving to North Carolina in the morning, so we really need to find him."

"Well, you obviously can't leave until you find him, right?"

"I don't know what we're going to do. Can you please call us if you hear from him?"

"I certainly will."

"Thank you, Ronnie. We'd really appreciate that"

Before hanging up, Will thought back to all of the times he and Ronnie had argued about Sam and Suzanne over the years. The arguments they'd had were nearly always due to Will's rigid and inflexible demands when it came to Lee's visitation rights. Ronnie had repeatedly tried to find some sort of a compromise that would make visitation easier, but to no avail.

"Hey Ronnie, I just want to say something."

"Sure, Will."

"I wanted to apologize for all of the disagreements we've had about the kids over the years."

"Oh…okay. Well, I'm sorry too, Will," she replied as she rolled her eyes, not even remotely interested in anything he might have to say about it.

"You know, when you think about it, it's kind of ridiculous anyway. I mean, they weren't even our kids."

Ronnie was floored that he would make such a statement, especially at a time like this. Finding no words to say, she was silent.

"Alright, well, I'm gonna go. Please call us if you hear anything."

Dawn paced through the house most of the evening, unable to sleep. By the following morning, they still had heard nothing about Sam's whereabouts. They had called everyone who may know anything, but everyone they talked to seemed just as stunned by the news as they were.

Against what her own feelings were, Will was able to convince Dawn that the best thing to do would be to go ahead with the move to North Carolina, leaving Sam behind. After all, everyone here would be looking for him, and once he was found, they could bring him there.

Feeling as though she was leaving a large piece of her heart behind, she agreed that it was probably the best thing to do. She understood that, had they forced him to go, he would more than likely just run away again as soon as he had the chance. Not only that, but if he did run away after coming with them, he would be doing so in a place where he knew nobody, and where he would have no choice but to somehow try to make his way clear across the country alone. At least here, she thought, he had friends and family members he could depend on if things got tough. She and Will loaded up the last of their belongings into the car, and after taking one last look at their home, she started the car and pulled away.

SEVEN

"Those were definitely some crazy days," Sam thought to himself as he continued staring out through the window, not really paying any attention to what he was seeing.

He and Angela continued to see each other for about a year after he had left home. They absolutely adored each other, but neither of them knew how to express their feelings in words. Sam had no doubt that he loved her very much, and he believed that she felt the same way. Their inability to express how they felt about each other became a serious problem within their relationship. It wasn't that either of them were demanding to know how the other one felt, but instead a lack of communication that left both of them feeling very confused.

A clear example of this came late one winter evening. They had made plans to get together with another couple on a Saturday night, and he decided that despite his fear of being rejected, he was going to tell her that he loved her. He was nervous about it all day, but he knew that he needed to tell her. He had a couple drinks as soon as he had arrived, trying to calm his fears.

His palms began to sweat as he sat on the sofa in her apartment, Angela sitting on the floor between his knees and leaning in toward him. He looked down as she carried on a conversation with their friends. He felt his face getting hot with nervousness as he looked down at this beautiful girl he was so very much in love with. Not able to control the urge any longer, the words rose up in his throat as if they were forcing themselves out from the deepest part of his soul.

"Angel?" he said as he reached down and touched her shoulder.

"Yeah, Sam," she answered with a smile as she looked him in the eyes.

"I love you…," he said quietly, almost holding his breath as he awaited her reply.

A look of panic came over her face as the words left his mouth. It wasn't that she didn't want to hear those words. It was that the timing was all wrong.

She had spent much of her life with alcoholic family members who would say all kinds of things when they had been drinking. It made her sick to her stomach, and she had learned to never take those words seriously. She also knew that Sam had been drinking, and had no idea if she could trust that he meant what he had just said, or if it was simply the alcohol talking.

Once he had seen the look of panic in her eyes, along with the absence of any type of a verbal response, Sam knew that he had just made a terrible mistake. He immediately assumed that she didn't respond because she didn't feel the same way about him, and he began to feel like an absolute fool.

As the next few days passed, Sam struggled to understand what their relationship was all about. He knew that they always enjoyed spending time with each other, but believed that she wanted no part of love.

Angela wanted him to love her, and she definitely wanted to hear him say those words to her, but she didn't want him to say it while he was drinking. She also loved him, and honestly wanted to express her love to him in words, but she was very much afraid of those feelings. She decided to wait and see if he would tell her that he loved her again, telling herself that if he never did, it would be because he didn't really mean it in the first place. It would simply mean that he was drunk, and said something he regretted saying the next day. Unfortunately, Sam decided that if she didn't want to hear those words from him, he would never say them again...And he never did.

As time passed, and their relationship grew deeper, they regularly showed their love for each other in many other, non-verbal ways. He found it impossible to be in the same room with her without reaching out to touch her continually; not doing so dramatically, but instead with simple things like putting his hand on the small of her back or stroking her hair. She loved the way he always felt the need to be touching her in some way. She could feel the absolute love in his touch, which always made her feel very warm inside.

Public displays of affection were also a very normal, regular occurrence for them. A simple walk around the neighborhood would almost always include stopping at some point so he could take her by her hands, look her in the eyes, and kiss her slowly and passionately.

Although their feelings for each other were very strong, the cares and concerns of their own personal lives prevented them from spending as much time together as they would've liked.

What would eventually be the fatal blow to their relationship came just a few weeks later. Both Sam and Angela had moved into different apartments, Angela moving into a basement apartment in her sister's house, and Sam moving into an apartment with his step-mother after finding that his mother and step-father had given up on looking for him. He had been homeless for a number of weeks, crashing at friend's houses, sleeping in his car, or anywhere else he could find. Out of desperation, he called his step-mother and asked if he could stay with her until he could find a better job and a place to stay. She reluctantly agreed, but made it very clear to him that it was only a temporary situation.

He had recently been in the dog house with his step-mother for continually staying out all night without calling to let anyone know where he was. Angela had invited Sam to come to her apartment for a visit, and as he was leaving, his step-mother gave him a very stern warning, threatening to throw him out in the streets if he failed to come home again.

Angela met him in the front yard as he pulled up in front of the house, greeting him with a loving hug and a kiss.

"Hey there, sexy!" she said with an enormous smile.

"Hey, Angel, " he replied, stepping back to admire her. "Wow! Look at you!"

"What?" she answered with a shy smile. "Do I have something in my teeth?"

"No, you look absolutely beautiful."

"You always say that to me, Sam."

"I know, and I always mean it when I do. You're the most beautiful woman in the world to me, Angel."

"Awe, thank you. I know you do," she replied, leaning over to kiss his cheek.

"Hey, I want you to come upstairs and meet my sister, okay?"

Sam had never met any of Angela's family before, so he was slightly surprised by her suggestion. Every time he had come to see her before, they would always just hang out in her apartment together.

"Okay," he replied, slightly confused, but willing to roll with it.

Once they entered the home, it became clear that she wanted them to spend some time there. Angela's sister had made dinner for everyone, and afterward she pulled out some board games they could all play together. Sam was truly enjoying the visit, and they stayed in Angela's sister's house for hours, laughing, joking, and playing games.

Eventually, Angela asked Sam if he'd like to go downstairs to her apartment. He readily agreed, and they said their good-bye's and headed downstairs. Sam looked at his watch to find that it was already past 11:00pm, and too late to call his step-mother to let her know what was going on. He knew he'd have to leave soon, or risk being thrown out on the streets. He pulled Angela close and kissed her, wrapping his arms around her.

"Sam?" she said as she pushed him away gently. "I want you to stay here tonight."

His heart sank as he heard those words. He wanted nothing more in the world than to do so, but he knew that staying there would lead to him being homeless again.

"Angel…I can't," he stuttered.

Angela felt her heart breaking a little due to what felt like him rejecting her.

"Why not?" she asked softly.

"I really, really want to," he pleaded. "But I can't. I just had a huge argument with my step-mother. If I don't go home tonight, she's gonna throw me out."

"Call her and tell her," she replied, motioning toward her phone.

"I can't, Angel…She's already in bed sleeping. She'll lose it if I wake her up."

Sam reached over to hug her again, but she pushed him away once more.

"Sam…I want you to stay here tonight," she repeated, looking into his eyes.

He could feel his heart breaking as he noticed the tears welling up in her eyes.

"I can't, Angel…I have to leave."

Angela was absolutely crushed as she started to walk him toward the back door, believing that he was rejecting the idea of being with her.

"Angel…I'm so sorry…I just can't," he said sincerely as he looked back at her through the doorway.

"It's ok…Just go," she replied with eyes full of tears.

Sam's heart felt heavier than it ever had before as he walked to his car and began the long drive home.

"Why tonight, of all nights?" he asked himself in frustration. Even though he still believed that Angela didn't love him, he remained insanely in love with her and the last thing he'd ever want to do was break her heart. He knew by the look in her eyes that he had done just that.

As he pulled into the parking lot of his apartment complex, he continued to think back on the events of the evening, and his heart sank even further as he realized why she had arranged for the evening to go the way that it had. Meeting members of her family, spending time with them, and then asking him to stay for the night...it all became clear to him. She wanted more out of their relationship. She wanted far more, and he had just rejected her. He began to feel absolutely crushed as he realized what he had just done. By her actions, she was expressing her love for him, and in response, he had walked away. Being as late as it was, he decided he'd call her the next day to see if he could make things right. Maybe she'd give him another chance, and if she did, he would do things right this time. He might even get the chance to tell her that he loved her again. And maybe this time her reaction would be different.

He tried to call her the next morning, but there was no answer. He tried again the next day, and the next. Weeks passed, and he was never able to reach her. In an effort to protect her from a man who she believed would never want a serious relationship with her, Angela's sister would answer the phone every time he'd call. Once she recognized his voice, she would immediately begin to tell him that Angela wanted nothing to do with him anymore. She went on to invent lies, saying that she was now seeing someone else, and that he should go away and leave her alone.

Being completely unaware of what her sister had been telling him, Angela continued to wait for him to call. In time, they both simply gave up hope, and they never saw each other again.

Sam leaned forward in his seat, his face flush with sadness as he thought back upon the heartache he still felt over how that relationship had ended. All these years later, he had still never loved anyone as deeply as he had loved her. He often wondered if, when she thought back to their days together, she felt the same way about the love she had once felt for him.

"Next stop, Gad," Gabriel called out.

Sam turned and looked out over the platform. The entire structure was filled with men in military uniforms, and the parking lot was full of various types of military vehicles.

Off to the side, on a separate track running parallel to the one his train was on, he saw a long row of olive green rail cars with military markings on the side. The doors on each car stood open, while men in uniforms mingled outside. Some were hugging loved ones; wives, parents, and children. Some appeared to be grabbing one last smoke before boarding, while others stood alone, taking in all they saw happening around them.

His gaze was suddenly fixed on an officer directly across from where he sat. He was leaning against the side of the red brick train station, his back to the wall, looking directly at Sam, expressionless. His uniform was different than the rest, all white with more decorations than he'd ever seen before on any military uniform. His eyes never moved from Sam until the doors on Sam's train began to close, at which point he nodded, touched the brim of his hat, and turned away.

As the train began to move again, Sam was able to see inside of the passenger cars through the open doors. He saw row after row of plain, simple, olive green bench seats, most of them empty. In front of the passenger cars there was a long row of flat-bed cars loaded with a multitude of various military vehicles and equipment.

"Wow!" Sam thought to himself. "I'm sure glad I'm on this train instead of that one...whatever this one is."

His thoughts were immediately interrupted as a group of three sailors, obviously drunk from a long day of partying, staggered into the car, shoving each other while shouting profanities with slurred speech.

"Oh baby!" one of them called out as he stood frozen in his tracks, looking back at the lady in the red dress behind Sam.

"Look at you...Mmmmmm," he continued while making a sexual gesture with his hips.

Sam looked back at the lady in the red dress. She was obviously embarrassed by his comments and turned to look out the window, not wanting to make eye contact.

"Hey, sexy lady!" the sailor continued shouting. "I'm talkin to you! Don't be shy. You know you want me!"

"Hey!" Sam shouted from his seat. "Why don't you leave the lady alone?"

"Are you talkin to me, old man?" the sailor replied, fixing his gaze upon Sam

"Yeah, I'm talking to you! Why don't you show some respect?" Sam said, standing from his seat.

"What's it to ya, pal? Why don't you mind your own business?"

"What's it to me?" Sam shouted back. "She's my wife! You got anything else to say, smart guy?"

With that, one of the other sailors walked up behind his buddy and put his hand on his shoulder.

"Knock it off, Man You're making a scene," he said as he pulled him back and then looked at Sam.

"I'm sorry, man...he's just had a few too many...You know how it is"

Sam stood his ground as the three sailors slowly turned away and found seats for themselves. Once he was sure everything was under control, he turned and walked back toward the lady in the red dress, taking the seat next to her.

"Thank you," she said quietly as she reached over and touched his hand.

"No problem," he replied, looking over at her with a smile.

"They don't mean any harm. They're probably on leave or something and just had a few too many drinks. I'm sure they'll pay for it in the morning," she said with a warm smile.

"Yeah…you're right about that," he replied with a chuckle.

Being a Navy veteran himself, Sam knew exactly where they were coming from. After leaving home, losing Angela, and also losing contact with most of his close friends due to not having a solid place to stay, he decided to enlist. He had seen many commercials promising that if he did so, he'd see the world. He liked the idea of seeing the world. There didn't seem to be anything holding him in the old neighborhood. In fact, looking back on his life, that neighborhood had brought him nothing but heartache, sorrow and disappointment. He started to believe that a change of scenery would do him some good.

Upon finishing boot camp and basic training, he was assigned to a submarine tender in San Diego. He felt a true sense of hope as he stepped off of the plane in LAX and felt the warm sea air blow around him. His entire life was about to change, and he knew it. The old neighborhood was gone, along with all of its painful memories. It felt as though he had boarded a plane in Chicago and stepped off into a whole new world as he looked around at the palm trees swaying in the breeze. He then boarded a small, two-engine plane heading to San Diego, and watched with excitement as he looked down across the coastline of southern California.

He had no idea what to expect as his taxi pulled into the submarine base on Point Loma. His eyes grew as big as saucers when he stepped out of the cab and looked up at the monstrous ship he had been assigned to. At over two football fields in length, and with a crew of over 1,500, the enormous gray beast towered far above him and stretched out as far as his eyes could see from the pier.

He grabbed his sea bag from the trunk of the cab and made his way up the staircase to the gangway.

"Machinist Mate Fireman Grace reporting for duty. Permission to come aboard, sir?" he said to the ensign as he saluted the flag.

"Permission granted," the ensign replied, looking down at his military I.D. "Wait here and we'll have someone come up and show you around."

"Thank you, sir," Sam replied as he boarded the ship and looked around at what would be his home for the next four years. He began to feel a very real sense of accomplishment in making through boot camp and all of his schooling. He walked over to the railing and looked down the coastline, taking in all of the new sights and sounds.

"Grace?" A voice shouted from behind him "Yes?"

"My name is Hawkins...Welcome aboard," a stocky, blonde man in navy dungarees said as he approached and reached out to shake his hand.

"Thank you, Hawkins."

"My name is Hawkins, but you can call me Hawk. That's what everyone calls me here. Follow me. I'll show you where your bunk is so you can unload your stuff, then I'll show you around."

Sam's eyes were open wide as Hawk led him down staircase after staircase, through the massive machine shop in the belly of the ship, and finally to the berthing compartment where he would be living.

"This thing is huge!" He said as he tried to take it all in.

"Yeah...it's pretty big...You can get lost in here if you're not paying attention.

After stowing away all of his gear, Hawk showed him around the ship, explaining where he'd be working, where' he'd go to eat, and eventually leading him topside, to the front end of the ship.

"Where ya from, Grace?" Hawk said as they stood by the railing looking down at the water below.

"Chicago...How bout you?"

"Ahhh...Chicago...I love that town. I'm from Grand Rapids, myself."

"So...is this your job here? Showing new guys around?"

"Nah," Hawk said with a laugh. "I got into some trouble, so I'm on restriction....I can't leave the ship for another week."

"So this is your punishment? Being a tour guide for the new guys?"

"Exactly...Hey, let me ask you something, Grace."

"Sure."

"Do you get high?"

"Uh....yeah," Sam replied hesitantly

"Well, hey...I do too. But you might want to be careful who you say that to around here. They kinda frown upon that"

"Yeah...I pretty much figured," Sam replied, wondering if he should've kept that little piece of information to himself.

"Hey...I've got some good weed stashed here on the ship. If you're interested, maybe we can get high a little later...You know, to welcome you onboard all proper."

"Right here on the ship?" Sam asked incredulously.

"Yeah...Don't worry, it's cool...We have our hiding places."

Sam chuckled as he noticed the slightly crazed look in Hawk's eyes, thinking that he'd just made a new friend who seemed to be ironically similar to his old friends back home.

"Alright...let's do it up," he replied with a grin.

Later that evening, Sam was sitting on the edge of his bunk, reading to pass the time.

"Hey…Einstein…Wanna go for a walk?" Hawk said with a laugh as he approached.

"Yeah…sure," he replied, putting his book away.

Hawk led him through compartment after compartment until they finally reached a door marked "ventilation room."

"Watch this," Hawk said with an evil grin as he opened the door. Sam heard a loud whooshing sound as the door's seal released, and felt a great deal of air being sucked into the room.

Sam looked around the dark, industrial looking surroundings as Hawk led him into a small inner compartment where about a half-dozen guys were sitting in a semi-circle around what appeared to be a ventilation duct, and then began to introduce him to this deranged looking group of men. They all appeared to be slightly insane, which made Sam feel right at home. There was Dan from Cleveland, who was referred to as "Steely Dan" due to his past adventures in thievery. Mark from Detroit, who spent a great deal of his younger years building race cars with his older brothers. Valdez from Sacramento, who had been caught dealing drugs and was given the choice of either enlisting or going to jail. Gene, also from Grand Rapids, was a very small, shy, quiet guy until he started drinking, at which point he'd want to fight everybody in the room with him. Ed, also from Detroit, was a big, dopey guy who just wanted to get high as often as possible.

"What's your name, dork?" Dan said with a chuckle through bloodshot eyes.

"My name?…It's your mother…My name is your mother," Sam replied, letting out a laugh.

"Alright," Dan replied, laughing. "Want a hit of this, mom?" He continued with a grin as he held out a smoldering pipe.

"Are you sure this is cool?" Sam asked Hawk as he took the pipe.

"Yeah, man…Just hold it next to the vent. It'll suck every last bit of the smoke right out of the room."

"Where does it lead to?" Sam asked suspiciously.

"The Captain's chambers," Dan replied, laughing hysterically.

"Yeah?" Sam asked as he brought the pipe to his mouth. "Does the Captain get high too?"

"If he didn't…he does now," Dan replied, causing the whole group to burst into laughter.

They all sat in the ventilation room for about an hour, passing the pipe around every so often. By the time they left, every one of them was nearly cross-eyed.

"Here…use some of this," Hawk said as he put a bottle of Visine into Sam's hand. "You don't want anyone to know you're baked."

"Cool…Thanks," Sam replied as he threw his head back and put a few drops in.

He returned to his bunk and laid back, thinking back about the old neighborhood. He knew that his old friends would laugh if they heard that he was sitting onboard a Navy ship, on a submarine base, stoned out of his mind.

Before he had left for boot camp, he was excited about the idea of getting away from the old neighborhood – away from his incredibly dysfunctional family, crazy friends, and all of the other drama that came along with it. He thought that he was heading toward a better life, but as is the case with many people who try to run from themselves, his dysfunctional, self-destructive attitude came along for the ride. But he was now finding himself in a far more volatile place. San Diego – with its close proximity to the Mexican border and being a major seaport - was in large part the drug capital of the western United States.

He started to think how rapidly things had changed for him over the past year, and how some things had remained the same. He thought about how he was sitting in the old neighborhood, feeling like he was going nowhere just a few short months ago. Now he was in southern California, in the Navy, partying with a bunch of new friends. He truly wanted to do well for himself. He wanted to work hard and learn new skills. He wanted to see places he'd never seen before, and he wanted to make his family proud.

His thoughts then turned to Angela, and how much he missed her. After all they had been through, he still loved her more than life itself. He wanted to write her a letter expressing his love to her, but he didn't know where to start or if she'd even read it if it was sent. He picked up a pad of paper and a pen he kept in his bunk and started to write, but the words failed him. Eventually, he gave up and drifted off to sleep.

Over the next few weeks, he spent a lot of time hanging around with the group of guys from the ventilation room. Of this group, Dan very quickly became his closest friend. All of them having been in San Diego longer than Sam, they showed him around town and brought him to the places where they all liked to party. They were all hard working guys, and very good at their jobs, but after hours, they were complete maniacs, partying for days on end when they could get away from the ship.

After going out drinking with them the night before, Sam was trying to sleep off a particularly brutal hangover the following morning when the curtain around his bunk flew open and he felt someone shoving him in the back.

"Wake up, dork!" Dan shouted as he shook him repeatedly.

"Leave me alone, you moron!" Sam replied. "I'm sleeping!"

"I said wake up, dork!" Dan shouted, shoving him more violently.

"Knock it off!" Sam yelled back. "I'm sleeping!"

"No you're not!....See?.....You aint sleepin. You're talkin and everything," he replied, continuing to shake him.

"Keep on shaking me and I'm gonna bust your head open!"

"Really? You're gonna bust my head open?" Dan said sarcastically as he shook him even harder. "Come on, dork! Bust my head open!"

Dan took off laughing as Sam rolled over and sprang from his bunk, fully intending to do him great physical harm.

He ran after him about halfway down the aisle separating the bunks, then stopped as his head began to pound, forcing him to return to his bunk and sit down. Within seconds, Dan came running back the other way, holding his face and screaming into his hands. Sam could tell something was very wrong.

"Aaaarrrggghhh! My face!" he shouted repeatedly

"What happened?" he asked as Dan sat down next to him, refusing to remove his hands from his face and letting out a scream every few seconds.

"Move your hands, man! What happened?"

Dan started to pull his hands away, but then covered his face again, leaning over with his face near his knees.

"Aaaaaarrrrgghh!" he screamed again, rocking back and forth.

"Dude! What the hell happened?" Sam insisted. "Move your hands!"

"I ran around the corner cuz you were coming after me...," he shouted as he continued rocking back and forth with his hands over his face.

"Yeah? Then what?"

"I thought I saw you coming, so I took off running as hard as I could. I got three strong steps in, pushing as hard as I could. Then I looked up, and ran face-first into the steel support beam."

Sam started to laugh.

"It's not funny, man!" Dan screamed into his hands.

"Come on, man. Let me see your face," Sam insisted, laughing so hard the tears were starting to fill his eyes.

Dan slowly pulled his hands away and looked at Sam.

"Whoa, dude!" Sam laughed as he saw a goose egg the size of a golf ball rising up on Dan's forehead, right between his eyes.

"You look like someone hit you in the face with a ball bat!"

"Shut up, man! It's not funny!" Dan shouted as he covered his face again.

"The hell it aint!" Sam replied, cracking up again.

"See that?" he continued. That's what you get for messin with me. I didn't even have to bust your head open. I made you bust your own head open!"

As much pain as he was still in, Dan began to laugh too.

"It almost knocked me out."

"Yeah? Well it should have, you moron."

Once Dan was able to gather his senses, he and Sam decided to get the rest of the guys and see where the next party was. By the time the afternoon had arrived, they agreed to rent a car at a cheap car rental place and head up to Los Angeles. They all pitched in their money, rented a beat up, twelve year-old Pontiac Tempest, bought some weed and a bottle of Jack Daniels, and got on Highway 5 north.

"Let's see what this thing can do!" Dan said as he punched the gas.

Before long, they were traveling at speeds over 100mph, jumping from lane to lane, and even passing cars by driving on the shoulder. Sam opened the bottle of Jack Daniels, took a swig and then passed it around the car as they swerved from side to side. Valdez lit a joint, took a hit, and handed it to Sam.

"Hey!" Dan yelled from the driver's seat. "Are you gonna give me some of that or what?"

Sam looked over at Valdez as Dan guided the car between two slower moving cars, flying past as if they were standing still.

"Why not?" Sam said with a shrug. "Might as well. We're all gonna die anyway."

He reached over the back of the driver's seat and held the joint up to Dan's mouth so he could take a hit. He slowed down to around 80mph as he took a hit, took a swig off the bottle, then punched the gas again, passing a group of cars on the left shoulder at around 110mph.

This continued throughout the entire drive from San Diego to Los Angeles, making the 2 hour drive in just over an hour. As they pulled into the parking lot of a trendy night club on Rodeo Drive, Sam was shocked that the old car made it that far under that kind of abuse.

"Piece of crap!" Dan said with a laugh as he slammed the driver's door. "Let's party!" he continued as he walked toward the club entrance.

"Can I help you?" the doorman said as they approached, already wasted from the drive up.

"Yeah, you can let us in so we can party with some of those fine lookin women!" Dan shouted as he looked in through the door.

"I'm sorry, but I can't let you in," the doorman said firmly.

"Is it because of the nasty goose egg on the ugly guy's forehead?" Sam said with a chuckle as he pointed at Dan. "If so, he has some makeup in the car he can cover that up with."

"No, sir. We have a dress code, and none of you are dressed appropriately."

"See that?" Sam said, looking over at Dan. "I told you that you should've worn that sexy little black dress I bought you."

"Awe come on, man!" Dan protested. "We just drove all the way up from San Diego to party. Can't you give us a break?"

"No. I'm sorry. Have a nice night," the doorman said as he turned away and closed the door.

"Now what?" Sam said as they turned away from the club, realizing they probably wouldn't be allowed in any of the clubs in the area.

"Alright!" Valdez spoke up. "Let's drive through Beverly Hills and mess with some rich people."

"Well, I *have* always wanted to see how the rich folk live," Sam replied with a shrug.

With that, they all piled back into the old Pontiac and headed up into the hills, continuing to pass around the bottle and the occasional joint.

"Look at these homes!" Dan shouted from the front seat as they drove past the elaborate mansions with gated drives.

"Whoa! Check her out!" Valdez shouted, noticing a nice-looking woman walking her dog in a jogging suit.

"Hey, baby! Wanna party with us?" he yelled out the window as they passed, causing her to look at the car with the same expression of disgust that one might have after eating a bad pistachio nut.

"Did you see the look on her face?" Sam said with a chuckle. "I think she digs you, Valdez."

"Yeah, she wants him bad!" Dan replied, laughing. "Hey!" he continued. "Check this out!"

With that, he pulled the car into the driveway of a home where a group of people were gathered in the yard, stopping the car just a few inches from the gate.

"Hey! Rich people!" he yelled out through the open window. "Open up! We wanna party."

"Oh man," Sam said as he began to laugh at the stunned expressions of the people in the yard as they stared at this group of maniacs in an old beater, sitting at their front gate. "We are soooo goin to jail," he continued.

"Nope. Not today," Dan replied as he slammed the car in reverse and pulled out of the driveway.

"Hey, where's all the lawn jockeys?" Valdez said with a laugh. "I thought all rich people had lawn jockeys."

"What the hell are you talking about, man?" Sam replied, shaking his head.

"You know. Frank Zappa sang about it," Valdez answered as he began singing.

"I'll take a ride to Beverly Hills just before dawn, and knock the little jockeys off the rich people's lawn. And before they get up…I'll be gone."

"You have serious issues, my friend," Sam replied with a laugh.

"Hey look!" Dan shouted excitedly as he pointed at a long row of construction pylons ahead of them. "A slalom course," he continued, punching the gas and beginning to weave in and out, passing the pylons on the right and left.

Cutting it too close, one of the pylons disappeared under the front of the car and became wedged underneath, making a loud grinding sound as it was being dragged across the pavement.

"Ok…*now* is when we go to jail," Sam chuckled.

"Back up, retard!" Valdez yelled from the back seat.

Dan threw the car in reverse and punched the gas, but to no avail. The pylon remained wedged under the car. He tried moving forward, then back again, but it was no use. Becoming frustrated, he threw the car in reverse and punched the gas again, this time continuing to drive as fast as the car would go for about half of a city block. Finally, with a loud thud, the pylon broke free and sprung back up in front of the car.

"Finally!" he shouted out as he put the car back into drive and began to pull away.

"Wait!!" Valdez shouted. "Somebody grab that thing! I want a souvenir!"

"Are you nuts?" Sam replied.

"No, I'm serious! Stop the car!"

Dan stopped next to the pylon, allowing Valdez to reach out and drag it in through the window.

"I'm gonna keep this forever!" he shouted with glee as he stuffed it down on the floor behind the front seat.

"You have some very serious issues, man. I mean it. You need to seek out some serious professional counseling," Sam replied.

"And you don't?" Valdez replied with one eyebrow raised.

"Point taken."

"And the defense rests, your honor."

"Hey, we'd better get out of here. I don't want to push our luck," Dan said as he began moving again. "You guys wanna head back?" he continued.

They all agreed that it would probably be the wise thing to do after drawing so much attention to themselves.

They made their way back to Highway 5 south and began the long ride back to San Diego as the sun began to set. After drinking and smoking for most of the afternoon, Dan decided to take it easy on the ride home.

A heavy fog began to roll in as the sky became dark. To make matters worse, the car's headlights began to flicker on and off, making it more difficult to see the road ahead. By the time they were about a half-hour out of San Diego, everyone in the car had dozed off except for Sam, who was sitting in the middle of the back seat keeping his eye on Dan to make sure he didn't nod off too.

He looked out across the landscape, with the flickering lights off in the distance covered by occasional patches of dense fog as they moved in and out of the valleys that dotted the hilly terrain. He turned his head to look back at Dan, just in time to see his head beginning to slump forward toward his chest.

"Hey!" he shouted, slapping him on the shoulder.

"What?" Dan replied as he jerked his head back up.

"You're falling asleep, man! Pull over. Let me drive," Sam insisted.

"Yeah…you're right," Dan replied as he pulled the car to the shoulder.

Within a few minutes of being back on the road, Sam looked in the rear-view mirror to see that Dan was sound asleep along with everyone else in the car. As loaded as he was from all of the partying they had done, he felt as though he had sobered up very quickly from the adrenaline rush he had just experienced. He knew that, had he not stayed awake to keep an eye on Dan, the consequences could've been horrific. He knew that, had Dan crashed, the car they were in would've been left unmovable on a major expressway, at night, in dense fog, and possibly with no headlights to alert oncoming traffic of the danger ahead. He didn't know why he decided to stay awake, or even how he was able to being as exhausted as he was. But he knew that everyone in the car was fortunate that he had done so. He put both hands on the wheel and kept his focus solidly on the road ahead of him until they made it safely back to the Naval base.

As the next few weeks unfolded, the near-death experience did nothing to slow down the drinking and drug use. If anything, it gave all of them more of a sense of youthful immortality as they laughed and told the stories about what had happened. Sam, Dan and Gene eventually rented a small house off base, which gave all of them more freedom to party as much as they desired while away from the ship. Many of the other sailors from their ship began to use their home as a place to party and crash, forcing them to lay down a strict rule that would need to be enforced. Anyone they knew was welcome to show up, party there, and crash there if they wanted to, but they couldn't show up empty handed. Before being allowed inside, they would have to show that they had either hard liquor, weed, or whatever other types of drugs they could get their hands on. This led to a constant flow of drugs and alcohol being brought to the house. On any given night one would not only find plenty of weed and alcohol, but cocaine, LSD, hashish, and opium also become very common party favors. Sam, Dan and Gene enjoyed being the recipients of whatever was brought there, and they took full advantage of the situation.

Sam and Dan were the only two at home one Friday night when there was a knock on the door. Dan opened it to see Drew - an acquaintance they both knew from the machine shop on their ship - standing on the front porch.

"Hey man, what's up?" Dan said as he moved to the side and allowed him in.

"Hey," Drew replied with a look of excitement. "I got something you guys are really gonna like," he continued as he reached into his pocket and pulled out a small packet with some yellowish powder in it.

"Do you guys like coke?" he asked with a sly grin.

"Yeah, I love the stuff," Dan replied.

"Well I've got something better."

"Better than coke?" Sam replied suspiciously. "What is it? Coke and a hundred dollar bill?"

"Not quite," Drew answered with a chuckle. "It's called crystal meth. Ever heard of it?"

"No, what is it?" Dan replied as he leaned forward.

"It's like coke, but turbo-charged," Drew answered as he dumped the powder on the glass top of their coffee table. "You guys gotta try this stuff," he continued.

"What the hell?" Sam replied. "Why not?"

Drew cut up a few lines on the table top, then handed a rolled up dollar bill to Sam.

"Have at it, man," he said with a smile.

Sam leaned forward and snorted it up his nose, feeling an immediate burn in his sinuses as he did so. He then handed the dollar bill to Dan, who did the same.

Within just a few minutes, Sam began to feel a sense of energy and alertness he had never before experienced. It felt as though a fog had been lifted and he could see clearly for the very first time. He felt incredibly strong, sharp, and energized.

"Damn!" he said with a laugh as he looked at Dan. "This stuff is amazing!"

"You aint kidding," Dan replied. "Wow!" he continued, shaking his head from side to side.

"I *knew* you guys would dig it," Drew said with a knowing grin. "You guys got anything to drink in this place?"

"Sure do!" Dan answered as he jumped up and headed toward the kitchen, returning a few seconds later with three beers.

"Let's party, you pansies!" he said as he handed one to each of them, then tilted his head back and finished half of his with one swig.

After a few more beers, Sam began to notice something strange about how he felt. No matter how much he continued to drink, he felt as though the alcohol was having no effect on him whatsoever.

"Dude, we're gonna need more beer," he said to Dan while raising one eyebrow.

"I was just thinking the same thing," Dan replied with a goofy smile. "Hey Drew!" he continued. "How much of that meth stuff do you got?"

"I dunno," Drew replied with a smirk as he reached into his pocket and pulled out a pile of plastic packets, dropping them on the coffee table. "How much do you need?"

"Whoa!" Dan replied as they all burst into laughter. "That should be enough for me, but I don't know what you guys are gonna do!"

"How much is this stuff?" Sam asked as he picked up on of the packets and held it to the light, flicking it with his finger.

"A hundred bucks a gram," Drew replied.

"Cool," Sam replied. "I'll pop for one."

"Yeah, I'll grab one too," Dan answered. "But first, we need to go on a beer run."

One of the benefits of the location of their house was its close proximity to the neighborhood liquor store. The three of them walked there, bought a couple cases of beer and a bottle of Jack Daniels, and returned for a long night of partying. That night lasted until the following afternoon, then through Saturday night, then through Sunday afternoon and into Sunday evening. More alcohol made its way into the house as various groups of friends stopped by at random intervals, continually replenishing their supply. Both Sam and Dan had bought more crystal meth from Drew as the weekend wore on, and Drew had thrown some of his own stash on the table as well. By the time Sunday evening had rolled around, they were all completely exhausted.

"Hey man," Sam said with slurred speech as he looked at Dan, who was slumped over on the sofa next to him. "We'd better stop now. We gotta work in the morning," he continued.

"Yeah," Dan replied in agreement, barely lifting his head.

"Hey Drew!" Sam called across the room, noticing that Drew had passed out in the chair that had been his home for 3 days. "Drew!" he yelled a little louder.

Drew didn't move.

"Hey," Dan said with a chuckle as he lifted his head from the table. "If he's dead, I'll grab the rest of his meth. You'll have to bury him in the back yard."

"He's too big to bury," Sam replied, laughing. "Can't we just drag him somewhere and hide him under some palm branches?"

"Ok, but I get his meth."

"Why do you get his meth?"

"Because I called it first."

"Ahh, but here's where you're wrong," Sam said with a sly smile. "Late last night, when he was really lit up, he looked me in the eye and said; 'Dude, I think we've become very close friends. When I die, I want you to have my meth.'"

"He told me the same thing."

"He told me you would say that."

Sam closed his eyes as he waited for Dan to respond. When he opened his eyes again, he saw shafts of light from the early morning sun coming in through the spaces between the blinds of the living room windows. He lifted his head slightly, feeling the worst hangover he'd ever felt, and looked around the room. It appeared as though a bomb had gone off. There were empty beer cans and liquor bottles strewn across the floor. The large ashtray on the coffee table was full of cigarette butts with ashes spilled over all four sides.

Drew had left while they were passed out, and Dan was hunched over the arm of the sofa.

"Hey!" Sam yelled as he slapped Dan on the shoulder. "Wake up, man. We gotta get back to the ship."

Dan groaned as he began to sit up.

"I feel like someone shot me in the face," he moaned.

"I know what you mean, man. You *look* like someone shot you in the face. We gotta get some more of that stuff," Sam replied with a chuckle.

"No kidding!" Dan said with a laugh. "That stuff is amazing!"

They had both fallen in love with this new drug, and over the course of the next few months, they began to buy larger quantities of it.

As the meth use became more frequent, and as the deals became more expensive, their behavior became more and more erratic. Twice each month, after receiving their paychecks, they would immediately cash them and buy as much meth as they could afford, leaving themselves with very little money to last until the next payday. Paranoia began to set in, causing them to become suspicious of everyone. They began to experience rapid weight loss due to being up for days at a time without eating, and a disturbing loss of body control. Dan began to experience what could only be described as fainting spells – passing out with no warning while trying to walk from one room to another. Sam – who was on the thinner side to begin with – had lost so much weight he could count his ribs if he took his shirt off. They were both dying slowly, and their death was being delivered to them through the drug they had no desire to stop using.

Everything came to a head for Sam on a Saturday morning when he was supposed to go to El Cajon with Dan to meet with Drew. They had spent the night on the ship so they could get a good breakfast in the morning. Sam awoke in his bunk, and then went into the bathroom, locking the door behind him. He then snorted up a large line of meth to wake himself up. This had become a daily experience for him, just as most people might start their day with a cup of coffee. But something didn't feel right. For some reason, he felt as though he couldn't pull it together. He walked up to the mess hall to grab some breakfast, thinking that might do the trick, but it didn't. Before he left the ship with Dan, he returned to the bathroom and drew out an even larger line that the one he had just done.

"That should do the trick," he thought as he put his head back, sniffed it deep into his sinuses and shook his head from side to side.

Within just a few seconds, blood began to pour out of his nose as if it had just been broken.

"What the hell?" he said under his breath as he quickly moved his head over the sink.

He put some light pressure on the side of his nose to stop the nosebleed. Once it had stopped, he washed the blood off of his face and hands and looked in the mirror. His complexion was very pale with what looked like a slight hint of grey.

"Well, that line just got washed down the sink," he thought to himself as he drew out yet another line on the top of the sink. Without thinking twice, he snorted it up the other nostril. He waited a few seconds to make sure that side didn't start to bleed, then left the bathroom and headed to Dan's car.

"Hey man," Dan said as he approached. "You alright?"

"Yeah, I'm fine," Sam replied. "Why do you ask?"

"Because you look like crap."

"Awe shucks. Thanks, man. I'll bet you say that to all the guys. I'll be alright. I just did a monster line, as thick as your arm," Sam replied with a sarcastic smirk. "You ready?"

"I was born ready," Dan said as he started the car.

"Then let's do this."

Sam didn't talk at all as they neared the expressway. His palms were sweating, his heart was pounding, his stomach was churning, and he began to feel as though he might pass out. He closed his eyes for a few minutes, trying to calm himself down.

"Hey!" Dan shouted as he reached over and shoved his shoulder. "Are you ok, man?"

Sam's head began to spin and the color had completely left his face.

"No, man. I don't think I am," he replied as he leaned his head out the window.

Within a few seconds, he began to vomit violently.

"Hey, man!" Dan shouted. "What are you doing? You better not be puking all over the outside of my car, you moron!"

Sam leaned more of his upper body out of the window and vomited again, this time even more violently than the last time.

Dan looked in his rear-view mirror and noticed all of the cars behind them slowing down, backing away and changing lanes.

"Hey man, you'd better knock it off," he said with a laugh. "You're gonna cause an accident. You got people swerving all over the road back there."

Sam continued to vomit until there was nothing left inside of him. Once he felt as though it was safe, he took off his shirt, wiped his face off, and then threw it out the window, collapsing back against the seat.

"Hey, we don't have to do this," Dan said as he looked over. "We can go back."

"No," Sam said under his breath. "Go ahead, man. I'll be ok."

Within a minute, he had completely lost consciousness. Dan continued driving to where the deal was supposed to happen.

"Hey man, we're here," he said, shaking Sam's shoulder. "Hey, wake up, dork!" he continued as he shook him a little harder. Sam didn't respond, so Dan left him in the car and went in to make the deal by himself. He was still unconscious when Dan returned, so Dan just let him sleep and headed back toward the ship. He began to shake him harder as they got closer to the naval base, but Sam didn't respond at all. He remembered what Sam had said about snorting a big line before they had left, and he began to think that going back to the ship wasn't a good idea. He pulled over and checked his pulse and his breathing, and then turned around and drove to the house. Sam was still unconscious when they arrived, so Dan went inside to see if anyone was there to give him some help. He walked inside, finding a few guys from the ship sitting in the living room.

"Hey, give me a hand for a second, will ya?" he asked as he turned and motioned toward the door.

"Sure. What's up?" Valdez replied as he stood up and followed him.

"It's Sam. He's messed up. We gotta get him inside."

"What do you mean?"

"He's just messed up, man."

"Messed up how?"

"I don't know. He was throwing up, then he passed out. I can't wake him up."

"Oh man!" Valdez shouted with a laugh as he looked at the side of Dan's car. "Did he puke all over your car?"

"Yeah, but he'll be washing it as soon as he wakes up! I can promise you that!"

Valdez reached in through the window and began slapping Sam's face.

"Hey man, wake up!" he yelled, slapping him repeatedly. Sam remained motionless, his body slumped against the passenger side door.

"He doesn't look good, man," Valdez said, shaking his head. "Maybe we should take him to the hospital or something."

"Are you crazy?" Dan replied incredulously. "He just did a bunch of meth! If we take him to the hospital, he's gonna get busted. We need to get him inside. He just needs to sleep it off," he continued. "You open the door and I'll grab his shoulders."

They managed to lift his limp body out of the car and then carried him into the house, laying him on the bed. He remained there, unconscious, for the rest of the day. Dan and Valdez checked on him occasionally to make sure he was still breathing, but as night fell they both went to bed.

When Dan awoke the following morning, he tried again to wake him up. He grabbed him by the shoulders and started shaking him.

"Hey, man!" he shouted as he shook his body. "Wake up! We gotta go to work!"

Regaining consciousness, Sam tried to push him away, but couldn't muster enough strength.

"I can't, man," he responded in a rough voice. "I'm really sick."

"You have to!" Dan shouted as he shook him more violently. "Come on! You gotta go to work or you're gonna be in big trouble!"

"I can't. I'm really sick," Sam repeated. "Leave me alone," he continued.

"Alright, man," Dan said sarcastically. "I tried."

Dan and Valdez left him there and drove to the ship to start their workday. They stood for the morning muster, listening nervously as their Chief Petty Officer went through roll call.

"Garrison?" he shouted.

"Here," came the response.

"Gerardi?"

"Here."

"Grace?"

The Chief Petty Officer looked up from his list of names.

"Grace?" he repeated as he scanned his men.

"Valdez. Where's your buddy, Grace?"

"I don't know, chief," he replied, not wanting to give up his location.

"Have you seen him today?"

"I saw him last night, chief. He was really sick."

The Chief scribbled on the page next to Sam's name, and then continued through the rest of the names on his list. When Sam didn't show up for the rest of the day, he was reported as being A.W.O.L.

Sam slept through the remainder of the day, waking up only to eat later in the evening. By the following morning, he was still too ill to report for duty, causing his Chief Petty Officer to report him as being A.W.O.L. a second consecutive day.

Upon returning to his ship the next day, he was immediately escorted to the medical bay to take a mandatory drug test, which he failed due to traces of THC – a chemical found in marijuana – being found in his body. He was placed on restriction and not allowed to leave the ship for any reason until he was brought before the Captain to face charges of being A.W.O.L. and for failing a drug screening. The Captain's decision was to send him to a program called "Correctional Custody" for ninety days, which was a disciplinary program held on a marine base. His daily routine consisted of waking up at 5:00am, getting dressed in his exercise gear, making his bed and standing at attention for roll call within 3 minutes. He was then led to the exercise area, where he and the rest of the prisoners would be put through a torturous workout administered by Nay Seals. They would then shower, eat breakfast, and participate in daily work assignments as issued. After dinner, they were forced to attend classes designed to enlighten them on the error of their ways. Their entire day was filled with activities from morning till evening, with an hour of free time before the call for lights out was announced.

Although the daily regiment was exhausting, it began to have a positive impact on him as time elapsed. He was eating healthy food, getting daily exercise, and being forced to think through the bad choices he had been making. More importantly, he hadn't used any crystal meth for quite some time, and at this point he had no desire to ever see the stuff again. He knew that it had nearly killed him, and it was only fate that had kept him alive. He respected his friends for hiding him until he had recovered, but at the same time he thought that was the dumbest thing they could've done. He didn't know how close to death he had been, but he was certain that he had been right at its doorstep. By the time he was released and returned to his ship, he felt very differently about everything. He resolved that he was going to change his ways, give up the drugs and alcohol, and work harder than he ever had before.

After being back on the ship for 30 days, he was brought before his Chief Petty Officer to review his one-month evaluation.

"Sit down, Grace," the Chief said as he pulled out his file.

"Grace, I've seen how hard you've been working since returning from Correctional Custody," he began. "Unfortunately, due to your failing your last drug test, it's impossible for me to give you a positive evaluation."

"I don't understand, Chief," Sam replied. "I've done everything you've asked of me and more."

"I know that, but I can't give a positive evaluation to someone who has failed a drug test," he said as he handed the evaluation to Sam for his signature.

Sam looked down at the evaluation, stunned to see the worst evaluation he had ever received.

"Oh come on, Chief!" he protested. "This isn't right!"

"I'm sorry, Grace," he replied in a matter-of-fact tone. "It's just the way it is."

His blood was boiling as he signed his evaluation and left the Chief's office. He knew that he had worked as hard or harder than anyone else in his shop for the past month.

In spite of his intense anger, he continued to show up for work the following month, working even harder than he had the month before. At the end of the following month, he again sat in the Chief's office, and he again received the same poor evaluation. He returned to the house after work, enraged at the unfair treatment he had received. He entered the living room, where Dan was rolling a joint and drinking a beer.

"Any more beer in the fridge?" he asked in an agitated voice.

"Yeah, man," Dan replied. "Help yourself."

He went into the kitchen and grabbed a beer, twisting off the cap and downing half of it on his way back to the living room, where Dan had just lit the joint he had rolled.

"Give me a hit of that," he demanded.

"What?" Dan replied in shock, knowing that Sam hadn't smoked any weed or drank as much as one beer since returning. "Are you serious?"

"Yeah, I'm serious," Sam insisted. "Screw it, man. I'm done with these morons."

He explained what had happened in the Chief's office and how poor his evaluations had been since returning to the ship. Dan had worked alongside him every day throughout this time, and he knew how hard he had been working. He also knew that Sam had completely cleaned himself up. He had been a model citizen for two solid months, and Dan knew it.

"That's just not right, man," Dan replied, shaking his head. "So what are you gonna do?"

"What can I do?" Sam replied, exasperated. "Screw it, man. I'm gonna get high. If they wanna bust me and throw me out, then let em throw me out. I'm done playing their game."

"Welcome back," Dan said with a chuckle as he handed the joint to Sam.

The following morning, Sam was seething as he looked at the Chief. In the middle of roll call, a sailor from the medical staff entered the room and interrupted the Chief.

"Chief, I need to see Grace for a minute."

"For what?" the Chief replied.

"Random drug test."

"Grace?" the Chief called out.

"Yes, Chief," Sam replied.

"Go with this man. You're being taken for a random drug test."

"No problem, Chief," Sam replied. "I'd love to."

Sam knew that he would test positive for THC a second time, which would lead to his being discharged. In his anger of the treatment he had been receiving, he welcomed such an opportunity. He followed him to the medical unit eagerly, knowing that his time in the Navy was about to end.

"Take good care of this," he said sarcastically as he handed the specimen to the doctor. "It's my ticket out of here."

As he had expected, his test returned positive for THC. He was again placed on restriction until his discharge paperwork could be completed, at which time he was released from active service.

He said goodbye to the friends he had made, exchanging phone numbers and addresses and promising to keep in touch, and then left the ship for the last time, being escorted off of the Navy base by M.C.'s.

EIGHT

"Next stop, Asher," Gabriel bellowed, shaking Sam from yet another daydream.

He looked out his window at the approaching platform to see what appeared to be a large celebration. There were many people gathered around a row of large tables, which had been arranged in a rectangular pattern surrounding a center table, which was larger than the rest. From his seat in the train, he could see that there was a wide variety of meats on this table. Turkey, beef, chicken, lamb, and various types of sausages were there in abundance. On the surrounding tables he could see many types of complimentary side dishes. There were various salads, vegetables, fruit, breads, and deserts, all arranged on different tables according the types of food found upon each.

The tables were all underneath a large, tent-like covering, which looked to be made of white linen with braided purple strands hanging down from each corner.

The people on the platform appeared to be very happy, smiling and laughing as they wandered about and mingled, stopping to enjoy whatever delicacy they chose as they passed each table.

As the doors closed and the train began to move forward, Sam locked eyes with a well-dressed man standing in the center of the crowd. Smiling at first, the man's expression changed to one of apparent concern as he looked back at Sam through the glass.

"Excuse me, sir," Sam heard a woman's voice say from just in front of him.

He looked up to see a woman holding the arm of a very sickly looking man and assisting him to his seat. She was attempting to navigate down the aisle while dragging a cart which was holding an oxygen tank, the long hoses of which were wrapped around the man's arm, leading to a mask that was hanging around his neck.

"Oh, I'm sorry," Sam replied as he pulled his feet away from the aisle to allow them to pass.

Behind them was a man wearing what appeared to be a very expensive suit. He took off his jacket, draping it over the seat across the aisle from Sam, and then sat down, letting out a sigh as he relaxed back into it. Sam looked at his left wrist, upon which was a gold Rolex watch. Gold cufflinks adorned the cuffs of his shirt sleeves, and he was wearing a beautiful ring on his right hand, decorated with numerous expensive gems.

"Check out Johnny Gotrocks over here," Sam thought to himself.

He looked back toward the front of the car, where Gabriel was leafing through a newspaper.

"Hi, how are you?" he heard from his left, looking over to see the man who had just sat down reaching over to shake his hand. "I'm Matthew."

"Oh…hi," Sam replied, reaching over to shake his hand. "I'm Sam," he continued, not at all eager to start a conversation.

"What brings you here, Sam?"

"Oh, not much. Just traveling," he replied dismissively.

"I wish I could say that," Matthew replied with a grin. "I'm on yet another business trip."

"Business must be good," Sam replied, looking down at Matthew's watch.

"Oh, I don't know if it's all that good, but at least it's consistent."

"What type of business are you in?" Sam asked, not really caring.

"I work for the I.R.S.."

"Great," Sam thought to himself. "A flippin tax collector."

"You didn't come here to audit me, did you?"

"You caught me, Sam."

"Well, good luck with that, pal," Sam replied with a sarcastic smirk. "I haven't earned a dime in years."

"Yeah? Well, we all have to be made accountable at some point. We can't even die without having our accounts settled."

"What a jerk," Sam thought as he looked back at the man with the oxygen mask.

The last time he'd seen a man looking so ill was when he had seen his father passing away. He had just returned from his bad experience in the Navy. Seeing as how he had been thrown out due to drug abuse, his family was reluctant to give him a place to stay. After all, he had no car, no job, and no money, and if he were to get a job, their fear was that he'd simply use that money to buy drugs and fall back into his old habits. After pleading with them to let him stay long enough to get a job, his step-mother reluctantly agreed to let him sleep on their dining room floor with a few blankets until he could get a job and find his own place. It was on that first night that his step-mother, Ronnie, broke the news to him.

Over the past few years, his relationship with his father had deteriorated to the point where they'd rarely speak to one another. While he was in San Diego, Sam had reflected back upon the relationship he had with him over the years, and had come to the conclusion that they never really had much of one. He had only lived with him for the first six years of his life, most of which he couldn't remember. What he did remember was a very mixed bag. There were times when he felt as though they were close, but those times were scattered between many other times when he believed that his father wanted nothing to do with him. He never felt as though he measured up in his father's eyes, always being told by him that he was lazy and useless.

As he had grown older, into his teen years, the tension between them had grown even stronger. Sam was looking at his father's life, comparing it to his own, and began to resent his father's continual belittling of him while his own life was a complete and total mess. Seeing him as being nothing more than an angry, hostile, violent alcoholic who couldn't keep a job for any length of time, Sam started to believe that it was his father who needed to get his act together, not him.

"We need to talk, Sam," Ronnie said in a solemn voice.

"Sure," he replied. "What's up?"

"It's your father," she said with a pause. "He's not here, Sam. He's in the hospital…He's very ill."

"What do you mean?"

"He has lung cancer," she said, her eyes welling with tears.

"How bad is it?" he asked, stunned by the news.

"It's bad."

"How bad?"

"The doctor says he only has a few months to live. There's nothing they can do. He'll be coming back home tomorrow, but I don't know how long he'll be here."

Sam stepped back, running his hands through his hair and letting out a deep sigh.

"I don't even know what to say," he replied as his mind began to race.

"Sam," she said as she took his hand. "I know that you and your father have never been close. I know that you've had a lot of differences over the years. But you need to try to find a way to make things right."

"I don't know how to do that, Ronnie."

"I know, but you need to try."

Sam knew she was right. He knew that much work would need to be done, and many fences would need to be mended, if he and his father hoped to somehow heal their relationship. Being suddenly aware of how short their time was to do so made it that much more important to him.

The following morning, he got up early and walked to an area nearby where there were numerous strip malls, hoping to find a job. After filling out as many job applications as he could stand, he returned to his father's house.

"Is he here?" he asked Ronnie quietly as he entered the living room.

"Yes, he's in the bedroom."

Sam walked into his father's bedroom and sat on the edge of his bed where his father was sleeping. He looked very ill, and he could tell that he had lost some weight.

"Hey dad," he said quietly. "How ya doin?"

Lee, startled from his sleep, looked over at him as his eyes began to adjust.

"Oh…it's you," Lee said with a look of disgust. "So they kicked you out, huh?"

"Yeah, they did," Sam replied, not wanting to get into it.

"How are you feeling, dad?"

"I feel like crap. How do you expect me to feel?" he snapped back.

"Can I get you anything?"

"Can you get me anything? Yes, you can!" Lee replied, his voice getting louder. "You can go out there and get a job!" You'd better not think you're gonna just sit around here doing nothing!"

Sam stared at him for a few seconds, his heart beginning to race as he felt the anger building through him.

"Dad," he said with a pause. "I know I screwed up, ok?"

"You sure did."

"I'm gonna make it right, dad. I was out filling out job applications for hours today. I'll find a job and I'll get back on my feet."

"You'd better do it quick, Sam!" he replied, his face red with anger. "You're lucky your step-mother allowed you to sleep on the floor! If it were up to me, I would've thrown you out in the street so you could live like the lazy bum that you are!"

"Alright, dad," Sam replied in exasperation. "I'm gonna go."

With that he stood up and left the room, feeling as though he wanted to put his fist through the wall.

"What happened?" Ronnie asked, seeing the anger in his face.

"What happened?" he replied in an exaggerated tone. "What happened is what has always happened! He acted like a jerk and started talking to me like I'm some kind of loser! Same old story!"

"Sam," she replied, taking him by the arm as he tried to walk around her. "He's very sick."

"I know that!"

"He's crabby because he's not feeling well. You have to try."

"I am trying, Ronnie, but I can't be the only one who's trying. He has to at least meet me halfway."

Over the next few months, Lee became more ill. He was eventually admitted to the local hospital where he could receive more care. Sam got a job in the stockroom of a local warehouse and was able to find a small apartment. He tried repeatedly to make amends with his father during that time, but it was clear to him that Lee wanted no part of it. All of their conversations felt forced and unnatural. There was simply no relationship between them to be restored. Feeling a very deep sense that he needed to try again, he stopped by the hospital to visit.

As he entered the room, he said hello to his aunts and uncles; the siblings of his father who he truly admired and respected.

"Hey dad," he said as he walked around the foot of the bed. "How are you feeling?"

Lee seethed at him from his bed, his eyebrows furrowed in anger as he stared at him.

"What are you doing here?" he demanded.

"I came by to visit, dad. I wanted to see how you're doing."

"I see you're still smoking," Lee snapped, noticing the pack of cigarettes in Sam's shirt pocket.

"Yeah, I know," Sam replied. "I gotta quit."

"Did you get a job yet?" Lee demanded.

"Yeah...I did, dad," he replied, becoming angry at Lee's attitude.

"Your hair is too long!" he snapped back. "Why don't you go get a haircut? You look like a slob."

Sam stopped in his tracks, staring at his father in disbelief that he would be talking to him in this manner.

"What?" Lee barked. "You got nothing to say?"

"You know what?" Sam replied with a sigh, waving his hand at Lee in a dismissive gesture. "I'm gonna get out of here, dad. I'll see you later."

As he left the hospital, he decided that he would never return. He could see no reason why he should continue to visit only to be treated with so much disrespect. If his father, even in his current condition, wanted no part of having any sort of a relationship with him, then why should he try?

As the weeks passed, Lee became more and more ill. Ronnie began calling Sam every few days, urgently trying to convince him to see his father before he passed away. He never did until Lee had finally slipped into a coma. At that point, knowing that he didn't have to fear being verbally assaulted, Sam returned one last time.

Upon entering the room, he saw a mere shell of the man he knew. Once being a 6'4", 265lb bar room brawler, he had dropped to 150lbs. He had an oxygen mask covering his face, and his chest would heave off of the bed with every breath. Sam took a seat at the front of the bed, staring at this shocking sight. He stayed for about 10 minutes, watching in disbelief as every breath seemed to take longer than the last one, waiting for the breathing to stop. He returned home and cried, knowing that he would never speak to his father again. As strained and as painful as their relationship had always been, he knew that there was still one thing he could do to at least find some form of closure. He decided that he would return to his father's room the following morning and ask to be left alone with him. He decided that he would then take his father by the hand and tell him that even though they've had their struggles over the years, he still loved him. He believed that his father would somehow be able to feel his touch and hear his words, and maybe, just maybe, both of them would find some peace in that moment. His father had always been the one who had control over their relationship, never allowing it to be a close one, but Sam knew that if he was able to do this one thing, he would be in control of how their relationship ended, and it would end with kind words of love.

He awoke the next morning, his mind immediately processing the words he would say and how he would say them. He began to speak the words aloud, as though he were rehearsing for a public speech of some sort. He didn't want to upset his father, so he needed to choose his words carefully. He knew these would be the last words he would ever speak to him, and that he would remember those words for the remainder of his life, so he wanted them to be perfect. He made himself a quick breakfast, took a shower, and had started to get dressed when the phone rang.

"Hello?"

"Sam...it's Ronnie."

"Hi Ronnie. What's up?"

"Sam...your father is gone."

The room started to spin as her words rang through his mind with, mixing with an incredibly deep sense of sadness and rage.

"Noooooo!" he cried out, throwing the phone across the room and collapsing in a heap next to his bed.

He knew at that very moment that any hope of having any form of closure or resolution between he and his father had been crushed. It was gone forever. He realized that the final conversation he and his father had would forever be one filled with his father's contempt, disgust and hatred. His body doubled over in spasms as the tears poured from his eyes, letting out guttural moans as he grasped at the air. He felt as though his entire world had just fallen down around him, crushing him in the process.

"Dad!" he cried out into the air. "Why, dad?! Why couldn't you give me just this one thing?!"

He remained on the floor, sobbing uncontrollably for hours, unable to lift himself to his feet. He spent the remainder of the day alone, refusing to answer his phone. Friends and family members attempted to call him throughout the day, but he had no desire to speak to anyone.

When the day of Lee's wake arrived, he drove to the funeral home and parked in the lot, staring at the building and wondering if he should even go inside. There was nothing there he wanted to see. His father was gone, and the only thing he'd see inside would be his father's lifeless body; a visual reminder that all hope had been lost. He knew that he had to be there out of respect for his father and his family, but he wanted no part of it. He remained in his car for another fifteen minutes, smoked one last cigarette, and then pulled himself together and went inside.

He felt numb as he was greeted by various friends and family members who offered their condolences. He then walked to the side of the room and stared silently at the casket for a few minutes. He could see the face of the man inside, but this man bared no resemblance of the father he knew. It was as if someone had removed his father's body and replaced it with the body of a far smaller, less imposing, and much older man.

"Hey," Sam heard a man's voice say from his side.

He turned to see his brother, Little Lee, and gave him a hug.

"How are you?" Lee said in a quiet voice.

"I've been better, bro."

"Yeah, I know. Me too."

They stood in silence for a few minutes, neither of them knowing what to say to each other.

"Have you gone up there to say goodbye?" Lee asked quietly.

"No," Sam replied, looking back at the casket.

"Do you want to go up there with me?" Lee asked.

"No...I can't, bro...That's not Dad."

"What do you mean?"

"That's not Dad, Lee...That's just his body...He's gone."

"Yeah, you're right, little brother. It really doesn't even look like Dad, you know?"

"No, it doesn't."

"Alright, well, I'm gonna go up there, ok? I'll be back in a few minutes."

Sam nodded and watched as Little Lee approached the casket. He could tell that he was beginning to cry – a sight that he didn't want to see – so he turned away and walked outside. He took a seat on the front steps of the funeral home and lit up a smoke when he heard someone approach him from behind.

"Hey, bro," his sister, Suzanne, said softly as she sat down next to him and put her arm around him.

"Hey, sis."

"Are you ok?" she asked quietly.

"Yeah, I guess so...As good as can be expected under the circumstances."

"Yeah, I know what you mean."

"So this is how it all ends, huh?" he said, shaking his head. "Ashes to ashes, dust to dust. Not with a bang, but with a whimper. This enormous beast of a man, reduced to nothing."

"Sam, I want you to know something, ok?"

"What's that?"

"I talked to Dad while he was in a coma. I talked to him about God and how Jesus died for his sins, and I explained to him about how all he needed to do is confess that he was a sinner in need of forgiveness. I said that it's never too late in a person's life to turn to the Lord with their whole heart, asking to be forgiven."

"Sis," Sam interrupted. "You know that I love you, and I mean no disrespect, but I don't believe any of that crap."

"I'm sorry, Sam....I know...I guess I was just trying to make you feel a little bit better." she said quietly as she rubbed his shoulders.

"Thank you, but I just don't buy it, sis. I mean, how could a loving God allow things like cancer to destroy people like that? How could a loving God cause people to suffer so horribly? How could a loving God allow you and I to go through everything we've gone through?"

"We live in a fallen world, Sam."

"So that's the answer?"

"God didn't want us to fall into sin, but we did."

"Well, I'm sorry sis, but I don't want any part of a God who would allow so much suffering. I don't believe there *is* a God, and if there is, he's not one I want to know."

The two of them sat in silence for a few minutes, Suzanne continuing to rub Sam's shoulders.

"I'm sorry, sis. I'm just upset, you know?" Sam said as he put his arm around her.

"I know, Sam. It's ok. I'm gonna go back inside, alright?"

"Alright...I'll be in there in a few minutes. I just need to clear my head a bit."

As she walked away, Sam's mind started to wander. He reflected upon his father's life, how it was spent, how it had ended, and began to think about the very different life he wanted for himself. While he saw many differences between he and his father, he could also see some similarities. As he pondered what he really wanted in his own life, he began to realize that he just wanted the simple things that most people take for granted. He didn't want to be rich or famous. He didn't want fancy cars or an enormous bank account. He simply wanted to feel normal. He wanted to fall in love, to someday have a wife who loved him, some kids, and the suburban house with the white picket fence. He just wanted to feel like everyone else. His life up to this point was a severely chaotic stew of dysfunction and drama, some of it self-imposed, and some of it brought into his life by others. He didn't want any more drama. He simply wanted peace.

He began to think about Angela, and how much he still loved her. A few days after his father was buried, he began to look for her. He tried to find her phone number, but had no luck. He searched for her address, but could find nothing. He drove down to the neighborhood where they had met, hoping that by some chance of fate he'd see her. He drove to the restaurant where they had worked together and went inside, asking if anybody knew where she might be, but nobody remembered her. After all, it had been four years since she worked there and most of the staff was new. He drove down the street where they had first held hands, to the apartment where she used to live, and to the last place he knew she had worked, but found nothing but memories. He drove to where he remembered her sister's house being, but it had been so long since he had been there, and the homes all looked the same. He drove up and down the street numerous times, trying to find something, anything that would spark a memory of which house it was, but found nothing.

With no options left, he drove to a popular mall in the neighborhood and sat down in the food court, watching the countless people walking back and forth, hoping to somehow find her in the crowd. After staying there for a couple of hours, he gave up and returned home. He repeated this search a number of times over the next six months, but never found a trace of her.

One day, as he was digging through his belongings, he found an old phone book that he had taken with him when he had joined the service. He flipped through the pages hoping to find anything he could use to help him find her, but again he found nothing.

As he looked through the names and numbers he had jotted down, he came across the phone number of another girl, Kim, who he knew from the old neighborhood. They were never very close, but he remembered her as being a very pretty girl, and they always enjoyed being around each other on the rare occasion that they were. It had been at least four years since he had spoken to her, so he didn't know if the number was still good. He picked up the phone and dialed.

"Hello?" a woman's voice answered.

"Hello. Kim?"

"Yes."

"Kim Cooper?"

"Yes, who is this?"

"Hi Kim. It's Sam. Sam Grace. Do you remember me?"

"Sam?" she responded with a laugh. "Of course I remember you, Sam! How are you?"

"I'm good. How about yourself?"

"I'm good. It's been...what...4 or 5 years since I've talked to you?"

"Yeah, something like that."

"What have you been doing with yourself, Sam?"

"Well, I joined the Navy since we last talked."

"You did? she said with a chuckle. "I've never thought of you as being the military type."

"Yeah, well, apparently I'm not."

"Are you still in?"

"No...we...uh... we had a bit of a falling out, the Navy and I. Let's just say we were divorced due to irreconcilable differences."

"I see. So how long have you been out?"

"About six months now."

"Where were you stationed? Are you back in the area now?"

"I was in San Diego for my entire tour, but yes, I'm back home now. How about you? What have you been up to?"

"Well, I went to Western and earned my degree in business management."

"Wow! That's amazing! Congratulations!"

"Yeah, it was a big accomplishment for me. I'm living back with my parents now. I found a job at a company nearby, but I'm looking for something better."

"Well, let me ask you something if you don't mind."

"Sure."

"Are you seeing anyone?"

"Um...no," she replied hesitantly.

"How would you feel about going on a date?"

"Um...I don't know, Sam," she said cautiously as the tone of her voice changed to one of skepticism.

"Hey, look at it this way," he replied enthusiastically. "You haven't seen me in over four years, right?"

"Right..."

"So for all you know, I could be an absolute slob, right?"

"Okay...," she said with a chuckle.

"But on the other hand, I haven't seen you in over four years either, so you could be an absolute slob too. It'll be just like a blind date!"

"I guess you're right, Sam," she replied with laughter. "Alright, let's do it!"

"Great! Does this Friday work for you?"

"Sure, what time?"

"I can pick you up around 7. Is that okay?"

"Sure is."

"Great! I'll see you then, Kim."

"Sounds good, Sam. I'll see you then."

Sam couldn't wait for Friday to come. He was hoping that Kim was still as hot as he remembered her being. He found himself staring at the clock all day at work that Friday, and as soon as the whistle blew, he drove home as fast as he could, took a shower, put on his best clothes and cologne, and then headed to Kim's house, stopping to pick up a red rose on the way. He could feel his palms beginning to sweat as he approached the front door and knocked. Kim's mother opened the door and peeked around the corner.

"Hello?" she said with a smile.

"Mrs. Cooper?" he replied nervously.

"Yes."

"Hi, I'm Sam. I'm here to pick up Kim."

"Oh, come on in, Sam. Kim will be down in a minute. She's still getting ready." "Thank you," he said as he stepped inside.

"I'll be right back, Sam. Make yourself comfortable."

"Thank you."

Kim's mother rushed upstairs and barged into Kim's room, closing the door behind her.

"Oh my God!" she said in an excited voice as she grabbed her by the hands.

"What?" Kim replied excitedly.

"He's absolutely gorgeous!"

"Are you serious?"

"Yes, I'm serious! Come on! Hurry up!"

"I will, mom!" she replied, laughing.

She glanced in her mirror one last time, quickly fixing her hair, and then followed her mother downstairs.

"Hi Sam!" she said with a wide smile as she entered the room.

"Hi Kim!" he replied, jumping to his feet and walking over to give her a hug.

"Wow!" he said with a broad smile. "Look at you! You look beautiful!"

"Why thank you," she replied, grinning ear to ear. "You're not so bad yourself," she continued, looking back at her mother with her jaw dropped open.

"Well, shall we?" he asked as he offered her his arm.

"Yes, we shall," she replied as she took it and followed him toward the door.

"Have a good time, kids!" her mother said excitedly as she saw them out.

Sam walked her to the car, opening her door for her as she climbed inside.

"Are you hungry?" he asked as he got behind the wheel.

"I'm starving!"

"Do you like Italian?"

"I do!"

"Good, because I thought we could get some Mexican."

"Mexican food gives me horrible gas."

"Chinese it is, then!"

Sounds great! I love Chinese food.

Sam was very impressed with how beautiful she was, He found himself continually looking over at her while he was driving. So much so, in fact, that he nearly ran over a row of mailboxes while staring at her.

"Whoa there, big guy!" she said nervously as he jerked the wheel to the left.

"Sorry," he replied. "I'm a very good driver...I really am."

"I can see that," she replied sarcastically.

"I was...well...to be honest, I was staring at you."

"Why? Is there something in my teeth?"

"No."

"Ear wax? I have ear wax, don't I."

"No, that's not it either. It's something else."

"My hair? Did my hair get all funky or something?" she said with a coy smile as she flipped down the visor to take a look in the mirror.

"No…I just can't get over how beautiful you are."

"Awe, who? Little old me?" she replied, batting her eyelashes.

"Ok…don't do that."

"Why not?"

"It's kinda creepy."

"Oh, ok. Is this better?" she said as she ran her hand through her hair and leaned back against the window, striking a slightly seductive pose.

"No, you *definitely* can't do that!"

"Why not?"

Because I'll crash, and we'll die."

"That would be a very disappointing first date."

"Indeed."

"And then I'd never get the chance to decide if I'd like to have a second."

"Whoa, lady! You're moving a little fast, aren't you? I mean, I haven't even seen you eat yet. What if you have horrible table manners?"

"Would that be a deal breaker?"

"I guess it depends on how bad they are."

"Alright. I'll try not to chew with my mouth open."

"Good plan."

"It's always good to have a good plan."

"Indeed."

"So, how did you like your time in the Navy?"

"Eh…," he answered, shrugging his shoulders.

"Eh…?"

"The accommodations were lousy, but at least the food was horrible."

"Well, it's always good to be able to look at the bright side. Did you see many places?"

"Not really. My ship didn't travel much. We went up to Seattle for a while. While I was there I was able to explore Victoria, British Columbia a bit. On the way back down we stopped in San Francisco for a few days, then headed to Mazatlán, Mexico."

"Oooh…a world traveler, huh? That's sexy."

"Well, what can I say? I try my best to strap on as much sexy as I can."

"I don't think you really need to try too hard."

"No?"

"No…I think the sexy just kinda pours out of you."

"Are you flirting with me?"

"Maybe I am."

"Hmm…Ok…I guess I might be able to overlook a few bad table manners."

"That would be very big of you."

"What can I say? I'm a giver."

"Apparently."

They were both really starting to enjoy each other's company. It was still very early into their date, but Sam was feeling a sense of comfort with her, as she was with him. That comfort only grew more throughout their dinner. Neither of them wanted the date to end, so once they had left the restaurant, they headed to a local dance club nearby. After having a few drinks and dancing until they were exhausted, they decided it was time to go home. Sam parked the car in front of her house and walked her to the front door.

"Hey, I had a really nice time tonight," he said as they paused on the stairway.

"Yeah, I did too," she replied with a warm smile as she turned to look at him.

"I'd like to do this again soon."

"Ah…so I guess I should assume that my table manners were up to snuff?"

"They were impeccable. I only saw you put your elbows on the table once."

"What can I say? she said with a playful smile. "I aim to please."

"Do you want to go out again, say, next Friday?"

"Sure, I'd really like that."

"Okay then, let's do that."

Sam began to feel a sense of awkward nervousness from wanting very badly to lean in and kiss her, but not being sure if she wanted the same.

"Um...Sam?" she said after a few seconds of awkward silence.

"Yeah?"

"Are you just gonna stand there like a dork or are you gonna kiss me?"

"I think I'm gonna kiss you," he replied as he leaned in, giving her a soft, slow kiss.

"Mmmm. That was nice," she said with a smile.

"Yeah...it was ok, I guess."

"Get outta here, you jerk!" she said, playfully smacking him on the shoulder.

"Alright, I'm gonna take off. Have a good night, Kim."

"You too Sam. Drive carefully."

Kim walked inside, leaned against it with her back, and let out a heavy sigh.

"Kim?" her mom called as she walked quickly toward the living room.

"Yes?"

"How did it go?! Tell me everything?!" she asked excitedly.

"I think I'm in love, mom."

"Really?" she replied. 'You had a good time?"

"Oh mom, we had such a good time. He's amazing!"

Sam walked back to his car feeling as though he were walking on air. He let out an enthusiastic shout as soon as he was far enough away from her home so that she couldn't hear. He couldn't wait to see her again, and he began thinking of plans for their second date before he had driven a city block.

The following Friday arrived, and their second date went even better than their first, as did their third and fourth. They fell very much in love with each other, and after dating for a little over a year, Sam stopped by her home while she was at work. Her father answered the door, which was exactly what Sam wanted to have happen.

"Oh hi, Sam. Kim isn't home right now," he said as he opened the door.

"I know, Mr. Cooper. I actually came here to talk to you," he replied nervously.

"Oh, ok. Come on in."

The two of them entered the home and took a seat at the dining room table.

"What can I do for you, Sam?"

"Well, Mr. Cooper, Kim and I have been dating for a little over a year now. I think she's an amazing woman, and I'm very much in love with her."

"But...?" her father asked cautiously.

"No, there's no buts, Mr. Cooper. I actually came by because I'd like to ask for your permission to marry your daughter."

"I see...," he replied, sitting back into his chair.

"You see?"

"Yes," he replied, offering no further answer.

"Well, how would you feel about that?" Sam asked, growing more nervous with every passing second.

"I don't know, Sam."

"You don't know?"

"No, I don't know. You see, I've lived with Kim throughout her entire life. I'm afraid that if you married her, she may just drive you completely out of your mind. She's not right in the head, Sam."

"With all due respect, Mr. Cooper, have you taken a good look at the guy who's asking to marry her? I mean, let's be honest here. I'm not exactly someone you'd want to elect as the president."

"Valid point, Sam," he replied as a smile broke on his face. "You're not right in the head either. If the two of you ever had children, God help us all."

"I'd promise to provide whatever therapy would be necessary, sir."

"Absolutely, Sam!" he said with a wide smile as he leaned forward to shake his hand. "I'd be honored to have you marry my daughter, Sam, and I'd be honored to call you my son-in-law."

"Thank so much, Mr. Cooper!" Sam said with an enormous smile on his face. "You scared me for a few minutes there. I thought I might have to bring the ring back, which would be impossible because I bought it from a street vendor."

"That's one of the things I've always liked about you, Sam. You're very practical."

Sam left, returning a few hours later to propose to Kim. He had been rehearsing his proposal for weeks, and he knew that it was time. He waited until he knew that her family would be finished eating dinner, and then returned.

"Hi, baby!" Kim said with a smile as she opened the door. "I didn't expect you to stop by tonight. To what do I owe this unexpected pleasure?" she continued as she wrapped her arms around his neck and gave him a kiss.

"Oh, I was in the neighborhood, so I thought I'd stop by. Do you feel like grabbing a cup of coffee or something?"

"Sure. Come on in for a second while I change."

"Hi, Mr. and Mrs. Cooper," he said with a smile, acting as though he hadn't seen them earlier.

"Hi Sam, how've you been?" Mr. Cooper replied, playing along.

"I'm good. I was in the neighborhood, so I thought I'd drop by to see if Kim wanted to go out for a cup of coffee."

"You were in the neighborhood?" he asked with a devilish grin.

"Yeah."

"But you live 20 miles away. What brought you into this neighborhood?"

Sam stared at him with a stunned expression, having no idea how to answer his question. He looked up the stairway to make sure that Kim couldn't hear their conversation and then leaned back toward him.

"I heard there was a professional smart-ass living in the neighborhood, so I drove down to see if I could find him. And look at that, will ya? I just did. Wow! It must be a Christmas miracle."

"Are you ready, babe?" Kim asked as she started back downstairs.

"Absolutely!" Sam replied with a smile.

"Have fun, kids! Don't do anything crazy!" Mr. Cooper said with a sarcastic grin as they headed out the doorway.

Sam's palms began to sweat as he drove to the local coffee shop. He kept repeating the words he had memorized in his mind. He was pretty sure that Kim would accept his proposal, but he didn't know for certain. His stomach was in knots by the time they arrived.

"Are you ok, babe?" she asked as they sat down at the table, reaching across it to hold his hand.

"Yeah...yeah. Why do you ask?"

"I don't know. You just seem really distracted. Is there something on your mind?"

"Well, to be honest, there is."

"Do you want to talk about it?" she asked with a concerned expression.

"Baby...," he began, pausing for a few seconds to collect his thoughts. He then brought both of his hands forward, holding both of hers and looking her in the eyes.

"We've been together for a while now. I think it's safe to say that there's nothing we don't know about each other. This past year has been amazing. I've enjoyed every single moment I've been able to spend with you."

"I have too, Sam," she said as her eyes began to well up with tears.

"Look...I'm not a perfect man by any means. We both know this," he continued. "Sometimes I talk too much. Sometimes I think too much. I can be an irresponsible dreamer at times. I can be annoying. I came from a working-class family, I have no degrees, and I've never accomplished anything to speak of. I'll probably never be rich or famous, but this much I know: I simply love you with all that I am. You are the most beautiful, precious woman in the world to me, and I can't imagine living a life that you're not a part of. I absolutely adore you with all of my heart, with all of my soul, and with all of my strength."

He then let go of her hand to pull a ring from his pocket, got up from his seat, and kneeled next to her.

"Oh Sam, I love you so very much," she said, bursting into tears.

"Baby, I know that I can't promise you much. But I can promise you this: If you will agree to be my wife, I will love you for the rest of my life. I will take care of you to the absolute best of my ability, and I will spend the rest of my days loving you more than any other man could possibly love any other woman. So what do you say, baby? Will you marry me?"

"Yes, Sam!" she cried out. "Yes, yes, yes, yes, yes!"

Sam put the ring on her finger, and then stood with her, wrapping his arms around her and holding her as tightly as he could.

"I love you so very much, Sam!" she said as she wrapped her arms around him and began kissing him repeatedly on the neck. "I love you with all my heart."

They planned to have a simple, humble wedding they could afford, saving as much money as possible over the next six months. The wedding was held in a public park where they had spent many days laying on a blanket, talking, and looking out over the small lake at its center. Both of their families helped out as much as they could, her mother making homemade center pieces for the tables and decorations to hang from the many trees which surrounded the small clearing where the tables were placed. It was obvious to everyone in attendance that they were very much in love, and nobody doubted that it would be a marriage that would last forever.

They moved into a slightly larger apartment in the northwest suburbs of Chicago, where Kim began to immediately replace Sam's bachelor décor with a more appealing, although slightly more feminine one.

Sam got a job driving a truck for a local municipality, doing construction work during the summer months and plowing snow through the winter. Kim got a better job with more pay than her prior job at a local logistics company just a few miles from home.

After living there for a few months, Kim began to feel slightly ill. It began in the early morning hours when she first awoke. She was experiencing slight nausea for the first few hours of the day, but it would subside before afternoon.

"Sam...," she said one morning as he was pouring her a cup of coffee. "I haven't been feeling well lately."

"No?...What's wrong, baby?"

"I don't know. I've just been feeling a little nauseous every morning."

"For how long?"

"Just for the past few days…maybe the past week."

"Hmm…Maybe you're pregnant," he said with a chuckle.

"Don't even joke about that!"

"I'm sorry. Do you think you should go to the doctor?"

"I don't know. It's not that bad. I've just been a little nauseous. It usually goes away within a few hours."

"Have you tried taking anything?"

"Yeah, I've tried some antacids. They seem to help a little bit."

"Well, maybe you should set up an appointment."

"Yeah, maybe I will. We'll see."

After Sam had left for work, Kim began thinking things over. "Maybe I am pregnant," she thought to herself. She thought that if she was, the timing would be terrible. After all, she had just started a new job, and where would a baby sleep in their small apartment? As the day wore on, she started to think about it more positively. She had always wanted to have children someday. Not right at the moment, but someday. She knew that she and Sam were very much in love, and many thoughts began to enter her mind about how beautiful it would be to have a child with him. She began to daydream about having a little girl, playing dress up, having tea parties, buying her pretty little dresses, fixing her hair and making her feel beautiful. Her thoughts would then shift to having a little boy, watching him play baseball, seeing Sam playing catch with him in the front yard, buying him toy cars and trucks. She thought about how should would decorate each of their rooms, and how much fun it would be to work with Sam picking out various wall colors, bedspreads, furniture and decorations.

By the end of the day, she had nearly convinced herself that she wanted to be pregnant.

She stopped by the local drug store on her way home from work and bought a pregnancy test, not telling Sam what she had done, but wanting to surprise him with the news if the test came out positive.

The following morning, while Sam was having his first cup of coffee, she took the test from her purse and took it into the bathroom. Her hands were shaking with nervous excitement as she pulled it from the package. After reading the instructions very carefully, she used it and then waited with great anticipation for the results to show up. After waiting as long as she could stand, she picked it up and looked at it.

"Oh my God!" she nearly shrieked as the positive result showed up.

"Are you okay in there, baby?" Sam called out, looking over his coffee.

"Yeah…um…I'm fine," she replied, covering her mouth with her hand and trying to pull herself together.

She put the test in her pocket, cleared her throat, took a deep breath, and opened the bathroom door. She walked over to where Sam was enjoying his coffee, slid it away from the edge of the table, and sat on his lap facing him. She then put her arms around his shoulders and began playfully kissing his neck, hiding her face behind her hair.

"Well, good morning to you too, beautiful," he said with a smile as he put his hands on her waist.

"Sam?" she whispered in his ear while continuing to kiss him.

"Yeah, baby."

"Do you love me?"

"Of course I love you, baby. More than anything in the world."

"Do you have any idea how much I love you?"

"I think so. Why do you ask? Did something change that I'm not aware of?"

"Well, yes. A little bit," she replied, sitting back to look into his eyes while pulling the pregnancy test from her pocket.

"You're gonna be a daddy," she said with a smile, holding the pregnancy test in front of his eyes.

"Oh my God!" Sam shouted as he jumped to his feet, nearly dropping her on the floor.

A sense of absolute panic set in immediately as he began pacing back and forth through their living room, nervously running his hands through his hair.

"Are you sure?!" he asked in a loud voice as he raced toward her. "Did you read it right?!"

"Sam," she said with a chuckle. "I'm a college graduate. I think I can read a pregnancy test."

"Oh my God!" he repeated. "You mean I'm gonna?...you're gonna?...we're gonna?.."

"Yes, Sam," she said as she put her arms around his neck and looked him in the eyes. "We're gonna have a baby."

"We're gonna have a baby," he repeated back to her with a stunned expression.

"Yeah...we're gonna have a baby," she replied, pulling him close to kiss him.

"Oh my God," he said again. "I love you so very much, baby."

Sam had to leave for work, so he hugged her tightly, kissing her repeatedly before walking out the door. He spent his entire day at work with his mind racing back and forth from thoughts of sheer panic to thoughts of incredible joy. He was very much in love with Kim and he loved the idea of having a child with her, but he had no idea how to be a father. There was no fatherly role model he could look back upon to form his ideas of what kind of a father he should be. He knew deep within his heart that he didn't have a clue. He thought about Kim all day long and how much he loved her. He couldn't wait to get back home so he could see her again. He drove home as quickly as he could as soon as he had left work, and then paced back and forth through their apartment continually looking at the clock until she arrived. He ran to the door as soon as he heard it open, wrapping his arms around her and hugging her so tightly she could barely breathe.

"Let me go, you crazy person!" she shouted with a laugh, struggling to get free.

"Hey there, baby!" he said with a smile, giving her a kiss.

"And hello to you too, baby!" he said with a chuckle as he bent down to kiss her belly.

"You are such a nut," she replied, laughing.

"I know. But hey, you knew what you were getting into when you married me."

"Not really," she said, rolling her eyes.

"Hey...guess what?" he said playfully.

"What?"

"We're gonna have a baby!"

"I know," she replied with a wide smile. "Isn't that beautiful?"

"It sure is," he said as he pulled her close and looked her in the eyes. "I can't think of anyone in the world who I'd rather have a baby with."

"Nobody?"

"Well, almost nobody," he replied nonchalantly. "There *was* this one girl..."

"Stop it!" she said, playfully pushing him away.

"No, I'm serious, baby. I'm so happy right now I could scream."

"Really?"

"Yes, really. I love you so very much, and If we have a girl, I'd want her to be almost as beautiful as you."

"Almost?...Why almost?"

"Because it would be impossible for anyone to be *as* beautiful as you."

"Awe, thank you. You are so incredibly sweet to me."

"Yeah, I'm pretty cool that way, no?"

"Yes, you are."

"And if we have a boy, I'd want him to be almost as tall, handsome, charming, witty, personable, confident, intelligent, loyal, faithful, strapping, kind, loving, and compassionate as me."

"Ahh, see? That's what attracted me to you...Your humility."

"Oh, that's right...I left out humble."

"I wonder why?"

"A mere oversight, my dear."

"Apparently."

"But all kidding aside...I couldn't be happier, baby."

"Are you sure?"

"Yes, I'm sure."

"You seemed pretty nervous about it this morning."

"I was...I mean, I am. But I'm happy at the same time."

"I know what you mean. I'm a little nervous too. I really wasn't ready for this right now, but then again, I guess nobody really feels like they are when it happens unexpectedly like this."

"It's just that...I don't think I know how to be a dad."

"Why would you say that?" she asked with a concerned expression as she pulled him closer.

"I don't know, baby. I just never had a dad who I could've learned all of that stuff from. You know my story. It's just hard for me to wrap my mind around all of this. I don't want to fail."

"Sam...I have so much confidence in you."

"Yeah?"

"Yeah...You're an amazing man, and you're an amazing husband. I have no doubt that you'll be equally as amazing as a father."

"Thank you, baby. That means a lot to me."

"I know how much you love me, and I know you'll love this baby just as much if not more. You're gonna be fine. Better than fine. You're gonna be awesome."

Over the next few weeks, Sam began to read everything he could get his hands on that dealt with pregnancy and parenthood. He doted over Kim as much as he possibly could, always being concerned about whether she was eating right, getting enough rest, and taking good care of herself. They both continued to work every day, and would then spend their evenings together either reading and discussing articles about the baby's growth progress or coming up with ideas on how to decorate the corner of their bedroom where the baby would eventually sleep. After a few months, they learned that their baby was a boy. Sam made a daily habit of putting his face close to Kim's stomach and talking to his son, reading him bedtime stories and saying things like "Hey, clean your womb." The closer they came to the delivery date, the more convinced Kim was that he was going to be an excellent father. When they were within a few weeks of the day, they packed a suitcase containing everything that she might need during her hospital stay. They placed it on the floor of the bedroom closet, leaving the door open so it was in plain view and wouldn't be forgotten when the moment arrived.

Three days before the expected delivery date, Sam came home exhausted from a long day of construction work. They were in the midst of a major project at work, and the weather was not cooperating, blasting them with temperatures in the upper 90's for the past few weeks. He took a cool shower as soon as he got home, had some dinner, and then decided to go to bed early. Tomorrow was going to be another long, hot day, and he wanted to get plenty of rest. He was awakened a few hours later by a nudge from Kim.

"Sam?" she said quietly.
"Yeah, baby."
"It's time."

"Okay, baby," he replied, still half asleep. "I'm right here."

"No, Sam," she said a bit louder. "It's time!"

Sam threw the covers off and jumped to his feet immediately.

"It's time?!...Now?!"

"Yes...right now."

"Okay...um...we need to...what do you need?!" he replied in a panic.

"Calm down, Sam. It's okay. We have time. Just help me get up and bring me to the car. Then come back inside and get my suitcase."

Sam helped her to the car, and then ran back inside, frantically looking around to make sure he wasn't forgetting anything. He grabbed the suitcase on the way out and ran back to the car. His heart was pounding as he tried to focus on his driving, looking over at Kim continually.

"Watch the road, Sam," she said with a slight chuckle between contractions. "Remember our first date when you nearly ran over those mailboxes?"

"Yeah, I do."

"Yeah? Well, let's not do that, ok?"

Sam looked over at her again, thinking back to how she looked to him on that very first date. Quite a bit of time had passed since that night, and she was now 9 months pregnant and having contractions every few minutes. But in his eyes, she was just as beautiful now as she was back then. Maybe even more so.

Although it was only a ten minute drive, the ride to the hospital seemed to take forever. Red lights seemed to stay red for 20 minutes, and he didn't remember seeing any green ones the entire way. They finally arrived at the hospital and he parked the car next to the emergency entrance and then ran inside.

"My wife is having a baby!" he shouted at the nurse's desk as he stormed inside.

"Alright, sir," the nurse replied calmly. "Where is she?"

"She's in the car, right outside the door!"

"Alright. Don't bring her in. We'll bring a wheelchair out."

Sam ran back outside and opened the passenger side door, kneeling down next to Kim.

"Are you okay, baby?"

"Yes, I'm fine," she replied, taking a deep breath with a contraction.

"They're bringing a wheelchair for you. Just try to relax, okay?"

"I'm more relaxed than you, tough guy," she replied with a slight chuckle as the contraction subsided.

"Good point," he said with a laugh. "But then again, you've always been tougher than me."

"And don't you ever forget it."

"I'll try to keep that in mind."

Sam followed closely as the orderly helped her into the wheelchair and then brought her to the examination room. Within a few minutes, the nurse arrived and examined her.

"Well...," she said as she removed her gloves. "You're definitely in labor, but you have awhile to go yet. Your contractions are pretty far apart, and you're only slightly dilated. We're going to check you into a room and keep you here, okay?"

"Okay," Kim replied with a nervous smile. "Thank you."

Once they had checked her into her room, Sam grabbed a chair and pulled it up to the bed next to her, taking her hand as he sat.

"Sam?" Kim said in a soft voice.

"Yeah, baby."

"You heard what she said. It's gonna be awhile. I know you're very tired. Why don't you try to get some rest."

"No, I'm gonna stay right here by your side, baby. I'll be ok."

"You can stay here, but why don't you shut your eyes and get some rest?"

"Alright, I'll try. But I want you to tell me if you need anything, okay?"

"I will. I promise."

Sam sat back in his chair, still holding her hand, and stretched his legs out, trying to get comfortable. He closed his heavy eyes and tried to nod off, but he couldn't. Every time he would hear Kim's breathing start to increase, he would open his eyes to look at her, rubbing her hand in an effort to comfort her. Her contractions continued throughout the night and into the early morning. The nurse would come into the room to check on her from time to time, but she was making very little progress.

"Hey, baby," he whispered into her ear as the sunlight began to shine through the window. "I'm gonna go get a cup of coffee and maybe something out of the vending machine. Do you want anything?"

"No, babe. I'm fine. Maybe you could just bring me some ice chips on your way back."

"You got it," he replied, bending down to kiss her forehead.

Sam felt as though his legs weighed 1,000lbs as he made his way down the long corridor toward the vending machines. He paused briefly at the window leading into the nursery where all of the new babies were, peering inside and feeling anxious to hold his son for the first time. He bought a cup of vending machine coffee and a bag of chips, and then returned to the room, stopping to get some ice chips on his way.

"How ya feeling, baby?" he whispered quietly as he sat down next to the bed, taking Kim's hand.

"I've been better, but I'm okay," she replied with a warm smile.

"Are the contractions getting more painful?"

"Not really. I'm just very tired."

"I know, baby," he said, leaning over to kiss her forehead.

"Do you think you could do me a favor?" she asked.

"Of course, baby. What do you need?"

"Could you find a wash cloth, wet it with some cool water, and wipe my forehead?"

"Sure can," he replied, getting up and heading toward the bathroom.

"How's that?" he asked as he returned and placed the cool washcloth on her forehead, and then wiped it across her cheeks and neck.

"That feels wonderful. Thank you."

"You're welcome. I hope this little guy makes an appearance soon."

"I know. Me too. You must be so exhausted."

"No, that's not it, baby," he replied, blown away that she would even be thinking of him while going through this experience. "I just can't stand watching you in pain like this. It's like watching someone you love with all your heart being slowly tortured."

"Oh babe, I'll be okay. I'm sure we'll be able to hold our baby boy soon, and when we do it'll be worth every second of this."

Despite their wishes, the baby had other plans, refusing to come out. Her contractions grew more powerful and painful throughout the rest of the day, and then well into the following evening. Her doctor was becoming concerned with the length of her labor and the toll that it had to be taking on her body. He was afraid that she might be too exhausted to push when the time came if it continued much longer. During the early hours the following morning, he decided that they would have to take the baby via cesarean section. They moved her into the operating room and started to prep her, but just before they had begun, the baby decided it was time to arrive. After 36 hours of labor, Sam stood in awe as he held his only son for the very first time.

"Hey there, little guy," he said, looking down at his son and beaming with pride as his eyes welled up with tears. "Let's go see mommy."

He walked over to Kim's bedside and placed him carefully on her chest, sitting down next to her and feeling a sense of love that can only be fully understood by someone who had experienced the same.

"We're gonna go ahead and clean her up, Mr. Grace. She's gonna be a little while," the nurse said.

"I can't be with her?"

"No, you can't."

"Okay. Hey baby, I'm gonna go get something to eat while they fix you all up. Do you want me to get you anything?"

"No, I'll be okay. Go ahead and eat. I know you must be starving."

"Yeah, I've had enough vending machine snacks. I need to eat. I'll be right back, okay?" he said as he leaned over to kiss her cheek.

Sam left the room, and began pumping his fist in the air, half walking and half running as he made his way toward the exit.

"I'm a dad!" he shouted at a group of nurses as he ran by. "I'm a dad!"

"Congratulations!" one of them shouted back.

He climbed into his car feeling an incredible surge of adrenaline pumping through his body. He then drove to the nearest restaurant he could find and ordered a sandwich to go, devouring it in the car on the way back to the hospital.

By the time he returned to Kim's room, they had just finished cleaning her up and were about to wheel her into recovery.

"Hey there, beautiful," he said as he entered. "How are you feeling?"

"I'm okay," she replied with an exhausted smile.

"Where's our son?"

"They brought him to the nursery. They'll be bringing him back soon."

"Are we ready?" the nurse asked as she entered the room.

"We sure are!" Kim replied.

They wheeled her into the recovery room, and then left once they knew she was comfortable.

"Hey, babe. I know you're exhausted," Kim said as she looked over at Sam. "Why don't you lay next to me for a little while and rest before you drive home. I don't want you driving when you're this tired."

"Yeah, that's probably a good idea," he replied, climbing into the bed and putting his arm around her. "I love you, baby."

"I love you too, Sam."

Within just a few minutes they were both sound asleep, holding each other in their arms.

NINE

"Next stop, Issachar," Gabriel shouted, startling Sam.

He looked out through his window to see a station that was clearly under construction. A large concrete slab sat at the center of the job site, and there were many trucks and large pieces of construction equipment scattered around it. There was a man operating a backhoe, digging a horizontal trench along the far side, while a group of laborers cleaned around it with shovels. He saw a few more men lowering a large piece of pipe into another trench, while a man in a skid steer backfilled gravel over the top of the plumbing that had already been laid.

To his left, he watched as a group carpenters worked together to raise a newly framed wall into place. Standing in the center of the concrete slab was a man who was apparently the job foreman. He was a rugged, muscular man with a dark tan due to working outdoors during the heat of day for many years. It was clear to Sam that he was in charge. He was watching the crews work, walking over to each crew while pointing and barking out orders.

As the train once again began to move, the man walked over to a large orange water cooler, filled a cup, and then drank it down. As he poured himself another cup, he raised his eyes to look at Sam through the window, paused for a second, and then nodded at him. It was a strange nod, Sam thought. It wasn't a type of silent greeting, but one that was more of an acknowledgment one might give upon seeing that what was being done was right and good.

Sam turned and looked at the I.R.S. guy sitting across from him, who had fallen asleep. Not wanting to have any more conversations with him, he stood up quietly and walked to the back of the car where he took a seat in the last row, put his head back, and then closed his eyes.

"It feels like I've been on this train forever," he thought to himself, starting to feel a bit more nervous about his situation and being increasingly curious as to where it was heading.

He opened his eyes and looked down at his watch. "Huh…it still says it's 11:15," he mumbled under his breath. "Great…now my watch has stopped too."

He slapped it a few times to see if the hands would start to move again, but to no avail. He closed his eyes again, hoping to nod off for a little while.

"Hey there! How are you?" he heard a loud voice say from the front of the car, opening his eyes to see a short, enthusiastic man as he reached out to shake hands with Gabriel.

"James, my good friend!" Gabriel replied as he shook his hand. "How are you?"

"I'm doing well, Gabriel," he replied. "And you?"

"You know me, James. I'm just happy to be doing the Lord's work!"

"Fantastic," Sam muttered. "Gabriel must be a Jesus freak too. I swear these people are everywhere. Flippin lunatics."

"Make yourself comfortable, James," Gabriel

said enthusiastically. "It's good to see you!"

"Thank you, Gabriel. It's good to see you too!"

James made his way through the car, greeting everyone he passed along the way with a cheerful smile.

"Don't sit here. Don't sit here. Don't sit here," Sam thought to himself as James passed row after row of seats, eventually reaching the row where Sam was sitting.

"Hi! How are you?" he asked in a loud, enthusiastic voice, smiling as he looked at Sam.

"Hi," Sam replied indifferently.

"I'm James! What's your name?" he said as he reached out to shake Sam's hand.

"Sam," he replied, offering a half-hearted handshake and then turning away to look out the window.

"So, what brings you out this way, Sam?"

"Oh…I don't know," Sam replied. "Just observing."

"Hey, me too! This train is fascinating. I can't even begin to tell you how many times I've been on it. Seems like millions."

Sam was tempted to ask him where they were and where the train was heading, but knowing that James was apparently a good friend of Gabriel's made the idea less appealing. After all, what if it was learned that he had no ticket? Furthermore, he had no money to purchase a ticket if it came down to it. Knowing that he would be thrown off the train in the middle of nowhere, he decided to remain silent about it.

"Hey, you wouldn't happen to know what time it is, would you?" Sam asked. "My watch seems to have stopped.

"Sure," he replied, looking down at his. "It's 11:15."

"Are you sure?" Sam asked with a puzzled expression.

"Yeah," he replied, looking at his watch a second time. "11:15."

"So, are you from around here?" Sam asked, shrugging off his confusion momentarily.

"Oh, no. I'm not from anywhere near here."

"But you said that you've been on this train many times."

"I have. There's just something about this train that keeps calling me back time and time again."

"Yeah…I can see why…it's pretty nice," Sam replied, looking around at the beautiful interior of the car.

"It sure is. And besides, I can think of far worse places we could be right now."

"Yeah," Sam agreed with a chuckle. "Like prison."

"Exactly…or being thrown off the top of a building, having rocks thrown at your head or being clubbed to death."

"What?!" Sam said, looking over at him with a puzzled expression.

"I'm just sayin," James replied, flashing him a peculiar expression while shrugging his shoulders.

Sam looked back through the window next to him. It felt as though he had been on this train for hours, but from what he could see, the sun hadn't changed its position in the sky even slightly since he had first awoken. He stood up and leaned into the glass, straining his neck trying to see where it was, but he couldn't find it. In fact, the sunlight he saw shining appeared to be more of a brilliant glow than direct sunlight.

"Must be something strange about this glass," he thought to himself as he ran his fingertips across it. He returned to his seat, putting his head back against the headrest.

"Hey, I didn't mean to freak you out, buddy," James said with a chuckle. "I just meant that things could always be worse."

Sam nodded in agreement, and then began to think back upon his days with Kim. That was one of her favorite things to say to him when times were tough. She was always so very optimistic when it came to how she viewed their life together. Such was the case when they brought their new son home for the first time.

After pouring through books full of baby names, as well as listening to well-intended suggestions from nearly every friend or family member they had, they decided to name him Lee, after Sam's father.

"I think we need a bigger place," she laughed as they put Lee into his crib and looked around at the enormous piles of baby clothes, diapers and toys they had received from friends and family.

"Gee...ya think?" Sam replied, having no idea where they'd put everything.

"Well, it could always be worse," she said with a smile as she laid on the bed, Sam climbing in next to her.

Sam raised his head and looked at the crib, which they had wedged into the corner of their bedroom. There wasn't even enough room to walk around it, forcing them to climb over the bed to get to the other side.

"Maybe we should see if they have a two-bedroom available," he replied.

"Or maybe we should think about buying our own home?" she answered.

"Are you serious," he asked, wondering if that were even a possibility.

"Well, we *do* have some money saved. Maybe we should look into it."

"It would be pretty amazing if we could pull that off, wouldn't it?"

"It sure would."

"Can we get one with an Olympic sized pool?" he asked with a chuckle.

"Sure, babe. Whatever you want."

"And a hot tub?"

"Absolutely. I mean, we can't have one without the other. That would just be unbalanced."

"Can it have a white picket fence?"

"I don't know…Are you gonna paint it?"

"Okay…scratch the white picket fence."

"Good thinking."

Sam looked back at Lee, who was sound asleep in his crib. He didn't know if it would be possible to buy a place, but he sure loved the idea of giving his family a place of their own where Lee could grow up. He imagined the two of them playing ball in the yard, jumping in piles of leaves in the Fall, making snowmen in the winter, and the countless other activities they might enjoy.

The following morning, he called a local Realtor whom Kim's parents had referred to him. After going through all of their information, the Realtor was fairly certain that he could find them a place. They were both absolutely thrilled with the news, and after Kim had recovered enough to start looking at some places, they began to comb through the local listings within their price range. After narrowing down their search to just a few places, they found one that they thought might work. It was a small, 3 bedroom ranch in a fairly decent neighborhood, and it was priced below the other homes they were looking at. It had been listed as a fixer-upper, in need of a bit of t.l.c., but the thought of putting some time and effort into a place didn't frighten them if the price was right. Sam called the Realtor and scheduled an appointment to look it over.

"Wow…they're apparently not very interested in curb appeal," Sam said with a chuckle as the Realtor pulled in front of the house.

"This is an interesting story," the Realtor replied. "The guy who owns this place got divorced from his wife a couple of years ago. Once she had moved out, he had a couple of his buddies move in with him. They all just sit around partying every day. The place is pretty much trashed."

Sam looked at the front yard. The grass was waist-high, looking as though it hadn't been cut in months. There was a large maple tree in the front yard, and the branches had grown down far enough that they were nearly touching the ground.

"Oh look, babe," Kim said with excitement. "There's a park across the street where Lee can play."

Sam glanced over at the small neighborhood park, and then looked back at the house. The home itself wasn't too bad. It was sided with aluminum siding, which appeared to be in fairly good shape. The paint was peeling off of the wood around the windows, but he knew that would be an easy fix.

"Wanna go inside?" the Realtor asked.

"Sure. Why not?" Sam replied as he opened his car door.

"Hello, we're here to look at your place," the Realtor said with a smile as a grungy looking man appeared in the doorway holding a beer.

"Sure," he replied. "Come on in."

Kim gasped as they entered the living room. The old, ugly carpeting was severely stained everywhere she looked, as the tenants were obviously not even slightly concerned about spills or even cleaning them up once they had occurred.

"Sam," she whispered in his ear as they made their way down the main hallway. "My feet are sticking to the carpeting."

"I know. Mine are too," he whispered back, laughing. "We'll have to stop on the way home and buy new shoes."

The three bedrooms at the end of the hall were small in size, but big enough to put a bed and a dresser in each of them. The doors and woodwork were in pretty bad shape, with two of the doors having holes punched in them. The bathroom was an absolute disaster. It had been paneled with a white, plastic paneling that had been painted over a number of times. The tub was badly worn with a few chips in the finish. Just above to top of the tub, mildew was growing on all three walls. The caulk around the tub had been reapplied numerous times, and it was also covered with mildew. The ceramic tiles on the floor were very old and dirty, and they moved under his feet as he walked. The toilet looked as though it had never been cleaned, the sink was old, worn, and outdated, and the cabinet beneath it was filthy and badly water-damaged. Sam knew that buying this place would mean completely gutting the bathroom, and probably even the drywall would need to be replaced due to the serious mildew problem, but if he was able to do the work himself, it might be worth the effort..

"Oh...my...God," Kim said quietly as they entered the kitchen, her hand over her mouth.

The kitchen cabinets were original, from the 1950's, and they had been painted over multiple times. A few of the cabinet doors were missing, as were half of the pull handles on the doors that remained. There was some very outdated mosaic tile on the backsplash behind the countertops with various tiles missing. The countertops themselves were also from the 1950's, and were worn through the original finish to the point where the surface of the wood underneath could be seen. All of the appliances were in need of replacement, and the vinyl flooring was worn through to the concrete.

"Let's take a look at the back yard," Sam said, wanting very badly to find something positive about the home other than the price.

"Wow...and the fun just keeps coming," he said sarcastically as the three of them stepped outside into the back yard. The lot itself was enormous compared to the small city lots that he and Kim had grown up being accustomed to. It looked to be at least a half-acre in size, and was fenced in on all four sides, but just like the front yard, the grass was waist-high. There were four large maple trees in the back yard, the branches of which were also growing down to the ground.

"Lee could have a blast in a yard this big, baby," Sam said with a smile.

"We'd never find him in this yard," she answered sarcastically.

"We could buy a dog and hang a pork chop around Lee's neck."

"We wouldn't need a dog. We'd need a goat."

"Maybe we can just tie a big bell on him."

"I'm gonna go out front and let you two talk it over, ok?" the Realtor said with a smile as he turned and walked toward the gate.

"What do you think, baby?" Sam asked.

"I know that the price is right, but it would need so much work," she replied, feeling a little defeated.

"I know. But all the yard needs is a good lawnmower and some trimming of the trees. That wouldn't cost anything. Just try to imagine everything back here all cleaned up. It wouldn't cost anything to do that," he replied as he stepped behind her and put his arms around her.

"We could barbecue right here on the patio, build a fire pit, a garden, maybe plant some flowers here and there."

Kim stood silently for a moment, trying to imagine what the yard would look like if it were well-maintained.

"Yeah, I can imagine that. It could be really beautiful. But what about all of the work inside?" she asked.

"Well, there's not a lot of floor space, so new carpeting would be reasonable. The bathroom and kitchen need to be completely replaced, but we can go take a look at how much it would cost us to replace everything. I can do all of the work myself."

"Sam, it's too much work for you. How are you gonna do all of that?"

"If you really want it, I'll find a way, baby. I promise. Maybe I can take some time off of work, at least enough time to replace the bathroom. We can replace the carpeting before we move in. The kitchen can be replaced a little bit at a time. If you think you could love this place once it's finished, I'll do whatever I can to make it happen."

"I *do* love this yard," she replied hesitantly. "And the park across the street is perfect."

"It sure is, baby. Why don't we sleep on it? After all, I can't see this place flying off the market overnight. If we decide that we want it, we can make a list of everything we'd need to fix it right and then see how much everything would cost before we make an offer, okay?"

The two of them thanked the Realtor for his time, telling him that they wanted to think it over for a day or two. They then went home and started to write down a list of everything they would need. After looking into how much it would cost them to make all of the necessary repairs, they came to the conclusion that it was something they could manage. They didn't have enough saved to repair everything, but with both of them earning their current salaries, they could fix everything within just a few months. The following day, they made an offer, which the buyer accepted, and within just over one month they were sitting at the closing table being handed the keys to their very first home.

"I think I just may be the happiest man in the world, baby!" Sam blurted out with an enormous smile as he grabbed Kim's hands and began swinging her around in circles in the parking lot of the title company.

"I know!" she replied enthusiastically. "Can you believe it?!" We're homeowners!"

"I know!" he yelled. "And I promise to help you

in any way I can while you do all of the remodeling work!"

"Oh no, Mr. Grace," she replied, laughing. "Do I look like a carpenter to you?"

"No," he said, leaning in to give her a kiss. "You look like the most beautiful woman in the world."

"Why thank you," she replied playfully. "You're not so bad yourself."

"But on the other hand, you *would* look pretty sexy with a tool belt on."

"Do you think so?"

"Absolutely!"

"Is that the only reason you married me? Cuz you think I'm pretty?"

"Absolutely not!"

"Good!" she replied in a matter-of-fact tone.

"I married you because my first choice backed out of the deal."

"Oh, is that right?" she replied, raising one eyebrow. "Well, I'll have you know that the only reason I married you was because I was bored."

"Needed a little flavor in your life, did ya?"

"Well, that *and* I felt a little sorry for you," she said with a chuckle.

"And because I'm drop dead sexy."

"Well, yeah, that *did* influence my opinion a little."

"And because I'm smart, and funny, and..."

"Hold on, babe. To be honest, I really just married you for your money."

"Hmm...that could be a problem," he replied, rubbing his chin.

"Oh? And why's that?"

"Because I think we just spent all of it."

"Oh...That *could* be a problem."

"Do you feel as though it's one you can work your way around?"

"I'll work on it."

Still having another week before they had to be

out of their apartment, Kim stayed home with Lee, packing their belongings with the help of some close friends while Sam spent his days gutting the bathroom and having the new carpeting installed. He tore out everything in the bathroom, clear down to the studs, and then replaced the drywall and floor tile. With the help of a couple of friends, he managed to wrestle the new bathtub into place, finished the painting, and installed the new toilet, sink and vanity they had picked out. He refused to let Kim see it until it was completely finished, which occurred the day before they were supposed to move in. He put all of his tools away, cleaned up the remaining mess from the construction, and then raced home to pick up Kim and Lee, excited to show them what he had done.

"Don't open your eyes," he said, covering her face with his hand as he led her down the hallway.

"I won't!"

"No peeking," he said playfully

"I'm not peeking," she replied with a laugh.

He led her right to the doorway of the bathroom, checking first to make sure that he hadn't left anything behind.

"Okay, baby! Open em!"

"Oh Sam!" she shouted out, her eyes starting to well up with tears as she looked at her new bathroom. "It's so beautiful!"

"You like it?" he replied, puffing his chest out a bit.

"Are you kidding?! I *love* it!" she said enthusiastically, turning around to hug him. "I'm so proud of you, babe! You did an amazing job!"

"Thank you, baby," he replied, beaming with pride.

"How do you like the carpeting?" he continued, leading her back into the hallway.

"It's beautiful!" she answered. "And it feels so soft under my feet!"

"Yeah, and they don't stick to it when you walk,

either!"

"No kidding," she replied, making an ugly face as she remembered how nasty the old carpeting was.

"I can't believe this is the same place, Sam! I think I'm starting to love it!"

"Look, Lee," he said, looking down at his son, holding him close to his chest as he walked into what would soon be Lee's bedroom. "This is your room! Do you like it?"

"He seems very unimpressed," he continued, noticing that Lee had fallen asleep in his arms.

"Oh, I don't know about that," Kim replied as she walked up to Sam and caressed Lee's face with her hand. "I think he feels very much at home."

They returned to their apartment, put Lee to bed, and then began to pack up the last of their belongings.

"It's gonna be sad to leave this place," Kim said as she looked around at the stacks of boxes and empty walls.

"Why do you say that?"

"I don't know. We've just had so many good memories here."

"Yeah, you're right," Sam replied, thinking back to how happy he was when they had first moved in, when they had brought Lee home for the first time, and many other happy moments.

"I was sitting right over there when you told me you were pregnant," he said, pointing toward the table he was sitting at when he realized that his life had changed forever.

"And it was right back in that bedroom over there that I became pregnant," she replied with a warm smile.

"Yes, it was," Sam agreed, returning her smile.

"Hey...," Sam said softly as he sat on the sofa next to her, putting his arm around her. "Don't be sad, baby," he continued. "We're gonna make a lot more beautiful memories in our new place."

"I know," she replied, resting her head back against his chest. "I love you so very much, Sam."

"I love you more, baby," he whispered, wrapping his arms tightly around her.

The following morning came far sooner than either of them would've liked. Both of them could still feel the soreness in their bodies from all of the work they had done over the past week. A number of friends and family members showed up to help them with their move, and within just a few hours they found themselves sitting on their sofa in the living room of their new home, both of them utterly exhausted.

There were boxes stacked in every room of the house, and the kitchen was a mess of full garbage bags and empty pizza boxes. Their helpers had all gone home after being well fed and thanked for all they had done.

"I think I'm gonna take a shower in our beautiful new bathroom," Kim said as she stood and started toward the bedroom for a change of clothes.

Sam put his head back and let out a heavy sigh, feeling very relieved that the move was over and he could finally rest. He could feel himself beginning to doze off within just a few minutes.

"Sam?" Kim said as she re-entered the living room, clothes in hand.

"Yeah, baby," he replied.

"We have no shower curtain."

Sam picked his head up slightly, opening just one eye to look at her, suddenly aware that their apartment had a shower enclosure with a sliding glass door, leaving no need for any such device.

"Ugh!" he said with a heavy sigh. "It never even occurred to me to buy one."

"It never occurred to me either," she replied.

"Alright, baby," he said, standing up and grabbing his car keys. "I'll go buy one. Is there any particular design you'd prefer?"

"Oh, I don't know," she replied with a smile. "Get something pretty...with flowers."

"I was thinking of more of a football theme."

"To be honest, I don't care what it looks like, babe. I just need a hot shower."

He drove to the local home décor store and began to browse through their selection, when his eyes landed on one that caught his eye.

"Perfect," he said out loud as he picked it up, chuckling a bit as he walked toward the register to pay. He then drove back home, stepped inside and handed it to Kim.

"You can't be serious," she said in a deadpan voice as she removed it from the bag and looked at it.

"What?" he replied, acting as though he were confused by her response.

"Superman? You bought a Superman shower curtain?"

"Yeah, baby," he said with a smile. "I thought it would remind you of me while you're taking a shower."

"You are such an odd man," she said, laughing and shaking her head.

She then headed toward the bathroom, returning after her shower. Looking into the living room, she saw Sam sound asleep on the sofa with Lee sleeping on his chest. Her heart melted as she sat on the chair across from them, watching for a while as they slept, knowing how much they all loved each other.

Over the next few weeks, they were able to find a day care center nearby that was reasonably priced. Although it broke her heart to do so, Kim dropped Lee off the first morning and then cried all the way to work. She had spent every hour of every day with him since he had arrived, and it felt as though she was abandoning him. While she never stopped feeling guilty about doing so, she really had no choice. They needed her income if they were going to rebuild their kitchen. She loved the idea of being a stay at home mom, but that simply wasn't possible at this point.

Sam found a cheap, used riding mower for sale in the local newspaper and was able to tackle the jungle out in the back yard. He then trimmed all of the trees properly, which improved the view tremendously.

After saving as much as they could over the next few months, the bought new, unfinished kitchen cabinets, which Sam finished himself after reading up on how to do so professionally. He ordered new countertops, installed a new kitchen sink, and replaced the flooring. As more time passed, they were able to purchase new appliances, and within six months of their moving into the home, it was barely recognizable compared to how it had looked when they had first seen it.

While at work one morning, he was assigned to pick up some construction materials right in the heart of his old neighborhood. Many memories began to come back as he drove through the very familiar streets he had spent so much time walking up and down. He had some time to kill before he could pick up his order, so he drove past the old home he had grown up in, past his old grade school and high school, and eventually found himself in the parking lot where he and Angela had first met.

While he was very much in love with Kim and was very happy in the life they were building together, he found himself reminiscing every now and then about the time he had spent with Angela. He couldn't understand it, but there was just something very different about her. There was something very different about the love he had always felt for her. He couldn't understand how she could've seemingly vanished off of the face of the earth. He knew deep down inside that – had he been able to find her when he'd returned from San Diego – it would've been her that he would have married and started this new life with. After all, he had met Kim after being forced to give up on the woman who would always have been his first choice.

He turned to look down the street they had been walking down the very first time he held her hand. He could almost picture the two of them walking together, and a sense of warmth filled his heart, along with a deep sense of sadness for having lost the woman he had loved so very deeply. What bothered him most was the way that it had ended. There was no clear reason as to why it had, and there was no sense of closure afterward. He wondered how she remembered him and how she thought of him these days. He found himself wishing that he could talk to her one last time, knowing that if he were able to do so, he would try to explain to her how much he had always loved her.

His memory flashed back to an evening with her that he would always remember. He had been working late one night, and called her before heading home. As exhausted as he was, he desperately wanted to see her. They agreed to stop for a bite to eat at a Thai restaurant in the neighborhood. After enjoying a nice meal, they went for a walk through the neighborhood, holding hands along the way.

It was a warm, summer's night, and there was a slight fog in the air. As they walked together, he suddenly stopped, taking her by the hands and looking deeply into her eyes. He leaned in to kiss her, but did so very slowly, wanting the moment to last forever. It would remain one of the most memorable kisses either of them had ever experienced, and one that he could still feel to this day if he closed his eyes and thought about it. He began to wonder if she remembered that kiss, and if she ever found herself thinking about the love they felt for each other that night. He wondered if she ever had moments when she missed the love they had felt for each other.

Shaking the memories from his mind, he picked up his order and returned to work. Throughout the rest of the day, he found himself thinking about her repeatedly. He knew that it wasn't good for him to be thinking about all of that, but he couldn't help himself. Deep in his heart, he had always felt as though she was 'The One,' and no matter how much he loved Kim, he couldn't get past that thought.

He returned home after work, still reminiscing about her. Kim had made it home before him, and was sitting on the patio with Lee in her lap as he walked into the back yard.

"Hey baby," he said with a warm smile as he walked over and gave both of them a kiss.

"Hi babe," she replied, smiling back at him. "How was your day?"

"It was good. How about yours?"

"It was crazy! I didn't have time to breathe!"

"I had an interesting day," he replied.

"Oh yeah? How so?"

"I had to drive down to the old neighborhood to pick up some materials today. I love that neighborhood. Lots of memories."

"Yeah, I know what you mean."

Sam sat in the chair next to her, staring out across the back yard for a few minutes.

"Sam?" Kim said quietly.

"Yeah, baby."

"I've been thinking about something."

"Uh-oh…that can't be good," he replied with a chuckle.

"Seriously, babe. I was thinking about Lee growing up. He seems to be growing so fast."

"Yeah, he sure is."

"Sam, I really don't want him to be an only child."

"What are you saying?" he replied, turning in his seat to look at her.

"I think I'd like to have another baby."

"Are you serious? Right now?"

"Well, I want Lee to have a brother or sister close to his age. Someone he can grow up with and be best friends with. I'm afraid that if we wait too long, there'll be too much of an age difference."

"That's very true," he replied, sitting back into his chair. "My sister and I are only a year and a half apart, and we've always been like best friends."

"See what I mean? I want that for him too. I want him to have that best friend."

"But how would we manage paying for day care for another baby? That would make things kinda tight for us."

"Well, that brings up something else I've been thinking about."

"What's that?"

"Sam, I've been thinking about this a lot, and I think I'd really like to be a stay at home mom."

"Are you serious?" he replied. "How can we afford that?"

"Well, I wouldn't stay at home forever. It would just be until the kids are in school full time. If we decided to have another baby, I'd work until the baby came and then take off for a few years. We could save as much as we can until then."

Sam looked out over the back yard again, thinking everything over for a few minutes.

"Sam?" Kim said quietly, looking for a response.

"I don't know, baby. That's a lot to think about."

"I know…It's just that Lee is only gonna be a baby for so long. Once those days are gone, they're gone forever. I'm just feeling as though I'd rather be the one who's with him all day. I know that the day care does a good job, but nobody loves a child like his own mother. I'd really like to give him that."

While he knew that everything she was saying was true, he began to feel slightly overwhelmed by everything. He had gone through so many drastic changes over the past few years, and this would be yet another major challenge. He loved the direction his life had taken since meeting Kim. He had gone through his unflattering dismissal from the military, the death of his father, wanting to find Angela to see if he could work that out, to being married to Kim, having their first child, and buying their first home. He wanted very badly to be a good provider for his new family, to give them everything they might need, but this would really put the pressure on him. He would become their sole provider. He began to wonder if he could do it. What if he was injured at work? What if he lost his job? On the other hand, he thought, what could be better for Lee than to be with his mother every day instead of being in day care?

"I have to be honest, baby," he replied. "That scares me a little bit."

"What scares you about it?"

"The unknown."

"Life is full of unknowns, babe," she replied, reaching over to take his hand. "We can either be afraid of them, or we can embrace the excitement of them."

"I just don't know if I can do it. What if I get fired? What if…"

"Sam," she said, squeezing his hand a little tighter. "I have so much faith in you. I trust you completely. You're an amazing man, Mr. Grace."

"That's me," he replied with a chuckle. "Amazing Grace."

"That's you, alright."

"So, if I agreed to have another baby, can we start right now?" he said with a smile, batting his eyebrows at her.

"Right this minute?" she replied.

"Yeah," he said, leaning over to put his arms around her. "Right here and right now."

"The neighbors might talk."

"Let em talk."

"Sam?" she said as he started to playfully kiss her neck.

"Don't talk right now, baby. I'm putting my moves on you."

"You're gonna smother Lee."

"Oh...is Lee here?" he laughed, leaning back to look at him. "Oh yeah, there he is! Hey, little guy, be a good wing man and go clean your room or something. I'm trying to put the moves on your mother."

"So, what are you saying, babe?" she asked, pushing him away slightly to look him in the eyes. "Do you want to have another baby?"

"Yeah," he replied, leaning in to give her a kiss. "I would love to have another baby with you."

"Oh, Sam!" she said with a sigh of relief, the joy welling up inside of her. "I love you so very much!"

"I love you more, baby."

"You make me so very happy."

"Yeah? Well you make me happier."

Within one month, Kim became pregnant again. A few months later, they discovered that they were going to have a baby girl. Both of them were thrilled by this news, and started to decorate her bedroom, eagerly awaiting her arrival. Kim continued to work until just before the baby was due, and then resigned from her job. Sam took on some additional hours at work so they could save more, which he decided he would continue to do once the baby had arrived.

Once it was clear that Kim had gone into labor, Sam dropped Lee off at the baby-sitter's and took her to the hospital, once again taking a place at her side, refusing to leave until their daughter was born.

"Sam?" Kim said between contractions. "Can you do me a favor?"

"Anything, baby," he replied, moving closer to the bedside.

"Can I hold onto a few of your fingers when I'm

having a contraction?"

"Sure, baby. Will that help you?"

"Yeah, I think so. Just let me squeeze them until the contraction is over."

"You got it, baby," he replied, putting two of the fingers of his left hand into her palm.

As the next contraction arrived, she squeezed his fingers together until it had passed.

"Did that help, baby?" he asked.

"Yes, it did," she replied. "I don't know why. It just did."

"Okay, baby," he said. "You just keep holding onto them. I'm not going anywhere."

Eight hours into labor, her contractions had grown progressively more intense. As their intensity grew, so did the intensity with which she would squeeze Sam's fingers. He started to think about asking her if she could squeeze something else instead, but she wanted his fingers, and he wasn't about to say *"Ouch, that hurts"* while watching what she was going through. At 20 hours into labor, she wasn't merely squeezing his fingers, but was instead crushing them together, and then twisting them violently from side to side. Finally, after a grueling 24 hours of labor, little Nicole Grace came into the world, immediately adored by both of her parents.

"Mr. Grace?" the nurse said after sending Kim to recovery. "We're gonna need you to sign some documents for us, okay?"

"Sure," he replied, following her outside of the delivery room.

"Okay…we need you to sign here, here, and here," she said, pointing to the signature lines on a number of pages.

Sam took the pen and lowered it to the page, trying to grasp it so that he could sign his name properly. No matter how hard he tried, he couldn't get them to cooperate.

"I can't write," he said with a chuckle.

"Excuse me?" she asked.

"It's my fingers," he replied, beginning to laugh out loud. "I think she broke all of em."

"Well, just do your best, sir," she replied, laughing along with him.

He scribbled across the pages to the best of his ability, and then joined Kim once they had moved her into her recovery room.

"Hey there, baby!" he said as he entered the room, gave her a kiss, and then took a seat next to her bed.

"How are you feeling?

"I feel pretty good," she said, reaching over to hold his hand.

"Oh my God!" she exclaimed, looking down at his swollen, bruised fingers. "What happened to your fingers?"

"Um…you happened to my fingers," he said with a laugh.

"Did I do that to you?!" she asked in a stunned voice.

"Yeah…it's ok. I'm fine."

"Why didn't you tell me I was doing that?"

"Well, you were a little preoccupied. Besides, what was I gonna say? Ouch, you're hurting me?"

"I'm so sorry, babe! You should've said something," she replied, pulling his fingers up to kiss them.

Sam stayed with her until she was ready to sleep for the night, and then drove home to get some sleep himself.

The following morning, he picked up Lee from the sitter's house, dressed him in his best clothes, and then stopped to buy some balloons and red roses for Kim before driving to the hospital

"We're gonna surprise mommy, okay buddy?" he asked Lee as he kneeled down next to him just outside of the door to her room.

"Here…I want you to take these balloons and

this rose and bring them to her, ok?

"Okay," Lee replied excitedly as he took them in his hands.

"She's right inside this door," he said, turning Lee around and pointing toward her room.

"Mommy?...Mommy?" Lee called out as he waddled into the room.

"Awe...Thank you, Lee!" she cried out with an enormous smile as she saw him coming around the edge of the bed.

"Here, mommy!" he said in a sweet voice as he reached up to hand them to her.

"Hey there, baby!" Sam said as he followed Lee into the room a few seconds later, holding the remainder of the roses. "These are for you too."

"Awe, thank you, babe! That was very sweet of you!"

"How are you feeling?"

"I feel pretty good. I can't wait to get back home, though."

"Well, we can't wait for you to get home either. There's a lot of dishes to be done and laundry to be washed," he replied with a chuckle.

"Oh, is that right?"

"That's right!"

"Well maybe you'd better leave now and get started on that," she replied with a laugh.

"How are we feeling, Mrs. Grace?" her doctor asked as he entered the room with a clipboard in his hand.

"I'm good, doctor," she replied.

"Good, good," he said, looking down at her chart.

"You know, just looking some things over here," he said, raising his eyes to look at her. "Are you happy?"

"I'm very happy, doctor. Couldn't be happier," she replied, looking up at Sam.

"Good," he nodded. "Listen, for whatever the

reason, you seem to experience some pretty difficult deliveries."

"You're telling me," she replied, rolling her eyes.

"Your labor lasted 36 hours with Lee, and 24 hours with Nicole."

"I know. I remember every single hour."

"Well, you have your boy, and you have your girl. I don't want to overstep in saying this, but maybe it would be best for you to stop there. Have you thought about that?"

"Yes, I have. I think I'm done having babies, doc."

"Okay, good," he said, standing up. "I'll be checking in on you from time to time. Please let me know if you need anything."

"Will do, doctor, and thank you."

"Are you sure that you'll never want any more?" Sam asked after the doctor had left the room.

"Yeah, I think I am," she replied. "He's right. We have our boy and our girl. I don't think I want to go through this anymore."

"Well, to be honest, I don't think I want to see you go through it anymore either. It's really hard to watch. I feel so helpless watching you suffer like that. I want to make it stop and make you feel better, but there's nothing I can do."

"Gee, I'm sorry it's so hard for you," she replied sarcastically.

"Hey, I'd have the babies if I could," he said with a laugh.

"No you wouldn't."

"You're right...I wouldn't. I'd buy a dog instead."

The next few months brought with them a difficult transition for both of them. Sam found himself working more hours than ever before, leaving home every day just after sunrise and not returning until late in the evening, completely exhausted. Kim was starting to feel a bit stir crazy from being at home all day long with a newborn and a toddler. This brought a bit of tension into their relationship, causing them to argue about the silliest of things.

Sam would find himself walking in the front door after a grueling day only to have Kim virtually drop both of the kids into his lap, completely exhausted from spending the entire day changing diapers, feeding them, cleaning up after them, and having no adults in her life to have an actual conversation with.

Knowing that they could both use a break, and without her having any knowledge of his plans, Sam arranged to have Kim's mother watch the kids for the weekend so that he and Kim could get away for a few days. Things were tight for them financially, but with the additional hours he had been working, he was able to save enough to book a room at a luxury resort in southern Wisconsin. They offered a spa package designed to pamper women who were guests there, so he booked appointments for her to get a pedicure, manicure, and a massage. He arranged to leave work early that Friday, giving them more time to enjoy their weekend.

"Hey, baby," he said with a smile as he walked in the front door, surprising Kim.

"Sam?" she replied with a stunned expression. "Why are you home so early?"

"I have a surprise for you," he said with a grin. "You and I are going away for the weekend. Just you and me, baby. Go pack some clothes for yourself."

"What?" she replied with excitement in her voice. "Where are we going?"

"Well, if I told you, it wouldn't be a surprise, would it?"

"What about the kids?"

"Your mother agreed to watch them."

"Are you serious?"

"Dead serious! Go ahead and start packing. I'll

get the kids ready."

Kim could hardly contain herself as she ran down the hallway into the bedroom. She desperately needed some time away, and she was ecstatic that Sam thought of it.

"What kind of clothes should I pack?" she shouted from the bedroom.

"Just pack something casual, but nice."

"How many days will we be gone?"

"Three, including today."

She was absolutely giddy as she began to throw her clothes into her suitcase, running back and forth from the bedroom closet to the bed. Unable to control her excitement, she ran out of the bedroom and jumped into Sam's arms, kissing him repeatedly on his neck and face.

"I love you so very much, Sam!" she said with a playful smile.

"I love you too, baby."

Sam got the kids ready, drove them to Kim's mother's house, and then returned home to pick Kim up.

"Woo-hoo!" she shouted as they pulled away from the curb. "Where are we going?" she continued, absolutely beside herself with excitement.

"I told you, it's a surprise," he teased.

After driving for about 45 minutes, he turned into the driveway of the resort. Kim's eyes grew large as she looked around at the beautiful landscape surrounding the buildings.

"Oh Sam!" she sighed, her jaw dropped open. "This is absolutely gorgeous!"

"Not as gorgeous as you, baby," he replied, reaching over and putting his hand on her knee.

He parked the car, and then leaned over to give her a kiss before grabbing their luggage and bringing it inside. Kim was in awe of the beauty of the place as she stood in the front lobby, taking it all in.

The lobby stood two stories high, with

enormous crystal chandeliers hanging from the ceiling, casting brilliant slivers of light across the highly polished marble floor. Across from the check-in desk, separated from the lobby by a long brass railing, there was a large lounge area, three steps lower than the main level, running alongside a two-story wall of windows that overlooked the immaculate gardens outside. To her left, a man in a black tuxedo was playing a beautiful grand piano while the guests relaxed on overstuffed lounge chairs, enjoying cocktails.

"Do you hear what he's playing?" Sam asked with a smile.

"Is that Amazing Grace?" she replied with one eyebrow raised.

"Sure is, baby. I love that song. Amazing Grace…that's me," he said, pointing at his chest with his thumb.

"That's you, alright," she replied with a chuckle as she turned to take everything in.

There were long corridors to either side, one leading to a fine restaurant and the other leading to a bank of elevators. Both were beautifully decorated with fine artwork along with the occasional alcove containing various large plants.

"Alright," Sam said as he stepped away from the desk. "Are you ready to see our room?"

"Absolutely!" she replied.

"Close your eyes," he said after they had found the suite he had reserved.

After struggling with the room key for a bit, he threw the door open and led her inside.

"Okay," he said cheerfully. "Open em!"

"Oh, my…," she replied as she opened her eyes.

Directly in front of her on the floor was a trail of red rose pedals, leading around the corner and covering the king sized bed. Past the bed was a large sitting area with two overstuffed chairs and a table.

On top of the table was a bottle of champagne, two glasses, and a dish of chocolate covered strawberries. On the wall directly across from the two chairs was a marble fireplace. On the far wall at the end of the suite was a separate exit leading to a small patio with two Adirondack chairs, overlooking a beautiful pond, surrounded by flower gardens on three sides. To her right there was a large bathroom with a Jacuzzi tub, marble floors and countertops, and a separate shower.

"Sam!" she gasped, turning to hug him. "This is so beautiful!"

"Yes, it is," he replied. "But it became a lot more beautiful when you walked in."

"Oh Sam...You are so sweet to me."

"I just wanted us to get away for a little while, baby. We've both been so stressed out lately with everything that's been going on. I've been working like a dog, and you've been trapped in the house all day every day. I just thought we could both use this."

"I know. I really haven't been myself lately. I'm sorry."

"Neither one of us have."

"Yeah, you've been a real turd," she said with a chuckle, flicking his nose with her finger.

"Oh, so this is how you treat me? I bring you to this amazing place and you call me a turd?" he replied playfully while putting his hands on her waist.

"You know I'm only teasing."

"Are you?"

"Yes...no...well...maybe."

"What do you say we put our things away and go for a little walk?"

"That sounds great," she replied enthusiastically.

After they had unpacked, they left the room, making their way outside to the wandering path that led them past an elaborate marble fountain, and then off into the massive garden area.

"Baby," Sam said as he reached down to hold her hand as they walked. "I was thinking a few days ago about how we used to be."

"What do you mean?"

"Before everything got so crazy. Before the kids, and before we got so involved with fixing the house."

"Yeah?"

"We were just different toward each other. We were nicer to each other. We talked more. We had fun all of the time, didn't we?"

"Yes, we did," she replied softly.

"It's really sad to me that we don't act that way toward each other anymore."

"I know…I've been thinking about that too. I guessed we've been so wrapped up in other things we kinda forgot about each other."

"Baby…," he said, stopping to face her and take her by the hands. "I don't ever want to be one of those couples that get so wrapped up in the busyness of life that they forget that they're in love with each other. I love you, baby. I'm *in love* with you. I don't ever want to lose that."

"Neither do I, babe. Maybe we just need to keep that in the forefront of our minds. We need to remember that first, before anything else."

"They say that marriage is a lot of work. That's very true, but it's worth the effort, don't you think?"

"Absolutely!"

"So can we start right now trying to put a little more fun back in our marriage?"

"I think that's a wonderful idea, Mr. Grace," she replied, drawing him closer. "And how do you propose we start doing that?"

"Hmm…," he replied with a curious expression.

Over her shoulder he noticed waterfall in the midst of the garden, made out of jagged stones and surrounded by tall, leafy plants.

"See that waterfall over there?" he asked with a

grin.

"Yes I do," she answered, turning her head to look.

"Wanna go make out under it?" he asked, batting his eyebrows suggestively.

"I kinda do," She answered playfully.

"I kinda do too!"

"Do you think we'd get arrested?"

"I don't know, but it would be a great story if we did, no? We'd both have the biggest smiles ever captured on a mug shot."

"True, but my hair would be a mess. If the tabloids got ahold of that picture, I'd be ruined."

"Funny, but I haven't seen any paparazzi," he said, looking around suspiciously.

"You never will. They're masters at hiding in plain sight," she whispered, leaning her back against his chest as she pulled his arms around her stomach.

"Maybe we should pass on that then."

"Yeah, probably."

After enjoying a leisurely walk through the gardens, they enjoyed a nice, romantic dinner and then returned to their suite.

"Would you care for a glass of champagne, Mrs. Grace?" he asked, throwing a towel over his forearm to act like a waiter.

"Why, yes I would, Mr. Grace," she replied in an overly formal voice.

He poured each of them a glass, and they then walked outside to relax on the deck for a while. There was a beautiful, soft summer breeze blowing Kim's hair slightly to one side. Across the pond, the sun was just beginning to set, casting brilliant streaks of orange, pink and purple light across the clouds.

"You look very beautiful tonight, baby," he said as he put his hand on hers.

"Thank you, babe," she replied, turning her head to look at him. "Can we stay here forever?"

"Sure," he answered with a chuckle. "As soon

as we win the lottery."

The two of them sat in silence for a few minutes, taking in the immense beauty of their environment.

"Something just occurred to me," Kim said, breaking the silence.

"What's that?

"I believe this is the first time I've seen you drink since our very first date."

"I think you're right," Sam replied, looking at his nearly empty champagne glass. "And I think I'm ready for another one," he continued, chuckling. "Would you care for another?"

"I don't know, babe. I think you may be trying to get me drunk so you can take advantage of me."

"I am," he replied in a matter-of-fact tone.

"Okay then," she answered playfully. "In that case, I'll definitely have another one."

The following morning, Sam awoke with the sunrise. Not wanting to awaken Kim, he slowly and quietly climbed out of bed, got dressed, and then made his way to the lobby, returning with coffee for both of them.

"Good morning, babe!" she said with a smile while rubbing the sleep from her eyes.

"Good morning!" he replied. "Did you sleep well?"

"I slept like a rock," she answered. This bed is amazing!"

"Well, you'd better get out of it soon. We have to get some breakfast before your appointment."

"My appointment?" she asked, puzzled.

"Yes! You have an appointment at the spa," he replied, grinning ear to ear.

"What kind of appointment?"

"Oh, just a little manicure and pedicure I scheduled for you. Then, of course, we don't want to be late for your full body massage, do we?"

"Are you serious?" she asked, her eyes

opening widely.

"I sure am!"

"Oh Sam!" she exclaimed. "You are so amazing!"

"I've been told that," he said with a cocky smirk. "And by some pretty amazing people, too."

After enjoying a wonderful breakfast, they made their way to the spa. The manicure and pedicure came first, followed by an hour long massage. Kim could feel every last ounce of stress being wrung out of her body as the masseur worked his magic up and down her spine, focusing a great deal of his attention on her extremely tight neck and shoulders. By the time he had finished, she didn't know if she had enough strength to pick herself up from the table.

"How do you feel, baby?" Sam asked as she walked into the waiting room.

"I feel like a washrag," she replied with a laugh. "I can barely walk!"

"Did it feel good?"

"Yes!" she exclaimed. "It felt incredible! Thank you so much, babe!"

"You're welcome. I knew you needed that."

"I sure did! I think I need a nap now!"

After giving her ample time to recuperate, they spent the rest of the day walking through the gardens, laughing, talking, and sitting on various benches they came across on their journey. They could both sense the old magic of their relationship beginning to come back as they recalled many of the funny, sweet, and warm moments they had shared with each other over the past few years.

After returning to their suite for a short nap before dinner, Kim took a shower and then took some extra time perfecting her hair and makeup. She then put on a short, sexy, black dress that she knew Sam was crazy about, taking one last look in the mirror before exiting the bathroom.

"How do I look, babe?" she asked with a knowing, confident smile as she came around the corner, stopping to strike a pose.

"Oh, my!" Sam replied, his jaw dropping with amazement at how gorgeous his bride looked. "You look absolutely ravishing!"

"Why, thank you, sir," she replied playfully.

"No, I'm serious," he said as he looked her up and down, unable to take his eyes off of her. "You look stunning!"

"Well, I wanted to look pretty for you, babe," she replied as she walked up and put her arms around him. "It's been a long time since I've gotten dressed up for you. I should do that more often. You deserve it."

"Any chance you could make yourself look like this every day before I get home?"

"Sure," she said with a chuckle. "As long as you don't mind hiring a full-time nanny to watch the kids all day."

"Let me see how much overtime I can get. It might be worth it," he replied, laughing.

Sam couldn't have been more proud as he walked through the hotel lobby with Kim on his arm. There seemed to be a little more confidence in his stride as noticed men's heads turning to look at her as they passed.

"Do you know who every man in this hotel wishes he was right now, baby?"

"No, who?"

"Me."

"Oh yeah?" she asked. "And why is that?"

"Because I'm with the most beautiful woman in this place."

"Oh thank you, babe," she replied with a sweet smile. "You always make me feel so beautiful."

"That's because you are," he said, pausing to open the door to the restaurant.

They enjoyed an absolutely delicious dinner

together, repeatedly gazing into each other's eyes over the candles at the center of the table. They both began to feel as though they had fallen in love all over again – a feeling that continued to grow for the remainder of the weekend.

"Sam?" she said as they neared her parent's home to pick up the kids.

"Yeah, baby," he replied.

"Thank you so very much for all of this. We really needed it."

"You're welcome, baby. I know we did."

After putting the kids to bed for the evening, Sam walked outside into the back yard and sat on the patio. He began to think about the many dreams he had about where he'd like to see his life lead just after his father had passed. He recalled thinking about how much he wanted to just have a normal life. He remembered how he wanted to have a simple home in the suburbs, a wife who he would love and who would love him, a child or two of his own. He smiled deeply as he looked out across their beautiful back yard, knowing that the wife and children he loved dearly were just inside the wall behind him.

"Well, Mr. Grace," he said under his breath. "I think you have arrived."

TEN

Sam shifted in his seat a bit, feeling himself growing weary of being on this train for such a long period of time. Thinking back to that evening on his patio, he thought that was probably the proudest moment of his life. It's a rare occasion when a man can come to the realization that he possesses everything he'd ever dreamed of having, and he had been there.

Looking toward the front of the car, he noticed that Gabriel was nowhere to be found. He gazed over his shoulder to the rear of the car and noticed a doorway that appeared to lead to an additional car. Being curious, he stood from his seat and walked toward it, grasping the handle with his hand, and then pulling it to the side. The door opened, exposing a small compartment between the two cars. Stepping into it, he noticed something very strange about this space. He'd been on trains many times before, and he'd walked from car to car many times while on them. He expected to hear the loud sounds of the train rolling across the track, but he heard nothing. In fact, it was just as silent in this space as it had been within the car. He paused, remaining completely still, and strained to hear any sound whatsoever, but heard nothing. What's more, the train didn't feel as though it was moving at all. He couldn't feel the rocking motion that one would feel as a train moved across the countryside. Shrugging it off, he leaned forward and grabbed the handle of the next door, pulling it open.

This car wasn't as well lit as the other one, and there was only one small window directly in the center of the car. After his eyes had adjusted to the darkness, he could see that it wasn't a passenger car, but instead a nearly empty box car of some sort. A single shaft of light shone through the window, landing upon a casket that had been placed in the middle of the car. He was bewildered, wondering why there would be a casket being carried by such an elaborate passenger train. Even if there was a very good reason for this, he thought, why would they put it where anyone who walked through the door would stumble upon it?

He walked closer to it, thinking that it must be the casket of someone very important or wealthy. After all, if this guy's family could afford to reserve and entire car on this train just to haul his body somewhere, they must be loaded. But as he looked at it more closely, he noticed that it wasn't very elaborate at all. In fact, it didn't even appear to be as well made as the one he had seen his father buried in.

As he walked slowly around the other side, it occurred to him that he didn't see any flowers along with it. There were no beautiful bouquets with banners reading *'Loving Father'* or *'Beloved Son.'* There was just a poorly build casket, sitting all by itself in a dark, unlit rail car.

Turning away from the casket, he noticed another set of doors on the other end of the car. He made his way to the end of the car and opened the first door, once again finding himself within a dead silent vestibule between this car and the next. He pulled open the second door and found himself in another passenger car, identical to the one he had been riding in. There was a wide variety of people in this car too, but his attention was drawn to a man who was sitting in the center of the car. While everyone else appeared to be very comfortable, this man looked very uneasy and out of sorts. He kept shifting in his seat, looking out the window and then back at the other passengers in the car. Sam noticed some small beads of perspiration on the man's forehead. It was clear that he was very nervous about something. He looked up at Sam with somewhat of a pleading expression, as if he needed help.

"Excuse me sir, but you're not allowed to be here," Sam heard from his right.

Sam shifted his gaze in that direction to see another conductor walking quickly toward him.

"You're not allowed to be here, sir," he repeated in a stern voice. "I'll have to ask you to return to your car."

"Oh, I'm sorry," Sam replied. "I was looking for.."

"Please return to your car, sir," the conductor interrupted, reaching for the door handle, and then pulling it closed in front of him.

While he was annoyed at the conductor's rude behavior, he didn't want to make a scene. He walked back through the car toward the one he had been sitting in, hoping that Gabriel wouldn't confront him upon his return. He made his way quietly through the double doors, looking toward the front of the car. Gabriel returned just as he returned to his seat, looking over at him as he lowered himself into it.

He looked out through his window, noticing that the train appeared to be entering a small town of some sort.

"Return to *'my'* car?" he thought to himself, replaying the conductor's words in his mind. "What did he mean by *'my car?'* How does *he* know what car I should be in?"

"Next stop, Dan," Gabriel yelled.

He looked out through the window to see the station approaching. It wasn't much of a station compared to the other ones he had seen so far. It was a very simple, wood framed building, small in size. There was a small sign hanging on the face of the building, at the very top of the peak at its center. He saw the name 'Dan' written upon it, with a carving of a set of scales underneath, similar to what you might see representing justice.

His gaze shifted to a larger building to the right of the station. It appeared to be a courthouse of some sort, having four large, concrete pillars rising up across the front of it. At the center of the façade, there was again the name 'Dan,' along with the same scales carved into the concrete.

There was a group of people gathered on the front staircase, apparently pleading their case before a man in a black robe. They were very animated in their discussion, while the man in the robe – apparently a judge – turned from side to side to discuss the matter with those who stood on either side of him.

As the train began to move again, the judge looked through the window, directly at Sam. His facial expression appeared to grow more solemn as he stopped paying attention to the crowd around him. Just before the station blocked his line of sight, the judge brought his right arm up, extending it straight out in front of him. He then made a fist, and turned his hand, making a 'thumbs down' gesture.

A chill ran down Sam's spine as he turned

away from the window.

"What the heck was *that* all about?" he muttered to himself.

He looked forward, noticing that a few more people had entered the car. A clean cut, middle-aged man was making his way toward the back of the car. Sam stared at the back of the head of the mysteriously familiar woman in red as the man passed her. He thought about striking up another conversation with her, but he didn't want to be a pest. There was still something so incredibly familiar about her, but he had absolutely no idea what it was.

"Hey there! Where ya headed?" the middle-aged man asked Sam as he took the seat in front of him.

"Oh...just doing a little sight-seeing," Sam replied.

"It's a good day for it!" the man replied. "It's gorgeous outside!"

Sam realized that, while it appeared to be a very nice day, he had no idea if it really was. Being stuck on this train, he hadn't been outside at any point today.

"Sure looks like it," he replied as he looked out the window.

"I'm Thaddeus," the man said in a friendly voice, reaching over the back of the seat to shake Sam's hand.

"Nice to meet you, Thaddeus," he replied, shaking his hand. "I'm Sam."

"Nice to meet you too, Sam."

Wanting to avoid exposing his situation, but at the same time nearing his breaking point from still not knowing where he was or where he was going, he looked at Thaddeus. He seemed like a nice enough guy from what Sam could tell. He began to wonder if he should explain his predicament to him. Maybe, he thought, this guy could help shed some light on what was going on. Looking around to ensure that nobody else could hear their conversation, he decided to go for it.

"Hey…," Sam said quietly as he slid forward on his seat, bringing himself closer. "I have a bit of a problem I was hoping you might be able to help me out with."

"Yeah?" Thaddeus replied, turning in his seat to face Sam. "What's up?"

"Well…You see…I think I boarded this train by accident. I don't know where I am."

"Well, I don't think anyone could possibly board *this* train by accident," he replied with a laugh.

"But apparently I have," Sam answered. "I have no idea where I am, or where this train is going. Can you help me out?"

"Sure. We just left Dan, and we're headed toward Joseph."

"That really doesn't help me out much," he replied with a touch of desperation in his voice. "I've never been to either of those places. I don't even know where they are."

"I don't really know what else to tell you, man. The stop after that is Benjamin. That's where I get off. Does that name ring any bells?"

"No…not at all. You wouldn't happen to have a map of some sort with all of the stops on it, do you?"

"No, I don't. Why don't you ask the conductor?"

"Nah…never mind. I'm sorry to bother you," Sam replied, feeling even more frustrated and wanting to end the conversation before Gabriel got wind of it.

"No problem, man," he replied, turning around in his seat again. "Hey, look at it this way," he continued. "Nothing happens by accident. Wherever you end up, that's where you're supposed to be. You might as well just enjoy the ride."

Sam turned to look out the window again, wishing he was anywhere but where he now found himself. He thought back to his marriage with Kim, and how that had all began to go south after such a promising start.

He had continued to work more and more hours trying to make ends meet after she had quit her job. She didn't return to work after the kids had started going to school full-time. She truly enjoyed being a stay at home mom, and she was very good at it. She was constantly taking them outdoors whenever the weather permitted. She'd take them to various parks, museums, and other local attractions she knew they'd enjoy. While doing so, she was always trying to be aware of the beauty of nature, and was continually teaching them to be aware of it themselves.

She was also a very good housewife for Sam. As much as it could be with two young kids in the house, their home was always exceptionally clean, and she always had dinner waiting on the table for him when he returned home from work. He couldn't complain about anything she was doing throughout the day. It was just that the pressures of the job and the stress that came with it started to wear on him. He started the habit of having a few beers after work every day to calm his nerves. Kim saw no problem with this most of the time, believing that he was a hard-working man who deserved a few after working so many long hours.

Lee had just entered 4th grade, and Nicole 3rd when a group of teenage boys began hanging out at the neighborhood park across the street. Sam didn't think much of it, as they would usually just hang out, playing an occasional basketball game when enough of them were around. It wasn't until their neighbor stopped by to speak with them that Sam started to think they might have a problem on their hands.

"Hey Sam," Beth said as she entered his front yard while he was pulling some weeds.

"What's up, Beth?" he replied, looking up at her as she approached.

"Not much...Hey, do you have a few minutes?

I'd like to show you something."

"Sure," he replied, standing up to follow her as she led him over to a wooden bench in the park.

"Do you see this?" she asked, pointing to some gang-related graffiti that had been painted on it.

"Wow...That's not good," he replied, looking around the park to see if there was more.

"No, it's not."

"Did you see who put it there?"

"Yeah," she replied. "It was those older kids who've been hanging out here lately.

"The guys playing basketball?"

"Yeah."

"Alright...well...I know how to solve that problem," he said with a grin as he walked back across the street, returning with a gallon of leftover paint and a paintbrush.

"Problem solved," he said as he opened it up and began to paint over the graffiti.

"Here comes one of em," Beth said as she looked down the street, seeing one of them approaching.

Sam continued painting, starting to whistle as he did so to make sure that the kid saw what he was doing.

"Y'all paintin my bench, huh?" he asked as he passed the park.

"Oh...this bench?" Sam asked sarcastically, raising his voice. "No...this isn't *your* bench. This bench is *my* bench. I'm painting *my* bench.

With that, the kid flashed a gang sign at him, causing Sam to lose his temper for a moment.

"Hey! That crap aint gonna happen here, pal!" he yelled, dropping his paintbrush and walking toward him.

"Sam, don't!" Beth yelled, grabbing him by the arm to restrain him.

"You can take that crap somewhere else, pal! Cuz it aint happening here!" he continued, returning to finish his work on the bench.

A few days later, while Sam was at work, a few of the neighbors were talking in their front yard when a car came racing down the street. As they passed the park, they began throwing bricks and empty beer bottles at the group of teenagers who were hanging out there. Both groups began to flash gang signs at each other as the group by the park chased after them. Beth called the police and told them about the situation, but they told her there was nothing they could do. They told her to keep an eye on things, to call them if anything else happened, and promised to start sending extra patrols through the neighborhood.

That Saturday morning, Sam spent a few hours mowing his lawn on his riding mower. As had become somewhat of a ritual for them, Lee and Nicole ran out to the patio, waiting for him to come around so they could climb up into his lap and ride around the yard with him a few times.

Once he had finished, he started to chuckle as an idea came to him. He had noticed a large plastic sled they had stored in the shed during the summer months. He pulled his mower close to the shed, and then went inside to grab the sled and some rope. With the kids watching from the patio, he tied the sled to the back of the mower, leaving enough rope to keep them a safe distance from it.

"Come on, guys! Hop on!" he yelled with an ear to ear grin as he pulled up next to the patio with the sled in tow. Both of them ran to the sled and jumped on it, laughing with excitement.

"Hold on!" he yelled as he put it in its highest gear and took off.

Hearing them laughing hysterically from inside the house, Kim got up and walked outside to see what was going on. Just as she stepped outside, Sam turned the corner and took off up the hill leading to the back of their lot, both kids holding on with all of their strength as the sled bounced over the bumps and divots along the way. She began to laugh out loud seeing how much fun they were all having while at the same time wondering if Sam had lost his mind.

"Be careful!" she yelled out to him as he circled the yard and went flying past her.

"I can't hear you!" he yelled back as he turned the corner once again.

"Look mom!" Lee shouted, letting go of the sled and throwing his hands in the air.

"You hold on, Lee!" she shouted back, afraid he was going to tumble off.

After circling the yard a number of times, Sam pulled the mower to a stop in front of the patio and turned it off.

"Wanna go for a ride, baby?" he asked with a sly grin as he batted his eyebrows at her.

"Sam Grace!" she replied with a chuckle. "I believe you just might be insane."

"Yeah? And what was your first clue?"

"I don't remember. It was a very long time ago."

As he got off the mower, he could hear voices yelling from across the street. He walked around the side of his house and into the front yard to see the same group of teenagers playing basketball at the park. To the left of the park he saw one of his neighbors – an elderly woman – motioning for him to come over.

"What's going on?" he asked as he crossed the street and approached her.

"It's those boys," she replied, pointing at them. "I'm trying to play outdoors with my grandchildren, and their language is horrible."

Sam looked down to see two small children playing in her front yard, and then looked over toward the park.

"I'll take care of it," he said as he started toward them.

"Hey guys!" he yelled as he walked up. "You wanna watch your language? There's a lot of little kids around here. They don't need to hear that crap."

"Yeah, sorry, man," one of them answered.

Sam looked over the rest of the crowd. Standing in the middle was a short, cocky looking Hispanic kid who just stood there glaring at him.

"Thank you!" Sam replied, staring the kid down.

He had seen this kid before. He knew that he was dating a girl who lived down the block because he had seen them together a few times. Something about this kid gave Sam the impression that he was going be trouble. He started to ask around, wanting to learn who this kid was and where he had come from. What he discovered was that he wasn't from the neighborhood, but had been involved in a number of confrontations with a few of the other neighbors. They all described him as being very arrogant, obnoxious, and with a bad temper. Sam looked out his living room window a few days later and saw him sitting on a swing at the park by himself. He went outside and walked across the street to the park, sitting down on the swing right next to him.

"Hey, how ya doin?" Sam asked, getting no reply as he sat.

"Hey, listen," he continued. "I've been asking around about you. I know where you live. I know where your girlfriend lives. I know that you think you're a pretty bad dude, but I have to tell you something.

Do you see all of these houses along this block?" he asked, pointing up and down the street.

"In every single one of these houses, there's a family. And in every one of those families, there's a man who has worked very hard to get what he has. So I want you to understand just one thing. You have no idea whatsoever what a man will do, or what he's capable of doing, when it comes to protecting his home and his family. Do you get my point?"

"I'm outta here, man," the kid replied dismissively as he stood up and started to walk away.

"That's right, you are!" Sam yelled out. "Just

keep on walking."

A few weeks later, and after a variety of small skirmishes between them and the kids at the park, Sam's neighbors invited him and his family over for a barbecue. They had been drinking for a few hours, discussing the situation at the park as well as the complete lack of concern shown by the local police over it. They had all called the police on numerous occasions, but the answer was always the same. Until one of them had clearly broken the law, there was nothing they could do.

"Did you see what that one kid did by your car earlier?" Beth asked him.

"Which kid?" he replied.

"The Hispanic kid who's dating the girl down the block."

"No I didn't. What did he do?"

"They were both walking down the street, and when they got to where your car was parked, he turned toward it and was about to kick the driver's side door when his girlfriend pulled him away."

"Did he really?" Sam replied, feeling the anger building inside of him.

"Yeah, he did."

"When did this happen?"

"Just a few hours ago."

Sam felt the anger within him turning into outright rage as he stood up, his beer still in hand, and walked out to his car, looking it over for any signs of damage. He looked down the block to see four or five of the kids – including the Hispanic kid – hanging out near his girlfriend's front porch.

He went inside of his home, retrieving a 9mm handgun he kept near his bed to protect his family in case an intruder broke in. He tucked it inside of his belt and made his way outside.

He walked back out to his car, sat on the hood, and began pounding his fist on it.

"Hey!" he called out in a loud voice, looking

toward the crowd down the street. "You want some of this? Do ya? Come on and get it!"

Hearing the commotion, a few of his neighbors left the barbeque and walked over to where Sam was sitting. Including Sam, there were four of them. Dave and Fred, who were both neighbors, and Fred's brother-in-law. They were all large men, and they were all fed up with what had been going on in the neighborhood recently. They had all been drinking for a few hours too, which didn't help to calm the situation any.

"What's going on?" Fred asked as he approached

"They wanna dance? Let's dance," he answered, looking directly at the group down the street.

"Hey! You wanna do something to my car?" he yelled down the street. "Come on! Do it now, tough guy!"

The group stepped away from the front porch and looked back at them, not saying anything. A few minutes later, one of them started walking toward them. He didn't say a word as he passed, not even making eye contact as he did so. He then walked completely around the block, returning to the group to tell them what he saw.

Sam began to have second thoughts about having a gun in his belt. If the police arrived, it wouldn't look good, and might even cause him to be arrested. He walked back inside of his house to put it away, but when he had returned, everyone was gone. He looked down the block where the teenagers had been, but there was nobody there. He walked into his neighbor's back yard, but the men were all gone.

"What's going on?" Kim asked with a concerned expression.

"Nothing," he replied, turning back toward the front yard. "Stay back here with the kids. I'll be right back."

322

Still unable to find anyone, he walked back to his car and leaned against the side of it. Within a few minutes, he saw four guys walking toward him in the center of the street. At first, he thought it was his neighbors, but as they drew nearer, he realized that it was the group of teenagers. While seriously rethinking his decision to put his handgun back inside, he nonetheless stood his ground as they approached. To his surprise, they all continued past him, none of them saying a word or even as much as looking at him. He looked down the block again, this time seeing his neighbors walking down the center of the street behind them. He fell in with them as they passed, following the group of teenagers to the end of the block where they stopped.

Neither group said anything to each other for a few minutes, until the Hispanic kid left the group and started walking toward them.

"Hey!" one of the others called out to him. "You're on your own, man."

He stopped in his tracks, not being eager to take on four grown men by himself, and then turned back toward his friends.

"Coward!" Fred yelled out as he walked away.

"What did you say?!" the kid yelled back stopping to turn around again.

"You heard me," Fred answered. "Coward!" he repeated a second time.

With that, two of the kid's friends grabbed him and pulled him back into the crowd.

"Do you hear that?" Sam said, suddenly hearing multiple cars racing toward them.

Instantly, three cars appeared in the middle of the intersection and came to a screeching halt. All of the car doors flew open, and at least a dozen guys jumped out of them. Some were holding clubs or baseball bats as they approached, talking things over with the guys Sam and his neighbors had been following.

"This might be a little painful," Dave said, looking over the much larger and better armed group.

"Sixteen of them, four of us," Fred said with a chuckle. "I like those odds."

"Here we go," Sam said as the group turned and began to walk toward them.

Before they had taken more than just a few steps, police cars came racing upon the scene from every direction. They jumped from their cars, guns drawn, and surrounded the group of teenagers, who immediately dropped their weapons and put their hands in the air.

"Are you guys out of your minds?" one of the officers asked as he approached Sam and his neighbors.

"I don't know what you mean, officer," Sam replied.

"You can't be doing stuff like this!" he insisted.

"Stuff like what?" Dave replied innocently. "We're just a few neighbors enjoying a nice walk on a warm summer night."

"Don't give me that crap!" the officer snapped back. "I told you to call us if anything happened. I told you not to confront these guys."

"We weren't confronting anyone, officer. We were escorting them," Fred replied.

"Yeah," Sam added. "They looked really lost and frightened. We were simply making sure they made it out of the neighborhood ok."

The officer shook his head and turned away from them. The other officers rounded up the group of teenagers and began questioning them. Before they had left, they arrested a number of them for various charges, warning all of them to stay away from the park or they would risk being arrested again.

"Sam...," Kim called out as she approached him on the sidewalk in front of their home.

"Yeah, baby."

"That was an absolutely crazy thing to do! Why

did you do that? You could've been killed!"

"What was I supposed to do? Just let em take over the neighborhood?" he replied, indignant.

"It's not your job to save the neighborhood!" she answered, raising her voice.

"Well, somebody had to do something."

"Sam, we have two kids! What would we do if something bad had happened to you?"

"Well, nothing did," he replied, bringing his beer up to take another swig.

"Sam, I think you've had enough to drink," she said, reaching to take the beer from his hand.

"What are you? My mother?" he replied angrily while pulling it away from her.

Kim stared at him for a few minutes, feeling heartbroken. She noticed that he was beginning to stagger slightly, and his speech was becoming a little slurred.

"Come on, kids," she said to Lee and Nicole as she looked down toward them. "It's time for bed."

"Are you coming inside, Sam?"" she asked, looking back at him.

"I'm gonna have another beer," he replied. "I'll be there in a little while."

He returned to Fred's back yard, sat down, and they all continued drinking until the early morning hours.

Kim was beginning to worry about his drinking. She'd never seen him drunk before, and she didn't like the way his personality had changed. She saw an anger and rage in him that she'd never seen before, and it frightened her deeply. She awoke the next morning to find him passed out on the living room sofa, still in his clothes, with a half empty beer on the floor next to him. Being afraid that the kids might walk out of their rooms and see him like that, she picked up the beer and threw it away, and then woke him up, telling him to go sleep in the bedroom.

Once the kids woke up and came out of their

325

rooms, she made breakfast for the three of them, and then left quietly to take them out for the day.

Sam awoke a few hours later to find them gone. His head was throbbing from a hangover, and he was feeling a little nauseous. He poured himself a cup of coffee and then walked outside, sitting down on the patio.

He looked over into Fred's back yard to see dozens of empty beer cans scattered everywhere. He hadn't seen a mess like that since his time in the Navy, when he and all of his buddies would stay up drinking all night long and then be forced to clean up the aftermath the following morning. He hadn't felt this hung over since then either. It was a very familiar feeling, but not one that he enjoyed.

After having a few more cups of coffee and a small breakfast, he began to feel a little bit better. He laid on the sofa watching t.v. for a few hours, allowing his head to clear a bit more. He wasn't really watching t.v. as much as he was just staring at the screen with a blank expression, his mind wandering.

An old, black and white movie he'd never seen before was playing, when a scene caught his attention. In this scene, a young man was sitting in front of his deceased father's tombstone, speaking to him as if he were there. The young man was very upset, crying uncontrollably as he poured his heart out within the words he was speaking.

Sam began to think about all of the things he had wanted to say to his father before he had passed away, but never had the chance to. When he had expressed his sadness over this to a few family members, they suggested that he say whatever he wanted to say now, assuring him that his father could hear him. He really didn't have any strong belief in the afterlife, so he doubted that this was true. At the same time, he understood that there could be some psychological benefit found in doing so. Kim and the kids had been gone for quite some time, and he had no idea when they might return. After thinking everything over for a while, and not wanting to just lay around the house by himself all day, he decided to drive into the city where his father was buried and express to him what was on his mind.

The last time he had been to his father's gravesite was the day he was buried. He wasn't exactly sure where it was, but he had a general idea. He pulled into the cemetery and drove all the way to the back, fairly certain he was close.

"Ok...Where are you at, dad?" he whispered under his breath as he began to walk slowly through the rows of gravesites, reading the names on the headstones as he passed each one. He didn't even remember what his father's headstone had looked like, so he had no idea what to look for.

As he was walking, he passed a row of small bushes. A robin flew from one of them, startling him for a second. He stopped and watched as it flew away to his right. Thinking this might be some sort of a sign, while at the same time thinking that he might be nuts to believe so, he walked along the path the bird had flown. After taking only fifteen or twenty steps, he looked down to see his father's headstone directly in front of him. He stopped for a second, stunned that this bird had apparently led him directly to it, and then sat in the grass in front of it. He kept silent for a few minutes, not sure what to say or how to say it. He couldn't remember ever having any conversation of any depth with him before, but at this point, he knew that he would be the one who controlled any conversation that might occur. Maybe he could hear him, or maybe he couldn't, but either way he knew he'd feel some sort of relief from saying what was on his mind. His eyes began to well up with tears as he thought everything through. He tried to speak a few times, but stopped himself, wanting to be sure that the words came out right.

He looked around him, scanning the horizon.

There was a busy road running along the back side of the cemetery, with heavy traffic moving in each direction. To his right, there was a run-down looking apartment complex with debris scattered throughout the common area. The fence surrounding the cemetery was covered with paper and plastic garbage that had been blown against it while caught in the wake of the fast moving traffic.

"So this is how it all ends, huh?" he thought to himself as he realized that his father's body had been laid to rest in such a cluttered, dirty section of the cemetery.

Gazing back upon the headstone, his thoughts turned to how much guilt he had felt ever since his father had passed away. He had wished many times that he would've put his own feelings aside and visited him while he was in the hospital. Had he done so, maybe the two of them could've said some things to each other that would've mended their relationship to some degree. Maybe there would've been some sort of closure for both of them.

"Hey Dad," he began, choking up a bit. "Listen…I don't know if you can hear me or not, but I drove all the way down here because there are some things I need to say to you."

The tears began to flow more profusely as he continued to speak, blurring his vision as he stared at the headstone.

"Dad, I'm so sorry," he whispered, breaking down inside. "I know that you and I had our differences. We never saw things eye to eye. We were just very different people, and we were never able to understand each other.

I don't know why things had to be the way they were. I don't understand why we couldn't have had a good relationship. Maybe I never will. I truly wish that we could've had that, but it just didn't turn out that way."

He turned away, looking off into the distance

while wiping the tears away that were now streaming down his cheeks.

"Dad…I should've visited you when you were in the hospital. I was just so very angry. I was hurt, but it was wrong of me to simply leave you there to die. I'm so very sorry, dad. You were there for months, and I never came by. I never called. That was so very wrong of me, and I can't even begin to express how sorry I am for doing that to you. You're my dad, and even though we had our share of differences, I want you to know that I love you."

He sat there in silence for a few more minutes, the tears continuing to flow. He raised his eyes and looked over at the apartment complex again. Suddenly, out of nowhere, a thought entered his mind. It wasn't a voice he heard in his head, but it seemed to him as though his father spoke directly to him through his thoughts.

"Sam," the internal voice answered. "The whole time I was in that hospital, there was a phone sitting right at my bedside. I was there for months, and at any given time I could've picked it up and called you to try to make things right…but I never did."

Sam stood to his feet feeling a sense of rage flow over him with an intensity he had never felt before. His mind flashed to a vision of the hospital room his father had been in the last time he'd visited. Just to the right of his father, as clear as day, he could see a telephone sitting on a small table, within arm's reach. It had never once occurred to him that his father bared as much responsibility for things ending the way that they had as he did. Even though Sam was a man at the time, he was a very young man, stubborn in his ways and without the wisdom to know that this guilt would remain in him for the rest of his life. His father surely should've had enough wisdom at that age to know that he should pick up that phone, but he never did. That thought left Sam with the incredibly painful realization that his father had somehow come to the conclusion that he'd rather die alone, with things remaining just as they were, than to make even the slightest effort to talk to his son before he died.

"How could you do that to me?" he said, stepping back from the gravesite in amazement. "I was your son! How could you do that?"

He turned away, the tears flowing even more heavily, and stormed back to his car. Once inside, he began beating his fists against the steering wheel. He felt incredibly hurt and humiliated that his father could think so little of him. He started his car and sped off, nearly causing an accident as he pulled out of the driveway into the heavy traffic.

The further he drove from the cemetery, the angrier he became. He regretted driving there in the first place. He felt like an absolute fool for ever feeling even slightly guilty about not visiting his father, and he swore to himself that he would never visit his gravesite again.

The house was still empty when he arrived back home, so he made himself some dinner, opened a beer, and then walked outside, sitting down on the patio chair. Kim returned with the kids a couple hours later, and after they had put them to bed, she joined him outside.

"How are you feeling?" she asked.

"Eh…I'm ok," he replied.

"How late did you stay next door last night?"

"I'm not really sure…I stayed a few hours after you went to bed."

"You drank quite a bit last night. Were you hung over this morning?"

"No…not really," he replied, wanting to downplay the amount.

"How many beers did you have?"

"I don't know…I wasn't really counting…Maybe 4 or 5."

"I think you had more than that."

"Please don't give me a hard time, ok? I'm really not in the mood," he replied, wanting to avoid the topic.

"Ok...I'm sorry."

They sat in uncomfortable silence for a few minutes, staring out over the back yard. Sam started to think again about what had happened at the cemetery earlier, and it began to wear on him.

"I went to see my dad today," he said quietly.

"You did what?" she replied, slightly confused.

"I went to see my dad...at the cemetery."

"Why did you do that?" she asked, knowing that he had never done so before.

"I don't know...I guess I just felt as though I needed to clear some things up between us. I felt like I had to say a few things to him."

"And how did it go?" she asked, concerned by his facial expression.

"Not so well," he replied, looking down at his beer.

"What happened?" she asked, reaching over to rub his arm.

"Well, I went down there to say that I was sorry for not visiting him while he was in the hospital. I apologized to him for that, and I told him that I love him, but something occurred to me as I was sitting there talking to him."

"What's that?" she asked, continuing to rub his arm compassionately.

"The last time I saw him, he talked to me like I was an absolute piece of trash. He humiliated me in front of my aunts and uncles."

"I know, babe...I'm so sorry," she replied, raising her hand to run her fingers through his hair.

"He had no reason to do that."

"I know he didn't. You're a good man, Sam."

"After I had left, I never went back. He knew that was the last conversation we'd ever had. He laid there, dying, for quite a few weeks after that. Through all of that, there was a phone sitting right next to his bedside. He could've picked it up at any time and called me to apologize, or if not to apologize, to simply try to make things right."

He paused for a few seconds, feeling himself starting to choke up as he spoke. He didn't want to break down in front of her, so he took another sip of his beer and cleared his throat.

"How could a fifty year-old man leave his own son behind like that, knowing that the very last conversation we would ever have had ended the way that it did? How could he possibly leave me, remembering that the very last words he spoke to me were so rotten?"

"Oh, Sam…," she replied, moving close to him and wrapping her arms around him. "I'm so sorry…He shouldn't have done that to you."

"It's just not right, you know?"

"No…it isn't."

"I would never do that to Lee…I couldn't. If I found out that I was dying, and he and I had a heated argument about something, the first thing I'd want to do would be to make things right with him."

"I know you would, babe."

"It's absolutely unthinkable. I mean, did he really hate me that much?"

"No, Sam. He was your father. I'm sure he loved you."

"Yeah? Well he sure had a funny way of showing it."

"Sam…," she answered, sitting back in her chair to look him in the eyes. "Some men have a very hard time expressing how they feel about others, especially men from that generation. They were raised to be tough and strong. They were taught that expressing your emotions was weak. They came from the John Wayne era. They didn't know any better. They weren't like you, babe."

Sam stood from his chair and walked into the

house, returning a minute later with another beer. Kim desperately wanted to talk to him about how much he'd been drinking recently, but she knew this wasn't the time.

"Are you ok?" she asked, reaching out to hold his hand.

"Yeah, I'm ok," he responded, shrugging it off. "It is what it is," he continued, throwing back another swig of his beer.

He continued to drink every night after coming home from work, which was really beginning to bother Kim. What was once just one or two beers per night was becoming three or four, and then five or six. The more he would drink, the angrier he became. Some nights he would sit outside by himself, literally drinking himself to sleep every night, while other nights he would scale it back a bit.

As the kids were growing up, he made a habit of reading them a bedtime story every night before tucking them in for the evening. It had gradually become every other night, and then every third or fourth night, leaving the kids wondering why he wasn't doing it much anymore. Instead of arguing, and trying not to make him feel guilty, Kim gradually took over that role.

"Mom, is dad mad at me or something?" Nicole asked one night as Kim was tucking her in.

"No, honey," she replied. "Why would you think that?"

"He never reads me bedtime stories or tucks me in anymore."

"I know, honey," she replied, kissing her forehead. "He's just been very tired."

"He never talks to me anymore either. He comes home after work, eats dinner, and then sits outside not talking to anyone."

"I know, honey. Your father loves you very much. He's just going through a hard time right now and wants to be left alone."

"Is he ok, mom?"

"Yeah…he's ok," she replied. "Go to sleep now, ok?" she continued, standing up to turn off the bedroom light.

"Mom?" she said just as Kim stepped away.

"Yes, honey?"

"I love you."

"I love you too, sweetie. Get some sleep, alright?"

Kim's heart began to break as she walked away. She walked through the kitchen, making her way outside to find Sam sitting on the deck chair with a beer in his hand.

"Sam, we need to talk," she said, sitting down next to him.

"About what?" he replied coldly.

"About Nicole. She just asked me if you were mad at her for something."

"Why would she think that I'm mad at her?"

"Because you never tuck her in or read her bedtime stories anymore. She also said that you don't talk to her anymore, and that all you do when you come home is sit out here by yourself."

"Are you serious?!" he asked incredulously.

"Yes, Sam, I'm serious!"

"Alright…I'll talk to her."

"Sam, this has to stop," she replied in a firm tone.

"What has to stop?"

"Your drinking. It has to stop. It's getting out of control."

"Why is this about my drinking all of a sudden?" he asked, feeling agitated.

"Because that's all you do anymore when you come home. You don't talk to me. You don't talk to the kids. You don't talk to anyone! You walk in the door, eat your dinner, and then come out here and start drinking one beer after another!"

"Hey, I'm a grown man! If I want a couple of

beers after working like a dog all day, I'm gonna have a couple of beers!" he barked back, his face turning red with anger.

"But it's too much, Sam!" she pleaded. "Can't you see how it's affecting everyone?"

"Yes, I do!" he snapped back sarcastically. "But do you know what's really odd to me? I'm the one drinking the beer, and yet it somehow transforms you into a relentless, nagging, pain in the neck. Leave me alone, will ya?!"

Kim stared back at him in stunned silence as he finished his beer and then walked inside to get another one, plopping back into his chair and opening it loudly as he glared at her.

"I don't even know who you are anymore, Sam," she said quietly, her voice cracking slightly.

"I'm me...The same guy I've always been," he replied without looking at her.

"You're not the man that I married. The man I married was kind and thoughtful and caring. The man that I married looked at me as though I was the most beautiful woman on the planet. The man I married used to go for long walks with me, and he used to talk to me. I don't know what happened to him, but I really miss him...I'm going to bed, Sam."

"Goodnight! Sweet dreams!" he shouted sarcastically as she walked away.

Her eyes were filled with tears as she made her way down the hallway and into the bedroom. She closed the door quietly behind her, and then laid down on the bed, sobbing into her pillow. She couldn't understand how Sam could've changed so much in such a short period of time. She still loved him with all of her heart, but she didn't like him very much at this point. She thought back to what might have happened to bring all of this on, wondering if maybe his experience at the cemetery had brought something out of him that was causing him to act this way. She began to wonder if maybe he needed some help, but she had no idea how she could help him.

After sitting by himself for an hour or so, Sam began to feel guilty about having hurt Nicole and Kim. He thought back to the days when he was a young boy, seeing his father drunk and out of control. He had sworn to himself that he would never be that guy, and he was beginning to see some similarities. That thought frightened him a bit. He would never have wanted to make Kim or the kids feel that type of fear. He finished his beer, and then walked to Nicole's bedroom, quietly opened her door, and kneeled down next to her bed.

"Hey, sweetie," he whispered. "Are you sleeping?"

Seeing no response, he leaned over and kissed her on the cheek.

"I love you, sweetie," he said softly as he stood up and left her room, turning to enter his bedroom.

Kim was sound asleep when he entered, having cried herself to sleep awhile earlier.

"Hey, baby," he said in a soft voice as he laid down next to her and put his arm around her. "I'm so very sorry."

Waking from her slumber, she reached back and started to rub his forearm, pulling his arm more tightly around her.

"I'm just getting worried about you, Sam. I'm worried about us."

"I know," he replied, kissing her cheek. "I'll stop the drinking, ok? I didn't realize that it was having such a negative impact on everyone."

"It's ok, babe," she replied, turning to face him.

"I don't want to turn out like my father," he whispered.

"You're nothing like your father, Sam. You're such a good husband and such a good father, and we're all very proud of you."

"Thank you, baby," he said, kissing her on the forehead. "I'm trying my best."

Sam came home from work the next day, ate dinner with his family, helped Kim clean off the table and do the dishes, and then took everyone out for ice cream. Throughout the entire evening, he went out of his way to connect with all of them. He could sense an immediate difference in how they reacted to him. He missed being the family they had been in the past, as did everyone. After a very nice evening together, he brought them back home, read the kids a bedtime story, and tucked them in.

"Thank you for a wonderful evening, babe," Kim said with a smile as he re-entered the living room.

"Thank you for being a wonderful wife, baby," he replied.

"Hey, I'm sorry for nagging you," she said softly, putting her head on his shoulder after he had sat down next to her. "I don't mean to nag."

"You had every right to," he replied. "I was being a bit of a jerk."

"Yes, you were," she answered, laughing.

"I know...I don't know why I was acting that way. I guess I was just stressed out from work and all of the nonsense that was going on at the park. I felt as though I just needed a little something to take the edge off so I could sleep."

"I can understand that," she replied. "I didn't mind you having one or two beers after work. It just got out of control a little bit."

"Yeah, I know. Thanks for showing me the error of my ways," he said, laughing.

"Well, *somebody* needs to keep you in line, Mr. Grace. It might as well be me," she replied, playfully flicking his ear.

Sam didn't drink at all over the next few weeks, and he tried his best to leave the stresses of work at the door, making sure that he didn't bring them home with him. After one unusually grueling day, he was really feeling the need to have a few on his way home. His boss had been on his back all day long due to problems that had nothing to do with him, and he left work feeling exceptionally tense and frustrated. Knowing that walking in through his front door with a case of beer would send Kim into a tailspin, he stopped at a local liquor store and picked up a small bottle of vodka. He knew that it would be difficult for her to detect it on his breath, and he figured that he could get away with taking just a swig or two after dinner without her being aware of it. He pulled over about a block away from home and opened the bottle.

"Just enough to take the edge off," he thought to himself. He looked around to ensure that nobody was watching, and then drank two or three mouths full before hiding it in his glove compartment.

Kim seemed completely unaware that he had been drinking at all throughout the entire evening. He made a point of being nice to her and the kids, knowing that showing any signs of irritability might alert her.

As evening fell, he read the kids their bedtime stories, tucked them in, and then walked outside to his car after Kim had gone to take a shower. Looking around quickly, he pulled the bottle from his glove compartment and took another swallow. Upon returning inside, he grabbed a bag of chips, eating a handful to cover his breath before opening a soft drink and then sat in front of the television.

"Snacking this late is gonna make you chubby," she said with a chuckle upon returning to see him with the chips.

"You've never seen me chubby before," he replied with a smile. "Who knows? Maybe you'll like it."

"I guess it's never too late to try something new."

"That's right," he said with a smirk. "Besides, there'd just be more of me for you to be in awe of."

"Good point…And you could keep me warmer

through the winter months with your pudgy little belly," she giggled, leaning back away from him.

"Warmer is good."

"I could even warm my cold feet on it," she said with a laugh, playfully sliding her feet underneath his shirt.

"So that's all I am to you?" he asked in a deadpan voice. "Your personal foot warmer?"

"No...of course not...But it's a nice perk."

"Just one of many fringe benefits I have to offer."

"Sam...I'm very proud of you," she said with a warm smile.

"For what?"

"For putting the drinking behind you, and for putting our family first."

"It's not a big deal, baby," he replied, feeling a little guilty inside.

"Well, *I* think it's a big deal," she said, leaning back against him.

Sam didn't reply, simply wanting that conversation to end. Deep down inside, he wanted to do what was right. He didn't want to drink. He didn't want to hurt Kim or the kids. He knew that if she found out that he had been drinking – especially in the sneaky way he had done so – it would break her heart. That being the case, he also knew that he needed something to calm himself down at the end of the day. He began to justify his actions in his own mind, believing that he deserved the small amount of peace he felt after a few drinks. He believed that if he was smart about it, he could have what he saw as the best of both worlds. He could get what he needed by sneaking off to take a drink if the mood struck him while keeping her from finding out, and therefore keeping her happily believing that all was well.. He managed to pull this off successfully for a number of months, stopping on the way home from work to drink a little bit, and then sneaking out to his car for a sip here and there while she was busy doing other things. She nearly caught him on a few occasions, walking outside just after he had put the bottle back in his car, but he managed to keep it hidden from her with some fast thinking.

As time went on, he found himself making more and more trips to his car throughout the course of the evening. His tolerance for alcohol began to increase, as did his desire for more. He managed to keep his temper in check, which was becoming increasingly difficult for him.

It all began to unravel for him one night when he had a little too much to drink. It was late in the evening, just before bedtime, and he had made one too many trips out to the car. He stood from his chair and stumbled to the side for a couple of steps, catching Kim's attention.

"Are you okay, Sam?" she asked with a puzzled expression.

"Yeah, I'm fine," he replied with slightly slurred speech.

"Sam?"

"Yeah, baby," he answered, not wanting to make eye contact.

"Come here a minute," she said, standing to step toward him.

"Hang on…I have to go to the bathroom," he replied, turning away and ducking down the hallway.

He entered the bathroom and locked the door, turning to look at himself in the mirror.

"Hold it together, dude," he thought to himself, knowing that she might be on to him.

He remained in the bathroom for a few minutes, rinsing his face with cold water, and then brushing his teeth in an effort to hide any trace of alcohol on his breath. He took a deep breath, and then opened the bathroom door to find Kim standing just outside of it.

"What were you doing in there?" she asked

suspiciously.

"I was just getting ready for bed, baby," he replied, stepping forward to give her a kiss.

"Sam...look at me," she said, pushing him away from her to look in his eyes. "Have you been drinking?"

"What?! Why would you ask me that?!" he protested.

"Why did you stumble when you stood up a few minutes ago? And why does your speech sound slurred?"

"I'm just really tired, baby. It's been a long day. I'm gonna go to bed. Are you coming?"

"Okay," she replied, not really believing him, but not completely certain that he wasn't telling the truth. "Yeah, I'll be there in a few minutes," she continued.

"Okay," he answered. "Goodnight, baby."

He walked into the bedroom, closing the door behind him. He climbed into bed with a sigh of relief, knowing that he had just dodged a bullet.

Kim returned to the living room and waited until he was asleep. After being fairly certain that he was, she went to the bathroom and began to look through the cabinet for any form of alcohol. Not finding anything, she went into the kitchen and began to search there. She opened every cabinet, moving things around to ensure that there was nothing hidden anywhere. She dug through the trash, looking for empty bottles, but found nothing.

She returned to the living room and sat on the sofa. She was nearly certain that he had been drinking, but began to think that maybe he was telling the truth. Maybe he *was* just very tired from a long day at work.

As she sat there thinking things over, a car came down their street and passed the front of the house. In doing so, the headlights shone across the side of Sam's car sitting in the driveway. Her mind instantly flashed back to the few times she had walked outside and had seen him reaching into the passenger side putting something away. She sprang to her feet and hurried outside. She opened the passenger side door and looked inside. She couldn't see much in the darkness, so she reached down with her hand, feeling around on the floor and under the seat. She sat inside of the car, looking into the back seat and feeling around on the floor there. She then felt under the driver's seat, but again found nothing.

Looking forward, her eyes became fixed upon the glove compartment. She reached forward and opened it, and when she did, a half-empty bottle of vodka fell out into her lap.

"Oh Sam!" she cried out, her heat sinking deep within her chest and her eyes filling with tears. "How could you?"

She sat in the car, weeping for a few minutes, unable to move. She felt so incredibly betrayed and crushed deep within her soul she could barely breathe. She kept staring down at the bottle in her hands, at a complete and total loss as to why he not only be drinking again, but that he would be lying to her about it also.

She stood from the car, holding the bottle in her hand, and quietly closed the door. She then walked back inside, tears streaming down her cheeks. She thought about waking him up and confronting him with what she had found, but remembering the angry confrontations they'd had about his drinking in the past, she didn't want to repeat those experiences.

She walked into the kitchen and poured what was left in the bottle down the sink. Wanting it to be the very first thing he'd see when he awoke in the morning, she then turned and placed it in plain view, on the center of the countertop. She then returned to the sofa, her heart completely broken, and cried herself to sleep.

ELEVEN

Sam looked through his window as he felt the train slowing down once again. He noticed that the land they were traveling through seemed to be very dry and sun baked, as though the area had experienced a severe drought of some sort. Off in the distance, he could see a dried up riverbed. It was clear to him that it had once been a fairly large river, so he imagined that this drought must have been going on for quite some time.

He put his head back and closed his eyes, thinking back to the morning he walked into his kitchen to find that empty vodka bottle on the counter. Although he knew he had hurt Kim very badly by continuing to drink behind her back while lying about it the whole time, it angered him that she wouldn't just allow him to have a few drinks if he needed them. After all, he thought, he had been a model citizen otherwise. He had been spending time with the kids, playing with them, being a good father, reading them bedtime stories every night, and a multitude of other things to make sure they knew they were loved. He had been a good husband too. He continually complimented Kim, he spent as much time alone with her as he could, he was faithful, and he continually encouraged her in whatever she was doing at the time. On top of all that, he thought, he was a darn good provider. He paid the mortgage every month, he maintained their home well, and he brought enough money home to put food on the table every night. In his eyes, he was doing everything right, so what else did she want from him?

The more he thought all of that through, the angrier he became. He was sick and tired of everyone trying to tell him what to do, micro-managing every area of his life, and trying to control him. No matter how much he did, he thought, it was never enough. He was never good enough in his father's eyes, in his boss's eyes, and now he wasn't good enough in hers.

He picked up the empty bottle and threw it against the kitchen wall, shattering it into a thousand pieces. Hearing the loud crash from the living room, Kim came running into the kitchen.

"What just happened?!" she asked him frantically.

"So!" he yelled, turning on his feet to face her. "You had to go digging through my car, huh?!"

"Sam...I was worried!" she pleaded, immediately feeling guilty for doing so.

"Let me ask you something," he shouted back at her. "Don't I provide you with a good life?! Don't you have everything that you need?!"

"Well...yeah...of course you do," she stammered.

"Have I ever said no to you whenever you've asked me to do anything?!"

"No..."

"And how about the kids? Do they have nice clothes on their backs? Is there food on the table every day? Have they ever gone hungry? Are all of their needs being met?"

Kim stood silently, terrified by the look of intense rage in his eyes and not wanting to say anything that would anger him further.

"Then why do you feel the need to snoop around trying to find something I'm doing wrong, and then pull some passive-aggressive stunt like this?"

"I'm sorry, Sam...I didn't know it would upset you."

"You didn't know it would upset me?!" he replied, raising his voice even louder.

"Please stop screaming at me!"

"Let me tell you something," he said with a growl, stepping closer to her. "I'm under a lot of pressure here, and I'm doing the best that I can. If I want to have a few drinks to relax a little bit, then that's exactly what I'm gonna do. And nobody – not you or anyone else – is gonna stop me from doing so. You got it?!"

"Sam...I'm sorry...You were just drinking too much before."

"Do you wanna know why I drink?... Huh?... Do ya?...It's because of you! You're the reason why I have to drink every night!"

"Me?! What are you talking about?! she asked incredulously.

"Because nothing I do is ever enough for you!" he barked back. "All the good things I do are completely ignored by you, but if I wanna have just one drink, you'll throw that in my face, acting like I just killed somebody!"

"I'm so sorry, Sam…I never meant to make you feel that way."

"Well, congratulations. You just did."

With that, Sam turned and stormed out of the house, not returning for a few days. Kim considered everything he had just said, and started to think that maybe he was right. He did do a lot of things right. She felt guilty for making him feel so angry and frustrated, and swore to herself that she'd be more aware of what she was doing to bring that on.

Thinking back as he sat on the train, he started to become angry all over again. In his mind, that moment was the beginning of the end of their marriage, and he blamed her for it. Had she not been so controlling, everything would've been just fine.

"Next stop, Joseph," Gabriel shouted.

Sam peered through the glass at the upcoming station, and saw what looked like some sort of farmer's market surrounding it. There were multitudes of people lining up to buy various types of food from what appeared to be an endless stockpile. Given the degree of what looked to him like a severe drought surrounding the area, this seemed very odd to him. He assumed that the food he saw must've been shipped there from somewhere else, but he couldn't imagine how such a large amount could've been moved there. His mouth began to water as he looked at the many carts bearing fresh fruit, vegetables, breads and grains. He couldn't remember the last time he had eaten, but he knew that it was a long time ago.

In the center of the merchants who were selling these items, he fixed his gaze upon a man wearing a very odd looking jacket. It was completely covered with various colored stripes, and as far as Sam could tell, it looked as though he wore it to draw attention to

346

himself for some reason, as if he wanted people to be able to find him in the crowd.

Sam watched as the man walked back and forth amongst the vendors, apparently giving them instructions as they waited on the people. Just as the train started to move again, the man picked up a basket of fruit, and then turned to look at Sam with a facial expression that seemed as though he was offering some of it to him. Sam's stomach started to growl as he thought about how delicious it would probably be. He looked away just as Gabriel was walking past his seat.

"Excuse me," he said, reaching out to catch Gabriel's arm.

"Yes, sir?" he replied, pausing in the aisle.

"I know this might be a strange question, but I'm very hungry. Are there any vending machines on this train where I might be able to grab a snack?"

"There are no vending machines, sir. There is, however, a complimentary buffet in the next car," he replied, pointing toward the front of the train.

"Oh, man! That's great! Thank you!" Sam said as he stood up.

"You're very welcome, sir."

Sam walked to the front of the car and then slid the door open, stepping into the vestibule, and then opened the following door to enter the next car. His eyes grew wide and his mouth immediately began to water as he looked around the car. There was a long table on either side, running the entire length of the car. Just to his right, there was a stack of fine china, cloth napkins, and what appeared to be very expensive silverware. Beyond that, there was an extremely elaborate salad bar with every possible salad topping one could imagine, followed by at least a dozen different types of salad dressings.

In the corner at the end of the car there was a bread table, piled high with rolls, bagels, and loaves of bread. From where he was standing he could see rye, pumpernickel, white, and wheat breads.

As he scanned the table on the other side, he saw many different types of meat and seafood. There were three carving tables – one for prime rib, one for ham, and another for turkey. Beyond the carving tables were large platters piled high with lobster, crab legs, shrimp, and salmon.

As he gazed around the room, it looked to him as if somebody had gathered together every single one of his favorite foods and then laid them out in front of him. He had no idea where to even begin. Everything he laid his eyes on looked more delicious than the next. The only thing he knew for certain was that he wouldn't be eating any salad.

He picked up a plate, and then walked directly toward the seafood table, loading it up with lobster tail, crab legs and shrimp. After devouring all of it, he loaded his plate with prime rib. He thought that maybe it was only because he was famished, but according to his own taste, everything he ate was cooked to absolute perfection. It couldn't have been prepared any better had he ordered it himself, asking that it be made just as he would've wanted it. Every bite seemed to taste better than the last, and he couldn't get enough of it.

"If you eat any faster you're gonna stab yourself with your fork," he heard a man say across the table from him.

He looked up suddenly, being so focused on the food in front of him that he was completely unaware that anyone else was even in the room.

"This food is amazing," he replied, looking over to see a man dressed from head to toe in camouflage sitting at the table with him.

"Yeah, it looks pretty good," he replied, looking down at Sam's plate.

"Have you tried any of it?" Sam asked, noticing that there wasn't a plate in front of him.

"No...I don't have much of an appetite right

now."

"Oh...," Sam thought to himself as he took another mouthful of prime rib. "So you thought you'd just sit here and bother a complete stranger while he's trying to enjoy a meal? Lucky me."

"I don't know how anyone can with this world being in the state that it is."

"Yeah?" Sam mumbled through his mouthful of food.

"Yeah!" he replied, raising his voice slightly. "This corrupt and completely inept government of ours has its hands in all of our pockets, taking everything we have, and for what!? So they can stuff the bank accounts of their rich friends and family members while our people starve in the streets?"

"Look," Sam said as he glanced across the table, slightly annoyed. "I'm not really into politics, and even if I was, I'd keep whatever opinions I had to myself."

"But don't you see? That's the problem! Nobody wants to talk about what they're doing. Everyone just goes about their business, trying to look after number one. People need to get involved. The only way things are gonna change is if we come together as a people and demand something more."

"Hey, no offense, man, but I'm trying to eat here. Do you mind?" Sam replied with an agitated tone.

"Yeah, go ahead!" the man answered harshly. "Go ahead and stuff your face while people are starving out there!"

"Listen!" Sam replied, his face growing red with anger as he pushed himself back from the table. "What's your name?" he asked sarcastically.

"Simon."

"Listen, Simon, all I'm trying to do is enjoy a meal here. I have no desire to know what your political beliefs are, and I'm even less compelled to talk about mine. Why don't you leave me alone and go find someone who cares, okay?"

With that, Sam stood up and returned to the food table, feeling extremely annoyed, but not wanting to cause a scene.

"We can't just turn our backs on what this government is doing!" Simon replied in a loud voice as he stood from the table and started to walk toward the door. "Those who refuse to fight for what's right are just as guilty as those who oppress the poor and needy. Every single day there are people dying in the streets while we sit back and do nothing to help them. You'll pay for your indifference! We all need to be zealous about doing what's right!"

"Yeah, yeah, yeah," Sam answered, waving his hand in a dismissive gesture. "Why don't you go be zealous somewhere else. I've got some crab legs that need to be eaten here."

Sam began to place some crab legs upon his plate, and then threw the plate back down on the table, feeling too annoyed to eat anymore.

"Thanks for ruining my appetite, you jerk," he muttered under his breath.

"Did you enjoy your meal, sir?" Gabriel asked as he returned to the passenger car and took a seat.

"What?" Sam replied with an irritated tone.

"Your meal.....Did you enjoy your meal?"

"Oh...yes," Sam replied. "It was delicious. Thank you."

"Good!" Gabriel replied. "People who have eaten here have gone as far as to say that if they were asked to choose their last meal, they'd want to come back here."

"Yeah?" Sam replied with one eyebrow raised. "That's quite a compliment to the chef."

"Indeed it is."

"How long is the buffet open?" Sam asked, thinking that he might want to return later if he was on the train long enough.

"It never closes, sir."

Sam hadn't eaten that well in a very long time. While he truly enjoyed dining at finer restaurants, he wouldn't even be allowed to enter one in his current state. Even if he could, there was no way he could afford to dine there. Thinking back, he couldn't even remember the last time he had been to one.

After his previous confrontation with Kim over the vodka bottle, his drinking not only continued, but grew to a point when he had begun to plan his entire day around when and where he could have his next drink. There grew an increasing distance between them, as he didn't want her to annoy him about it and she didn't want to be around him when he had been drinking. They had grown so far apart over the years that it didn't even feel as though they were in a relationship anymore. They merely existed together under the same roof, keeping the family together only for the sake of the kids. Because of the tension that was evident in their home on a daily basis, Lee and Nicole each rented apartments with friends as soon as they were old enough and able to move out. This left Sam and Kim alone in their home, and it took away any reason for Sam to stop drinking, much less slow down.

After staying up far too late one evening, drinking until just a few hours before sunrise, Sam passed out on the sofa. He awoke a few hours later, jostled from his slumber by the sound of the telephone.

"Hello?" he answered in a raspy voice.

"Sam?"

"Yeah?"

"It's Johnny. Where the heck are you? Are you coming to work today?"

"Oh...yeah. What time is it? My clock must've stopped," he replied, trying to think fast.

"It's 7:15. You're already late."

"Alright. I'm sorry Johnny. I'll be there within the hour."

He staggered toward the bedroom, getting a change of clothes, and then took a quick shower. He was still feeling a little drunk from the night before, so he poured himself an oversized cup of coffee, drinking it quickly to try to snap himself out of it. Once he had finished it, he poured himself a cup to go and headed for work.

Upon arriving, he was able to successfully avoid any lengthy conversations with anyone. He was given his assignment, and then immediately walked outside to get into his truck, relieved that nobody had noticed his inebriated condition.

He knew that all he needed to do was to make it through the first few hours of the day without incident. After that, he'd be just fine.

He started his truck, and then pulled out of the lot, heading for the open road. He could feel the effects of his intoxication, making him less sure of what was going on around him. He rolled down the driver's side window to allow the fresh air in, thinking that it might help.

As he approached the first major intersection, his coffee bounced out of the cup holder, landing on the side of his leg. He reached down quickly to pick it up, taking his eyes off of the road for a second. Panic struck him as he looked back up to see that he had inadvertently pulled the wheel to his right while looking down, and his truck was heading straight for the ditch along the side of the road. He quickly jerked the wheel back to the left, but it was too late. The gravel shoulder had grabbed his passenger side front tire, dragging the truck closer to the ditch. As the rear tires hit the gravel, the entire truck sank toward the slope of the ditch, causing it to roll onto its side as it slid. He hung onto the wheel with all of his strength as it came to a crashing halt against a large tree just off of the road, showering him with small pieces of broken glass and debris as all of the windows blew out.

He could feel a sharp pain from his ribs, and blood beginning to drip from his forehead where a small piece of metal had flown through the windshield and struck him. He raised his hands to feel it, but it didn't seem to be too serious. He reached down and began to struggle to release himself from the seat belt he was now hanging from. After a few minutes, he was able to break free, sending himself tumbling head first into the passenger side door.

"Hey man! Are you ok?" a voice yelled from outside of the truck.

"Yeah...I think so," Sam replied, wincing with pain as he struggled to his feet inside the cab.

"I was right behind you, man. I called the police, and they're on their way."

"Alright...thanks," he replied, knowing that the police were the last people on earth he wanted to see at the moment.

After a few failed attempts, he managed to pull himself over the dashboard, climbing out of the truck through the hole that had been left by the missing windshield. After he was on his feet, on level ground, he staggered backward a few steps to survey the damage. The entire truck was destroyed. The tree had nearly ripped the roof completely off of the cab. The fiberglass hood had flown off upon impact, and was lying about 30 feet away. Three of the tires had been torn from their rims, and from where he was looking, it appeared as though the frame of the truck had been bent and twisted.

"Hey, you'd better sit down, man," the motorist said, putting his hand on Sam's shoulder and leading him over to a clearing in the grass.

Sam sat in the grass, wishing that he would've just called in sick this morning. He knew that if the officer arrived and detected that he had been drinking recently, his life would be over as he knew it. He'd lose his job immediately, along with the benefits and pension he had worked so very long to accumulate.

He tried to think of anything that could somehow explain how this had happened without causing the officer to suspect anything. He remained seated on the grass when the officer arrived, not wanting to stand up in his presence.

"Are you alright, sir?" the officer asked as he approached.

"I don't know, officer. I hit my head pretty good," he replied

"I can see that," the officer replied. "Are you feeling light-headed or dizzy?"

"Yeah, a little bit."

"Okay. Don't try to get up. You stay right there. An ambulance is on the way."

"That's perfect!" Sam thought to himself as he remained seated. "If I can convince them to take me to the hospital, I can get away from this cop," he reasoned.

"Can you tell me what happened here?" the officer asked as he pulled out his note pad.

"Yeah," Sam began, holding his forehead with his hand. "I on my way to a job site, and as I was coming up to the intersection, a deer ran out of the woods right in front of me. I tried to avoid it by cutting the wheel to the right, but I guess I overdid it. The gravel grabbed the steer tire and sucked me right in."

"All right," the officer replied. "Just relax, okay? I'm gonna take a look around."

The officer stood and walked over to the truck, looking over the damage. He looked to the rear and saw the tire tracks leading into the ditch, and then saw the rut dug into the gravel where the tries had slid into it.

"I was right behind him, officer. I saw everything," the concerned motorist said as he approached from behind.

"You did?" the officer replied, not yet seeing anything strange about Sam's story.

"Yeah. He was driving along like nothing was

wrong, when he all of a sudden began to drift off to the right. Next thing I knew, the whole truck just turned over on its side."

"He said that a deer ran out in front of him. Did you see a deer?"

"No, I didn't see any deer, but maybe the truck blocked my vision."

The officer looked back behind where the truck had gone off the road, but he didn't see any evidence of skid marks from hard braking or steering. From what he could see, it appeared as though the truck had simply driven straight into the ditch. As the ambulance arrived, he looked down the road, ahead of where the truck was. He saw nothing that would've necessarily blocked the vision of the trailing driver, and thought that he more than likely would've seen a deer, had it run out from the woods onto the road. He returned to where Sam had been sitting as the paramedics were putting him on a stretcher.

"Are you taking him?" he asked.

"Yeah, he's got a pretty good cut on his head, and he may have a few broken ribs."

"Alright," the officer replied, pulling him off to the side. "Make sure they give him a drug and alcohol screening, ok?"

"Will do," he replied.

As they loaded him into the ambulance, Sam was certain he had gotten away with it. His story seemed reasonable, and the officer didn't give him any reason to believe he wasn't buying it. After investigating the scene further and checking the truck for any open containers, the officer radioed in to have his dispatcher notify Sam's boss, Johnny, of the accident. Johnny immediately contacted the hospital to inquire about Sam's condition, and after learning that he was going to be alright, he asked them to perform a drug and alcohol screening, as it was the company's policy to do so whenever there was an accident involving one of their drivers. He then drove to the hospital to pick him up and bring him back to work.

Sam was treated and released from the hospital after his x-rays showed no sign of broken ribs. They cleaned up the cut on his forehead, which required five stitches to close the wound. By the time Johnny arrived to pick him up, he was completely sober.

"How are you feeling, Sam?" Johnny asked as he approached him in the hospital lobby.

"I've been better," Sam replied, shaking his head.

"What happened?"

"I had just left the yard, and I was driving to the job site. Just as I was reaching the intersection, a deer ran out of the woods, right in front of me. I tried to move to the right to avoid it, but I guess I went too far. The gravel grabbed the tires and sucked me right into the ditch."

"Why didn't you just hit it?" Johnny asked, knowing that the truck would've sustained far less damaged if that were the case.

"I don't know. I probably should have. It was just a knee-jerk reaction on my part."

"Alright, well, let's get you back to the yard," he said as he turned to exit the lobby.

As the investigating officer was wrapping up the accident scene, he received word that Sam had tested positive for alcohol, and he was above the legal limit. Learning that Sam had already left the hospital, he drove his squad over to the facility where he worked, pulling into the lot just as Sam and Johnny had arrived.

"Mr. Grace," he called out as he got out of his car.

"Yes?" Sam replied, turning to face him.

"You'll have to come with me," he said, reaching for his handcuffs as he approached.

"What do you mean?" Sam replied, his

stomach sinking.

"Your blood test from the hospital came back positive for alcohol, above the legal limit. I'm going to have to place you under arrest for DUI."

"Are you kidding me?!" Johnny exclaimed as the officer turned Sam around and handcuffed him.

"I don't know what he's talking about, Johnny!" Sam protested in disbelief as the officer led him to the car. "I wasn't drinking anything!"

The officer drove him to the station, booked him, and locked him in a cell. Sam felt his entire life crashing down around him as he thought about the ramifications of his actions. Not only was he certain that he would lose his job, but he also knew that Kim would completely lose her mind when she found out what had happened. He knew that he would need to get another job immediately, but had no idea how that would be possible. He was a truck driver, and he didn't have any other job experience to offer. He also knew that trucking companies would never hire a driver with a DUI conviction, especially if that conviction came while driving a truck for another company.

He sat on the cold, metal bench in his cell, put his head back against the cinder block wall, and let out a heavy sigh, wondering how he would break the news to Kim. There was no way he could hide the truth from her at this point, and he knew that she would be completely devastated. She had pleaded with him to quit drinking countless times over the years, saying that it was destroying everything, but he had refused to listen, believing that he was fine. He had convinced himself that their problems didn't stem from his drinking, but instead from her trying to control him. Now, here he was, sitting in a cold jail cell, and about to be fired from a job that had provided for his family for many years.

He had his credit cards with him, and he had the ability to post his own bail, but the only way he could leave would be if somebody came to pick him up. He could then get a ride back to work, where he could pick up his car and try to talk things over with Johnny. He was fairly certain that he would be fired, but maybe not. He began to wonder if he needed to tell Kim anything. Maybe he could have somebody else pick him up – someone he could trust to keep things quiet. Hopefully he could smooth things over at work, but if not, maybe he could somehow find another job fast enough to keep bringing home an income. He knew that she would find out eventually, but he also knew that it would be much easier to tell her the news if he could reassure her that the bills would continue to be paid. He knew that her first thought – after getting past the anger and frustration she was certain to feel toward him – would be the very real fear that their home would be lost because of this.

After thinking all of this through for a while, he asked the officer on duty if he could make a phone call. The only person he knew he could trust with anything was his sister, Suzanne. The officer opened his cell and led him to the phone, telling him that he had just two minutes. He took a deep breath, and then picked up the phone.

"Hello?" Suzanne answered.

"Hey, sis. How are you?"

"Oh, hi, Sam," she replied, happy to hear his voice. "I'm fine. How are you?"

"Not so good."

"What's wrong?" she asked, her voice changing to a tone of concern.

"Well, I could use a little help," he replied, hesitating for a few seconds.

"With what?"

"I'm in jail right now, and I need someone to come pick me up."

"In jail?!" she replied in shock. "Why?! What happened?! Are you okay?!"

"Yeah, I'm fine. It's a long story. Can you come and get me? I'll explain everything when you get here."

"Absolutely, Sam. I'll leave right away."

"Thanks, sis. I really appreciate it."

"No problem, Sam. Where did they take you?"

"I'm at County."

"Alright. I'll be there in about a half hour."

"Hey, sis? Can you do me another favor?"

"Sure, Sam. What is it?"

"Don't say anything to Kim, okay? I want to tell her myself, but not over the phone."

"I understand."

"Thanks again, sis."

He hung up the phone, and then asked to be brought to the cashier where he posted bail. A few minutes later, he was led outside and took a seat on a public bench on the front lawn of the courthouse, turning his back to the public sidewalk to ensure that nobody he knew would notice him if they walked by. Within about 25 minutes, he looked up to see Suzanne's car pulling up. He stood from his seat and walked quickly over to the passenger side door, keeping his head down until he climbed inside.

"Hey, sis. Thank you so much for coming to get me," he said with a sigh of relief as he leaned over to give her a hug.

"Of course, Sam!...So, what happened to you?" she asked, looking over to see the large bandage on his forehead..

"Well, I got into an accident at work today."

"Oh my!...Are you okay?"

"Yeah, I'm fine. It wasn't that bad of an accident. Nobody got hurt. I was on my way to a job site when a deer ran out in front of me. I tried to avoid it, but I over-steered and ended up putting the truck into the ditch."

"Oh no!" she gasped. "Are you sure you're ok?"

"Yeah. They brought me to the hospital and

359

checked me out. I'm fine. Just got a few stitches on my forehead where a piece of debris came in through the window."

"So...why did they arrest you?" she asked with a confused expression.

"Well, I was up pretty late last night, and I had a few drinks before I went to bed. I guess they picked something up on the blood test they gave me at the hospital. I don't know how that's possible. It couldn't have been much at all, because I felt fine when I went to work."

"Oh, Sam," she replied as her heart sank. "What does that mean? Are you gonna lose your job now?"

"I don't know, sis. I have to talk to my boss and see what they want to do about it. I hope not, but none of that is under my control. I guess it's gonna be what it's gonna be."

"What are you gonna do if they fire you?"

"I guess I'll just have to find another job somewhere. I'll be alright."

Suzanne turned into the lot where Sam worked, turning to give him a long hug before he got out of the car.

"Please let me know what happens, ok?"

"I will, sis."

"And if you need anything, please call me."

"I will. Thanks again for your help," he said as he opened the door and stepped out.

He turned and looked at the building, dreading what he was about to hear. He paused for a few seconds before stepping inside, trying to think of anything he could say that would help him to keep his job.

"Here goes nothing," he said under his breath as he opened the door and walked into Johnny's office.

"Sam," Johnny said with a solemn voice. "Hey, close the door and take a seat, okay?"

Sam turned around and closed the door, and then sat in the chair in front of Johnny's desk. He'd been in that seat many times before, usually for mundane things such as reviewing the employee evaluations he had been given. He was never even slightly concerned about sitting there at any given time, but this time it felt to him as though he was about to sit in the electric chair, awaiting the pulling of the switch by his executioner.

"Sam...We have a real problem here," Johnny said as he opened a file on his desk. "The hospital sent us the results of your drug and alcohol screening, and it's not good."

"I know, John," he replied, staring down at the paperwork.

"What were you thinking, Sam?"

"I have no idea how this could've happened, Johnny," he replied, trying to plead his case. "I'll admit it...I had a couple of drinks last night before I went to bed, but I felt fine this morning."

"Don't lie to me, Sam."

"I'm not lying, Johnny, I swear!"

"Sam, you didn't even show up this morning until I called you. You gave me some bogus story about how your alarm clock must've stopped, and then you show up drunk and hour later and destroy one of our trucks!"

"I wasn't drunk, Johnny!" Sam insisted.

"The hell you weren't!" Johnny answered, raising his voice as he pulled a piece of paper out of the file and slid it across his desk. "Take a look at it, Sam! The numbers don't lie! You were well over the legal limit!"

"I don't see how that's possible," Sam replied, looking down at the report.

"I don't see how it's possible that you could do something that stupid! Why didn't you just call in sick? Why would you come here and climb into a truck knowing that you were loaded?"

"I don't know...I felt fine."

"Sam, I really hate to have to be the one to tell you this. You've been a good employee here for a lot of years, and I've never had a problem with you. But there's nothing I can do about this, Sam. We're gonna have to let you go."

"Johnny, please....Don't do this to me."

"It's out of my hands, Sam. I wish I could do something to help you out, but you did this to yourself... I'm sorry."

Sam sank back into his chair, unable to think of anything more to say. He knew that Johnny was right. It was the company's policy to terminate anyone who was caught driving under the influence, even if they weren't involved in any type of accident.

"Why don't you take a few minutes to clean out your locker. I'll keep everyone out of the locker room until you're done so you don't have to answer any questions."

"Alright, Johnny... Thank you."

Sam stood up and made his way into the locker room, grabbing a large garbage bag on the way to put his belongings into it. He cleaned out everything, and then carried it out to his car and put it into the trunk, looking back at the building he had worked out of for so many years, knowing that he'd never be welcomed back again.

After leaving the lot, he drove over to the local coffee shop and went inside. He had to give Kim the appearance that nothing was wrong – that he had simply gone to work that morning, returning at the usual time. He remained there, drinking coffee and watching the clock until it was time to go home.

"What the heck happened to you?!" Kim asked, noticing the bandage on his forehead as he walked in the front door.

"Eh...Nothing, really. I tripped on a shovel at the job site today and ended up hitting my head," he replied nonchalantly.

"Are you okay?"

"Yeah, I'm fine. Just got a couple of stitches," he replied as he walked into the kitchen to pour himself a drink and then walked out into the back yard to sit on the deck.

Kim didn't ask any more questions, accepting his explanation without feeling the need to know any more about it. Their relationship had deteriorated to the point where any conversations they might have were only casual, semi-polite expressions. Unless there was something that needed to be addressed regarding the kids, neither of them felt any desire to discuss anything of real importance.

The following morning, Sam awoke at the usual time, left the house, and then spent the majority of the day looking for a new job. He did so everyday throughout the entire month, applying for every and any job that might be available, but could find nothing. He continued to receive the paychecks he was owed by the company for the hours he had already worked, but after two weeks, those stopped coming. He then began to draw money out of their savings account, depositing it into their checking every pay day in the same amount that his paychecks would've been had he still had his job. In an effort to make the money last as long as he could, he stopped making their mortgage payments, thinking that he could catch up on them once he found a job. After just a few months, he had nothing left in savings, and he still had not found any work.

One day, while Sam was out pretending to be at work, Kim walked to the mailbox to get their mail. On the top of the pile was a letter from their mortgage company with writing on the envelope which read *"Important information regarding your account – Do not discard."* Curious as to what this might be about, she opened the envelope and read the following:

"Dear Mr. and Mrs. Grace: We have attempted to contact you repeatedly with regard to your account,

*which is now 90 days past due. Having been unable
to reach you, and hearing nothing from you about this
matter, we are writing to inform you that we are now
beginning the foreclosure process. To avoid
foreclosure, it is absolutely necessary that you contact
us immediately."*

Feeling an enormous knot building within her
stomach, she walked quickly to the phone and dialed
the number on the letter, certain that there must be
some sort of a mistake. After talking it over with the
account representative, she learned that there was no
mistake. Sam had not paid their mortgage payments
for three months.

She hung up the phone, and then called Sam's
workplace, asking to speak with him.

"Hello?" Johnny answered.

"Hello…is this Johnny?"

"Yes it is."

"Hi, Johnny, this is Kim. Sam's wife. I need to
speak with him right away. Is there any way you can
have him call me?"

Johnny paused for a few seconds, suddenly
aware that Sam had obviously not informed Kim of his
termination.

"Hello?" Kim said nervously.

"Um…Yeah…Listen, Kim, I'm not exactly sure
how to say this, but Sam doesn't work here anymore."

"What?! What do you mean?!"

"He doesn't work here anymore. He's been
gone for a few months now."

"Are you serious?! Why?! What happened?!"
she replied in shock.

"I really don't think I should say anything about
that. You'll have to ask Sam."

Kim dropped the phone, her mind spinning with
a thousand different thoughts, and even more
questions.

"What the hell is going on?!" she thought to
herself, trying to imagine any reason why Sam

would've lost his job, and more importantly, why he wouldn't have told her for three months.

She walked over to the living room sofa and sat down slowly, feeling completely numb. None of this made any sense to her. Sam losing his job was definitely a very serious problem, but it was one that could've been overcome if he had told her. She could've looked for work herself and possibly kept up with the mortgage payments until he found another job. It was unthinkable to her that he would've hidden that from her, and risked losing their home in the process.

As the panic began to grip her, she grabbed her car keys and drove directly to the bank. She wasn't sure how much money they had left in their savings account, but she hoped it would be enough to at least bring their mortgage payments up to date.

Upon arriving at the bank and speaking with one of the tellers, she learned that not only had their savings account been completely drained, but it had also been closed.

She walked back to her car, shaken to her very core by everything she had just learned. She sat in the driver's seat, brought her hands to her face and began to sob uncontrollably, rocking back and forth in her seat as the muscle spasms gripped her stomach. She stayed there for about a half hour, completely unable to move. Once she was able to pull herself together enough to drive, she returned home, finding Sam's car in the driveway when she arrived.

The shock and sadness she was feeling turned into a sense of intense anger as she stared at his car, thinking about how he had left every morning, pretending to go to work and acting as though nothing was out of the ordinary. She thought about how he had lied to her every single day for what had to be months at this point, returning home at his usual time every evening. She picked up her purse, along with the letter from their mortgage company, and stormed toward the front door.

"What is this, Sam?! How can you explain this?!" she yelled as she entered and found him sitting on the sofa.

She then threw the letter at him, waiting to hear whatever the lies were that he might come up with to explain the situation. He looked down at the letter, not saying a word.

"Explain this to me, Sam!" she insisted. "How did this happen?!"

"I lost my job a few months ago," he replied, bringing his hand up to his forehead as he slumped forward in his seat.

"And you then thought it would be a good idea to hide that from me? Why?"

"Because I thought that I could find another job before you found out. I didn't want you to worry."

"Oh, so because you didn't want me to worry, you completely drained our savings account and didn't pay our mortgage for three months?!" she shouted. "Had you told me about this earlier, I could've found a job and helped out! But you chose to hide this from me, lying to me every single day for months while allowing our home to go into foreclosure?! Why would you do that?!"

"I just didn't know how to tell you," he replied in a defeated voice.

"Why did you lose your job, Sam?"

"I got into an accident."

"What do you mean? What kind of an accident?"

"I was on my way to a job site, and a deer ran out in front of me. I tried to avoid it, but I over-steered and put the truck into a ditch."

"And they fired you for that? That doesn't make any sense, Sam!" she insisted, knowing full well that an accident of that type would not be enough to cause him to lose his job, especially since he had worked there without any problems for so many years.

Sam sat silently, not wanting to admit to her that he was fired because of a DUI conviction, but also knowing that she knew too much about his job and how they deal with accidents to buy his story.

"Talk to me, Sam!" she insisted. "Tell me the truth!"

"When they took me to the hospital to check me out...," he began, and then hesitated for a few seconds.

"What happened, Sam?!"

"They gave me a drug and alcohol screening."

"And...?"

"I had a few drinks the night before the accident, and I tested positive for alcohol."

Kim stepped back, absolutely enraged that his drinking – which was the source of all of the problems within their marriage for so many years – had now caused him to lose his job, and would now probably result in their losing their home.

"I can't do this anymore, Sam...I just can't," she replied, exasperated.

He remained seated in silence as she turned away and headed down the hallway toward the bedroom. She pulled a suitcase out of the closet and threw it on the bed, and then began to gather some clothes, laying them on the bed. She then walked into the bathroom, grabbing her toothbrush and some toiletries.

After listening to her rustling through the bedroom closet for a few minutes, and then hearing the zipper on the suitcase open, Sam got up and walked toward the bedroom.

"What are you doing?" he asked, standing in the doorway.

"I'm leaving, Sam."

"What do you mean you're leaving?"

"I'm leaving...I can't do this anymore," she replied, refusing to make eye contact.

"Where are you gonna go?"

"I don't know. Maybe to my mother's."

"For how long?"

"You don't get it, Sam. I'm leaving."

"What are you saying?"

"I just can't live like this anymore, Sam!" she cried out, turning to face him. "I've begged you to quit drinking for years! I've begged you to get some help! I've tried everything I could think of, but you just wouldn't listen! It's over, Sam! I'm finished! I want a divorce!"

"Kim...please," he said softly, stepping toward her to put his hand on her shoulder.

"Don't you dare touch me!" she shouted, pushing his hand away. "I'm through with you, Sam! I'll be back to pick up my things later. We can put the house on the market and try to salvage whatever is left of the equity. We'll figure out what to do with the furniture when the time comes."

Sam stepped away, speechless, as she turned back toward her suitcase and began to put her clothes inside. He couldn't believe that she was really leaving him, but he knew that he couldn't blame her for doing so.

"Can we talk about this later?" he asked quietly, hoping that maybe she'd change her mind once she had calmed down.

"No! There's nothing to talk about, Sam! It's finished! Do you understand me?!"

"Alright," he replied under his breath, turning to walk toward the kitchen.

He pulled a glass out of the kitchen cabinet, put some ice in it, and then filled it with straight vodka. His hands were shaking as he brought it to his mouth and drank nearly half of it with his first sip. He then refilled it and stepped outside onto the patio, collapsing into his chair as he stared out over the back yard.

Kim didn't say another word to him as she finished packing and then loaded everything into her car. Sam listened from the back yard, hearing her car door open and close, the engine starting, and then listening closely as the sound of the engine faded off into the distance.

He gazed around the back yard, remembering all of the good times they had shared there. He thought about the kids playing happily, almost able to see their smiling faces as they ran through the grass. He thought back upon how the yard had looked the first time they had seen it, laughing to himself as he remembered what a mess it was. He thought about the countless times that he and Kim had sat of the patio together, holding each other's hands as they watched the endless sunsets and talked about how happy they were with each other. He recalled the laughter of his children as he dragged them through the yard on their sled, driving his riding mower as fast as he could.

"It's all gone now," he whispered as he took another sip of his vodka. "All of it."

He then thought back to the very moment when he had sat on the patio, in the early morning hours, watching the sun rise as he drank his cup of coffee, and thinking that after all he had been through, he had finally arrived.

A deep sadness gripped him as he thought about how horribly everything had disintegrated into nothing. He couldn't remember the last time he'd felt truly happy or hopeful. It seemed as though it had been many years since he had actually smiled a genuine smile. His life had somehow become nothing but an enormous heap of lies. Everything he had once believed in or hoped for had been reduced to absolute rubble.

He finished his drink, and then poured himself another. Having nobody there to stop him or even slow his drinking down, he continued to drink until he passed out in his chair, remaining there until sunrise the following morning.

Over the course of the next few weeks, Kim refused to see him or even speak to him. She would drive past the house to see if his car was gone, and if it was, she would go inside to gather more of her things. She spoke with their Realtor, explaining their situation to him, and after determining the fair market value of their home, she asked to have it listed. Due to the urgency of their situation, and in hopes of a quick sale, their asking price was set at slightly less than what they knew it was worth. Once all of the paperwork had been signed, the Realtor then stopped by the house to discuss everything with Sam. Not wanting to argue about anything, Sam agreed to everything she had decided to do and signed off on it.

Still unable to find any work, Sam began to sell off his tools, lawn mower, and various other items while waiting for the home to sell. Due to the depression he felt about everything, his drinking increased dramatically. He stopped looking for work, instead staying home all day long, drinking straight vodka throughout the day.

Within just two months, their home sold for a price that was agreeable to both of them. Sam gave Kim everything that was in the home, including all of their furniture.

Having nowhere else to go, he found an apartment for rent in the basement of the home of an elderly couple. They had never brought in a renter before, but they wanted to do so to supplement their retirement income. They were looking to rent it to someone who would be quiet, not wanting to have to deal with loud music or wild parties. They weren't interested in performing a background or credit check, and Sam was able convince them that he'd be the perfect tenant. It wasn't much to look at, and it was in a rapidly declining neighborhood in Chicago, but he needed something he could rent quickly, and something that wouldn't require a credit check. He also liked the idea of being back in the city where he had grown up. It wasn't in his old neighborhood, but it was within walking distance, which gave him a certain degree of comfort. He also knew that being back in the city would give him more opportunities to find work, and he was fairly certain that he'd be able to.

At the closing of the sale of their home, Sam asked only for enough to pay his rent, utilities, and minimal living expenses for the next six months, giving Kim everything that was left after that. Not wanting to face any difficulties down the road, and wanting to further convince his new landlords that he was a good choice as a tenant, he immediately paid them six months of rent in advance. Knowing that he would need to find some type of work before the money ran out, he was able to tone down his drinking during the day long enough to fill out a number of job applications each day before returning to his apartment.

Having already sold their home and agreeing upon who would take the rest of their belongings, Sam and Kim's divorce proceeded very quickly through the court system. They were divorced within just a few months and went their separate ways.

After the divorce was final, Sam found himself thinking a lot about Angela, wondering where she was and how she was doing. He would wander through the old neighborhood at least a couple of times per week, stopping to rest and watch the people as they passed, hoping to see her. He had no idea if he would even recognize her if they stood face to face. After all, so many years had passed since they were together, and both of them were sure to have gone through many changes with age. Even if he did see her, he wondered what the chances were that she would be even slightly interested in speaking with him. He had written to her so many times when he was in the Navy, expressing his deep love for her, but she responded only once or twice, and never spoke of what her feelings were for him when she did so. He wondered if she hated him for leaving, or if she even remembered him at this point. Still, he wanted so very badly to just speak to her one more time, knowing that if he could, he would simply want to tell her that she was the only woman he had ever truly loved with all of his heart. Even if she wasn't at all interested in him at this point in her life, he wanted so very badly for her to know that.

He wondered how differently his life would've turned out had they never parted. He wondered if, given the chance, they would've eventually married each other. He thought he could see very clearly the love she had for him in her eyes whenever she looked at him, but maybe it was all just his imagination running away with him. All these years later, there were still so many questions in his mind about how she really felt, and what he believed they felt about each other. He had come to terms with the fact that he would probably never know the real answers to any of those questions, but the questions remained, eating away at him whenever they came to mind.

He continued to search for her as often as he could, but she was nowhere to be found. He eventually gave up all hope of ever finding her again, forcing himself to face the reality of his situation. He was alone, and he would probably always be alone. After all, everything he once had was now lost, he didn't have a job or any form of income, and he lived alone in a dark, dirty basement apartment where he would drink himself to sleep day after day. He wondered what woman in her right mind would ever want anything to do with him. He had never imagined that his life would come to this, but he couldn't ignore the fact that it had. He knew that something had to change, but he felt completely incapable of making those changes.

As he was sitting on a park bench near his apartment, resting after a few hours of walking from business to business to ask if they were hiring, he looked up to see a young couple walking toward him.

"What are you smiling about?" he thought to himself as they approached, seeing the wide smiles on their faces.

"Excuse me, sir," the young man said, stopping in front of him. "Do you mind if I ask you a question?"

"Sure, why not?" he replied, not really wanting to be bothered.

"If you were to die today, do you know where you would go?"

"Yes," he replied with a smirk. "Into a box, and then into the ground, just like everyone else."

"So...I take it that you don't believe in heaven or hell?"

"I've got news for you, kid. There is no heaven, and I've already been through hell."

"Then you don't believe in God either?"

Sam didn't answer, shaking his head and letting out a heavy sigh, annoyed that this person would have a belief that there was a God, and even more annoyed that he would be bothering him with this nonsense.

"You know, the bible says that Jesus is the way, the truth, and the life, and that anyone who comes to him can have eternal life," the young man said enthusiastically.

"Hey!" Sam blurted out, turning to face him. "Let me save you a lot of time and effort here, ok? If you want to live your life out of some 2,000 year-old book, that's up to you. But I live right here in the real world, and I have no interest in your book, your Jesus, or your God. Why don't you go bother somebody else with that nonsense, because I don't want to hear about it."

"Alright," the young man said quietly. "I'm sorry to have bothered you."

Sam looked away, not responding. He could feel the anger welling up within him, greatly offended that some absolute stranger would have the nerve to just walk up and try to push his beliefs on him.

"Before I go, I just want you to know that whether we believe in Jesus or not, we're all going to meet him face to face some day. And when that day comes, every knee will bow, and every tongue will confess that he is Lord."

"You know what?!" Sam replied, raising his voice as he stood up. "I hope you're right! I hope that I do see this Jesus after I die, because if I do, I'm gonna ask him why he's been just sitting up there in heaven for 2,000 years, doing nothing while innocent people are killed, women are raped, and children are being molested! What kind of a God would allow all of that?"

"That's a very good question," the young man replied calmly.

"You're damn right it is," Sam bellowed.

"This world is a sick, depraved, dangerous place to live. It wasn't created to be that way, but through mankind, sin entered the world, and we've been living through the ultimate consequences of that sin ever since. The bible doesn't claim that, if we give our lives to Christ, we will never again be affected by the sin that's in the world. It simply says that no matter who we are, we're all guilty of our own sins. If we want to spend eternity in the presence of God, those sins need to be forgiven, and the only way we can be forgiven is to confess that we are sinners, asking Jesus to forgive us, and then giving our lives over to him."

"So that's your answer?" Sam shouted. "People spend their entire lives living through this kind of hell just so some God can wait to see if they'll admit that they did something wrong in their lives? They suffer through all of this until they die, and then they're supposed to be grateful that they can spend eternity with the same God who allowed all of it to happen?"

"God loves us, sir. He loves us enough to want

us to spend eternity with him. That is why he sent his only son to die for our sins, so that we might be forgiven. Our lives here a very short when compared to eternity. If we turn to him, whatever bad things happen to us in this life will be as nothing compared to the love we will feel from him forever. But if we don't turn to him and confess, the place where we spend eternity will be far worse than anything we could possibly face here, and it will be an eternal reminder of how we refused to accept the free gift of his grace and forgiveness here when we had the chance."

"I'm sorry, kid," Sam said as he turned to walk away. "I've done the best that I could with the life I've been given. I don't need to be forgiven by your imaginary God. He doesn't exist."

"Yes, he does exist," the young man shouted as Sam continued to walk away. "And you'll be face to face with him someday."

"And if I am, I guess we'll sort all of that out when it happens, won't we?" Sam replied, stopping to look back at him.

"Yes...you will," he replied with a solemn expression.

Sam was absolutely infuriated as he walked quickly back to his apartment. He couldn't believe the nerve of this kid. His hands were shaking as he fumbled with his keys, throwing the door open and then slamming it closed behind him as he walked inside. He walked over to the kitchen counter, poured himself a drink, and guzzled the entire glass down. He then poured himself another, taking a seat at the foot of his mattress.

Just as he was beginning to calm down a bit, the church bells down the block began to ring, making him feel as though they were somehow purposely mocking him. He put his hands over his ears to block out the sound until they stopped ringing, finishing his second drink as soon as they had, and then leaned his back against the wall, letting out a sigh of relief.

TWELVE

In the months that followed, Sam was still unable to find any work. The money he had from the sale of his home had dwindled down to just a few hundred dollars, which he kept in an old shoebox next to his bed. With plenty of public transportation available to him in the city, he decided to sell his car in an effort to buy himself a little more time. That lasted for just a couple more months, and he was coming dangerously close to running out of money completely. He considered selling his 9mm handgun, but decided to keep it because of the dangerous and unpredictable neighborhood he was living in.

Due to the affordability of such items, his diet consisted mainly of peanut butter sandwiches, hot dogs, or grilled cheese. He also cut down on the number of times he would eat during the day, having peanut butter toast for breakfast, and then not eating anything else until early evening. He also changed his drinking habits, buying only the cheapest liquor he could find. Doing so left him feeling very ill every morning, but there was simply no way he could afford the more expensive brands. His physical appearance began to deteriorate rapidly, as did his health.

He found himself in an extremely dire situation, being in the last month of the six he had paid to rent his apartment. He knew that, within a few more days, his landlord would be asking him for another rent payment – a rent payment that he not only didn't have, but one that he had no idea how he would be able to come up with anytime in the near future.

In an effort to save as much money as he could, he had drastically reduced the frequency with which he'd wash his clothes, sometimes wearing the same clothes for a week before changing. Due to his shabby appearance, he began to be mistaken for a homeless man as he walked the streets looking for work. Local business owners who had at one time welcomed him inside to fill out employment applications were now more likely to quickly escort him out of their places of business, not wanting his presence to frighten away potential customers. Beginning to give up all hope of finding work, he started to take a bottle of liquor with him as he wandered through the neighborhood.

Finding an open space on a bus stop bench one morning, he sat down to rest, taking his bottle out of his pocket for a quick swig. He was completely unaware of his surroundings when a very attractive, well-dressed woman approached and sat down next to him.

"Hey…are you okay?" she asked in a soft voice.

"What?" he replied, surprised by her sudden appearance.

"Are you okay?" she repeated with a look of concern in her eyes.

She looked very familiar to him, but he couldn't place where he might have seen her before. Having spent so much of his time roaming the streets, he assumed that their paths must've crossed somewhere in the neighborhood.

"Oh…Yeah…I'm alright," he stammered. "Why do you ask?"

"Well, I saw you sitting here from across the street, and it looked as though you were having a hard time. Have you eaten today?"

"What do you mean?" he asked with a puzzled expression.

"Have you eaten today?"

"Um…yeah," he replied, shrugging his shoulders.

"Here," she said softly. "I want you to have this."

Sam looked down at her hand, noticing a beautiful gold ring she was wearing as she pressed a twenty dollar bill into his palm. His initial response was a feeling of shame, realizing that this woman had come to the conclusion that he was homeless. He wanted to refuse her money, but he knew that he really needed every penny he could get.

"Go get yourself a hot meal, okay?"

"That's very kind of you...Thank you so much," he replied, tucking the bill into his shirt pocket.

"You're very welcome," she answered with a warm smile as she stood and walked away.

He sat back on the bench, watching her walk down the street until she was out of view. After taking a few more swigs from his bottle, he decided to walk back home. He was too drunk at this point to talk to anyone about a job, so it was pointless to even try. He stopped at the local liquor store on his way back home, buying a large bottle of liquor with the twenty dollars he had just been given.

Once he had arrived back home, he opened his shoebox to throw the change inside. Picking up the crumpled up bills inside, he started to count how much he had left. If he really stretched what was there to the best of his ability, he might be able to buy enough food to eat for a few more days. After that, he had no idea what he would do. He started to regret buying his last bottle of liquor, but at this point, it didn't really matter. He didn't know how long he could hold off his landlord, but the writing was on the wall. He knew that within a very short period of time, he would be homeless and penniless. He drank himself to sleep, figuring that if he wasn't awake, he wouldn't have to eat.

He awoke the following morning and looked around his apartment. Having just one crust of bread and a small amount of peanut butter in the bottom of the jar, he made himself a small breakfast, washing it down with a swig of liquor. Once he felt awake enough to start his day, he went to his shoebox and collected the last of his money, and then started the short walk to the grocery store to buy what would be the last of his meals.

As he cut through the neighborhood park, a group of rough looking teenaged boys began walking toward him. Not wanting to get involved in any kind of altercation, Sam moved to his right as he walked, trying to avoid walking directly past them.

"Hey! Look at the bum!" one of them shouted to his friends. "Hey! Bum! What are you doing in our park?"

Sam continued walking, looking down at the ground and trying to ignore them.

"Hey! I'm talking to you, bum!" he called out, turning directly into Sam's path. "We don't like bums hanging around in our park! Why are you here?"

Sam picked up his pace, trying to make it to the other side of the park where there were more people, and where it was less likely that he'd be confronted.

Undeterred, the teenager ran in front of him, and then turned to face him, bumping him with his chest.

"I'm talking to you, bum! What are you doing here?"

"Hey, man. I don't want any trouble, okay?" Sam said nervously as the other teens surrounded him.

He tried to step to the side and walk around him, but the teen stepped in front of him again, this time shoving him backward.

"Where you going, man? I asked you a question!"

"I'm serious…I really don't want any trouble."

"Well, I don't care if you don't want trouble. I'm telling you that you just found some."

With that, the teen reared back and then punched Sam in the face, knocking him slightly off balance. Sam staggered to his right for a second, and then lunged forward, trying to break through and run away from them. He only made it a few steps before one of the teens tackled him from behind. He tried to get back to his feet, but was immediately shoved back to the ground.

"Hey, look what I found!" one of them shouted with a laugh, picking up the bottle of liquor that had fallen from Sam's pocket in the commotion.

"Please!...Don't!" Sam cried out as he reached for it.

"Is this yours, bum?" he asked, pulling it away from his reach as he circled him. "Do you want this?"

Sam started to answer when he suddenly felt a searing pain from his side as one of them kicked him in the ribs, knocking him sideways.

"You want a drink, bum?" he said mockingly as he opened the bottle.

"I think he does!" another replied. "Give him a drink, man!"

"Here you go, bum! Have a drink!" he said as he poured the entire bottle all over Sam's head and shoulders.

Sam got up on all fours, trying to get back on his feet when one of them stepped forward, kicking him in the face. He collapsed in a heap, face down on the ground as he felt blood beginning to drip from his cheek. He strained to pull himself up again when all of them started to kick and punch him relentlessly. His head began to spin as blow after blow reached his face, back, and sides. He then felt a severely sharp pain on the back of his head as the empty liquor bottle came crashing down on it, sending shards of glass flying all over his head and shoulders. He fell face down in the dirt, absolutely defenseless as everything around him faded to black.

"Go through his pockets, man!" one of them

said after realizing he had been knocked unconscious.

Reaching down to sift through them, he looked up with a smile as he pulled out the small, crumpled wad of bills.

"Seventeen dollars!" he yelled as he put it in his own pocket. "The bum just bought us lunch!"

The teens grabbed him by his feet, and then dragged his lifeless body through the grass, hiding him behind a group of overgrown bushes. They then walked away, laughing and high-fiving each other.

"Next stop, Benjamin!" Gabriel bellowed, shaking Sam awake.

As he turned to look out the window, his mind once again drifted back to what had happened the day before he found himself on the train. It was only yesterday, but he couldn't remember anything that had happened, not even the beating he had just taken. No matter how hard he strained to remember, he had no recall whatsoever of the events that had taken place.

He turned in his seat and looked around the train, which had become quite crowded by this time. Every seat had been taken with the exception of one – the seat right next to the woman in the red dress. He thought about it for a few seconds, and then stood up, walking over to her.

"Excuse me," he said with a smile. "Do you mind if I sit here?"

"No, not at all," she replied, smiling back at him.

"Hey, this isn't a pick-up line or anything, but I could swear that I know you from somewhere," he said, desperately trying to think of why.

"Maybe you do."

"Do I look familiar to you?" he asked

"Yes," she answered, looking away.

"Help me out here. Where do I know you from?"

"It was a very long time ago," she replied.

"How long ago?" he asked, drawing an absolute blank.

"Oh...many years ago. We were just teenagers."

"Now you really have me confused," he replied, staring intently at her face and trying to remember.

"We used to work together."

"Where?"

"At a restaurant. You were they guy who made ice cream sundaes, and I was a waitress."

"Wait a minute!" he replied, putting his hand on her cheek and turning her face toward him.

He looked deeply into her eyes, feeling his heart beginning to grow in size as he suddenly realized he was suddenly looking at the only woman he had ever truly loved.

"Angel?" he said, his eyes starting to well up. "Is it really you?"

"Yes, Sam...It's me."

"Oh my God!" he shouted. "I can't believe this! I've been staring at you this whole time, convinced that I knew you from somewhere, but I didn't recognize you! You look so very different!"

"Is that a good thing or a bad thing?" she asked with a coy smile.

"Oh, believe me, it's a very good thing! You look absolutely beautiful! But then again, you always did."

"Awe...thank you, Sam."

"How long have you known it was me walking around here?"

"I knew it as soon as I saw you."

"You did? Why didn't you say anything?" he asked incredulously.

"I didn't know if you remembered me."

"You didn't know if I remembered you?! Are you kidding me?! How could I ever have forgotten you? I've been looking for you throughout my entire life!"

"Have you really?"

"Yes! I looked everywhere! As soon as I returned from the Navy, I went everywhere and anywhere I thought I might find you. I went to the restaurant, to your old apartment, to the bank where you used to work, everywhere. I tried to find your sister's house, thinking that I might see you. I thought that, even if I didn't, I could ask her where you were, but all of the homes there looked the same. I couldn't remember which one it was."

"Well, I have a little secret for you, Sam."

"What's that?" he replied, feeling like an excited little boy inside.

"I looked for you for a very long time too."

"Did you really?"

"Yes, I did. I drove to all of those same places, hoping to come across you. I tried many times to find your name in the phone book. I even called your old high school, asking if they had any information as to your whereabouts. I went as far as trying to contact the ship you were on in the Navy, asking if you had left any forwarding addresses."

"Are you serious?!" he asked, amazed that she had been looking for him just as desperately as he had searched for her.

"Yes, I'm serious. I would even go to the mall in the old neighborhood, scanning the crowd and hoping to see your face."

"I did the exact same thing!" he replied with a chuckle. "I would sit in the food court for hours, watching everyone who walked by!"

"That's crazy," she said, smiling widely.

"I wonder how many times we just missed each other, or walked by each other without realizing we had just done so."

"That's a very real possibility, I guess."

"That kinda breaks my heart."

"Yeah, mine too, Sam."

"So, tell me all about yourself. Where have you been all these years? Are you married?"

"No, I'm recently divorced. I was married for twenty years, and I have two kids. I still live in the old neighborhood, in the home my ex-husband and I bought when we were first married. How about you?"

"I was married for a little over twenty years too. I got divorced earlier this year."

"Oh, I'm sorry to hear that," she replied, putting her hand on his.

Sam started thinking back to what he knew he had always wanted to say to her if they were ever to meet again. He wasn't sure how she might respond to him at this point, but he couldn't hold back from saying it any longer.

"Hey, I have to tell you something, okay?" he said, softening his voice.

"What is it?"

"Maybe this it's a little sudden for me to say this, and maybe this isn't the right time, but I swore that if I ever saw you again, there was something I would say to you...Something I've wanted to say for many years."

"What?" she replied, looking into his eyes.

"Angel, way back when we were together, I loved you with all of my heart. You were the most precious, beautiful, amazing woman I have ever known, and I've kicked myself throughout all of these years for ever letting you go. It was the biggest mistake of my life, and one I will always regret."

"Oh Sam...That's so very sweet of you. But that was a very long time ago."

"I really mean that, Angel, I've never loved any woman as much as I loved you."

"Thank you so very much for saying that, Sam. That really means a lot to me. I really loved you too. In fact, I have a secret to share with you."

"What's that?"

"During the last few days before my wedding, I

385

started to search all over for you. I so desperately wanted to find you."

"Why?"

"I don't know. I guess that I thought I wanted to make sure that there was no chance we'd ever be together before I went ahead and married someone else."

"What would you have done if you had found me?"

"I don't know. I only know that I really wanted to."

Sam sat back in his chair and let out a heavy sigh, feeling incredibly blessed that this woman he had always loved so very much had also felt the same way about him, while at the same time cursing fate for not allowing them to find each other.

"Sam...there's something I want to show you," she said, reaching down for her purse.

She brought it up onto her lap, opened it, and then reached inside of it, pulling out a pile of what appeared to be very old, folded pieces of paper in a plastic baggie.

"Take a look at these," she said as she handed it to him.

Sam carefully opened the baggie and pulled the papers out, unfolding them slowly as he stared at them. They were hand-written letters, which had obviously been penned many years ago. As his eyes began to focus on them, he recognized the handwriting. It was his. He then looked at the heading at the top of the page, recognizing the letter head from the ship he had been on while in the Navy. His eyes opened wide, suddenly realizing that what he held in his hands were the letters he had written to her many years ago.

"Wait a minute!" he said with a gasp. "You've kept these all this time?"

"Yes, I did."

"I...I can't believe this!"

"Well believe it, because it's the truth. What do you think about that, Sam?"

"I'm speechless...Astonished."

"How do you think I must've felt about you, keeping those letters for all these years?"

"I think you must've been very much in love with me."

"I was...Sam...Maybe this is the wrong place and the wrong time to say this to you, but I just have to say it, because if I don't, I may never get the chance again. Sam," she continued, taking both of his hands to look him in the eyes. "I have never felt as loved by anyone, nor have I ever loved anyone else, as much as I loved you and felt loved by you. I don't know why, and I don't know what that means now. I only know that it's the truth."

Sam sat back into his seat, absolutely amazed by what he was hearing. He wanted to pinch himself to see if this was only a dream.

"Oh Angela...Why didn't you ever tell me?" he asked with sadness in his voice.

"I was afraid, Sam."

"Of what?"

"I didn't know if you felt the same way, and I was so afraid of being hurt."

"But I told you that I loved you. Do you remember?"

"Yes, I do."

"Why didn't you say that you loved me too?"

"Because, deep down inside, I didn't know if you really meant it. We had all been partying, and I thought that maybe you just said it because you were drunk. I decided to wait until you said it to me again when you weren't drinking, and if you had, I would've told you that I loved you too...But you never said it again."

"Oh, Angel," he replied with a sigh. "I wanted to say it to you so very badly, but you looked absolutely terrified when I did. I assumed that it was the last thing you wanted me to say."

"No, I always hoped that you would say it again."

"I really wish I would've."

"I really wish you would've too."

"You know, I've often wondered about how differently my life would've turned out if we had stayed together. I've wondered if we would've gotten married, had kids, etc.. I've even tried to imagine what those kids would've looked like."

"I've wondered about those things too, Sam."

Sam began to feel his heart break as he thought about how little it would've taken for him to stay with her. He knew deep down in his heart that, had she just been able to tell him that she loved him, he would've done anything for her. He would've stopped partying if she had asked him to. He never would've enlisted and lived through that disastrous part of his life. He looked down at the letters again, laughing at how ridiculous his writing was.

"I was such a dork," he said, laughing as he read aloud the words he had written.

"No, you weren't a dork. You were cute!"

"Angel, I remember writing you and asking you to come to San Diego to be with me. I remember telling you how much I loved you and missed you. Why didn't you ever respond to that?"

"I didn't think you really meant it, Sam. I thought you were just some heartsick, lonely boy who wanted some company. And besides, how was I supposed to get down there? I was only 19, and I didn't have either a car or a driver's license at the time."

"I would've bought you an airline ticket, a bus ticket, a train ticket, anything! Heck, I would've walked back to Chicago and carried you all the way there on my back if I had to!"

"Now you're sounding like that crazy, 19 year-old boy again," she replied with a chuckle.

"Hey, do you remember how we always used to talk about running away to Maui?"

"I sure do!" she replied with an enormous smile. "You said you were going to build us a treehouse we could live in, near a waterfall and with no windows – just curtains hanging so that nobody could see in, and we could go to sleep every night feeling the cool ocean breezes flowing through."

"That still sounds really beautiful, doesn't it?"

"It sure does, Sam."

"Do you remember the first time I walked you home?"

"Yes, I do," she replied with a warm smile.

"I'll never forget the way I felt that night. I thought that you were so very beautiful, and I couldn't believe you agreed to let me walk you home."

"Well, I thought you were very handsome too."

"Did you really? I thought I was such a dork."

"No...You were very handsome."

"I remember reaching down to hold your hand, hoping that you'd let me. I'll never forget your facial expression once I was holding it. You broke into such a beautiful smile."

"Did I?" she replied, blushing slightly.

"You really did. I can still see how beautiful your face looked under the streetlights. I was absolutely mesmerized by your beauty."

"You always said such sweet things to me, Sam. You were always telling me how beautiful I was."

"I always meant it when I said it too."

"I know you did."

"I have a secret to share with you if you're interested," he said with a smile.

"Yes, I'm interested," she replied.

"As beautiful as I thought you were back then – which was exceptional – I think you're even more beautiful now. You're absolutely stunning."

"Oh, thank you so very much, Sam. See?

There you go again, picking up right where you left off."

"I guess some things just never change, huh?"

"Apparently not."

Sam turned away, gazing out through the window as a million different memories of the two of them together swam through his mind.

"What are you thinking about, Sam?" she asked, rubbing his hand.

"I was just thinking about the very first time we kissed. Do you remember?"

"Of course I do. It was by the front door of my apartment after you had walked me home."

"That's right. I can still remember it like it was yesterday. I can picture the whole scene."

"So can I."

The two of them sat silently for a few minutes, leaning more closely toward each other and beginning to feel as though all of the old magic they had felt so many years ago had never gone away, but had only hibernated for what had turned out to be an extremely long winter in both of their lives.

"Sam? Do you know what I'm thinking?"

"No, what?"

"I'm thinking about how much I would love to feel that kiss just one more time."

Sam turned sideways in his seat, facing her, and then looked her in the eyes. He then leaned forward, slowly pressing his lips against hers. Both of them immediately felt the same deep, profound sense of love for each other that they had shared at the moment of their very first kiss. After lingering there for a while, he leaned back away from her, looking deeply into her eyes. He them put his arms around her, pulling her close and holding her chest tightly against his. They both suddenly felt their heartbeats lock into step with each other, almost as if their two hearts had started beating as one.

"Did you just feel that?" he said, leaning back

away.

"I think I just did," she replied, stunned by what she had just felt.

"Our hearts were just beating as one."

"I know…That was wild. I've never felt anything like that before."

"Neither have I…That was amazing!"

For the first time in many years, Sam suddenly felt a sense of true hope about his future again. He didn't know if Angela would have any interest in starting over with him, but at this point, it certainly seemed as though she would.

His heart began to sink as his mind went back to his current living conditions. Even if she would be interested in starting over with him, he knew that he had absolutely nothing to offer her. First and foremost, he was a severe alcoholic, which he knew would be a deal-breaker for her or any other woman. If there was any hope of them being together again, he would have to put that behind him once and for all. That was something he didn't know if he could do at this point in his life. The more he thought about everything, the more hopeless it all seemed to him. After all, even if a miracle occurred and he was able to stop drinking, she would eventually find out that he was flat broke, without a job, with no hope of even finding one at this point, and just a few days from being hungry and homeless. How would he even begin to explain all of this to her?

He looked back at her as he reasoned through all of these things. She looked so incredibly beautiful to him, and she was so very well put together. It was apparent to him that she had done very well for herself. He knew that, even if her love for him was still as strong as it once was, there would be far too many obstacles to overcome. There would be far too many things about his life and who he really was that she could never possibly accept.

He looked down at her hands, which she had

folded in her lap, and knew instantly that he had seen those hands before – not back when they were teenagers, but very recently. He looked closely at the beautiful gold ring she was wearing, and panic struck him deep inside as his mind flashed back to where he had last seen it. It was when he had been sitting alone on the bus stop bench. Feeling a great sense of shame, he suddenly realized that she was the attractive woman who had pressed the twenty dollar bill into his hand. He had no desire to mention this to her, hoping desperately that she had no recollection of that moment.

"Sam?" she said with a soft voice, putting her hand on his.

"Yeah?" he replied.

"I know…"

Sam looked into her eyes, puzzled.

"You know what?" he asked.

"I know about your situation."

He sat back into his seat, closing his eyes, and let out a heavy sigh, completely embarrassed. He pulled his hand away from her, bringing it up to his head to brush his hair back.

"I'm sorry…I didn't mean to embarrass you," she said, taking his hand once again, her eyes welling with tears.

"How do you know?" he sighed.

"I started searching for you again, just a few months ago. I started asking around, trying to find anyone who might have any information about you. I came across a group of people from your high school alumni association and asked if they knew where you were. Nobody knew for certain, but a couple of them said they thought you had moved back into the city, in the neighborhood you now live in. Hoping that I might be able to find you, I drove to the neighborhood and walked around for a little while. I then stopped for a cup of coffee, watching for you as I sat by the window. That's when I saw you sitting on the bus stop bench."

"I can't even begin to express how embarrassed I am right now. I wish you wouldn't have found me like this."

"It's ok, Sam," she replied, rubbing his arm.

"It's just been a very rough patch for me the past few years."

"I know."

"Angel, I have to tell you something. I don't know where you are in your life right now, and I have no idea what it is that you want for your future. I don't know what all of this means. I don't know why we're sitting here with each other once again after all these years. But from what both of us have just said, we've been in love with each other throughout our entire lives. I just can't help but to wonder what it would be like to start all over again with you and give whatever this is between us a fighting chance to be something beautiful. I know that I'm in a very bad place, and I know there's no reason a woman like you would ever be even slightly interested in a man like me. I just want you to know this: I've thought about you throughout the entirety of my life. I've loved you like I have never loved any other woman, and whenever my mind has wandered toward imagining what it would feel like to me if we were given another chance someday, I've always come to the same conclusion. If I were ever given the chance to be with you again, it would feel as though I had truly come home for the very first time in my life."

"Sam...I..."

"I know. This isn't the right time or place for me to say these things. You don't have to answer right now. I just wanted you to know."

Feeling the train beginning to slow down, he turned his gaze out through the window again. As the station approached, he saw a large group of men dressed in camouflage gear, gathering around a very large, stainless steel table. A few of them were carrying hunting rifles, while others were unloading the carcasses of various wild animals from four-wheel drive vehicles.

Off in the distance, he saw more men in hunting gear, some of them walking toward a heavily wooded area a few hundred yards behind the station, while others seemed to be returning from the wooded area with their prey.

Behind the stainless steel table, there were large, steel hooks hanging on chains from the steel beams above. They appeared to be mounted to the beams with a type of roller system, allowing them to glide freely as they were pushed or pulled. Some of the hooks hung empty, swaying in the breeze as the wind from the train flowed past them. Others had deer, antelope, and other wild game hanging from them.

In the center of this area, Sam saw a man with a large carving knife who was feverishly dressing the animals, removing their skin and internal organs, and then pushing the cleaned carcasses away from him.

Directly behind him, there were a few men who were pulling the carcasses off of the table, and then hanging them on the hooks as other men brought more animals toward the table. They were all working together with the precision of a major assembly line, each man performing his duties diligently.

As he looked to the right, he saw a brick building with a large opening where the animals would be pushed through one by one. At the other end of the building was another opening where the now empty hooks would be pushed back outside, back toward the men who were loading the animals upon them.

Startled by some commotion he began to hear inside the train, Sam turned his gaze to the people in the car, all of whom were standing up and gathering their items. He looked at Angela, who was putting the old letters back into her purse.

As all of the passengers started to make their

way down the aisle, each of them reached over, putting their hands on Sam's shoulder as they passed, nodding at him with expressions of sincere empathy. One by one they passed by him, leaving the train in the same order they had arrived. The first to exit was the family with the young boy who wanted to drive the train. Next was Paul, the businessman who had sat with him at the bar talking about his 1965 Pontiac. After him was the young Marine from Decatur, Alabama.

"I have to go now, Sam," Angela said in a sad voice as she stood from her seat.

"Wait!" he replied in desperation as he stood next to her. "I'll go with you."

"You can't, Sam," she replied, turning to hug him one last time.

"What do you mean?" he pleaded. "Please, Angela! Let me come with you!"

"Sam, you can't. You and I are going very different places."

She pulled away slightly, reaching up to put her hand on his cheek as she gazed into his eyes.

"I will always love you, Sam," she said as the tears began rolling down her face.

"Wait!...Angela!" he cried out as she turned away from him and started down the aisle.

He felt as though his heart was shattering into a thousand different pieces as he watched the only woman he had ever truly loved walking away from him once again. He understood that they were very different people at this point in their lives, but he also knew that she was the only woman in the entire world whom he could love enough to put all of the drinking behind him forever. He realized that there was no way any woman as beautiful as her would ever want a man like him, but at that very moment he desperately wanted to change all of that. He wanted it more than anything he had ever wanted at any point in his life. If she could only hold onto the love he knew that she felt toward him, he was positive that his love for her would be the only thing in the world that could save him.

He pushed himself from between the seats, stumbling as he turned down the aisle after her. Just before she had reached the exit, he lunged forward, taking her by the arm and turning her around.

"Angela, please!" he pleaded. "I know we have our share of differences, but I know that the love we've always had for each other can overcome anything. I love you so very much, Angel! I'll change, I swear! I'll do whatever you ask of me! Please, I can't let you walk away from me again! Just give us one chance, please!"

Angela looked at his face as the tears ran down his cheeks, dripping from his chin and landing on the front of his shirt.

"I can't, Sam," she replied, taking his face in her hands and wiping his tears away as she felt her heart breaking deep inside. "It's too late."

She then turned away and stepped quickly through the exit. He tried to follow her, but was stopped suddenly by Gabriel's forearm as he stepped in front of him.

"Let her go, Sam," Gabriel said quietly as he held him back.

Unable to free himself from Gabriel's grip, Sam watched in horror as the doors closed behind her. He ran to the window, pressing his face against it as the train began to move once again.

"Angel! No!" he cried out, pounding his fists against the glass as she walked out of his sight.

Just as the train began to move again, he collapsed in a heap on the seat just in front of him, curling his knees up and holding his stomach as the most intense heartache he had ever experienced gripped his entire body. He began to moan loudly, not even able to form any words as the tears poured from his eyes and his stomach convulsed in excruciating agony. Unable to control himself any longer, he fell from the seat and into the aisle, curling up into a fetal position and rocking back and forth.

"I'm sorry, Sam," Gabriel said as he kneeled next to him, putting his hand on his shoulder. "I'm so very sorry. She loves you with all of her heart, Sam. She always has. It's just too late."

THIRTEEN

As he lay on the floor, his face contorted and his body writhing in the most intense, excruciating emotional pain he'd ever experienced, Sam suddenly concluded that he no longer wanted to live. He had absolutely nothing left to live for when he had boarded this train, but somehow he now felt as though he had far less. As bad as his life had gone for him up to this point, he was at least still able to hold onto the dream, however unrealistic, that maybe someday he and Angela would find each other and be together again. He had at last found her, and now she was gone forever, taking with her the only reason he had left to live.

As he tried desperately to bring himself to his feet, he no longer cared if Gabriel or anyone else knew he didn't belong on this train. He wanted off, even if that meant throwing himself from it as it raced along the countryside. He brought himself up to his knees, holding onto the leather seat next to him, and then pulled himself to his feet.

"I need to get off of this train," he said, turning to look at Gabriel as he rose.

"I'm afraid that's not possible, Sam," Gabriel replied in a calm voice.

"We'll see about that!" Sam snapped, walking quickly toward the doors on the side of the car.

"Sam...," Gabriel said firmly. "You can't leave."

Sam reached the side doors, attempting to pull them open with all of his strength, but they wouldn't budge.

"I said that I want off of this train, Gabriel! I don't belong here!" he shouted.

"Yes, Sam...you do," Gabriel answered.

Feeling a tremendous sense of panic washing over him, he ran to the front of the car, throwing the doors open that led into the buffet car. He paused for a second, looking around to see that the entire car had changed. All of the tables had been cleared off, no longer piled with the bountiful array of delicacies he had seen earlier. The tablecloths, china, and silverware had also been removed, leaving only the tables and chairs. He looked over at the windows, and then fixed his gaze upon the large center table where he had been sitting earlier. In desperation, he ran over to the table, picking it up, and then threw it against the glass with all of his strength. To his surprise, the table bounced off of it and came crashing to the floor. He picked it up once again, this time driving it toward the window like a battering ram. He repeated this a few more times, but the glass refused to shatter.

Undeterred, he ran to the front of the car and threw the doors open to find himself looking at the engine room. He immediately ran inside, looking through the entire compartment for the engineer, hoping that he'd be able to force him to stop the train so that he could get off. After searching through it, he found no one. He walked to the front of the car, looking down at the controls in front of him, searching desperately for something that looked like a brake or a throttle. To his left, he saw a lever sticking straight up out of the side panel, next to the engineer's seat. He climbed up into the seat and examined it more closely, seeing the word 'stop' written on the faceplate at the rear of its travel. He grabbed the lever, pulling back on it as hard as he could, but it didn't move. He then braced his feet against the dashboard for more leverage and pulled back again, this time using his entire body against it. It still wouldn't move. He stood up with his back to the dashboard, raised his leg, and began kicking against it with all his might until he couldn't kick any longer.

Giving up on the throttle control, he turned to the window on his right to see if maybe it was a slider that he could somehow crawl out through. Upon doing so, he saw in the distance about a half-dozen other trains, very similar to the one he was on, all heading in the same direction. He turned to look out the window to his left, and saw about a half-dozen more on the other side. Turning to look out through the front windshield, he saw something before him that seized him with terror. Off in the distance, there was a very large chasm, and beyond that, nothing but complete and total darkness, blacker that the darkest of nights. He froze where he stood, absolutely motionless for a few seconds. He then looked down at the ground directly in front of the train, suddenly realizing that there was no track laid out before it.

He backed away slowly, gripped with fear, wondering if he had somehow gone completely insane. He continued to back away in terror as the chasm continued to move closer. He then turned around, running as fast as he could back through the buffet car, tripping over the table he had thrown to the floor in the process. Making his way back to the rear of the car, he threw the doors open as fast as he could and re-entered the passenger car to find Gabriel sitting calmly in the front row of seats. Behind him, all the way in the back row, there sat a man Sam hadn't seen before. He was dressed in black from head to toe, his skin was as pale as that of a dead man, and he glared at Sam with eyes as dark as night.

"What's going on here, Gabriel!" Sam shouted as he ran up to him, grabbing him by the lapels. "What is this train, and where is it taking me?!" he demanded.

"What happened to you yesterday, Sam?" he replied calmly as he reached up to pull Sam's hands off of him.

"What are you talking about?! What does that have to do with anything?! And how do you know my name?!"

"What happened to you yesterday, Sam?" he repeated. "Think back and try to remember."

"Have you lost your mind?!" Sam shouted. "Who cares what happened to me yesterday?!"

"Sam!" Gabriel shouted in a voice like thunder, grabbing him by his wrists and shaking him for a second. "What happened to you yesterday?! Think!"

Frightened and unable to release himself from Gabriel's grasp, he began to think back upon the previous day, suddenly remembering the beating he took in the park.

"I was walking through the park..."

"And...?"

"There were some punk kids there...teenagers."

"Go on..."

"They were trying to confront me, calling me a bum, and asking me what I was doing in their park. I tried to get away, but I couldn't."

"And what did they do to you, Sam?"

"Why are you asking me these things?!" he shouted, trying to break free. "What difference does it make?!"

"What did they do to you, Sam?!" he replied, holding him more tightly.

"They beat me," he answered, feeling ashamed. "They beat me very badly."

"And then what happened?"

"I don't know..."

"Think, Sam! Try to remember!"

"I don't know. I must have been knocked unconscious. I woke up a little later. I don't know how long. I was laying in some bushes."

"And then what did you do?" Gabriel asked, loosening his grip slightly as his voice softened.

Sam thought back, suddenly remembering

waking up in a great deal of pain. He was bleeding badly from the back of his head, and both of his eyes were nearly swollen shut. He managed to get himself up on his feet, and then stumbled over to a park bench to sit down for a few minutes. He then reached into his pockets and realized that the last few dollars he had were gone. A sense of absolute hopelessness fell over him immediately. He had nothing left, nothing to eat, and nothing to drink.

He brought himself back upon his feet, and then began to walk back to his apartment, his head still spinning from the beating he had taken. He winced with every step, feeling a sharp pain in his ribs from where he had been kicked repeatedly.

Along the way, he could feel the cold stares of horror and disgust falling upon him from everyone he passed. He had never before felt so incredibly ashamed of himself, of his life, or of who he had become as a man. In spite of the searing pain, both emotional and physical, he kept pushing forward until he made it back to his apartment, where he wanted nothing more than to lie down on his bed and die.

"I walked back to my apartment," he replied.

"And then...?"

"I sat on the edge of my bed, wanting to die."

"And what did you do next, Sam?"

Sam thought back again, remembering sitting on the edge of his bed, staring into the corner. He then remembered pulling his 9mm out from under his bed and staring at it for a while. He began to think that there was no reason for him to live anymore. There was no way he could pull himself out of the depths to which he had sank, and even if he could, there was nobody left who would care had he done so.

As the tears ran down his face, he took the gun and placed the barrel under his chin, gently touching the trigger with his finger, gliding back and forth over it, firmly believing that this was his only choice.

"I'm so very sorry, Angel," he whispered as he

gripped it more tightly in his hands, pressing it harder under his chin. Just as he was about to pull the trigger, he was startled by a voice from across the room.

"Go ahead…do it," the voice whispered.

"Who are you?!" he stammered, crawling quickly back into the corner as he aimed the gun at a shadowy figure sitting in the opposite corner.

"What does it matter?" the voice replied.

"I said who are you?!" he demanded, shaking the gun at him.

"I aint nobody, brother…just a voice in the darkness."

Sam rubbed his eyes, trying to make out the face of this mysterious visitor through his blurred vision. In contrast to the dark hooded sweatshirt he was wearing, his skin looked very pale, like that of a dead man, and his eyes looked as though they were merely deep, dark holes with nothing behind them.

"Why are you here?!"

"Look at yourself, Sam. Look at what you've become. You're not even a man anymore. Just a shriveled up, nasty, drunken bum."

"Get up and get out of here, or I swear I'll blow your brains all over this room."

"No you won't," the voice replied with a chuckle. "And besides, even if you did, you'd still be the same piece of garbage you've always been. Look at yourself, Sam. Nobody cares about you. Nobody ever has, and nobody ever will. Your father, your mother, your step-father, your wife, your kids…where are they, Sam?"

Sam kneeled on his bed, completely frozen in silence as the voice continued speaking to him.

"And what about your precious little Angel? Where is she now? Face it, Sam, you'd be doing everyone a favor if you just put that gun back under your chin and did the job. At least that way there'd only be one last mess to clean up."

"Is that why you came here?! To watch me die?!"

"No...I just came to make sure you did the job right. Go ahead, Sam. Do it."

"You don't think I will?!" Sam barked back, putting the gun back under his chin.

"Nope...I don't think you have it in you."

"Oh yeah?! Are you sure about that?!" he asked, pressing in hard and putting his finger on the trigger.

"No...I don't."

With that, Sam squeezed the gun with all of his strength, pulling the trigger.

"Sam!" Gabriel shouted, bringing his attention back to his current situation. "What did you do next?"

"I woke up here," he whispered.

Sam immediately spun around to look at the man sitting in the back of the car, studying his face for a few seconds.

"It was you!" he shouted, pointing his finger at him. "You were in my apartment! Who are you?! Did you bring me here?!"

"Sam!" Gabriel shouted, grabbing him by the arm and turning him back around to face him.

"You said that you woke up here. What time was it when you arrived, Sam?"

"It was 11:15," he replied, looking down at his watch.

"That's right, Sam. It was. You were in your final hour."

"What is this, Gabriel?! Where are you taking me?!" he insisted as the panic began to wash over him.

He had never believed in any form of afterlife, but from what others had told him they believed, there was only one of two places a person would be heading if they were to find themselves in it.

"What have you been thinking about while you've been on this train, Sam?"

"What do you mean?! I don't know?!"

"What have you been thinking about, Sam? With everything that you've seen and heard, what did all of these things cause you to think about?"

"I don't know!" he insisted. "Everything!"

"Everything?"

"Yes, everything!"

"About your entire life? From start to finish?"

Sam immediately began to think back upon all of the things he had thought about during this journey, from the young boy with the nickname of 'tiger,' who reminded him of his earliest memories, to the memories of being alone in his apartment. He suddenly realized that his entire life had just passed through his mind while sitting on the train.

"Yes...my entire life," he replied.

"It is written: *"For nothing is hid, that shall not be made manifest; nor anything secret, that shall not be known and come to light,"* Gabriel answered.

"What did you notice about all of the stops on this route, Sam?" he continued.

Sam's mind went back to all that he had seen during this strange journey. In his mind's eye, he saw the vast multitude of people gathered at the first few stops, none of them boarding the train, but instead standing off at a distance, staring at it. He thought about the twelve men standing on the platform at one of the stops, and how they all turned to look at him just as the train began to move again. He pictured the large river – brilliant and seemingly alive. He pictured all of the people who were gathering around it at various points. He thought back upon the man running through the large open field, with deer running along with him. He then remembered the strange sight of the couple being married at the train station, the large collection of military equipment at another, and the enormous feast that had been going on at yet another. He remembered one of the stations appearing as though it was under construction, and the section of land that appeared to have experienced a long drought. He remembered thinking it was very strange that, in the midst of this drought, there was some sort of a farmer's market with an enormous selection of produce that went on forever. He then thought back upon the strange scene of the judge, standing on the courthouse steps, turning to look at him as the train began to pull away. A sudden chill ran down his spine as he recalled the judge flashing a 'thumbs down' hand sign at him.

"Gabriel," he said, barely able to mouth the words. "Where are you taking me?"

"All that you have seen has been shown to you to bear witness to the truth," Gabriel answered, ignoring his question.

"The great multitude you saw on the platforms when you first arrived were the many saints who have gone on before you. They came to bear witness that the decision of the Lord is right and good."

"What decision?!" Sam insisted.

"There were twelve stops we passed throughout this journey, Sam…Twelve…The number twelve represents completeness. Do you remember their names? There was Reuben, Simeon, Levi, Judah, Naphtali, Zebulun, Gad, Asher, Isaachar, Dan, Joseph, and finally, Benjamin. Do you know what those names represent, Sam?"

"I don't care about any of those names, Gabriel!" Sam shouted. "You said there was a decision made! What decision are you talking about?!"

Gabriel stood and then began pacing back and forth slowly, ignoring Sam's question as he explained further.

"These were the twelve tribes of Israel, Sam, all of whom also came to bear witness to what is to come.

"Reuben, the first-born…He was the sign of his father's strength. He watched from the station as you passed, agreeing that it was good. After Reuben came Simeon. You remember Simeon, Don't you Sam?"

"No!" he replied, lost in confusion.

"Simeon was a very violent, angry young man. He glared at you through the glass, fists clenched. Behind him there was a large multitude of people. None of them moved or said a word as we sat there. These were more saints who have gone on before you, Sam, and they also came to bear witness against you."

"Against me?! For what?!" he protested.

"After Simeon came Levi," Gabriel continued, once again ignoring his question.

"After Levi, there was Judah. You saw him standing amongst the other eleven of his brothers, explaining to them that you were on your way to the destination you have chosen for yourself. As we left them, they all turned to look at you, and then turned back to him in agreement of all he had said.

After Judah, there was Naphtali. It is written that when his father blessed him, he said that he was as a 'doe set free.' You mocked him as he ran through the open fields, with a number of deer running with him, but it was he who had come to judge you, not the contrary.

Do you recall what you saw off in the distance, running throughout the countryside at that time, Sam?"

Sam stood in silence, remembering how he had laughed at the man he saw running. He then pictured the large river he had seen off in the distance.

"That's right, Sam. You saw a large river. It was a river of living water. It is written:

'They shall hunger no more, neither thirst anymore; the sun shall not strike them, nor any scorching heat. For the Lamb in the midst of the throne will be their shepherd, and he will guide them

*to springs of living water, and God will wipe away
every tear from their eyes.'*

Sam thought back upon all that he had seen
there – The many people who were coming to this
river. They were running toward it, dipping their hands
in it, drinking from it, and even immersing themselves
completely into it.

"After this came Zebulun, and then Gad. It was
written of Gad that he would be attacked by a band of
raiders, but that in return, he would attack them at
their heels. All of the military equipment you saw,
Sam, belonged to him. You saw him, dressed in his
uniform with his back against the wall. He too
acknowledged that what had been decided what just
and true.

After Gad came Asher, of whom it was written
that his food would be rich, and that he would provide
delicacies for a king. You saw him in the midst of the
banquet tables, piled high with an abundance of every
type of food imaginable.

After Asher came Issachar. It was written of
him that when he sees how good is his resting place,
and how pleasant is his land, he would bend his
shoulder to the burden and submit to forced labor.
You saw him too, Sam. He was overseeing the
construction in the midst of the land of his inheritance.

After Issachar, you saw Dan – the judge of his
people. You remember him, don't you Sam? As he
saw you from the courthouse steps, he judged
righteously with regard to you.

And then there was Joseph…ah, Joseph – the
favorite of his father. He was the one you saw
standing in the midst of many, wearing the coat of
many colors that his father had given him. Just as he
had done in Egypt, you watched as he supervised the
distribution of food in a place of severe drought.

And the last stop you saw was Benjamin, the
youngest of the twelve, and the final one to bear
witness to all of these things. You see, Sam, the

verdict has been rendered, and all of those whom you have seen are in agreement."

"Why are you telling me all of these things?!" Sam demanded as he began to grow weary of all that he was being told. "Who are you, anyway?!"

"I am Gabriel – archangel of the most high God!" he shouted in a voice like thunder, knocking Sam back into his seat.

"I am telling you these things because I have been commanded to do so, not for your benefit, as if you are owed anything, but in order that you may know that the decision of the Lord is just and true!"

"What decision?!" he begged once again.

"Who did you meet on this train, Sam?" Gabriel continued, once again ignoring his question.

"I met a lot of people! I don't remember!" he replied as beads of sweat began to roll down his face.

"Think, Sam! What were their names?!"

Sam struggled desperately to recall all of them while trying to fight off the panic that was now completely overwhelming him.

"There was the family with the young boy...tiger," he answered. And his father...Peter? Was his name Peter?"

"Yes...Go on."

"Then there was the man at the bar...The one who was restoring an old car. I think his name was Paul."

"Very good, Sam. And who was next?"

"I don't remember! Please stop asking me all of these questions!"

"Who was next, Sam! Answer me!"

"The marine, from Alabama! Andrew! His name was Andrew!"

"And...?"

"I can't remember! There were too many people!" Sam insisted, drawing an absolute blank.

"Then allow me to help your memory, Sam. There were twelve men who boarded this train along the way, nine of whom you were aware of, two of whom remained silent, coming only to bear witness against you, and one whom you have yet to meet.

There was the couple who sat in front of you with the young boy. Do you remember? She had just returned from a long business trip. Her husband – the one who wasn't jealous of her being away with other men, his name was James, was it not?"

"I don't know," Sam replied, holding his face in his hands.

"The missionary, Sam. He sat next to you and began reading his bible. You didn't like that one bit, did you Sam? His name was Bartholomew. There was Matthew – the tax collector. There was James, the friendly man who shook my hand. You didn't want him to sit next to you, did you?"

"No...I didn't."

"Why not, Sam? Why didn't you want him to sit next to you?"

Sam sat silently, not wanting to reply. He knew that the only reason he didn't want James to sit next to him was because he had made a comment about doing the Lord's work when he had first greeted Gabriel.

"There was Thaddeus – the man who sat directly in front of you. I'm certain you remember him. He was the man you asked about this train – what it was and where it was going. Do you remember his response? When you became frustrated with not knowing where you were going, he said that wherever you ended up, that's where you're supposed to be.

Sam..," he continued. "What were your thoughts upon entering the buffet car? Did it seem to you as though every type of food available there was prepared exactly to your specific tastes? Did you feel as though it had all been prepared just for you?"

"Yes..."

"That's because it was, Sam. It was your last meal, prepared just for you. Do you remember the man you met in the buffet car?"

"Yes, I do," he replied, feeling the anger welling up inside of him once again.

"His name was Simon. He was very zealous, wasn't he? That's why he was given the name 'Simon the zealot.'

"The names of the people you met on this train…do they sound familiar to you?"

Sam remained silent, staring down at the floor.

"Wait a minute!" Sam suddenly demanded, completely ignoring Gabriel's question. "Angela was here! Why was Angela here?"

Gabriel took a seat next to him, reaching over to put his hand over Sam's while letting out a sigh.

"She was your first love, Sam. She was your only true love. She was brought here for two reasons, first to show you that throughout all of your life, you should've loved the Lord your God just as you loved her. Secondly, in his unsearchable grace and mercy toward you, she came that you might feel that love once more before she was taken away forever."

"Where are you taking me, Gabriel?" Sam asked in absolute despair.

"You will know the answer to that question soon enough, Sam, but there's something else you need to be shown first.

There's a good reason why I asked you if the names of all of these men sounded familiar to you, for the eleven men who boarded this train were the eleven apostles who walked the earth with our Lord, Jesus Christ. They also came to bear witness that the Lord's decision was pure and good. If you know anything about the apostles, you'll know that there were not eleven apostles, but twelve. Do you know who the twelfth apostle was, Sam – the one who has been purposely excluded from this group?"

With that, the man in black who was sitting in the back of the car stood, and then began walking toward them. As he turned slowly to look at him, Sam could see what appeared to be severe rope burns around his neck.

"The twelfth apostle was Judas, Sam," Gabriel said as he stood and began to walk toward the front of the car.

"Welcome home, Sam," Judas hissed at him through clenched teeth. "I've been waiting for you."

A deep darkness suddenly fell over the train as Sam jumped to his feet. It was a darkness that could not only be seen, but one that he could feel to the core of his soul.

"Gabriel!!" he screamed as he began to backpedal away from Judas. "Wait! Where are you taking me?!"

"You're being taken to the place you have chosen to go, Sam. To the prison of your own making, far removed from the God whom you have chosen to reject throughout the entirety of your life."

"Wait, Gabriel!" Sam pleaded. "You don't understand!"

"That's where you're wrong, Sam. I do understand. I understand completely."

"This isn't fair, Gabriel! How was I supposed to know?!"

"You were given every chance to turn to the Lord your God, Sam. He didn't choose to reject you. He reached out to you countless times through your church, your sister, and numerous prophets who were sent to you in his name. But you despised those prophets, didn't you? You have no right to believe that he has unfairly rejected you, because it was you, Sam, who rejected him."

"No!" Sam protested. "I didn't know! You don't understand! You don't know how difficult my life has been! You don't know how I was treated! How could I have been expected to see God after being beaten down and mistreated so badly by the very people who claimed to know him?!"

As soon as those words left his mouth, the

ceiling of the train faded away as if it had simply vanished. In its place, Sam looked up to see a vision beginning to appear before him. To the right and to the left, there was a large gathering of people from ancient days, shouting insults, spitting, and throwing rocks at a man in the center of them who had been severely beaten. His body was covered in blood from head to toe, and his face was severely bruised, cut, and contorted in extreme agony. Upon his head was a crown of thorns, and he was being whipped from behind as he was forced to carry his cross over the rocky, jagged terrain.

That vision slowly faded away as another one began to appear. In this second vision, Sam watched in horror as this man was placed on his back, screaming in agony as nails were driven into his hands. Once the cross was raised, Sam heard him cry out *"Father, forgive them, for they know not what they do."*

"Lord Jesus, forgive me! Please! Forgive me as you had forgiven them!" Sam cried out as he fell to his knees, suddenly feeling more ashamed and remorseful than he had ever felt before.

"I'm sorry, Sam," Gabriel said quietly from the front of the car. "It's too late."

Sam looked up in horror as Gabriel lifted his hands toward the heavens and then vanished from his sight, leaving him alone with Judas. A loud crash hit the side of the car, sending it rocking sideways. He sprung to his feet and tried to look out into the darkness that surrounded him. Upon doing so, he watched in absolute horror as thousands of demonic beings began to attack the trains he had seen riding alongside of his from the engine room. They were all flying through the air with incredible speed, crashing into the cars, and then tearing through the steel with their immense claws.

As he continued to watch, terrified by this horrific vision, he heard a man screaming from the car behind him. He quickly ran through the doors at the rear of the car, entering the box car containing the casket he had seen earlier. Another loud crash hit the side of the car, knocking him to the ground and breaking the casket free form its moorings. He jumped back to his feet, just barely able to avoid it as it slid against the wall, breaking open. He froze as he looked down into it, seeing his own body lying inside.

"No!" he screamed as he ran past it, trying desperately to get to the next car.

He could hear the man screaming again from inside as he threw open the doors. As soon as his eyes were able to adjust to what was taking place, an enormous, demonic being reached through a hole in the side of the car, burying it's claws directly into the chest of the man he had seen within that car earlier, and then dragging him out into the darkness as he tried desperately to free himself from its grip.

Knowing that there was nowhere left for him to run, he collapsed in a heap on the floor of the car. Within just a few seconds, another demonic being entered, dragging him helplessly into the dense, black nothingness.

After all of the passengers on the numerous trains had been dragged off – their horrible screams fading off into the distance until there was nothing left but cold, dark silence – the trains slowed to a complete stop. The wreckage, which had been strewn in every direction, covering the countryside, began to slowly disintegrate. The trains themselves also began to do so until there was nothing left of them.

Meanwhile, In the parking lot of the funeral home in Sam's old neighborhood, a small group of people were gathered, dressed in black clothing and with somber expressions upon their faces. There's a light rain falling upon them as they make their way toward the main entrance, offering each other heart-felt condolences.

Inside of the funeral home, in a room on the

left, a few more people are gathered around the closed casket where Sam's body rests. His mother, Dawn, sits on a chair in the front row, besieged with grief over the loss of her only son. In her mind, he left this world far too soon. She sits in silence, mourning the loss of a relationship that had actually been lost many years ago.

Next to her is Suzanne, heartbroken beyond words over the loss of her baby brother and the very best friend she'd ever had. Her mind continues to drift back to many laughs they had with each other, picturing the contagious smile she used to see on his face back in happier times.

Standing next to the casket is Little Lee, brushing back a few tears as he remembered the way that Sam had always been able to make him laugh, even in the midst of the very worst of circumstances. He shakes his head, thinking about how the last time he had seen him was on the very day that their father had been buried.

A small group of old friends from the neighborhood stand off to the side, remembering better days and discussing what they knew about that last days of his life.

"Hey bro...are you okay?" Suzanne asks Lee as she approaches him, putting her hand on his shoulder.

"No, I'm really not," He replies, choking back the tears.

"I know...This is such a sad day."

"Yeah, I can't say that I'm surprised it happened. I just didn't expect it so soon. I kept hoping he'd pull himself out of it, you know?"

"I know, bro. I did too."

"Have you talked to him recently?"

"No, we haven't talked in a while. You?"

"No...I tried to call him a few times, but he never answered."

"Same here," she replied, looking down at the

casket.

Hearing a commotion coming from the back of the room, they looked up to see Kim, Lee, and Nicole entering the room. Feeling extremely saddened and uncomfortable, Lee and Nicole walked over to a row of seats in the back of the room and sat down. After giving Kim a hug, Suzanne walked over behind them and put her arms around both of them.

"Hey guys," she said quietly. "How are you?"

Both of them remained silent, having no idea how to express the emotions that were stirring inside of them. They were both very angry with their father for abandoning them the way that he had, but at the same time they were feeling an unspeakable sense of sadness that his life had come to this.

"Hey," Suzanne said as she leaned in more closely. "I want both of you to know that you father loved both of you more than life itself. You meant everything to him."

"Thank you," Lee responded, reaching up to hold her arm.

"I remember so many good times with Dad," Nicole said, her eyes welling up. "I remember him reading us bedtime stories. He would always change his voice to sound like the different characters in whatever stories he was reading."

"Yeah...I remember that too," Lee answered with a laugh. "Do you remember how he used to wait until the grass was really high before he cut it, and then cut paths through it so we could walk along the paths through the tall grass, acting like we were explorers out in the jungle?"

"Yeah, and I remember how he would always pick us up on the patio and let us ride on his lap," she replied.

"He was always so happy when he could spend time with both of you," Suzanne said with a warm smile. "You were his entire world."

In the front of the room, Kim nervously made

her way toward the casket. She felt very out of place, knowing that Sam had told his family about their divorce, but having no idea what he may have said to them about it.

"Hi, Kim," Little Lee said as he stepped forward and gave her a hug.

"Hi Lee," she replied. "How have you been?"

"I've been a lot better," he answered, shaking his head.

"I know. Me too."

"Kim…" he said, clearing his throat. "I know that you really tried."

"Yes, I did," she answered softly. "I truly did."

"I know that Sam had a tendency to be his own worst enemy. I know that you tried to make him a better man."

"I didn't want to make him anything, Lee," she answered as a tear ran down her cheek. "I only wanted him to be the man that I knew he already was deep down inside."

"In spite of his problems, he was still always a good man. They just got the better of him in the end. It's such a shame," Lee answered quietly.

"It sure is, Lee. He struggled so very much. I know that it was very hard for him. You know, coming from where he came from, I guess that he really did the best that he could. He came so close to breaking out of it so many times, but it always seemed to just suck him right back in."

"It sure did."

"You know, Lee, maybe we should be happy for him now," she replied, forcing a smile.

"Why's that," he asked with a confused expression.

"Because his struggle is over. He doesn't have to fight it anymore. He can finally rest."

"You know, you're right, Kim," Lee replied, looking back at the casket. "I'm sure he's in a better place now."

FOURTEEN

In her small family home on the city's northwest side, Angela glances over at the clock as she puts in her earrings. She then rushes to collect her things and heads outside, knowing that she has only a few minutes to make it to church on time. After checking one last time to ensure that she has everything before leaving, she steps outside and locks the front door behind her.

"What a gorgeous day!" she thinks to herself as she looks to the skies above her.

She gets into her car and pulls from the curb, turning up the music on the Christian music station she has grown to love. She sings along to the music cheerfully as she drives along, feeling exceptionally inspired and uplifted by what they're playing. Within just a few minutes, she arrives at her church, and after greeting a few friends in the lobby, she makes her way into the sanctuary, finding a seat near the rear of the room.

She doesn't understand why, but for some reason she's feeling incredibly blessed this morning. Maybe it was just because of the beautiful weather, or maybe it's something else, but she's feeling a deep sense of joy she can't explain.

After sitting there for a few minutes, the church bells begin to ring to alert those outside that the service is about to begin. She watches as the last few parishioners straggle in, smiling widely at them as they pass. Before long, they are all seated, and the music begins.

Just a few blocks away, Sam is awakened by the sound of the bells. He immediately jumps to his feet, shaken to his very core by the incredibly realistic nightmare he had just experienced.

"Oh my God!" he exclaims as he runs his hands through his hair. "I'm alive! It was a dream! It was all just a dream!"

He looks toward the left side of his bed, and seeing his 9mm lying next to his pillow, he leaps for it, picking it up to examine it closely. He immediately pulls the chamber out and inspects it."

"It wasn't loaded!" he says in disbelief. "The damn thing wasn't loaded! Kim must've unloaded it at some point while she was still at home!"

Once again, he can hear the church bells ringing off in the distance, but for the very first time in his life, they don't sound as though they're mocking him. This time they sound as if they're inviting him. He immediately races across the room, grabbing his shoes and a pair of socks as the bells continue ringing, sounding as if they're becoming louder and louder. He puts his shoes and socks on as quickly as he can, and then races into the bathroom, puts his head under the sink, and then pulls a towel over his head, drying himself off. He then drags a comb through his hair and exits the bathroom. Finding his keys, he runs over to his front door and heads outside.

Temporarily blinded by the bright sunlight, he carefully makes his way to the sidewalk and heads toward the church, his pace growing faster and faster until he's nearly at a dead run. He races toward the front steps, climbing them as fast as he can, and then bursts through the front doors into the lobby. As he makes his way toward the sanctuary, he can clearly hear the choir as it sings Amazing Grace, the song he had always liked to believe was about him.

He pushes his way through the doors of the sanctuary just as the song is ending. Seeing an open seat to his right, he quickly makes his way to it, and then sits down. Feeling completely overwhelmed by the emotions within him, he immediately falls to his knees and begins to pray silently.

"My God!" he cries from deep within his soul. "Please forgive me!"

Within just a few seconds, he begins to sob uncontrollably, reaching his hands up to support his weight on the back of the seats in front of him.

"Our reading today is from the book of Psalms," the pastor says as he steps to the microphone. "From the 116th chapter," he continues.

"I love the Lord, for he heard my voice. He

heard my cry for mercy. Because he turned his ear to me, I will call on him as long as I live. The cords of death entangled me, the anguish of the grave came over me. I was overcome by distress and sorrow. Then I called on the name of the Lord: "Lord, save me!""

Upon hearing those words, Sam feels whatever is left of his strength leaving him. He doubles over, sobbing out loud as every words seems as though it was being spoken just for him.

Hearing the sound of a man crying, Angela looks over to her right to see him kneeling on the floor as the tears stream down his face. Feeling an intense sense of compassion rising up within her, she immediately rises from her seat and walks over to him, kneeling down next to him as she puts her arm around him.

"Shhh...It's okay," she whispers in his ear as she rubs his back while the pastor continues to read. She has no idea who he is, or why he is breaking down in this way, but she feels as though she has no other choice but to try and comfort him in his distress.

"The Lord is gracious and righteous; our God is full of compassion. The Lord protects the unwary; when I was brought low, he saved me. Return to your rest, my soul, for the Lord has been good to you. For you, Lord, have delivered me from death, my eyes from tears, my feet from stumbling, that I may walk before the Lord in the land of the living."

"Oh, my God!" Sam whispers as another heavy stream of tears burst from his eyes. "I'm so very sorry, Lord! Please forgive me."

"It's ok," Angela again whispers into his ear while continuing to rub his back.

Suddenly more aware of this kind stranger who had kneeled down next to him in an effort to comfort him, Sam wipes the tears from his eyes and looks at her, completely astonished at the vision now before him.

"Angela?" he whispers, barely able to even speak her name. "Is it really you?"

"Oh my God!" she replies in utter amazement. "Sam?"

"I can't believe it's really you!" he answers, immediately wrapping both of his arms around her.

"I know, Sam!" she replies, putting her arms around him in return.

Suddenly becoming aware of his condition, he begins to feel a tremendous amount of shame that she would see him like this.

"I've been such a fool, Angel," he whispers, holding her close to prevent her from taking a closer look at him.

"Shhh. It's okay, Sam," she whispers in return.

"I hate that you're seeing me like this after all of these years," he continues. "I've made such an incredible mess of my life."

"I know…but you're here now. Maybe all of that is about to change."

"I want that so very badly, Angel. I really do."

"I know you do. It's gonna be okay, Sam."

As he continued to hold her, pulling her into himself as tightly as he could, he can suddenly feel their hearts beginning to beat as one.

"Did you just feel that?" he asks softly.

"I sure did," she replies, amazed by what she had just felt.

"I'm so glad that you're here right now, Angel."

"I am too, Sam….Hey…," she whispers, pushing him away gently so she could look into his eyes, and then bringing one hand up to rest it on his cheek. It's gonna be okay."

Sam rocks back slightly, eager to look at her face once again.

"Hey Sam?" she says, wiping the tears from his cheek.

"Yeah, Angel?" he replies, once again amazed at her beauty.

"Welcome home."

Made in the USA
Lexington, KY
03 December 2014